D0042119

PR

BLO

"Another winner from Eilee
many ac
have no

"The we
exciting
revealed
to give
action . . .

"Fast-pac ... reading . . . I really like this story line and the characters, so I highly recommend you add *Blood Lines* to your library." —*Fresh Fiction*

"The magic seems plausible, the demons real, and the return of enigmatic Cynna, along with the sorcerer, hook fans journeying the fantasy realm of Eileen Wilks." —*The Best Reviews*

"Intriguing . . . Surprises abound in *Blood Lines* . . . A masterful pen and sharp wit hone this third book in the Moon Children series into a work of art. Enjoy!" —*A Romance Review*

"If you enjoy beautifully written, character-rich paranormals set in a satisfyingly intricate and imaginative world, then add your name to Eileen Wilks's growing fan list and savor *Blood Lines* to the very last page." —*BookLoons*

"Quite enjoyable, and sure to entertain . . . A fast-paced story with plenty of danger and intrigue." —*The Green Man Review*

"Those in search of paranormal tales that are rich and multifaceted will get exactly what they're looking for in the brilliant Wilks's exceptional supernatural stories." —*Romantic Times*

continued . . .

MORTAL DANGER

"Terrific . . . The cat-and-mouse story line is action-packed . . . A thrilling tale of combat on mystical realms."

—*The Best Reviews*

"*Mortal Danger* is as intense as it is sophisticated, a wonderful novel of strange magic, fantastic realms, and murderous vengeance that blend together to test the limits of fate-bound lovers. An intricately crafted, loving, lavish tale."

—Lynn Viehl, *USA Today* bestselling author of the Darkyn series

"A dramatically told story . . . It is this reviewer's hope that this series will have many more stories to come."

—*Romance Junkies*

"I've been anticipating this book ever since I read *Tempting Danger*, and I was certainly not disappointed. *Mortal Danger* grabs you on the first page and never lets go. Strong characters, believable world-building, and terrific storytelling make this a must-read for anyone who enjoys werewolves with their romance. I really, really loved this book."

—Patricia Briggs, *USA Today* bestselling author of *Moon Called*

"[A] complex, intriguing, paranormal world . . . Fans of the paranormal genre will love this one!"   —*Love Romances*

"A thoroughly enjoyable read. I'll be looking out both for the previous volume and the next book in what promises to be a series well worth following."

—*Emerald City Fantasy and Science Fiction*

"Gripping paranormal romance."   —*Fresh Fiction*

TEMPTING DANGER

"A story whose characters I remember long after the last page is turned." —Kay Hooper, *New York Times* bestselling author of *Blood Dreams*

"An exciting, fascinating paranormal suspense that will have you on the edge of your seat. With a mesmerizing tale of an imaginative world and characters that will keep you spellbound as you read each page, Ms. Wilks proves once again what a wonderful writer she is with one great imagination for her characters and the world they live in."
—*The Romance Readers Connection*

"Fantastic . . . Lily and Rule are a fabulous pairing . . . Ms. Wilks takes a chance and [her] readers are the winners."
—*The Best Reviews*

"Wilks's heroine is so top-notch." —*The Romance Reader*

PRAISE FOR THE PREVIOUS NOVELS OF
EILEEN WILKS

"Fun [and] very entertaining!" —*The Romance Reader*

"Should appeal to fans of Nora Roberts." —*Booklist*

"Fast-paced." —*All About Romance*

Books by Eileen Wilks

TEMPTING DANGER
MORTAL DANGER
BLOOD LINES
NIGHT SEASON
MORTAL SINS
BLOOD MAGIC
BLOOD CHALLENGE

Anthologies

CHARMED
(with Jayne Ann Krentz writing as Jayne Castle,
Julie Beard, and Lori Foster)

LOVER BEWARE
(with Christine Feehan, Katherine Sutcliffe, and Fiona Brand)

CRAVINGS
(with Laurell K. Hamilton, MaryJanice Davidson, and Rebecca York)

ON THE PROWL
(with Patricia Briggs, Karen Chance, and Sunny)

INKED
(with Karen Chance, Marjorie M. Liu, and Yasmine Galenorn)

NIGHT SEASON

EILEEN WILKS

BERKLEY SENSATION, NEW YORK

THE BERKLEY PUBLISHING GROUP
Published by the Penguin Group
Penguin Group (USA) Inc.
375 Hudson Street, New York, New York 10014, USA
Penguin Group (Canada), 90 Eglinton Avenue East, Suite 700, Toronto, Ontario M4P 2Y3, Canada
(a division of Pearson Penguin Canada Inc.)
Penguin Books Ltd., 80 Strand, London WC2R 0RL, England
Penguin Group Ireland, 25 St. Stephen's Green, Dublin 2, Ireland (a division of Penguin Books Ltd.)
Penguin Group (Australia), 250 Camberwell Road, Camberwell, Victoria 3124, Australia
(a division of Pearson Australia Group Pty. Ltd.)
Penguin Books India Pvt. Ltd., 11 Community Centre, Panchsheel Park, New Delhi—110 017, India
Penguin Group (NZ), 67 Apollo Drive, Rosedale, North Shore 0632, New Zealand
(a division of Pearson New Zealand Ltd.)
Penguin Books (South Africa) (Pty.) Ltd., 24 Sturdee Avenue, Rosebank, Johannesburg 2196,
South Africa

Penguin Books Ltd., Registered Offices: 80 Strand, London WC2R 0RL, England

This is a work of fiction. Names, characters, places, and incidents either are the product of the author's imagination or are used fictitiously, and any resemblance to actual persons, living or dead, business establishments, events, or locales is entirely coincidental. The publisher does not have any control over and does not assume any responsibility for author or third-party websites or their content.

NIGHT SEASON

A Berkley Sensation Book / published by arrangement with the author

PRINTING HISTORY
Berkley Sensation mass-market edition / January 2008

Copyright © 2008 by Eileen Wilks.
Excerpt from *Mortal Sins* © 2008 by Eileen Wilks.
Cover art by Don Sipley.
Cover design by George Long.
Interior text design by Kristin del Rosario.

ISBN: 978-0-425-22015-3

BERKLEY® SENSATION
Berkley Sensation Books are published by The Berkley Publishing Group,
a division of Penguin Group (USA) Inc.,
375 Hudson Street, New York, New York 10014.
BERKLEY SENSATION and the "B" design are trademarks belonging to Penguin Group (USA) Inc.

PRINTED IN THE UNITED STATES OF AMERICA

10 9 8 7 6 5

PROLOGUE

IN the east, dawn smeared a promise across the inky sky, but air and earth were dark yet. At an abandoned house just outside Midland, Texas, a pair of headlights shut off. A man and a woman climbed out of a 2005 Toyota Corolla.

"I keep thinking we've forgotten something," the woman said as she popped the trunk. She was tall and angular, with a runner's build and with strong shoulders—not pretty, but striking. She wore jeans, hiking boots, and a dark sweater. No makeup. Her hair was long and straight, a medium brown; her skin, an indeterminate tan that looked more Anglo than not; but she had the broad, high cheeks and strong nose of her mother's people, the Diné. Navajo, as outsiders named them. "I always forget something."

The man gave her a singularly sweet smile. He, too, was tall, angular, and athletic; his only remarkable facial feature was his eyes. The gray of a winter sky, they were heavily lashed and set off by the dark slashes of his brows. Some might guess him to have Native American blood as well, based on his coppery skin and black hair. They would be wrong.

"We have everything on our list," he said as they pulled camping equipment from the trunk. "If we failed to plan for some need, we'll make do." He paused. "You're frightened."

She nodded, though she looked and sounded almost placid. "Not all the way to real panic yet. About a six on the *ohmygod* scale."

"Well, then." He put down the duffel bag he'd been holding and folded her in his arms. "Let's see if we can get it down to a four, at least."

"Mmm," she said after a moment, the sound muffled by his neck. "Yes, but we won't get much done like this. My anxieties say inaction would be fine, the lying rats. That we can just can stand around and nuzzle each other. But your queen is going to expect promptness, I think."

"Among other things. She's a great one for expectations." He let a few inches come between them without releasing her. "You're all right, Kai?"

"I guess I can be scared and okay at the same time. Excited, too. It's a whole new world, after all. I'm all boggled about it." Kai drew air in through her nose, sighed it out, and nodded once. "Let's get moving."

She shrugged into her backpack and tucked the sleeping bags beneath her arms. They'd not be afoot long, so the weight wasn't a major issue. Still, he carried more of their gear, which was sensible. Nathan was probably five times as strong as she normally was, and she wasn't normal now. Hunger gnawed at her, a hunger food couldn't satisfy since it wasn't hers. She tired quickly.

Not for much longer, though.

Kai's backpack held a change of clothes, thermal underthings, plenty of clean socks and underwear, their medical kit, and a few more odds and ends. Nathan's carried the heavier items—their cleverly compact tent, camping tools, and trade goods: several packets of cinnamon; a roll of zippable plastic bags; a pair of small, sharp axes; four very fine knives; two boxes of nails; a hammer and a small spade; and a pound each of gold and silver made up into chains.

Nathan lifted the oversize duffel and they walked slowly away from the car. Kai's friend Ginger would retrieve it later today. Ginger knew Kai was leaving with Nathan, but had no inkling just how far they meant to travel. The story Kai had given her for abandoning the vehicle out here was pretty lame, as Ginger had pointed out several times, but Kai was used to Ginger's inquisitiveness. And Ginger was used to not getting all of her questions answered.

Kai hoped hard that she would see her friend again. "You're looking forward to this."

"Parts of it, yes. Your home is lovely, but I've been here a long time. And even with the recent influx of magic, it's still a bit thin here for me." Without breaking stride or changing tone he added, "You'll do, Kai. I know you've doubts, and that's as it should be, for this quest is a testing. But you'll do."

And that, of course, was where the *ohmygod* scale came from. Not a fear of running out of tampons. Though she sincerely hoped she'd packed enough; if she hadn't, she'd make do. The fear that she couldn't learn enough, understand enough, to do what she was supposed to—oh, yes, that was huge.

One step at a time, she reminded herself, following him through the darkness around the side of the old house. He could see here, she thought. She couldn't, not yet—certainly not in the shadow of the derelict building. She couldn't hear his footsteps, either. Just her own.

They reached what she would have called the backyard had it possessed anything other than dirt, trash, and dead weeds. Kai could see those weeds now, their rustly skeletons smudging air on its way from black to gray. The sky had lightened from ink to charcoal overhead, with a band of steel along the horizon. She moved up beside Nathan.

Like Grandfather said, swallowing tomorrow's troubles will give you gas today. And yet . . . "I don't see why we're doing it this way. You could find it. That's what you *do*."

"I could, once I got the scent. But that isn't what my queen wishes. And no," he said with a sideways smile for her, "while her wishes are sufficient for me, I don't expect you to accept them without a question or two. I imagine she saw something that led her to send us this way about things, rather than another."

"By 'saw' do you mean foreseeing? Or farseeing?"

"Likely both. Odds are, she has her hand on a pattern developing there, and this is the best way for it to proceed."

"Or she may just want to make this as hard as possible on me."

"That's also possible. Eh." He rubbed his nose with his free hand. "You're all puckered with worry, and a bit angry, too, and I'm still giddy with relief, which is a bad match in our moods. But it will work out, Kai. You'll see."

Nathan was giddy because his queen hadn't killed her six days ago. Kai had been pretty relieved herself at the time. The queen and her brother had thought she was a binder, a rare and dangerous type of telepath who could bind others to her will. Nathan had stood for her, placing himself between them and her, though he couldn't have stopped them. They'd all known that.

But he'd bought a pause, one in which the queen had listened, because she loved him enough to give him that much. In the end, Kai was allowed to live—for now. But not here. Not where people couldn't protect themselves from her.

She felt the bitterness coating that thought. She also saw it, strings of greasy gray wrapping the thought as if to mummify it. Oh, she'd seen what happened if you held on to such thoughts, seen people trapped by bitter thoughts too long hoarded, how the grayness strangled all the color out of them. She took a breath and did her best to let the thought and the bitterness go, and was rewarded as they faded away.

Kai wasn't exactly a telepath. She wasn't a non-telepath, either, just as she wasn't exactly a binder, yet could do some of what binders did. Her Gift baffled everyone, including herself. Maybe herself most of all. She didn't read minds, but she saw thoughts and the emotions connected to those thoughts. And sometimes, when conditions were just right—or wrong—she changed minds. Literally.

After a lifetime of suppressing that particular talent, now she had to learn how to master it. Quickly. Before it mastered her.

She felt the purr before she heard it, a low rumbling in her mind. A moment later a lumpy spot ten feet ahead of them shifted and stretched, becoming eight feet of dappled gray cat. Kai smiled. "Dell's purely glad about this, anyway."

"She understands we're leaving now?"

"Oh, yes." The bond they'd formed was very new, the intimacy of it sometimes unsettling, and some concepts didn't travel well between minds so different. But Kai knew Dell understood that her long hunger was nearly over.

When Dell's hunger ended, so would Kai's.

They'd reached the rendezvous. Kai set one of the sleeping bags down so she could rub behind one tall, tufted ear as the big cat stropped herself against Kai's legs. Dell had learned that her human was easily unbalanced, so her affection was tempered by care. "She's eager."

Dell would be much better off where they were going, and that gave Kai a happiness to hang on to. If the magic here was somewhat thin for Nathan, it was starvingly low for the chameleon-cat—which was why Kai had begun to tire. The familiar bond ran both ways, and the power the queen had generously offered Dell to sustain her while Kai and Nathan readied themselves for the trip was gone now.

"Best pick up the sleeping bag. It's time, Kai."

"What?" But she stooped to retrieve it. "I don't see . . . is she here?"

"She doesn't have to be here. It isn't a true gate. I explained that."

He had, but that wasn't to say she understood. Somehow Nathan's queen was reaching him though she wasn't even in this world, broadening his innate ability to cross between realms so he could take with him things that were his—clothes, gear, and Kai. Who would bring Dell with her.

"Focus on your bond with Dell." His voice was low. He stared ahead at something she couldn't see.

She took a breath and did her best to slip into the state she'd avoided all her life, the condition she called fugue. At first it wouldn't come. She allowed the frustration to wash through her, focusing only on Dell, the clear, simple colors of her familiar's thoughts.

Gradually her breathing eased and her mind slid into that other place, where the colors and shapes of thoughts drew her, their shifting endlessly fascinating . . . a place where she could lose herself. Had lost herself as a child. A place where her own thoughts could reach out and touch the minds of others, change them. Where the compulsion to do just that could be overwhelming.

But Dell's thoughts were clear and true, triggering no urge to meddle. Kai's heartbeat steadied and she found the bond between them, a smooth, pale tube just tinged with yellow, and she smiled it stronger. Brighter.

She felt Nathan's hand on her shoulder. "Now," he said, his voice the only thing in the world besides the colors, "we walk forward."

So she did, trusting him, smiling at how beautiful his colors were, and how intricate, the shapes flowing into a new pattern, then another, each elegant and enticing, fascinating . . .

A sharp pain in her cheek made her gasp—and brought her back, dizzy, into the world of the senses. A world different from the one she'd been in only moments ago. Snow whirled through the night air, damp and cold on her skin. She looked around, but could see neither buildings nor road, only the endless, muted white of the storm.

But Dell was warm beside her, gloriously excited and urgent. Nathan stood before her, worry tilting his brows down. "I'm back," she said, "though we really need to find something other than pain to get my attention." The hot sting in her cheek suggested he'd had to slap her out of fugue this time.

"We need jackets. Gloves for you." He unzipped the duffel.

She hugged the sleeping bags close. "I was expecting something more inhabited."

"There's a village or holding east of here."

Relief swept through her. "You know where we are, then."

He found a smile, this one apologetic. "No. I smell wood smoke. Here."

They shuffled burdens between them so both could don their jackets. Hers was quilted, hooded, good to sub-zero temps if she added the lining. She didn't. It was cold, but not much below freezing. She'd warm quickly once they started moving. "Dell's hungry. Can I—?"

"Yes. Don't worry." The last was addressed to the cat, not Kai. "I'll watch out for her."

In spite of her eagerness to hunt, Dell studied Nathan a moment. Kai could feel the big cat considering whatever communication she'd received from him—not the spoken words Kai had heard, but something. Then she vanished into the snow-blurred night.

Kai tugged on her gloves. Dell considered her too weak to survive on her own. In this place, she was likely right. "Can you tell if the others have come through yet? The ones we're to follow?"

Nathan tilted his head as if listening, though she had no idea what sense he was actually consulting. "We have

two or three weeks, I think. I stepped somewhat backward as we came through."

"Backward?"

"Time isn't entirely congruent between Earth and
Edge. There's enough flex to allow me some choice. Forward would be tricky, but it wasn't so hard to slide it back
a bit."

She stared. "You can adjust time?"

"No." He was patient. "But when two realms aren't
time-congruent, time becomes one of the choices I make
when crossing."

He thought that made sense. Ah, well. She had a great
deal to learn about him still. They'd been friends for two
years, but lovers for only six days.

And now they were supposed to rescue this world—or
play a part in its rescue, anyway. If she could make her
Gift work. "We'd better get moving."

ONE

❧

IT looked like a digital thermometer. There were two little windows in the plastic casing, one showing a deep purple the other, a pale teal. Cynna tilted it, squinting. Maybe the light was fooling her.

Still purple. Not the pretty teal she'd been praying for. No matter how hard she stared or squinted, or what angle she used, it stayed purple.

The knock at her door made Cynna jump. She dropped the tester, scowled at it, and left it lying on the floor. She slammed the bathroom door as she hurried to the other door—which was only steps away. Hotel rooms always put the bathroom right off the entry door.

"Coming, dammit. I'm coming."

No, she wasn't. Not now, but she had last month. Three times. Which was why the color of doom had showed up on the godforsaken tester.

Cynna checked the spy hole, unlocked the door, and swung it open. "Hey," she said with frantic cheer. "I'm ready. Let's go."

The woman at the door was a full head shorter than Cynna. Her hands were tucked into the pockets of a long

sweep of coat as black and perfect as the shorter sweep of
her hair, and a small frown was tucked between the arch
of her brows. Her eyes were dark and steady. "You need
a coat," Lily Yu said, not moving. "It's February, so you
need a *heavy* coat. And maybe your wallet? If we're going to shop—"

"Oh, yeah. Right. I'll get them." Cynna started to shut
the door in her friend's face, but stopped herself in time.
"Come in, but don't go in the bathroom."

That sent the eyebrows up. Cynna ignored that, grabbed
her denim tote and her jacket from the pile of clothes on
the bed. "I sure do need to wash clothes," she said brightly.
"Let's go. Oh, one more thing. No one is to say the p-word
this afternoon, or allude to it in any way."

Lily nodded thoughtfully. "Okay. No allusions to the
p-word."

Wow. That was easy. Should have tried that a month
ago and spared herself any number of gentle, tactful, or
blunt interventions. Lily had been so sure Cynna wasn't
facing reality.

Turned out Lily was right. The bitch. "So where are
we going?" Cynna asked as they headed down the hotel
hallway to the side exit.

"I thought we'd give the Fashion Center a try."

"Sure. Uh . . . do they have those snooty clerks who
look at you like you're about to boost a pair of panty
hose?"

Lily gave her a look. "How long have you lived in
D.C.?"

"Seven years. Why?"

"The Fashion Center is a mall. They've got all kinds
of clothing stores—Macy's, Talbot's, The Gap, Kenneth
Cole—"

"So I don't shop much. So sue me."

Lily patted her arm. "You will today."

That's what she was afraid of. Whatever had possessed
her to ask Lily to help her pick out some new things?

She glanced down at the woman beside her and sighed.

Envy, that's what. Lily always looked *right*. But she was tiny and . . . well, not cute. You wouldn't call a bullet cute, no matter how small and shapely it was. Bullets were also notoriously hard to stop, and that was like Lily, too.

And now, because Cynna had opened her big mouth, all that deadly determination was focused on her wardrobe. She'd actually used that word when she talked to Lily about helping her shop. A new wardrobe, she'd said. For work.

Clearly she'd been insane. She didn't have a damned wardrobe. She had clothes.

They left through the side door. Cold sucked at Cynna's face and made inroads along her front, so she zipped her jacket. It was an unusually cold winter for D.C., but she wasn't about to say so. It was too much fun needling Lily, who'd lived in San Diego all her life.

Lily grumbled under her breath and headed for her car—a plain white Ford exactly like Cynna's, only cleaner. The FBI must buy the things in droves.

The day was as sunny and still as it was cold, the sun a bright ball in a sky so blue and clear you'd think smog had never been invented. So when the shadow passed overhead, Cynna looked up.

The sinuous shape was growing familiar, though she still felt a chill of awe at the sight. Against the brightness of the sky it looked dark, but she'd seen the photographs. Who hadn't? Up close the scales would be red and shiny, the color of rubies or fresh blood.

"Is vanity a dragon thing?" she asked, one hand on the car door, her head tipped back to watch legend crawl lazily across the sky.

Lily opened her door. "What do you mean?"

"All the photos. Mika doesn't talk much, but he sure likes getting his picture taken." Technically, Mika didn't talk at all. Mindspeak wasn't the same as talking. But the ruby dragon seldom bothered to speak in any manner to the humans around him, much to the frustration of reporters. "Is Sam vain like that?"

Lily snorted. "Haven't seen a bunch of photos of him on the Internet, have you? I guess if you already know you're the biggest, baddest dude on two wings, you don't need a picture to prove it. Mika's young," she added as she got in.

Young was a relative term, but since Mika had probably been born before a passel of Pilgrims washed up on a big rock near Plymouth, Cynna thought Lily was stretching the limits of the word.

But dragons stretched a lot of limits.

For years people had believed they were myth, fairy tale, no more real than Odysseus's Cyclops. Even when twenty-two of them ended their long exile last November to return to Earth, it had been easy for people to dismiss the sighting since they'd vanished right away.

Probably some publicity stunt, right? It happened in California, and much of the country considered that explanation enough for any oddity. Since the government sat on its information—which included radar, both still and video images, and the reports of two of its own agents, namely Cynna and Lily—there had been no solid proof. Talk show hosts had had a field day with dragon-sighting jokes.

When they showed up again, no one was laughing. This time, the world *needed* them to be real.

The realms had done one hell of a bump-and-grind, knocking streams of magic loose from nodes all over the world. Loose magic has a randomizing effect on technology, especially anything run by computers . . . which was just about everything. It turned out that, in addition to being strong, beautiful, and deadly, dragons made dandy sponges. They soaked up all the excess magic in their vicinity.

Two days before Christmas, the black dragon had landed on the White House lawn. Sam—whose other call-name was Sun Mzao—had negotiated for the rest, assisted by Lily's grandmother. Much to Cynna's frustration, no one would tell her why Madam Yu had been involved. She had some guesses, though they were so preposterous . . . but so was Lily's grandmother.

Sooner or later, Cynna promised herself, she'd worm the truth out of Lily.

So far the Dragon Accords were working. Computers operated normally in the nation's capital, on Wall Street, and in and around the twelve U.S cities and eight throughout the world that had a dragon. True, dragons ate a lot, and the animal protection people were not happy about their preferred presentation style—the dragons insisted on catching the evening's cow or pigs themselves. But they'd stuck to their agreement to leave people and pets off the menu.

Problem was, there weren't enough dragons.

Cynna watched Washington's dragon bank and head down. Looked like he was heading for Rock Creek Park. He'd claimed the amphitheater there while governmental types argued over where to build his permanent lair.

"You coming?" Lily said.

Cynna slid in the car and buckled up. "Do you ever wish we'd gotten Sam instead of Mika?"

Lily shrugged and started the car. "Sam wanted to be near Grandmother. Or else Grandmother wanted him near. Or maybe he just wanted to be warm. It's never warm here."

"Bitch, bitch, bitch. If you're still around this summer, you'll be complaining about the heat. It's not a dry heat like you're used to."

"San Diego isn't as hot as you'd think. Hotter in the mountains, of course. As you move away from the coast, you don't get the cooling effects of the ocean."

"You miss it."

Lily sighed and pulled out. "More than I expected. This was supposed to be temporary."

Lily had originally been posted to Washington, D.C., for two purposes: to assist the Secret Service in an investigation and to take an abbreviated version of the standard FBI training at Quantico. Like Cynna, she belonged to a special unit in the FBI's Magical Crimes Division, one that until recently very few knew existed. Lily had been recruited last November. She was a touch sensitive, able to feel magic tactilely yet impervious to its effects, but her background as a homicide cop was as valuable to the Unit as her Gift. A lot of the Unit's agents lacked that kind of law enforcement training and experience.

Lily had finished up the assist-the-Secret-Service part of her assignment, but what with demon assassins and the Turning and all, her training still wasn't complete.

"There is an upside, I guess," Lily said. "Being parked at Headquarters puts twenty-six hundred miles between me and my mother."

"Yeah, but planes are flying again, cell phones are working—"

"Don't remind me."

Cynna smiled because she was supposed to, but she wondered . . . if her mother had lived, would she be as mom-averse as Lily? Some of her other friends were like that, too. A few seemed to be close to their mothers, but a lot of them had issues.

Not that she didn't have issues. You didn't have to have a living mother to find knots tangled all over your heart tagged "from Mom." Which was a damn good reason for never . . . not going there, she reminded herself. "How's Rule?"

"He's good. The mantles have settled into peaceful co-existence . . . which you'd know if you hadn't been avoiding us. I—oh, God."

"What? What is it?"

"I sound like my mother."

Cynna laughed. For the first time in hours—days—well, a long time, she felt like laughing. Maybe she'd been isolating.

You think? whispered a snide inner voice.

"I'd better get over that," Lily added casually. "It looks like I'm going to be a mother myself soon. Of sorts."

Cynna jolted so hard she nearly gave herself whiplash. "You—you're going to have a baby?"

"No. Oh, no, though—well, I can't say what I'm thinking without making a forbidden allusion. I was talking about Toby."

Toby was Rule's son, and Rule was . . . well, just about everything to Lily, except a husband. Lupi didn't marry. "You mean he's going to sue for custody? Or did Toby's mom finally agree to let him live with Rule?"

"Alicia didn't agree, but her mother has. I think Mrs. Asteglio approves of me, and with Rule and me going down there so often after she broke her leg—"

"She broke her leg?"

"Fell down the stairs. It was a wake-up call for her. She's sixty-three, you know, and has some other health problems that make it hard for her to care for a child Toby's age. And she knows Toby wants to live with his dad."

Since the boy had run away just before Christmas so he could spend the holiday with his father, Cynna agreed that Toby's preference was obvious.

"I feel sad for her," Lily added. "She loves Toby. It's hard on her, giving him up, but we'll make sure she gets to see him often."

"But Toby's grandma doesn't have legal custody, does she?"

"Toby's grandmother," Lily said tartly, "has raised him. His mother sure hasn't. Alicia visits on the occasional weekend, but even that's dried up now that she's in Lebanon. She's huffing and puffing and dragging her feet, but for the first time Rule has a good chance of winning if she does contest the suit. We're hoping she won't. It'll be easier on Toby if we can come to an agreement."

For years Rule had had no legal rights to his son. Toby's grandmother had allowed the boy to visit his father, but his mother—a reporter for the Associated Press—hadn't even put Rule's name on the birth certificate.

Rule had never taken the matter to court. The son of the best-known werewolf in the world would have been irresistible to the paparazzi. Besides, Rule had been certain he'd lose. The courts weren't exactly friendly to lupi.

Until a few years ago, some states had allowed people to shoot them on sight. Most lupi had actually preferred that to the federal government's policy—forced registration and drugs that prevented them from Changing.

But those were the bad old days. A few years ago the Supreme Court had ruled that lupi were citizens. As such, they were entitled to all the rights and protections of the law . . . when they were shaped like humans, that is. It was still legal to shoot one in wolf form.

After a few moments Cynna sighed. "I've been an ass, haven't I? So busy doing the poor-me bit I didn't have a clue what was happening in anyone else's life."

Lily gave her a smile. "It's okay to play turtle for a while, as long as you don't get too fond of your shell. You're out of it now. How much of your money do I get to spend today?"

"Oh, a couple hundred. I usually buy myself a Christmas present, but this time I never got around to it, what with the demons and all."

"Triple it."

"What? I'm not going to—"

"You said you wanted a new work wardrobe. Unless you've changed your mind? For example, you might have some reason to think your size could suddenly change—"

Cynna made a beeping sound.

"What?"

"That's the allusion alert."

Lily slid her an amused glance. "We'll start with the basics. Two good jackets—"

"I have jackets."

"Sure, and they might work if you were eighty pounds heavier. And eighty years old. *And* not interested in fashion. You look great in jeans, but the suits you pick . . ." She shook her head. "Is that what you think an FBI agent is supposed to look like?"

"All right, all right—but I look like crap in suits. I'm not built like you. I can't wear those teeny little fitted jackets."

"You can wear clothes that fit, though. As for how you're built . . ." Lily snorted. "You don't like looking like Xena, Warrior Princess? You're tired of wiping the drool off men's faces?"

"Well, but—"

"You've got a goddess's body, Cynna. Not the Maiden, but the Mother or some fertility deity."

Cynna gave her a dark look. She did not care for fertility deity references.

"Add in the butch haircut and tattoos, and I'm thinking we need to go for simple but dramatic. Whatever we get will probably have to be tailored, but—"

"Tailored?" Cynna squeaked.

"Most likely. We'll start with two jackets, like I said, and four pairs of slacks to mix and match. You could add a skirt, but I've never seen you wear one, so I thought we'd stay in your comfort zone and go with slacks."

"You've got a weird notion of my comfort zone."

"And of course you'll need things to wear under the jackets. Tees, a long-sleeved shirt, a sweater or—"

"There's a Wal-Mart about a mile from here."

"You didn't buy those jeans at Wal-Mart. They're killer."

"Thanks. But jeans aren't like suits. They have to fit exactly right, and most of them aren't long enough, so . . . quit looking at me that way."

"Uh-huh. How much did you pay for the jeans?"

Too much. "Sales. There are bound to be sales."

TWO

THE Fashion Center turned out to be a three-story temple to consumerism. It was midweek and the middle of the day—somehow Lily had persuaded her to take a day off for this insanity—so the teens and tweens were missing. But everywhere Cynna looked, a mom had stuffed a baby in one of those enormous touring devices they called strollers.

There was a muffled little lump of infant in one not ten feet away when Cynna emerged from the dressing room. It was staring at her with enormous, wary eyes.

It gave her the willies. She scowled at Lily. "They don't make clothes for people with breasts. Have you ever noticed that?" She tried tugging the jacket across her chest. The ends wouldn't meet. "See that? If you're more than a B-cup, forget it."

"Shut up, Cynna, and try this instead."

Maybe she'd been tactless. Lily was kind of small on top. Cynna slipped off the too-tight jacket and eyed the leather duster Lily was holding out. It was a dark, rich brown like baking chocolate, but . . . "It's not black."

"Black is so not your color."

She loved black. She'd always worn black. "You keep saying that, but black goes with my tattoos." They weren't precisely tattoos, but Cynna generally used the word other people recognized, not the Swahili that truly named the patterns overlaying her skin like heavy lace. The spells were *kilingo*; the core patterns she used to Find things were *kielezo*. Neither had been applied with ink and needles.

"Black makes people just see the tattoos, not the skin. Try on the duster."

Dubious, Cynna shrugged on the long duster. "Can you wear something like this to Headquarters?"

"I couldn't. I'd look ridiculous, like I was dressing up in my big sister's clothes. But on you, with those slacks . . ." Lily shook her head and sighed. "Check out the mirror."

Cynna turned. And stared. After a moment she felt a smile stretching her cheeks. The dangerous-looking woman in the mirror smirked right back at her. "Hey, is that me? I look hot."

"You do, except for the bag."

The brown slacks Cynna had been complaining about looked wicked cool now. So did the copper sweater, but her old denim bag was all wrong. Even she could see that. "I guess I could get a new one. Purses don't hold enough, so I usually get a tote or something, but . . . hey." While she spoke she'd tried buttoning the duster. Lo and behold, button met buttonhole. "It fits! How'd you find one that fits?"

"I asked one of those snooty clerks to help me. Ah . . . it didn't come from the sale rack."

Cynna gulped. Leather. Not on sale. And in this store . . . She grabbed her courage in both hands and looked at the price.

"Steady." Lily put a hand on her shoulder.

"I can't . . . there's no way I can afford this." Though part of her brain was scrambling to come up with a way . . . She had plenty of credit, but she hated paying interest. She had savings, too, but—

"If you're sure . . . ?"

"I am." No way was she compromising her security by pulling money out of savings for clothes.

"Then I guess you'll just have to accept it as a late Christmas present from me and Rule."

Cynna stared. "Get real. Christmas was weeks ago. Besides, this—this—no one gives Christmas presents that cost this much."

"Rule does. He gave me his card today and told me to buy you something you ought to have but were too cheap to spring for. Well . . . he put it more tactfully, but that was the gist." She nodded at the coat. "This would be it."

"It's too much. Way too much."

"Rule can afford it—and trust me, he'll be paying for the lion's share. He gave Cullen a diamond."

An image flashed into her head of Cullen Seabourne with a diamond winking in his ear. She ignored the quick flutter in her belly and cocked an eyebrow at Lily. "Right ear or left?"

Lily shook her head. "You can ask? Never mind. Your eyes are glazing over. I hate to mess with your fantasy, but the diamond is on a ring for his finger, not his ear. He has to be able to watch what he's doing when he feeds sorcéri into it."

So it didn't go *bam*. She knew that. Feed raw magic into a diamond too fast or slightly wrong and you'd end up with diamond chips, which was why so few practitioners tried it. Cullen could pull it off because he could see the sorcéri as he fed them in. That's what made him a sorcerer.

Envy bit again. Damn, she needed to go to confession. "Big bling?"

"Huge. Roughly five carats, but it's lab-grown, not natural. The outfit Rule bought it from has this new technique that makes big, clear diamonds that are atomically identical to natural diamonds. The process is so new the stones aren't on the market yet, but Rule got a deal on one because he promised a report on its magical properties. You haven't asked how Cullen is doing."

"He's got an ankle again and most of his foot." At Lily's raised brows she snapped, "He called, okay?"

"He said he hadn't spoken to you."

"He, uh, left a message." Lots of messages. Every night. Every blasted night he called, always between eight and nine, and left a message on her voice mail. Never putting pressure on her—oh, no, he was too canny for that. Most of the messages weren't seductive, either, though he'd left a couple that . . . never mind. Usually he said something funny or stupid or just *hi, checking in again.*

The man had no scruples. "Maybe I should try on a skirt with this," Cynna said brightly. "Get a new bag. You said . . . you said something about my bag." Weird. Her head was floating a foot over her shoulders all of a sudden.

"Are you hyperventilating?"

Could be. Her fingers were tingling and her lips were numb. "It was purple, not teal."

"What?"

"You know, that greeny-blue color. Teal." The words came out all rushed and shallow. "I was sure it would be teal, but I peed in a cup this morning and the tester came up purple."

Lily gave her one of those flat, appraising looks all cops master in cop school. "Okay. We're going to walk around now." She put an arm around Cynna's shoulders. "Hold your breath for three steps, let it out on the fourth, then hold it again."

"I'm not—"

"You can't talk and hold your breath at the same time."

True. Cynna counted steps and held her breath for half of them, her head floating along above her shoulders like a helium balloon on a short tether. They walked up to a sales clerk—short, skinny, and dressed in black.

Everyone got to wear black except her.

"We'll take the whole outfit," Lily told the woman and ripped the tags from the pants, the duster, and the sweater still on Cynna's body. She handed them to the clerk along with a charge card. "I'll be back for the card later."

The woman shook her head firmly. "You cannot—"

"We're having a health event here." Lily flashed her FBI ID. "Charge the clothes to the card and hold on to it for me."

The clerk yes-ma'am'ed her. Cynna didn't. Her breath whooshed out. "You are not buying the slacks and sweater."

"You'll pay me back. Keep counting."

A small, imperative hand at Cynna's back kept her moving past aisles of dresses and through the scented air of the cosmetics section, where Lily glared their way past the designated puffer trying to spritz them with cologne. Then they were in the concourse.

She remembered the place from some news story. There was supposed to be a small node near the fountain. At the Turning it had leaked, just like the rest of them— but this one had leaked a goblin along with the magic overflow. Shoppers had freaked.

So had the goblin. They were mean as hell in bunches, but didn't cope well outside the herd.

The incident didn't seem to have hurt business much, Cynna noted as they passed the fountain—dry now with an Under Repair sign parked in the middle basin. There were plenty of people out spending money or just hanging. She drew some stares, but she was used to that. Tattoos weren't uncommon these days, but Cynna's weren't the usual flowers or whatever. And there were a lot of them.

By the time they passed the escalators, Cynna's hands had almost stopped tingling and her head was back in a normal relationship with her shoulders. Funny, she hadn't realized panic felt so much like helium. "I'm okay."

"Good. Keep walking."

She didn't. She stopped and looked at Lily. "I didn't get you a Christmas present."

"I noticed that, and it was really tacky of you."

"Or Rule. I thought about it, but what do you get someone who has ninety times as much money as you do? Are you okay with this?"

"With Rule having more money than you do?"

"No, with him spending so much on a gift for me." Years ago, Cynna had been involved with Rule. That had caused a few problems when she and Lily first met—mostly, Cynna admitted, because she hadn't wanted to accept that Rule was taken. Who ever heard of a monogamous werewolf, after all? But that's just what Rule was, because of his mate bond with Lily . . . something Cynna hadn't known existed.

The rest of the world still didn't. Mate bonds were supersecret. Cynna knew three things about them: the bond wouldn't let Rule and Lily be too far apart; it gave them a directional bead on each other; and they were rare. Really rare. She wouldn't know that much if the clan's priestess hadn't decided Cynna was her successor. Which was just crazy.

"Of course I'm okay with it. Like I said, he bought . . . can I say Cullen's name without you freaking?"

"It's not him, it's . . . well, he's involved, or was involved, but he . . . it isn't about him."

Lily nodded. "Purple, huh?"

Cynna gulped in a breath, held it, and started walking again without being told. After a moment she said, "They teach you that in cop school? What to do when a witness hyperventilates?"

"No, my sister used to have panic attacks, and of course she didn't want our folks to know, so I'd walk with her. Wonder if she still has them." Lily tilted her head, considering that. "I haven't walked her through one in years, but maybe her new husband does. It's not easy being perfect."

"That's your older sister, then. The doctor."

"Uh-huh. Maybe I'll ask her about her panic attacks next time she calls."

"That seems like the kind of question a big sister might resent from a younger one."

Lily smiled. "Yeah."

"You're meaner than you look."

"She only calls to tell me to ditto whatever my mother's been saying—now that Mother's speaking to me again, that is. It usually involves a lot of criticism couched as advice. Why am I not married, what am I doing in D.C. instead of . . . Hey, the food court's up ahead. Are you ready to stop for a minute, grab a Coke?"

That was girl-speak for *Are you ready to talk?* Cynna walked on in silence for a moment, then stopped and looked right at Lily. "I never boosted panty hose because I didn't wear them. Copped some lipstick, though. Jewelry. A wallet once."

Lily didn't seem shocked or even surprised by the subject. "So did my cousin Jenny when she was fifteen. Makeup, I mean, not a wallet. I'm not supposed to know about it, but my cousin Freddy told me once when he was proposing."

Ick. "Your cousin *proposed*?"

"Second cousin, but we all just say cousin."

"You've got a lot of family."

Lily nodded and waited.

"I don't have any sisters or cousins. I had an aunt— she's the reason I'm not more messed up than I am—but she never had kids." Cynna jammed her hands in the pockets of her new coat. "I was pretty much a cliché growing up, you know? Not just poor, but ghetto poor. Funny how they don't call it that anymore. We have 'urban poor' these days."

"I guess some people think if they keep renaming it, maybe it will go away."

"Yeah. Doesn't work, does it? Kids still grow up like I did—absent father, drunk or junkie mother. I dodged some of the clichés, mostly because of Aunt Pat. I didn't drop out of school or do drugs or get . . . get . . ." She stopped, swallowed.

"Pregnant?" Lily said gently.

Cynna tipped her head up and stared at the girders crisscrossing the vaulted glass roof. The sky was blue and bright. After a moment she said, "I didn't hyperventilate. I guess that's progress."

"I guess it is. You want to go to the food court?"

Cynna shook her head. "We'd better head back and get Rule's card. I don't trust that clerk."

"Okay." They reversed direction. "Did you mean it about trying on a skirt?"

"No."

Lily grinned. "Temporary insanity does not constitute— oh, my God." She stopped moving. "What's *she* doing here?"

Cynna couldn't figure out who Lily was talking about. There were a number of "*she*s" directly ahead—an older woman with a Talbot's bag, a young mom with a toddler, two teens who should have been in school.

All at once a runty bald *something* was standing ten feet away. It had breasts, orange skin, and pointy teeth. It—she?—wore a tight yellow dress with purple polka dots, and it was grinning at them. "Hi, Lily Yu!"

The teens screamed. A nearby man in a suit gaped, then swung his briefcase at it.

"Hey!" It grabbed the case with both hands. That's when Cynna saw the tail—long and prehensile, it lashed around to grab the man's ankle. "Did you see that? He tried to hit me! Can I—"

"No," Lily said loudly, hurrying forward. "Turn loose of him and give him back his briefcase."

"But he—"

"Wasn't expecting you," Lily said, tugging on the briefcase. "You startled him."

"What in the hell is that thing?" the man demanded.

My words exactly. Cynna didn't say them, though. Lily seemed to have the whatsit situation under control, so she dealt with the teens. One of them was sobbing and clinging to the other, who glared at Cynna suspiciously.

"Great effect, isn't it?" Cynna said cheerfully. "You didn't see . . . ah, her coming, did you?"

The dark-haired one frowned harder. "No."

"Great! And your name is—?"

"Shauna. And this is Deanna." Shauna was still suspicious, but her friend stopped crying long enough to protest Shauna's making free with their names, which Mom had told them never, ever to do.

Probably Mom had also told them not to cut school, but never mind that. The girls weren't hysterical anymore.

Lily recovered the briefcase and restored it to its owner. "Sorry for the shock, sir."

"But he tried to hit me!" the orange whatsit exclaimed. It was child-size, but built like a squashed sumo wrestler. With breasts. Big breasts. And that tail. "Can't you shoot him or something?"

"No," Lily said shortly. "Gan, what are you doing here?"

Gan? Cynna looked closer. The body had changed the most, but the face was different, too. Same orange skin and bald head, same ridiculously wide eyes with Maybelline lashes, but the rest of the features were . . . well, you couldn't call them normal, but it was amazing what a difference a nose could make. Cynna would never have recognized the little demon.

Former demon, she supposed. Gan had been staying with the gnomes while she underwent some kind of mysterious transformation. Cynna ought to have recognized the voice, though—high-pitched and squeaky, as if one of those yappy little dogs decided to talk.

A crowd was gathering. "I'm calling the police," Briefcase Man announced.

Gan ignored him. "I'm going with you, of course. Didn't they tell you I was coming?"

"They?" Lily said. "Who?"

Gan looked around, frowning—an interesting sight, given the lack of eyebrows. Then she rolled her eyes. "Great. They got the timing wrong. Wouldn't you know it! They're supposed to be such hotshot gaters, but they couldn't even sync the—"

The screaming interrupted her.

Cynna and Lily locked glances for a split second, then took off running. The screams were coming from back near the fountain.

The China Doll was smart, she was tough, but Cynna's legs were a lot longer and she knew how to run. As Cynna pulled ahead, she heard the little demon piping away—somehow, despite her runty legs, Gan was keeping up with Lily. "Are you going to shoot someone? Who? I want a gun, too."

Gun. Right. Probably a good idea, so Cynna fished in her purse for her weapon without breaking stride. She had only two offensive spells—one that worked only on demons, and one that required physical contact. If whatever was up ahead required subduing, she'd rather not have to waltz with it.

She swerved around two young men running flat out and nearly collided with one of the stroller-mobiles. Damned bloody things were everywhere! She skidded, managed to dodge it and its terrified mom-motor—and stopped dead.

There were three of them. They stood beside the empty fountain, looking around. The short one wore a short green robe and tights. He looked like a gnome—small, wrinkled, long beard, big nose. A pair of oversize ears parted his scraggly hair, their tips covered by the absurd pouf of a hat he wore. The middlesize one was the color of wet clay, his skin damp and shiny, as if he was sweating. His lips were the weirdest part of him, being dusky black. He was as bald as Gan, but the effect was different . . . maybe because he wore only a loincloth and some sort of fancy boots.

Never mind the funny skin. This dude was beefcake.

The third one was gray, tusked, eight or so feet tall, with tight little curls on his head—no, her head. Those were breasts beneath the brown tunic, not just great pecs.

Didn't matter. Not when she was holding a sword big enough to gut an elephant. Cynna slid into firing position. "Put down the sword!"

They all looked at her. The gnomish one smiled and said something, but the syllables did not add up to English.

"Hold your fire," Lily told her as she skidded into place on Cynna's left, weapon ready.

"Hey! You can't shoot them," Gan squeaked, sounding disappointed as she, too, came to a stop. *"Harazeed,"* she called out to the trio—or something along those lines. *"Ke antar essy isclaum* Lily Yu *si* Cynna Weaver. *Ke relan* English, you idiot!"

"Ah!" said the little one in the funny hat, beaming. He put one hand on his chest and bobbed his knees once. "Welcome me-you-us, Lily Yu and Cynna Weaver. Please to take us to your leader."

THREE

GAN liked cars. She'd been in cars a few times back when she'd been sent to this Earth realm to help that idiot Harlowe. That was before Harlowe got himself killed, which had kept Gan from possessing Lily Yu like she was supposed to, and then they'd been dragged off to Dis, where she ended up liking Lily Yu, which made her start growing a soul so she couldn't be a demon anymore.

Things had sure been simpler back then. Simpler, but not as interesting.

Because life was more interesting now, Gan had decided to forgive Harlowe. When she'd told Jenek that, though, he had laughed in that whispery wheeze of his and said that wasn't really forgiveness, oh no. But he wouldn't tell her what forgiveness really was.

Gnomish elders were like that.

Gan had enjoyed the fuss when she blinked out of dashtu and surprised everyone, with people screaming and all. There'd been even more fuss when the three from Edge showed up, but Lily Yu didn't like fuss. She'd called someone on her *cell phone*—Gan wanted one of those—and a

bunch of cops had come, and things were dull for a while.
But now they were leaving.

"Where are we going?" Gan asked as she climbed into
the back of the police van with Lily Yu and Cynna Weaver
and the delegation from Edge. There were benches along
the sides, and the delegation from Edge sat on one bench
while Gan sat between the two humans on the other. A
metal wall divided their sitting place from the driving place.

"To see my leader," Lily Yu said. The other female,
Cynna Weaver, snickered.

"Not Rule Turner, though," Gan said. She did not like
the wolf. "*He's* not your leader."

"We're going to see a man called Ruben Brooks." Lily
looked at the three beings opposite them. "If I understood
you correctly, sir, you're from another realm."

The councilor smiled. "Is so. The our home . . . English word for realm is Edge. Edge is close many realms,
is for trade many realms. Is hub. Many gates in Edge.
Many trade."

"You're here for trade?"

"Is for trade, yes. We very good with gates, with the
making and maintaining. This for your leader and we to
talk of. Many details to agree with, yes? We is also here
for the Lily Yu and the Cynna Weaver."

"M-me?" Cynna Weaver stuttered. "You're here for
me and Lily?"

The councilor nodded, smiling that stupid smile. He
probably wasn't stupid, though. Gan wondered if she
should warn Lily Yu about that.

Maybe later. "We don't have any windows," Gan said,
frowning as they jolted into motion. The cars she had
been in before were called *taxis*, and they hadn't gone
very fast. She'd hoped the *police van* would go faster, but
even if it did, it wouldn't be much fun without windows.
"Do we have a siren?"

"We don't want to draw attention," Lily Yu said.

"Why not?"

"In Dis you knew the dangers and I listened to you.

Here, I know the dangers. Drawing attention would be bad." She turned toward the councilor. "Sir—"

"But this is made of metal. Even a Claw would have trouble opening it up, I bet. At least for a minute or two. Not that you have any Claws here."

Lily Yu glanced at Gan. "People can be dangerous, too, especially if they have weapons."

That made sense. Gan had seen some of the human weapons on television, though not lately, because the elders didn't allow television in the underways. "Do you have a television?"

Lily Yu gave her one of those thinking looks, but before she could answer, the councilor spoke. He told Gan to be quiet or he would have the half-half squeeze Gan's throat until her eyes exploded. He used the trade tongue, so Gan understood him but the humans didn't. He smiled the whole time.

Gan stuck her tongue out at him. Humans thought that was very rude, but he might not know that.

"So what did he say?"

That was Cynna Weaver asking, not Lily Yu. Lily Yu was asking the councilor questions, like what his name was. Which was rude, but she didn't know about gnomes. Gan would tell her . . . oh, the councilor was explaining now. Harazeed gnomes didn't even use call-names except with family. The others did, though, so he introduced them: Wen of Ekiba and Tash.

Then Lily wanted to know how he'd found her and Cynna Weaver at the mall, which was a very good question, but she should have asked Gan. The councilor just talked nothing-stuff back at her about that.

Gan turned to look at the woman who'd gone to Dis to find Rule Turner but hadn't gotten to keep him or even do sex with him. For some reason lots of human females wanted to do sex with Rule Turner. Gan didn't get it.

Cynna Weaver was interesting to look at with all those patterns on her skin. She wasn't as dense to Gan's *üther* sense as Lily Yu, but she wasn't thin, either. In fact, now that she looked closely . . . "Hey, you're pr—"

A flat, human hand clamped Gan's mouth shut. "I'd rather you didn't mention that."

Gan perked up. Secrets were almost always useful. She nodded, and Cynna Weaver removed her hand. "It's secret?"

"For now. Are you going to answer my question?"

Gan shrugged. "He told me to shut up or the half-half would choke me." Cynna Weaver's eyebrows went up. That eyebrow motion could mean all sorts of things, but Gan thought that this time it meant surprise. Gan's gaze drifted. "You've got great breasts. What do you think of mine? Pretty nice, huh? Jenek told me to keep 'em covered out here. He said humans have rules about that, but I see breasts on television sometimes."

"Human sexual customs confuse us, too, but keeping most of your breasts covered is usually best. I notice that you're talking and no one is choking you."

"I'm not talking to Lily Yu." The councilor didn't care if Gan talked to Cynna Weaver, which was interesting. Shouldn't he be trying to get Lily Yu on his side? "You're a Finder, right?"

"Right. Is the little guy your boss?"

"Huh! You mean the councilor? He's not in charge of me, but he is in charge of the half-half, who probably isn't strong enough to make my eyes pop out. I'm pretty strong, too. But she does have those tusks."

"Not to mention a great big sword, if we're talking about the same person—the one the councilor called Tash. She's a half-half?"

"Uh-huh. That's what they call them, all the ones who aren't just one thing or another. Half-halfs."

"Who's 'they'?"

"Gnomes. That's who I know about, anyway, but I guess everyone in Edge calls them that. There's a lot of half-halfs in Edge because of all the magic."

"You been to Edge?"

Gan nodded, preening. "I can still cross." That was rare—hardly any demons could cross between realms without being summoned, but Gan could. She hadn't lost the ability when she started growing her soul, either. This made her very special.

Cynna Weaver recognized that. Gan could see the admiration in her face and hear it in her voice. "I wish I could cross like that. Is it harder to do now?"

"Well, I don't have as much juice, but . . . hey, do you have any candy? *Chocolate* candy."

"My, you have changed. Not gobbling live bugs these days?"

Gan sighed. "I can't eat *ymu* anymore, so I have to eat dead things. But chocolate's different. I like chocolate."

"I think I've got some." Cynna Weaver pulled her big bag up into her lap and started digging around in it. "You've been staying with the gnomes."

"Uh-huh. What kind of chocolate?"

"How did you know that the councilor and the others were coming here?" She pulled out a candy bar. Gan tried to grab it, but Cynna Weaver held it up too high. "Answer the question first."

"I'm stronger than you. I can just take it."

"Do you have money?"

Gan's forehead scrunched up. "Huh?"

"If you have money, you can buy your own chocolate. If you don't have money, you'll either have to steal things— which can get you in lots of trouble—or get someone to give you what you want. I might give you more chocolate later if you don't make me mad. If you make me mad," she added, "I might zap you."

Gan eyed her. Cynna Weaver was bigger than her, of course, but that didn't mean much. Even big humans were pretty puny. But she'd seen Cynna Weaver kill a red-eye with a spell. Red-eyes were tough to kill. "Lily Yu wouldn't like it if you killed me."

"I have more than one spell. My zap spell hurts but doesn't kill. Usually."

"Yeah?" Gan perked up, interested. "Show me. Not on me," she added hastily. "On the half-half, maybe. Or the councilor."

"Not now. How did you know the Edge people were coming here?"

"I'd like to know that, too," Lily Yu said.

Gan looked up at her. It made her feel funny to see Lily Yu again. Good-funny and bad-funny all mixed up.

While Lily Yu was in Dis, she had died. Well, part of her had, since she'd accidentally gotten herself split in two—which wasn't Gan's fault, or not all her fault, anyway. Being human, Lily Yu had a soul, so the part that died hooked up again with the part that lived, which was the Lily Yu sitting beside Gan now.

It was complicated, but Gan more or less understood what had happened—as much as she understood anything about souls, anyway. The confusing part was the way she felt right now, as if she'd eaten something bad, something she couldn't quite swallow all the way. "Most of you doesn't remember me, huh?"

"Some of me does."

The way Lily Yu said that made the tight, unswallowed feeling in Gan's throat feel better. "You recognized me. Even though I look a lot different now, you knew who I was."

"I did, right away. Are you going to answer Cynna's question?"

Gan stole a glance at the candy, but Cynna Weaver still held it out of reach. She sighed. "Some of it I can't tell, but—"

The councilor tried to interrupt, but Lily Yu told him she wanted to hear what her friend said. The councilor made a huffy sound. "Little orange one is being mostly demon still. Not is friend."

Gan liked the way Lily smiled at the councilor, as if she might hit him in a minute but wanted it to be a surprise. "Really? I wonder how you would know who my friends are." She looked at Gan. "How did you know about this?"

"The councilor is a Harazeed, see—that's one of the gnomish people. So the Hragash—they're the ones I've been staying with—knew he'd be coming, or at least the elders did, because they talk to each other. And it's time for my testing, so they sent me here so I could take the next step."

"Next step?"

"Going with you to get back the—"

The councilor burst out with a lot of words, some of them in the trade tongue, none of them in English, but Gan caught the gist, which was *shut up*. Gan looked at him. "I'm supposed to help you, but you are not in charge of me. I can tell them that part if I want to, and I do . . . if I get my chocolate."

Cynna handed her the candy bar. Gan grinned and ripped off the paper. She stuffed half of it in her mouth, closing her eyes to savor the experience, and spoke through the thick pleasure. "They lost something. They want you to Find it."

"Some reason you didn't want her to tell us that?" Lily Yu asked the councilor.

"No, no," he assured her. "Is that the loss is secret—as the Gan knows."

The chocolate was almost gone, melting away inside her mouth. Gan swallowed and opened her eyes. The councilor wasn't smiling now. She shrugged. "Not a secret from these two, is it?"

"Is for speaking only when is shielded. No shield here."

"Excuse me," Cynna Weaver said, "but do you mean 'shield' or 'wards'? Because we can do wards, but . . . well, when we speak of wards we're talking about spells to repulse specific intruders—fleas, demons, whatever. Usually they'll send a warning if something does get through, as well. But a shield spell would create a true barrier, one that keeps out everything, including the mental stuff."

The Harazeed bobbed his head. "Is meaning that kind, yes. Shield for everythings' keeping out."

"Sorry. We can't do those."

"Is needing shield! Wards is not closing off the farsee-ing, farhearing, the elementals, the . . . wards is not being enough!"

Lily Yu spoke. "Can you make a shield?"

The councilor talked to the others in upset murmurs. They used trade tongue, but spoke so fast and low Gan didn't catch all of it. When the gnome turned back to Lily Yu and shook his head, though, the negative matched what she'd heard. "This one is not able. Others not able. I is having knowledge of spell for shield, but is not having . . ." He waved his hands. "English is not having word for this. My magic wrong for making shield."

"But you know how to make one?"

"I know spell."

"Cynna?" Lily Yu's face was all shut down so Gan couldn't see what she was thinking.

"I don't know," the inky woman said. "An unknown spell . . . ee-way ant-cay oh-nay ut-whay it-way eally-ray uz-day."

"Hey!" Gan said. "What language is that?"

"Pig Latin."

Pig Latin? Gan had heard of Latin, but she didn't think pigs spoke it. Or any other language. She frowned and took another bite of candy, smaller this time, wanting to save some for later . . . a couple minutes later, anyway.

Lily Yu reached across Gan to pat Cynna Weaver's knee. "You can do spells, but for something like this . . . an unknown spell and all . . . well. Better call in the expert." She looked back at the councilor. "I know someone who can probably work that spell of yours."

The councilor looked relieved. Cynna Weaver didn't. She looked . . . what was the word? Oh, yes. Appalled.

Wouldn't it be interesting to find out why?

Gan popped the last of the chocolate in her mouth and wiggled with pleasure. She was having so much fun. Even without the windows.

FOUR

❦

CULLEN could walk without crutches now, if he had to. It had been nearly five weeks since a giant flying monster from hell had chowed down on his foot and related bits. He didn't heal as fast as some lupi—his talents lay in other directions—but he'd finished regrowing the lower leg and his ankle now ended in a foot bulb, a knobby projection with everything a foot might need. It was curled up in an unfootlike shape, but the parts were all there.

But it hurt like hell to walk on the blasted thing. Tarsal and metatarsal bones, itty-bitty phalanges, and all those tendons were curled around one another, the bones still soft, nothing finished, nothing in its proper position. So he swung along on crutches beside the Fed who'd been designated to bring him to some supersecret location in the bowels of FBI Headquarters, aka the J. Edgar Hoover FBI Building, feeling foolish and annoyed.

Make that pissed. Lily gives him a call . . . and he'd answered his phone, hadn't he? Okay, maybe that was because he wanted to know how the shopping with Cynna had gone, whether the dippy woman had finally deigned to acknowledge reality. But he had answered.

And what does she do? Asks him to drop everything and come to this big, ugly block of a building named for the asshole who ran the FBI back when lupi were pretty much "shoot on sight" to the Feds. Wouldn't tell him why, either. She gave him this "can't tell you on an unsecured line" bullshit.

In spite of that, he'd agreed. Lily didn't make a habit of yanking him around, which meant something was up. He wanted to know what. But he'd been in the middle of an elaborate setup for a spell, an important one.

Cullen had the most impenetrable mental shields on the planet. They weren't some freakish natural ability, but something that had been given him—or done to him— while he was unconscious last September. It was driving him crazy. He possessed incredibly sophisticated spells, but passively. He didn't *know* the spells, couldn't cast them or learn from them. That was intolerable. He'd spent weeks creating a spell he hoped would read and copy the ones that had been used on him.

Of course, his shields were designed not to be tampered with, and reading them was akin to tampering. This would be his third attempt. He thought he had the parameters down, but only the casting would tell.

Lily knew all that. She knew how much this mattered. So when he'd told her he would come in tomorrow, he'd expected her to accept that.

Instead, she'd gotten Rule to order him to come here.

Oh, technically Rule hadn't ordered him. Technically, being heir to Nokolai clan didn't give him that authority. But if your Lu Nuncio tells you the clan needs you to do something, you're damned well going to do it, aren't you?

Especially if you've spent the better part of your life clanless. Outcast.

Cullen knew Rule wouldn't kick him out of Nokolai for failing to jump fast enough. He *knew* that. Yet here he was, and if a good half of his mad came from fears he had no intention of acknowledging, that didn't make him feel one whit more agreeable.

So maybe he was less than tactful when his escort turned him over to a pair of idiots in bad suits who were guarding a dull stretch of hallway holding three doors— one on the right, two on the left. The idiots wanted to search him.

He did keep his tone polite. "First you'd better search for some damned brains. I'll help. Bend over."

"Sorry, sir," said the first asshole, lying like a politician. "Orders. You're lupus. We have to search you before you can go any farther."

This was a perfect opportunity. All he had to do was exactly what he wanted—tell them to admit him immediately or else explain to their superiors why he'd left. They wouldn't back down. He could tell. They'd refuse to let him pass and he could leave.

Problem was, the bastards would think they'd won . . . and he'd told Rule he would do this. If he didn't follow through, he made himself a liar. Which he was, of course, when necessary. Lying was a fine and useful skill, one he'd honed well over the years. But he didn't lie to friends. He might occasionally forget to mention this or that, but he didn't lie to them.

So that was out.

Maybe he should just clobber these assholes and look for Lily on his own. An appealing notion . . . not smart, but definitely appealing. "First, I was *asked* to come here. Second, I've already been patted down, just before they issued me this nifty little badge that's supposed to admit me everywhere but the executive washroom."

"Yes, sir," said Asshole Number Two, who was enjoying himself. "But we have to conduct a more thorough search."

Cullen asked very sweetly, "Are you by any chance talking about a strip search?"

The first asshole wasn't as dumb as he looked. He took a quick, involuntary step back.

"Because if you are, you should know that I strip for a

living. If you want me to take my clothes off, it will cost you."

"You can start with those crutches." Asshole Number Two smiled a tight, smug smile. "Hand them over."

Cullen's fingertips itched. It would be easy to singe that smirk right off the man's pudgy face. "I'm missing my foot, and you want to take away my crutches."

"They might be used as weapons."

Cullen nodded thoughtfully. He'd better do what the man said, hadn't he? One crutch would go to Asshole Number Two—a head shot, he thought. Clip him across the front of the skull, which shouldn't do any lasting damage as long as Cullen minded his strength. The other would go in the stomach of Asshole Number One, who wasn't quite as much of a prick.

One of the doors behind the assholes opened and a little over five feet of slender Asian woman emerged. "Chill, Cullen."

He spun to glare at her. "Did you tell this pair of shit-for-brains to strip-search me?"

Lily's eyebrows went up. She inspected the two guards, settling with admirable instinct on Asshole Number Two. "That your idea, ah . . ."

"Baxter," he said, still smirking. He really wasn't very smart. "And I'm following orders."

"Whose? No, never mind." She spoke over her shoulder to someone on the other side of the doorway. "Ruben, I'd like to bring Cullen in before he burns someone. Could you clear him?"

The whirr of a motorized wheelchair preceded the man she'd spoken to. Cullen's curiosity shot up, eclipsing his temper for the moment. He'd met the head of the secretive Unit 12 once, but he'd been blind at the time. He knew how Ruben Brooks smelled, the sound of his voice, but not what he looked like.

Gaunt, erect, and with a beak of a nose, it turned out. Brooks's navy suit was beautifully tailored; his tie, silk—and knotted with all the clumsy disinterest of a five-year-old. His shoes were polished; his socks, brown. Those details said "married" to Cullen, though he supposed it was possible the man's style-conscious partner belonged to his own sex.

A quick glance at Brooks's left hand found a gold ring, giving weight to the married theory. Long fingers, Cullen noted, though the joints were swollen. Arthritis? The product of whatever condition kept him in that chair?

Behind the chair stood a skinny, red-headed gun freak, Brooks's bodyguard du jour. Steve Timms was human, intense, and barely back on duty after a month's medical leave. Cullen knew all this because he was the man's roommate at the moment.

Ah, Cullen thought, amused, when Timms failed to reveal by the flicker of a sandy eyelash that he knew Cullen, *my little boy is growing up. Hope he doesn't shoot me.*

The wheelchair required Brooks to tilt his head back to study the assholes. "The problem is, Agent Yu," he said mildly, "that I've already cleared Mr. Seabourne. So I'm confused, gentlemen. Whose orders were you following?"

Asshole Number One was puzzled. "It's standing orders, sir."

"And yet I didn't issue those orders, and you report to me. I remain mystified."

Asshole Number Two wasn't puzzled. He didn't like Brooks, thought he'd one-upped the man, and was stupid enough to let it show. "Orders issued by Acting Director Hayes last month, sir. All nonhumans are to be given a level one search before entering a level one secure area."

"Ah!" Brooks's exclamation landed soft and cold in the hallway. "You are oddly ignorant. Those orders were rescinded two days after being issued. The President," he went on in that chill, quiet voice, "did not consider them helpful. Nor do I. You will call Mr. Croft now and inform him you are to be replaced here at once, as you are temporarily suspended from duty. Mr. Seabourne." He looked at Cullen. "I appreciate your promptness and apologize for the insult. Please come with me."

He reversed his chair. Lily followed him promptly. Cullen paused to give the two guards a cross-eyed grin.

Childish? Sure. But fun.

Behind the door on the right was another hallway, this one short and ending at yet another door.

"MCD idiots," Lily muttered as they headed for that door.

"You're MCD," he reminded her.

"They're regular MCD. Not Unit."

MCD stood for Magical Crimes Division, a section of the FBI that had a bad rep with the clans. MCD had been tasked with enforcing the registration laws before the Supreme Court decided that werewolves were citizens.

The Unit was different from the rest of MCD. Most of its personnel were Gifted, for one thing. On paper the Unit looked like part of MCD, but in practice it had always operated independently of the rest of the division—even, to some extent, of the entire FBI bureaucracy.

Then came the Turning. The number and severity of magical disturbances shot right off the scale. The Unit was the only law enforcement agency with trained, Gifted agents, but there weren't enough of them to deal with everything. So they'd recruited from the ranks of regular MCD agents for some positions . . . leading to the presence of cretins like the two Cullen had just encountered.

Brooks stopped his chair a few paces away from the door at the end of the hall and put it through a tidy maneuver that left him facing Cullen and Lily. "I'll ask Agent Yu to brief you in a moment, Mr. Seabourne. First, though, I have a question. In your opinion, did those two agents act in honest if regrettable ignorance? Or did their actions arise from prejudice?"

Cullen shrugged. "Asshole Number One is stupid—probably doesn't read much, so he never knew about the search orders being rescinded. He thought he was 'doing his dooty.' Asshole Number Two—"

"Sort that for me, please."

"Asshole Number One's the blond. Number Two is the

African American, and if he didn't spend his formative years as an agent shooting lupi, he wanted to."

"Thank you. Mr. Timms? Your opinion, please."

His bodyguard was startled by the request, but answered promptly. "Baxter's an asshole, like Seabourne said. Likes to push around anyone who can be pushed. Carter's okay."

"Thank you. May I say, Mr. Seabourne, I'd like to meet you sometime when you're in possession of all of your parts. Is the regrowth painful?"

"You ever had a wound heal to the itching stage?"

"I have."

"It doesn't itch like that all the time. Just most of it. Inside, where I can't scratch."

"I see. That could be quite annoying." He nodded at Lily. "Please bring Mr. Seabourne up to date as briefly as possible."

"Yes, sir." She looked at Cullen. "We've got visitors. They say they came from another realm, and circumstances back that up. They arrived at the node at the Fashion Center mall two hours ago. Just before their arrival Gan showed up, obviously aware they were on their way, though a little confused as to the timing. There are three of them—a gnome, a man who looks human but isn't, and the third . . . I don't know what to call the third one. The gnome won't give his name—we're to call him councilor. The one who looks human is Wen of Ekiba, and the other one is called Tash, no surname. They claim they're here for trade . . . and for me and Cynna. Gan says they want us to find something, but they're not talking. Or rather," she added, "the councilor talks without saying much and they all talk among themselves, but not in English."

Cullen's eyebrows hitched up. "How did they communicate with you at all?"

"The gnome knows some English, but he won't discuss anything of substance without a shield. He's not talking about wards. Cynna asked about that. He claims he knows a shield spell, but can't use it. His magic isn't the right kind. That's why you're here."

Excitement rose and exploded in a dizzy froth. "Real shields," he repeated carefully. "This gnome is talking about a spell that erects a true shield over a space, not just a person?"

"One that blocks farseeing and farhearing, apparently, among other things. He was shocked to learn we didn't know how to make one."

Delight widened Cullen's grin. "How big a space?"

"Ask him."

Oh, he would. He'd ask the gnome from another realm—another realm!—a great many things. Cullen couldn't stop grinning. "I forgive you."

"I thought you would," she said dryly.

THE door at the end of the short hall led to a small, dark, crowded room. Monitors lining the far wall held the rapt attention of three of the four men in the room. The fourth sat at a keyboard to one side, presumably doing tech things connected to the images on the screens. He wore headphones.

Three of the men were strangers. Cullen knew the fourth one, a beefy fellow with a fine frizz of white hair exploding around his face like an excited dandelion. Cullen rather liked Fagin. The man was a top-notch scholar specializing in pre-Purge history. He was also the head of the Presidential Task Force created at the onset of the Turning.

Not that any of them mattered. Not with what Cullen saw on those screens.

For some reason they had the sound turned off. There were five screens; two were dark. The large, central screen showed a room furnished with institutional lack of imagination: a beige sofa and a couple of chairs. The gnome Lily had mentioned sat in one of the chairs. His feet dangled well off the floor. He was talking to a small, bald, orange female who must be Gan; they were roughly the same size. Behind Gan and the gnome stood a gray-skinned . . . call her a warrior, he decided. Whatever else she was, she carried herself as a fighter.

The big blade sheathed on her back was a clue, too.

His gaze flicked to one of the other screens, which had a view of the room's other occupants. The bald fellow apparently lacked interest in clothing, though he wore a silver necklace with a small silver disk as pendant . . . inscribed?

Cullen squinted and frowned. The resolution wasn't good enough for him to be sure. The man was talking to the only other person in the room, a tallish woman with her back to the camera. His lips, tongue, and palate were dark gray like a chow's. The woman . . . hell!

Cullen spun to glare at Lily. "What the hell are you thinking? Get Cynna out of there!"

Brooks answered smoothly. "Agent Weaver is acting on my orders. We've been assured it would offer grave insult to leave our guests in a room without someone present to act as host. Apparently that's gnomish custom."

"Gnomish *custom* is to exchange hostages. That's her real function—hostage, not host."

"Is this your so-called expert, Ruben?" a slick-looking man in a pricey suit drawled. "Doesn't seem well-informed. Everyone knows gnomes are harmless."

"Everyone knows a lot of damned silly things," Cullen snapped. "Who the hell are you?"

"Adam McClosky. Assistant Undersecretary of Commerce."

"When we're ready to trade something, be sure to speak up. Till then shut your—"

"Cullen," Lily said.

He caught his breath and tried to catch hold of his temper.

"Mr. Seabourne is an expert practitioner," Brooks assured the smooth man. "He's consulted for us before. I have great confidence in his skills and knowledge."

Brooks had done a nice job of stepping around the word "sorcerer." Since sorcery remained illegal due to the impenetrable stupidity of most lawmakers, Cullen appreciated that. "And I'm ready to consult. Get me in there and get Cynna out."

"Soon. Rest assured that Agent Weaver is as safe as we can make her. The room has defenses that aren't obvious."

"The room can't defend her against a magical attack."

"No, she'll have to handle that hersclf, should the need arise."

Cullen took two quick steps, but the place was too damned crowded. He nearly bumped into another one of the strangers, who stepped aside, eying him warily.

Timms spoke without leaving Brooks's side. "It's her job, Cullen."

Cullen scowled. Lily put a hand on his arm. "I think she'll be okay. I've shaken hands with all of them."

The touch startled him enough to break through his urgency. Lily didn't touch often or easily. "And . . . ?"

"They're all of the Blood, but only the gnome is Gifted. It isn't a Gift I've encountered before, but his magic isn't . . ." She waved a hand. "I don't know how to describe it, but his magic felt like it's bound up in itself. Or in something. He doesn't have much juice for other things."

"Of the Blood" meant they were innately magical beings. This was true of most of the nonhuman races, from gnomes to lupi to any number of less common beings and creatures. What Lily meant was that those of the Blood were seldom able to work spells—their magic simply wasn't available that way.

Excepting the Fae, of course. And Cullen, who was both of the Blood and Gifted. As was this gnome, apparently. "Maybe he's using most of his magic for something else right now. I'd very much like to know what, wouldn't you? That doesn't make Cynna safe."

"She's doing her job. And she's pretty good with spellwork herself."

Okay. Okay, he knew that, but . . . Cullen ran a hand

over his hair. "You'll know if something's been done to her. You'll check."

"Of course."

"What's the problem?" demanded the Deputy Under-whatever.

Cullen decided it would be easier to keep a grip on his temper if he ignored the man, so he did.

Fagin blinked sleepily, looking like an aging refugee from the sixties. "Why, if those three come from a high-magic realm—and they do—we have no idea what they might be able to do, magically."

"Why do you believe they come from a high-magic realm?"

Stupidity was so hard to ignore. Cullen managed not to roll his eyes. "They got here, didn't they?"

On the screen, Cynna had moved closer to the gnome. Gan was saying something. Then the councilor spoke.

Damn, but he hated watching remotely this way. He couldn't smell them, couldn't see any of the energies involved. Bet he could hear them, though, if he moved closer to the tech guy with the headphones.

"Exactly." Fagin beamed at him. "Assuming their arrival was purposeful—"

One of the other men broke in. "What do you mean?"

"We've recently seen many examples of creatures crossing accidentally, haven't we? Fairies, brownies, gremlins, even banshees were blown in on the power winds during the Turning. But these visitors arrived without that impetus, and Gan was expecting them. This argues that they did come here intentionally, using a gate, as the councilor claims. This means we're dealing with a culture that's quite sophisticated magically."

"And has plenty of power available," Lily added. "Gates gobble power."

"Very true. There's also the shield spell itself, of course."

"Break that conclusion down for the rest of us, please," Brooks said.

Or just shut up. That would be better. Even with his hearing, Cullen was hard-pressed to listen in on the tech guy's headphones with all the chatter in the room. Couldn't any of them think for themselves long enough to see the obvious?

"Our knowledge of other realms is largely theoretical," Fagin began, "since interrealm travel has been impossible since before the Purge—impossible for humans, that is. Some of the Fae have always been able to cross, though they chose not to. And imps or demons have crossed from time to time, although—"

Brooks spoke dryly. "Fagin, we aren't in class. I believe everyone here is aware of conditions prior to the Turning."

"Of course. The point I was wandering toward is that desert dwellers do not develop shipbuilding capabilities. Due to our relative dearth of magic, we've had no need for shields and haven't hung on to that knowledge. Their realm, apparently, does have a need."

"That makes sense," said one of the men Cullen didn't know. He looked at Cullen. "I understand you know something about gates, Mr. Seabourne."

Cullen twitched one shoulder in an impatient shrug. "Something. Theoretical knowledge, of course," he added in his first lie of the day. Three months ago he'd assisted in making a hellgate, but since that was even more illegal than being a sorcerer, he wasn't planning to add it to his résumé.

"These, ah, people arrived at a node. Is that typical?"

"For a gate? It's necessary. Nodes are the points of greatest physical and temporal congruence. Also, you need the power. Like Lily said, gates gobble power."

"So you believe the councilor created a gate to come here."

"Ah . . . no. Is he claiming he did it alone? Gate building is a team effort. Even the dragons have to work together to do it."

"Dragons? Do you mean they . . . what are you *do-ing*?"

Cullen had yanked the headphones off the tech guy's head and was holding them close to his ear.

On one screen, the inky tracery on Cynna's face stood out in sharp relief against her sudden pallor. He saw her throat work as she swallowed. From the headphones came the thread of her voice saying, "No way."

The tech tried to grab his headphones back. Two of the men started toward Cullen. He looked at Lily. "That bastard just told Cynna he's got her father."

FIVE

"**YOU** is not believing of me," the little gnome said. "So the Daniel is saying . . . is said? English verbs difficult."

Daniel. Her father's name had been Daniel. Daniel Weaver.

Cynna's mouth was dry. Spiking feelings jabbed at her—disbelief, anger, a nameless feeling all shaky and fierce . . . the shaky part seemed to be winning. "Maybe I'll just sit down for a minute." But she didn't move.

"Is hard talking of the father?" The gnome's voice was gluey with sympathy.

"I don't have a . . . I mean, he's gone. Long gone." She'd been two days shy of her third birthday when he walked out on them. She had a couple photos of him. She had a half load of his genes. That was about it.

"Gone from here, yes. Gone to Edge. The Daniel is being one of the Theilo . . . fall-through-cracks people. Fall into our realm."

"He didn't . . . you're saying that he didn't go there on purpose."

"This realm is being closed then. No one of Earth is coming to Edge on purpose. He fall in. Accident." The short green robe the councilor wore wrapped around his skinny body was held at the waist with a wide leather belt. It was a fancy thing, that belt, with gems and scrollwork and several little pockets sewn on, their flaps tied down. He unfastened one of the pockets, reached inside, and frowned, muttering in that other language.

He had to be lying. Didn't he?

The gnome undid another pocket and dug inside it.

He knew her father's name. He knew English . . . more or less. He knew Cynna was a Finder. How could he know any of that? Gan could have told them some things, but Gan didn't know about the sperm donor.

That's how Cynna thought of Daniel Weaver—as the sperm donor. He sure as hell hadn't been anything else to her.

Actually, Cynna didn't see how Gan could have told them anything at all. Communication between realms wasn't possible. No, it wasn't *supposed* to be possible, but what did that mean anymore? Gan had said the gnomish elders talked across the realms. Gan had expected the others to show up. And they had—almost on top of her and Lily. Surely that wasn't coincidence.

But . . . *her father*.

"The Daniel is said you not believing the words, so I giving you a thing from him." The gnome was holding something out in his soft little hand. A ring. A man's gold wedding ring. "You Finder. Check. See if I is speaking of true."

She stared at that ring as if it might leap up and bite her.

The room's only door opened. Lily, Cullen, Ruben, Timms, and a guy in a suit came in, and a whole bunch of stuff happened all at once.

Cullen swung toward Cynna on his crutches. The guy in the suit swerved around Ruben's chair, holding out a hand and yammering about how he was some kind of undersecretary. The gal with the tusks got nervous. At least, Cynna guessed that was why she drew that sword of hers in a single hiss.

Everyone stopped moving . . . except Timms, who drew his weapon. And Gan, who hopped up and down in excitement. "Swing it! Swing it! But not at Lily Yu. Lily Yu, stay back so she—"

"Put that damned thing away." That was Cullen, irritated, talking to the swordswoman.

"—doesn't cut you in half!" Gan yelled.

"Calm down, Gan." Lily said.

"Welcome to America, sir." The guy in the suit.

"Hold your fire, Mr. Timms." Brooks.

"Kethe mi notasi." Bald dude with shiny skin.

Reluctantly, the tusked woman sheathed her blade. She added a few words that might have been a curse or a prayer or a request for directions to the ladies' room.

"I am sitting down now," Cynna announced. And did.

"**So** while the guy from the Commerce Department was making nice with the councilor guy, Lily held the ring and I did a scan on it," Cynna finished. "The dominant pattern was new to me. Daniel Weaver's, I guess. But my mom's was there, too."

The sun was down, the smell of tomato and peppers hung in the air, and the twenty pounds of cat in Cynna's lap was purring. Rule stood at the counter, tearing lettuce as he listened. Lily stood beside him, cutting tomatoes into meticulously correct slices. She'd done most of the briefing; she was good at it.

Cynna, barred from helping by kitchen ineptitude, sat at their big, round table petting Dirty Harry and trying not to drool over the enchiladas baking in the oven. Trying not to think, too. Thinking hadn't brought any answers. It just put twitchy little wires in her veins, making it hard to sit still.

"Told you so," Gan said. "Are there more little fishies?"

Lily told her to look in the pantry, and Gan hopped down from her chair in search of "little fishies." Apparently sardines were one of the few dead things she liked.

Dirty Harry flexed a front paw, letting his claws prick Cynna's new slacks. She took the hint and resumed petting him. "He's not bothered by Gan at all."

"He?" Lily paused, her knife hovering over a tomato. "Oh, you mean Harry. He does seem pretty clear that she isn't a demon."

Cats hated demons. Harry had proved that his demon radar worked exceptionally well, but he was ignoring Gan. That pretty much proved Gan wasn't a demon anymore, to Cynna's way of thinking. She gave Harry a good rub behind the ears, and he rewarded her by turning up his engine.

"You're sure about the pattern, then." Lily said that in a way that left it hovering between statement and question. "It must have been faint. The ring didn't belong to your mother, and she's been gone a long time, hasn't she?"

"Dead" was the word Lily wasn't using. People sidestepped that word the way they'd step around a pile of dog shit on the sidewalk. Her father was gone. Her mother was dead. Big difference. "She died twenty years ago, so yeah, the pattern was old and very faint. And it was my mother's."

"You can pick up a twenty-year-old pattern from an object that didn't even belong to her?"

"Wedding rings are different. They carry a charge from—"

Gan's piping voice interrupted her. "What's this?" She'd emerged from the pantry with a bag of Goldfish. "It has fishies on it."

"Those are crackers," Lily said. "Cynna, if these people are truly sophisticated spellcasters, is it possible—"

Gan stuffed a handful of the little crackers in her mouth. And immediately spat them out. "Yuck, yuck, yuck! That's not food!"

"Some nutritionists would agree with you," Lily said dryly. "That doesn't make it okay to spit it out on the floor. Get some paper towels and clean it up."

"Don't want to." Gan turned to go back into the pantry.

Rule ripped off a handful of paper towels and walked over to the little not-quite-demon. He grabbed Gan's shoulder. "You made a mess. Clean it up."

Gan glared up at him. "Ow! That hurts!"

"It can hurt more."

"I liked you better when you were a wolf. And I didn't like you at all then." But she took the paper towels.

Lily watched, frowning. "She doesn't challenge you as much as she used to."

"She probably doesn't heal as fast as she used to," Cynna said dryly. Then she noticed the way Rule had stopped moving to look at Lily with a sort of tender surprise. "Hey—you remembered something from your lost time, didn't you?"

"Snatches." Lily tilted her head to smile at Rule, who came up behind her. They clasped hands. "They've been drifting in more often lately."

Like Cullen said, the mate-bound were touchy-feely. The wires thrumming along Cynna's veins tightened. Cullen. He was still at Headquarters talking spellwork and theory with the gnome, all frothy with excitement. With all the to-do, he hadn't had a chance to talk to her.

Or else he'd forgotten they had something to talk about. He was like that. She'd been amazed, really, at how regular he'd been about calling. She'd expected him to give up after a few calls—either that or come pounding on her door. He wasn't a patient man.

Maybe his wolf was patient, though. She didn't know that part of him at all.

After a moment, Rule released Lily's hand and moved to the coffeepot to refill his mug. Rule loved coffee. Cynna wasn't sure why. He couldn't get a caffeine buzz— his system threw off the effects of drugs too fast for them to have much effect. So it must be the taste he liked, which just proved that demons weren't the only ones with weird taste buds.

He leaned against the counter, sipped, and looked at

Cynna. His eyes, dark and steady, had been the second thing she'd noticed about him when they met all those years ago. "These people are way ahead of us with spell-work. Is there any way the gnome could have fooled you about the pattern?"

"Theoretically, sure, anything is possible. But some things are so unlikely we can cross them off. You aren't likely to wake up as a cat. I'm not likely to make a mistake about patterns, especially one I know so well. If they're good enough to fool me about that, they don't need a Finder."

"If that's really what they want from you."

Unease prickled down Cynna's spine as she considered the possibility. "Gan said they need me to Find something."

"They also want Lily for something, and she's not a Finder. And Gan isn't exactly reliable."

"She can't lie. At least, demons can't . . . Hey, Gan, can you lie yet?"

Gan's voice came, muffled, from the pantry. "Who wants to know?"

"The woman who stopped on the way here and bought a couple more candy bars."

Gan popped out of the pantry, chewing something. "Chocolate candy bars?"

"Yes."

"I can almost lie." She padded up to Cynna. "Ask me something."

"How old are you?"

"Three." Her round face split wide in a grin, showing all those pointy teeth. "Gimme my chocolate."

"Not yet. Three what?"

"That's why it's almost lying. I'm bound to be three somethings, depending on how you're counting and what time's doing in some realm or other. So I can say three and I'm not quite lying, but close. Give me my candy."

Cynna leaned down to get her purse. "Do the Edge people really want me to Find something?" She retrieved a Hershey bar, unwrapped it, and broke it in half. "Answer first. Then chocolate."

"I already said they did."

Cynna hadn't had much experience with former demons, but she'd dealt with the regular sort in her previous life as a Dizzy. She knew better than to let one get by with an answer like that. "Answer plainly."

Gan rolled her eyes. "Yes, they want you to Find their thingee. I'm not supposed to say what it is because of it being secret. Not because *he* said so, but Jenek told me not to." She wiggled that small, imperative hand.

The second Cynna handed over the candy it vanished into Gan's mouth. The little orange whatsit closed her eyes in bliss.

Lily tipped her head. "You think chocolate's some kind of drug for her?"

"You think it isn't for the rest of us?" Cynna broke off a bite and popped it in her own mouth. "Who's Jenek?"

"Gan's been staying with his family."

"He's my minder," Gan said, and ran her tongue over her teeth to get the last of the chocolate.

A gnome, then. There was a lot Cynna didn't know about gnomes, but she'd bet she knew something the others didn't. "Is that what you are now—a gnome? Or what you will be, when you finish your transformation?"

Gan shrugged. "Can't be a demon with a soul, can I? I haven't decided which family I'll marry with yet, but . . ." Her features squinched up in a suspicious frown. "I think you aren't supposed to know about that."

"I used to be Msaidizi. I know a lot of things demons know, and they know where gnomes came from."

"What's a mizzay-dizzy?"

"Demon rider." Among other things, not all of them bad.

"Oh. Well, don't tell anyone. I want to watch television," Gan announced, turning to Lily. "Where's your television?"

"Upstairs. I'll show you. Do you know how to order pay-per-view?"

"No. What's that?"

"Good. Come on."

Cynna grinned as Lily and her orange sidekick left the room. "It's like raising the demon child from hell, isn't it? Literally. Bet you're glad Toby isn't here right now."

Rule's eyes widened. "God, yes. I hadn't thought of that. I may have nightmares . . . Cynna, how did you guess that Gan was becoming a gnome?"

"I'm not supposed to tell. Got any candy?"

"Gan cleaned me out," he said dryly.

"Your credit's good. Here's the big secret, passed on to me by a demon I knew in my bad old days: gnomes started out as demons. Not all of them—I mean, they're a separate race now and have children and all that, so most of the ones alive today were born as gnomes. But that's where gnomes come from—demons who for some reason developed souls."

Rule shook his head. "That explains why Max took Gan to his people, but I'm . . . amazed. Max hates demons. He says all gnomes hate demons."

"Guess humans aren't the only ones with parent issues."

His mouth twitched. "I guess not. Cynna . . ." The timer dinged. He turned to slip on a mitt, then opened the oven.

Harry lifted his head, sniffed, and jumped down to stalk over to the stove, where he announced his willingness to sample chicken enchiladas.

"You're right, Harry. That smells fantastic." Cynna heaved a theatrical sigh. "The man's good in bed and he cooks, too. If only Lily were a little less conventional! Threesomes aren't *that* unusual these days."

Rule slid the glass casserole onto a cooling rack. "I ought to take you up on that just to see how high you jump and how fast you run."

"Hey, you're supposed to pretend you don't know I don't mean it." She didn't, not anymore, which made the flirting comfortable. The mate bond really did change everything, even the vaunted lupus distaste for fidelity.

Of course, she now knew where that distaste came from, why they were taught that sexual possessiveness was wrong and marriage was forbidden. Cynna's good mood evaporated. Unconsciously, she touched her stomach.

Rule studied her. "You're thinking about going to Edge, aren't you?"

She wrenched her thoughts back on topic. "Yeah. If they can get me there, I'm going. If you're worried about Lily—"

"I'm worried about you."

And that was the first thing she'd noticed about Rule, way back when. He cared. "I'm not buying into their story about Daniel Weaver all the way, but I think . . . well, thinking isn't good enough. I have to know. It, uh, it sounds like you don't plan to go there yourself." Which gave her a queasy feeling. She'd assumed they'd all go.

"I can't."

"But . . ." Her voice trailed away. She'd been so busy avoiding thinking about her own stuff, she hadn't given any thought to other people's problems. Again. "The mantles."

He nodded grimly.

Rule had been tricked into assuming the heir's portion of the mantle of another clan—his clan's oldest enemies. Cynna didn't understand mantles, didn't know exactly how or why it had happened, but she knew that the leader of the other clan was hanging on to life by a thread. If he died, the full mantle would go to Rule. "I guess it would be bad if you were in another realm when the Leidolf Rho died, huh?"

"Bad is one way to put it. I don't know if the mantle would cross to another realm to reach me. If it didn't . . . some lupi who suddenly lose their connection to their clan simply die. Most survive the death shock, however, becoming lone wolves."

Cullen had been a lone wolf for years before Rule's clan, Nokolai, formally adopted him. "Lupi don't do well as lone wolves."

"Usually they go insane. Cullen is very much the exception. Most sundered lupi don't stay lone wolves long, though. They gather in packs. Packs are dangerous to the humans around them—worse in that respect than lone wolves."

Worse? Cynna swallowed. "Are you sure you should tell me all this?"

Rule smiled gently. "Yes."

Because she was supposed to become the Rhej of his clan. Cynna had told him—told everyone—that wasn't going to happen. A Rhej was, among other things, the clan's priestess. Cynna was Catholic. She didn't worship the lupi's Lady. And even if she could get past that, who in their right mind would pick her for some kind of holy woman?

"Look, Rule—"

"I'm not saying you'll accept the Lady's offer. Just that it's okay for me to speak of these things to you. The Rhej has given permission."

That was okay, she supposed, as long as he wasn't expecting too much. She wouldn't spill his secrets. "I see that you can't go, but . . . it's probably none of my business, but, ah . . . does that necessarily mean Lily can't go? I mean, when you were in Dis and she—or part of her—was here, the mate bond worked as if you were still physically close."

Rule turned to look at the doorway a second before Lily appeared there. "Neither of us passed out then," Lily said, "because Earth and Dis are physically analogous. Edge isn't. I asked Gan about that earlier." She looked straight at Rule. "I've already told Ruben I won't be able to go."

Rule moved the way only a lupus can, all grace and speed. One second he was standing still. The next he was holding on to Lily and murmuring things Cynna couldn't quite catch.

She gave them a moment, then drummed her fingers on the table. "I could go watch TV with Gan, I guess."

Rule turned a smile on her. "Sorry. I'm feeling emotional. Lily thought of the clan. She understood what my duty must be without my telling her, and chose to put her own duty second." He bent his head and whispered something in Lily's ear.

Lily laughed and pushed out of his arms. "Later. Maybe. We'll see." Her smile faded into a sigh. "I couldn't tell Ruben why I can't go. He doesn't know about the mantles."

"Will this cause problems for you, *nadia*?"

She shrugged. "Not with Ruben. I told him it was clan business, nothing I could explain, and he was okay with that. But he's getting pressure from higher up to give the Edge delegation what they want."

"Including people?" Rule snapped. "Will Cynna be ordered to—"

Cynna broke in. "Rule, I'm going. Orders or not, I'm going."

Rule and Lily exchanged one of those couple's glances that say all kinds of things without using a word. Cynna could read some of it, though. They weren't happy with her decision.

Well, she wasn't exactly thrilled herself. She'd thought she would have friends at her back. Now . . .

The sound of gunfire came from the TV upstairs. Cynna's eyes widened as a thought struck. "What about Gan?"

"If I understood her correctly," Lily said, "she has to go to Edge to fulfill her . . . she called it a testing."

"She doesn't know you aren't going."

Lily shook her head.

So instead of Lily and Rule, Cynna would have a pissed-off former demon for backup. "Well, shit."

SIX

THE enchiladas were great. The company was strained due to the elephants at the table.

One elephant was the allusion ban, which Lily and Rule both honored. Cynna didn't know why they showed such restraint, but she was damned glad of it. The other subject they avoided—or tried to—was their opinion of her decision to go to Edge.

Hard to ignore, those elephants. Fortunately, there were other subjects to discuss. Like gnomes.

Rule knew one gnome pretty well. Max was crude, ill-tempered, oversize for his species, and unforgettably ugly. He was also very much Rule's friend. He'd gone to hell with them to rescue Rule—bitching about it all the way, but he'd gone.

"Max won the down payment for his club playing liar's poker," Rule said as he dished himself a second helping. "He's been banned from Vegas because he bluffs so well. To a gnome, lying is an art. I have the idea there are rules, ethical considerations, among his people about lies, but I've never figured them out."

"So we shouldn't take what the councilor says at face value," Lily said.

"If the gnomes in Edge are anything like the ones here, then no. They'll expect us to lie, too."

Cynna snorted. "No problem. I'm guessing Underass from Commerce sees lying as an art form, too."

Lily grinned. "Underass. You're talking about Mc-Closky, I take it."

"Got it in one."

"The government can and will look out for itself," Rule said. "You have to do the same. Just because the gnome says your father's in Edge doesn't make it so. He knew the man's name, yes. But he also knew Lily's name, and he didn't learn that from Daniel Weaver."

"He has a wedding ring with my mother's pattern on it."

"Cynna." Lily touched her hand. "That suggests Daniel Weaver—or his ring—was once in Edge. It doesn't prove he's there now."

ALL in all, it was a relief to close their front door behind her.

The air was cold and still. Cynna grabbed a lungful and held it in, hoping to quiet the jitters. Somewhere nearby a dog was barking. Somewhere even closer a lupus was watching her, though she couldn't see him. Rule's father had decreed that he'd be guarded from now on, and he'd spoken as Rho. Cynna didn't have to see the guard to know he was around.

She stuffed her hands in her pockets and grimaced. Dammit. She'd forgotten all about the coat. She hadn't thanked Rule, who didn't even know he'd bought it for her. Lily had left that out of her briefing.

Shit, she still owed Lily for the slacks and sweater she was wearing. She'd forgotten to ask how much they'd cost.

She wasn't going back inside to find out. Not tonight.

Her government-issue Ford was parked at the curb. She didn't go there. "Tell them I went for a walk," she told the unseen guard. She dropped her keys in her bag, slung the strap over her head so that it crossed her chest bandolier-style, and started moving.

The new coat was lined and supple and surprisingly warm. The swing of her arms made the leather whisper to her: *shh, shh, shh.* The sound reminded her of tires on pavement or an eraser wiping a blackboard. Motion.

Walking was Cynna's healthiest coping mechanism. She might prefer fighting, but she'd stopped acting on that impulse. Mostly. Anyway, there was no one around to punch tonight unless she headed back and socked Lily, who'd probably put her on her ass pretty fast. A second-degree black belt didn't take shit from a measly brown. And Rule might let her hit him, but that wasn't a fight.

And why was she even thinking these things? She wasn't mad at Lily or Rule . . . who had *not* abandoned her. It was stupid, irrational, to feel as if they had.

Dammit. She scowled at the dark street ahead as she stepped off the curb.

There was only the slightest sound behind her for warning. She spun.

Just under six feet of lean, angry man stood an arm's length away, crutches propped under his arms. Messy hair the color of cinnamon without the sugar framed a face sculptors would kill to commit to stone. He wore the same torn jeans and dirty denim jacket he'd had on earlier. The scowl was fresh.

"For God's sake," Cullen snapped, "didn't your mother teach you to look both ways before crossing the street?"

Her heart was pounding like mad. That pissed her off. "I don't remember. She may have, before she finished drinking herself to death."

"Poor little Cynna."

The mockery cut. Guilt rubbed salt in the wound, because Mama hadn't always been a drunk—not the helpless, hopeless kind, anyway. When Cynna was small, there had been vegetables with the boxed mac and cheese. Tucking in at night, sometimes a story. Walks to the park and pushing in the swing.

She turned abruptly and started across the street.

"Oh, stay and fight." He swung along beside her. "You're longing to belt me one. I might even let you."

"Why are you here? Why aren't you at Headquarters drooling over your new spell?"

"I'm stalking you."

That stopped her.

"Isn't that what they call it when a man follows a woman who wants him to get lost?" He freed one hand by tucking the crutch against his side and pushed at the small of her back. "Move it. There's a car coming."

The car was three blocks away and cruising sedately, but the street probably wasn't the best place for this discussion. Cynna started walking again. "Maybe I *will* belt you one."

Cullen didn't say anything. For the next half block he didn't say a word, and neither did she. The crutches didn't give him much trouble. He kept up easily.

Strangely, the jittery wires started to loosen. Maybe it was the walking. Maybe it was the inevitability of the conversation they were about to have . . . dream monsters were supposed to go *poof* if you turned and faced them, weren't they?

Her monsters weren't going away, but panic had dulled to dread. She'd done plenty of things she dreaded. She could do this, too. Cynna jammed her hands back in her pockets. "You're waiting for me to admit it."

"Yeah. I am."

Cynna dragged in as much air as her lungs would hold, letting it out in a whoosh. "I'm pregnant."

"I know," he said gently.

Oh, dammit, she hated it when he used that voice.

Cynna walked faster, but she couldn't leave her thoughts behind. Or her feelings. Or *him*. He kept pace beside her, silent.

"It's given to us to know," Cullen had told her that night, their one time together, his eyes shiny with tears. Tears that had scared the crap out of her.

Lupi knew it if a woman they had sex with got pregnant, but this knowledge was one side of a cruel coin. The other side was that it didn't happen often. Magic played hell with procreation, and limited fertility was the reason behind so much about them. Their determined promiscuity, for one. The way a Rho's son became heir, for another. Maybe even their looks. Cullen's physical perfection was an extreme example, but Cynna had never met an ugly lupus. The male of the species—and lupi were all male—were like peacocks or butterflies, their beautiful plumage designed to attract mates.

Mates, plural. Always plural with a lupus.

When Cullen had informed her that she was pregnant, she'd known about only one side of the coin, the low-fertility part. She hadn't believed him about the "special knowledge" side . . . partly, yeah, because she'd been hip-deep in denial. But dammit, she was on the pill. Cynna might take chances in other areas, but never about birth control. She'd been so sure she couldn't be pregnant.

For the past five weeks she'd waited for her period to show up. Finally she'd bought the damn test. "You're happy about it," she said, bitter.

"Happy is such a thin word . . . Cynna." He moved in front of her, stacked his crutches against his side, and gripped her shoulders in both hands. "This changes everything for me, too. Everything."

"But you wanted this. You wanted a child. You said you'd given up hoping."

"Yes." He dropped his hands. "After so many years . . . ah, I'm older than I look."

"I figured that." Another top-secret bit of lupus lore: they aged much more slowly than humans. "You can shock me with your true age later. Better believe I'll ask, but not now."

"What are you going to do?"

"I don't know. God, how could I know?" She threw up her hands, her voice rising. "Until this morning I didn't believe it. Even when I saw the tester, I couldn't believe it. What could God be thinking? I've got no fucking business raising a kid. I don't *want* to raise a kid!"

That truth slipped out and hung there between them: she didn't want his child-to-be. Cynna felt queasy. She put her hand on her stomach. Something was growing in there right this second.

"What are you going to do?" he repeated.

His eyes burned into hers. No, they just seemed brighter than usual because all the color had been sucked from his face. She stared at him as, slowly, she understood what he meant. "Cullen, I'm Catholic. You know that. I mean, I'm pro-choice because everyone isn't Catholic, so they should make their own decisions, but *I'm* Catholic."

"You take the pill. You have sex when you want to. Those aren't exactly Catholic beliefs. Are you saying that—"

"Yes. Yes, I am." She took a step toward him. He was hurting. It had to be bad, because Cullen never let anyone see him hurt or afraid or vulnerable. "I don't know what I'm going to do, but not abortion. That's out."

His crutches clattered to the ground. He grabbed her and held on tight.

Too tight. "Hey! I like to breathe!"

"Shut up." But his arms loosened. He didn't top her five-foot-ten by much; when he leaned his cheek against her hair, his breath stirred it. "You don't make sense. I don't understand you."

"Me, neither. But about this . . . see, if sex is a mistake, it's one that just affects the adults making that decision. So maybe the Church is right, maybe I'm right, but whichever way it falls out, no biggie. But abortion . . ."

Her voice trailed off. "We're talking about babies here. Not that I think what's inside me is a baby, not yet, but that's where it's headed, isn't it? I'm not up to making that decision. I don't understand enough about right and wrong. That's one of the reasons I went to the Church in the first place—for help with the big decisions."

His voice was dry. "And the pill? Does that fall in the 'no biggie' category?"

She snorted. "You may have noticed that the Pope's a guy? Not married, not fooling around . . . I don't see how he gets a vote."

"You don't buy the whole papal infallibility bit?"

"See, that's a funny thing. Papal infallibility doesn't mean popes are perfect or right about everything. Well, just look at the history of the Church—people being burned for witchcraft or put on the rack for saying the world was round? That's not right. It's more that they're supposed to be right about what the Church teaches, and not everyone agrees when a particular teaching is infallible. The last one everyone is sure of was issued in 1952, about the assumption of Mary."

Cullen rested his hands at her waist and looked at her, a smile playing on his lips. He was amused, or wanted to be. "You've given this some study."

"If you come to the Church as an adult, you have to think things over, understand what you're agreeing to." She grimaced. "Or not agreeing with. Father Jacobs says I'm a cafeteria Catholic."

His mouth crooked up. "Picking out the beliefs you like, leaving the others on the buffet?"

She nodded. "But Father Michaels says that's okay, as long as I keep thinking about the rest of it. Maybe I'm convinced I don't like fish, or won't care for the sauce it's in, but I should try it sometime, you know?"

"You've got a priest. Two priests." Cullen shook his head. "It boggles the brain."

"That's what Rule says, too. Is your foot okay? Can we walk some more?"

He answered by bending to pick up his crutches. "You aren't in this alone, you know."

By "this" he meant the pregnancy. The word made ripples in her. She started moving. "I get that."

"You don't have to raise the child. You could give it to me."

Not ripples this time—big, dizzy waves. "I'm not ready to decide. I'm barely able to say . . . to say 'pregnant.' I can't make decisions yet."

"Just so you know that option is part of this particular buffet."

She didn't say anything until they reached the next street. No cars. She started across. "You said 'it.' You don't know the sex?"

"For that you'll need ultrasound."

When? When did the growth inside her become enough of a baby to have a sex? She had no idea. She knew nothing about babies—carrying them, bearing them, raising them.

She knew one thing, though. If this one was a boy, it would be a lupus. It would Change when it was old enough, but that was okay because it would have a clan, people who cared about it, knew how to help it through the Change. But . . . "If it's a girl, it will still be Nokolai, right?"

"Yes."

There was such satisfaction in his voice. Because his child wouldn't be clanless, as he had been? Maybe because he would give his adoptive clan something wonderful. Lupi were nuts about babies.

All of the above, Cynna decided. And that was all she was ready to decide tonight. She'd had enough shocks for one day—that damned purple color in the tester window, the arrival of Gan and the delegation, the news about her father . . .

My father. Two words that had never held much meaning for her. Even in prayers it was "Our Father," not "my father." Now . . . *uh-oh. Thinking again, and not the productive kind.* "So how come you aren't still at Headquarters? Don't tell me you left a shiny new spell just to stalk me."

"Don't tell me you aren't curious about that shiny new spell."

"Now that you mention it . . . how's it sourced?"

He grinned. "Outside the caster."

The law defined sorcery as magic sourced outside the spellcaster—which was, as Cullen often said, a nice blend of stupidity and blinding ignorance. Even Wiccans drew on power from other sources, though the plants and gems they used didn't have much juice. "Think Congress will hold an emergency session to rewrite the law?"

"They'll come up with some way around it. They want this too much."

Trade with another realm . . . yeah, that was huge. Cynna didn't figure it could be kept quiet much longer. "What kind of spell is it?"

"Full draw."

That meant it drew on all four elements. "Balanced draw?" The more balanced the draw from the elements, the harder the spell, because spellcasters weren't themselves balanced. Cullen found Fire ridiculously easy and was good with both Water and Earth, not so good with Air. Cynna aced Air, did okay with Earth, and struggled with Water and Fire.

"It's ley line magic."

"Jesus!" She immediately felt guilty and apologized to God for using His son's name that way. She was trying to break herself of the habit. "Definitely a balanced draw, then. Uh . . . have you ever worked a ley line spell?"

"A few times. I'll in-blood the elements."

"That's—"

"The best way I know to do it."

Ley lines carried magic throughout the Earth, but as that magic left the nodes where it originated, it lost its uncolored intensity, splitting into the rainbow colors of the elements. That's why you had to use a balanced, full-draw invocation to tap one. In-blooding was a risky way to achieve balance, but so was every other technique if you were dealing with ley line energy. After a moment Cynna nodded. "You'd know what works best for you, I guess."

"I'm weak in Air. You're strong there. Keep an eye on me after the in-blooding. If I get distracted and lose the balance, I'll probably stop breathing. Remind me."

"I'll do that. What about the rest of the spell?"

He shrugged. "There arc material components for the invocation. The list he gave me is interesting in one way—Edge must be Earthlike if we have the same herbs."

"Unlike Dis."

"Right. But he's not revealing more without payment. When I left, negotiations had stalled while they flew in some gnome expert who lived in the underways for a few years."

"So you're waiting for the government to pay this councilor dude for his spell."

He tilted his head. "You're thinking that's why I left to stalk you—that I'd still be there if I had the whole spell to play with. You're wrong."

"And you are not telepathic." A good guesser, maybe. Uncomfortably good.

"This baby means more to me than the spell. More than anything."

It was the way he said it—matter-of-factly, no dramatics—that made her eyes water. Or maybe her hormones were already crazy. She took a second to answer so she could be sure her voice didn't wobble. "That's good. Every kid should have someone who puts him first."

"Did you?"

"Shut up, Cullen."

"For me it was my mother. She wasn't exactly June Cleaver, but she loved me all the way."

He'd started this, hadn't he? That made it okay to ask one of the questions she'd wondered about. "What about your father? Lupi are supposed to be nuts for children."

"Oh, sure, when I was a kid . . . but it turned out that he loved what he wanted me to be. Not what I was."

"A sorcerer."

"He thought I could give it up. He didn't . . ." The breath he drew was ragged. "He didn't fight for me. When the Rhej said I couldn't remain both Etorri and sorcerer, he didn't argue with her or the others. He argued with me. He fought me, not them. When I couldn't give up so much of what I am . . . after the *seco*, he didn't speak to me again."

"Jesus." Etorri was his former clan. The *seco* must be some kind of kick-him-out ceremony. Never to speak to him again after he'd lost his clan . . . that was a bigger betrayal than her own father's disappearance. Cullen had grown up believing the man *loved* him. "Never?"

He swiped a hand through the air, brushing away the past and her question. "I don't want any damned sympathy. I want you to know that it doesn't matter to me what this baby is—boy or girl, stupid or clever, clumsy, Gifted, whatever. It doesn't matter. I'm on his side."

"Or hers."

"Or hers. I don't want to just see her for a month or two in the summer, either. I want to be part of my child's life right from the start." His voice hardened. "I *will* be part of its life."

Did he think that things would have been different if his father had been a bigger part of his life? "How much did you stay with your father?"

"Point for Cynna." He licked his index finger and drew a 1 in the air. The numeral glowed faintly, then faded. "Summers, for a month. He lived in Canada. Mum and I lived in England."

"I thought I caught a bit of an accent. How long have you—"

"Cynna." He stopped and looked at her. "You're trying to steer the talk to me so you don't have to talk about the baby."

"Well, yeah. Of course."

A smile tilted one side of his mouth and bled into his eyes. "Your turn. Did you . . . damn!" His phone was beeping. He pulled it from its holster on his belt and glanced at the screen. "It's just Timms."

"You still staying with him?"

"Yeah. He's okay. Doesn't bother me much." He frowned at the phone in his hand. "Doesn't call me much, either. Doesn't call me at all."

"Maybe you should answer it."

For some reason, that seemed to be a major decision, but finally Cullen shrugged and held the phone to his ear. "You better not be calling to ask me to bring a loaf of bread home." A long pause. "She said *what*? Shit! No, you handled it right . . . Yeah, tell me about it . . . Well, you were there. Did she . . . no? Now that's interesting . . . I will. With Rule, probably. Thanks." He disconnected with a scowl.

"What? What is it?"

"A reporter from the *Post* has called him twice, asking to talk to his 'stripper friend.' Asking if I'm really a lupus. She's camped out across the street from Timms's place now."

SEVEN

CYNNA dug in her purse. "I'd better call Ruben and warn him. You call Lily and Rule."

"She asked to talk to his *stripper* friend."

"I heard you." She hit 3 on speed dial. It was after eight o'clock, but she was betting Ruben hadn't gone home yet.

"You don't get it. The reporter didn't ask him about weird beings from another realm. They wanted to talk to the lupus who takes off his clothes for a living." Cullen frowned into space for a moment. "Guess I should let Rule know, though." He punched in a number.

"Ida? This is Cynna Weaver. Is Ruben there? . . . Okay, you decide if he should be interrupted. Some reporter has been calling Timms, asking about Cullen. Cullen Seabourne . . . Yeah. Okay." Cynna waited while Ruben's secretary got him out of a meeting and Cullen talked to Rule.

After a moment she heard Ruben's voice, calm and courteous as always. "Good evening, Cynna. Ida tells me there's a problem with the press."

"Maybe. They might be onto this Edge deal already. Some reporter is camped out by Steve Timms's place, waiting for Cullen. He's . . . yes, Agent Timms. Sure, I'll hold." She waited again, this time while Ruben had Ida get Timms on another line.

The friendship that had sprung up between Timms and Cullen had taken everyone by surprise—except maybe Rule. Rule said Cullen had a habit of picking up strays.

Steve Timms was an MCD agent—regular MCD, the ones who used to track and forcibly register lupi. He was also one hell of a good shooter. Just after the first power wind he'd been assigned to back up Cynna when she went hunting a demon. Cullen had elected himself her consultant, and he and Timms had not hit it off. Timms was more used to shooting lupi than palling around with them, and Cullen enjoyed annoying people.

Then Cullen saved Timms's life, and all of a sudden they were best buds—at least in Timms's mind. The strange thing was that Cullen didn't object. When he was injured and Timms offered him a place to stay, he'd accepted. He'd even put in a word for Timms, via Lily, when the president told Ruben he had to have bodyguards 24/7.

Ruben was back, asking to talk to Cullen. "Sure. Just a sec." Cullen had finished his own conversation, so she held her phone out. "Ruben wants to talk to you."

Not for the first time, Cynna wished for a lupus's hearing. All she got was Cullen's side of the conversation, which was mostly "Hmm" and "He would, wouldn't he?" and "Yes, I thought so, too."

"Well?" she demanded as soon as he'd disconnected.

"Reporters are asking about the 'strange events' at the mall, but not about a diplomatic party from another realm. Brooks will warn his people, but he doesn't think the press has been tipped about the Edge delegation. He thinks this is personal."

"How so?"

"I met a couple MCD assholes today. One of them in particular didn't like me. Brooks thinks this guy knew about me staying with Timms from office gossip. He probably gave the reporter a juicy story about Brooks's personal bodyguard living in sin with a lupus stripper."

Cynna pursed her lips in a soundless whistle. There was no such thing as a gay lupus, but why let facts get in the way of a good scandal? "Ruben is not going to be happy."

"Nope." But Cullen was. He held out one hand and smacked the other into it. "*Whomp!* He'll come down on Asshole Number Two like a ton of bricks. He'd better, or Timms may decide to prove his manhood by shooting the idiot."

When he'd moved his hands, a flash had caught Cynna's eyes. "Hey, that's your new bling, isn't it? I want to see."

"Sure." He held out his right hand.

Cullen's hands were as close to ordinary as any part of him came. His palms were narrow, his fingers neither long or short. The nail beds were rounded, the nails cut blunt and short. No nicks or scars, of course, since he healed everything.

She had carnal knowledge of those hands.

Big deal, Cynna told herself, ignoring the sweet, sharp tug of lust. Lots of women had intimate knowledge of Cullen's hands. Not an exclusive club, the number of females who'd tripped him and beat him to the floor. "Wow," she said, focusing on the big, fat diamond on his index finger. "Is it loaded? Can I scan it?"

He considered her request a moment, then nodded. "Carefully. I've taken the safety off."

"Safety?" She looked at him sharply. "If you mean you leave it locked down most of the time—"

"It wouldn't exactly be safe to walk around with it ready to trigger."

"It would if it were keyed to you."

He was curt. "I don't know how."

Man, he hated to admit that. She grinned. "I do. It's a pattern spell—Air, so it won't come easily to you, but I can teach you. But first I want a peek." Cynna shook her hands to clear them of any muddy energy, then held her left hand over his right one. She fed a trickle of power into the tattoo circling her wrist like a dainty bracelet.

Finding was Cynna's Gift. She didn't need a spell to do that. Being a Finder meant she had an affinity for patterns, but her Gift didn't read, interpret, or remember them. For that she needed spells. She had several scanning spells scribed on her skin; the *kilingo* she'd activated would tell her how much magic was stored in Cullen's diamond.

Her wrist turned searing hot. "Son of a bitch!" She snatched her hand back, shutting down the *kilingo*. "You planning to burn down the city?"

"I didn't store it as Fire energy."

"No, that's how I measure power. As heat. You've got one hell of a lot of magic stuffed in that stone. Lots more than in the little one on your necklace." Which had held enough power to create mage fire on at least two occasions.

Cullen regarded his hand smugly. The diamond winked back at him. "I do, don't I?"

"There isn't that much stray magic around, not with Mika soaking it up."

"Makes a difference when you can see the sorcéri."

She supposed it did, and sighed. No denying the twist of envy. "Lily said you had a spell that lets others see sorcéri."

"It's not exactly a spell. I twist a few sorcéri together in a way that makes them visible to the eyes. It doesn't last long, and it's kind of tricky to do."

She stared at him, appalled. "You work with them *directly*?"

"What do you think mage fire is?"

"I thought you shaped it with a spell!"

"It's fire, isn't it? I call fire. I don't need spells for that, though it did take me a while to get the knack of calling mage fire. It's a ticklish business, but—"

"No duh!" Mage fire was one of the most dangerous

of the forbidden arts. Supposedly a lost art, actually, which was the only reason no one had bothered making it illegal. Three months ago, Cullen had reinvented it. She knew that, knew why he'd done it, and agreed with the necessity, but . . . "You don't shape it all?"

"You might say I ride it. Mage fire has to be sourced from raw magic, which is why only sorcerers should attempt it. If you can't see the energies, see what you're doing with them . . ." His hands shaped a mushroom cloud in the air. *"Boom."*

"Sometimes you scare the shit out of me."

"How sensible of you." Cullen reached out, touched the collar of her coat. "Great coat."

Her eyebrows shot up. "Thanks."

His fingers, restless, moved to her face, then tugged at a strand of her hair. "You keep this short so it won't interfere with the spells on your skin, right?"

His touch stirred thoughts of an activity that worked great to calm the jitters, one more pleasant than fighting. *Down, girl.* She nodded.

"But why do you bleach it?"

"You've heard of style? I like it blond."

"It stinks."

Offended, Cynna jerked her head back. "My hair stinks?"

"Not to a human, I guess. But since it's a lupus you're involved with—"

"We aren't involved." She stressed the last word. Involved meant committed. Cullen seemed to be wholly committed to the . . . *Oh, get over it. Use the word.* Cullen was committed to the *baby.* He wanted it, wanted it badly. He wasn't committed to her.

"No?" He smiled in an agreeable way she distrusted. "If you say so. Want to go visit Mika with me?"

"What?" She shook her head. "Your mind jumps around like a flea."

"I need to obtain one of the spell components. A dragon's scale."

That shouldn't pique her interest, not when she was so annoyed with him. "I hope you're not planning to steal one."

He laughed. "No, you were hoping I was, though you think you shouldn't. Sorry to disappoint you, but I'm after a trade, not a theft."

"I'm not disappointed." Much. It would be stupid to prefer sneaking a scale to bartering for one. Dragons were notoriously possessive. There hadn't been any incidents here in D.C., but the Toronto dragon had rebuked a hedge-witch who tried to steal a scale from his lair.

The witch had been lucky. Broken bones healed.

"If it cheers you any," he said, "we will have to sneak past a couple guards. The authorities don't think people should wander into a dragon's lair at night."

"I am the authorities." Strange as it still seemed.

"Are you going to badge your way into the park, then?"

"Well . . . I probably couldn't get you through that way." And it wouldn't be as much fun. She shook her head, disgusted with herself, and turned to head back. "So what are you going to trade? What do you have that a dragon might swap for?"

"Not me. You."

"You're dreaming. I don't have anything a dragon would want."

"You'll trade a service, not an object. Ever since that Canadian hedgewitch tried to swipe a scale, Mika's been fretting. If he sheds a scale in flight, how could he know? Anyone might pick it up. You can offer to Find any scales that aren't in his lair."

Cynna's eyebrows raised. "You've been chatting with Mika?"

"I amuse him. You'll take a fee for your Finding, a percentage of the scales you Find. We'll ask for one in three, but I doubt he'll let us have that many."

"Us? What's this 'us' I'm hearing?"

Cullen ignored that. "He'll want you to hunt scales every day. We can't agree to that, obviously, and there's no need. Mika's paranoia aside, dragons don't shed many scales. I'm thinking a Finding once a week should be enough, with flexibility built into the agreement for the times your duties take you away from the capital. And of course you won't be able to start until we get back."

Without any input from her brain, her feet quit moving. She spoke carefully. "There's another 'we.' You'd better explain this one."

He stopped a pace ahead and looked back at her, irritated. "You're an idiot sometimes, but you aren't stupid. Surely you didn't think I'd let you go traipsing off to Edge without me."

There was an odd constriction in her chest. "You're assuming I'm going, then. And you aren't trying to stop me?"

He snorted. "Are you crazy? I'm not Superman, able to stop a locomotive with a flex of my biceps. That little bastard waves a father in front of you, you'll go. The trick will be persuading them that I'm going, too, but I've got an idea about that."

Relief hit so fast and dizzy it felt almost like joy. Cullen's determination was about the baby, not her. She knew that. She didn't care. She wouldn't have to do this alone. She'd have a friend with her—an annoying, sometimes obsessive friend, but a friend nevertheless.

Cynna grinned, high on that soaring relief. "Of course you've got an idea. You always do when it comes to getting what you want. Wait. Shit!" Her grin slipped. "Is there a moon in Edge? What if there's no moon?"

"I'd go anyway, but I asked. They have a moon."

"Okay, then." She nodded like a bobblehead doll. "That's okay. So what's the dragon's scale for?"

"Part of the elemental invocation." Cullen frowned. "You aren't angry."

"Nope. I will be, I'm sure, off and on during the trip—you'll see to that."

"I'm not giving you a choice about this, and you aren't mad."

She shrugged. "There's always a choice. Come on. Let's go negotiate with a dragon."

IN spite of the dragon living in its southern end, most of Rock Creek Park remained open to the public during daylight hours. The park was a long, woodsy sprawl of nature covering better than seventeen hundred acres, with some parts groomed, some as close to wild as humans ever permitted within their urban sprawl. There were bike trails, paths, buildings, and bridges . . . trees, birds, and the occasional raccoon, deer, or coyote.

But it wasn't daylight, and the area around Mika's lair was off-limits at all hours. Which made things fun . . . mostly.

"Ow!" Cynna stumbled, then slapped at Cullen's back. "Damn branches. Slow down. It's a lot darker under these trees for me than it is for you."

He obeyed. Cynna had a hand hooked into the waist of his jeans so she could follow him in what was, for her, nearly pitch blackness. He was enjoying that hand. "Not a nature girl, are you?"

"I like nature fine in small, orderly amounts. Are you sure Mika won't mind us dropping in?"

"He hasn't offered to eat me since my first visit. Like I said, I amuse him."

"Maybe he isn't there now."

"If he . . ." A sound caught Cullen's attention. He stopped beside a large oak, cocking his head.

"What?" she whispered.

"Shh." Yes, those were footsteps on a paved path, not the random rustlings of some animal in the brush. He pivoted on one crutch so he could bend close and whisper near her ear. "Park police about fifty yards downwind. We'd best wait a moment."

He didn't mind waiting. The moon was just past new, her song all but inaudible, but the touch of wilderness here called to him almost as sweetly. The air was full of lovely smells—earth, vegetation, the musky traces of wild creatures that had passed this way recently.

And woman. Cynna always smelled delicious to him in spite of the chemical assault she waged on her hair. She was standing deliciously close, too. He let one crutch rest against the trunk of the oak, leaned in and ran his free hand up her arm to her throat, letting his fingers drift across her pulse there. "Mmm. It occurs to me we don't have an appointment, so we can't be late."

She shoved his hand away. "I'm not in the mood for seduction."

"Cynna! I'm shocked by such blatant untruth. Your scent says otherwise."

"Well, quit sniffing me! It's annoying for you to—to—"

"Know things you'd rather I didn't?" He captured her hand and drew circles in her palm with his thumb.

"Draw stupid conclusions! There's a difference between sex and seduction, as any man of your age and experience ought to . . . That reminds me. How old are you, anyway?"

He shook his head, surprised. "Why is it so easy to underestimate you? You're right—seduction's as much mental play as it is physical. If you don't want your mind played with right now, why don't I just toy with your fabulous body?"

In the dimness he caught the shape of her smile in the curve of her cheek—and the reluctance of it in the tone of her voice. "How about you quit playing altogether and answer my question."

"I'll turn sixty next month."

"Jesus!"

Anxiety pinched, an irritation without focus. Why should he worry about Cynna's reaction? True, Lily had had a hard time accepting Rule's real age, but his situation was hardly the same. Unlike Rule, he wasn't dealing with a bonded mate . . . just with the mother-to-be of his child.

Anxiety had teeth, yes, it did. "You knew I'm older than I look."

"Yeah, but . . ." She snorted. "A sixty-year-old stripper! If your groupies only knew."

"I don't have groupies." He touched the corner of her mouth, tucked up at the moment in amusement. "You have to be famous to have groupies. I may dance in a mildly notorious club . . . or did. I think Max has fired me again. But most people have never heard of me."

"Quit it. You may not be famous, but . . ." Her voice dropped back to a whisper. "What was that?"

The thud had apparently been loud enough for human ears. "Mika, I believe. He's been redecorating."

Her brows twitched into a frown. "*Not* the park policeman you heard earlier, then. If you did hear him."

"Oh, I did. Perhaps I forgot to mention that he went the other way." Cullen dropped a hit-and-run-kiss on her scowl and jumped back, grinning, before her fist could connect.

She heaved a sigh. "You're pissing me off, Seabourne. How can a man on crutches move that fast?"

"Shall I drop the other one and let you have another swing?"

She tilted her head, considering it. She was definitely considering it. Lord, but the woman delighted him almost as often as she annoyed him.

"I guess not," she said at last. "I'd feel guilty if I hit you and even madder if I didn't. So you haven't learned anything yet about the shield spell?"

He knew what she was doing—distracting him with talk of spellcraft. It would probably work. He retrieved his crutch and swung around to resume their trek through the trees, going slowly so she could keep up. "Very little, aside from the physical components. I do know it's a drawn spell."

"Right up my alley."

He grinned at the casualness of her voice. "You'll get a look at it. I'm not so egotistical I can't ask for expert advice. Speaking of which, I've suggested that Ruben bring in Sherry and her bunch." *Suggested* might be a euphemism, but he thought *blackmailed* would overstate the case. *Required?* Yes, that's the word he wanted. He'd required Ruben to ask Sherry and her coven to perform a particular task. "They'll need your snazzy new coat."

"Are you talking about Sherry O'Shaunessy?" Disbelief coated Cynna's voice. Sherry O'Shaunessy was high priestess of a very old, very powerful Wiccan coven who occasionally consulted for the Unit. "I can't believe you called them in. You don't play well with others, and you don't like sharing your toys. And what would they need my coat for?"

"It isn't my spell to share or not, is it? I'm not paying for it. But Sherry and company aren't going to be learning the shield spell, at least not right away. They'll be casting personal protection spells. Yours goes on your coat."

"I've got a protection spell."

"Speaking of egotistical . . ."

"All right, all right. Sherry's coven can undoubtedly put lots more zip into spells than I can on my own. But why? Isn't the whole point of a shield spell protection?"

"You're assuming it's really a shield spell."

"I'm not assuming anything, but odds are that it is. And you'll be able to tell once you see it, right?"

"It's a drawn spell," Cullen reminded her. "Will a spell from another realm use glyphs we're familiar with?"

"Some of them, but . . . okay, okay, you're right. We can't expect to recognize all of the graphic components, so you'll be relying on the gnome's explanations of the glyphs. Which may not be complete, and could be nonsense." She brooded on that a moment. "Still, the gnome and the others will be in the circle with us, and I'm guessing they don't want to go *boom.*"

"I doubt the spell causes physical harm. But think how handy it would be for a diplomat negotiating trade agreements to cast a good persuasion spell."

She did, apparently, think that over, keeping silent as they emerged from the softness of leaves and loam onto a paved path. There was plenty of room to walk side by side here; the trees lining the path had been knocked down and shoved into untidy piles.

"What in the world—?" Cynna stopped, looking at the woody debris.

"Mika likes this path."

"I guess he needs a little more room than we do."

"A little. Come on."

They started down the path. Cullen missed having her hand snugged in his jeans, but she must have been able to see well enough, now that they weren't under the trees.

For him, the world was drawn in crisp grays with pools of ebony shadows. What did it look like to her? His first Change was so many miles and years and heartaches ago . . . he couldn't call up a clear sensory memory of how the night looked back when he'd had merely human eyes.

"Okay," Cynna said at last, "here's how I see it. If the councilor tries something sneaky, you won't be affected because of your personal shields, but he doesn't know about them. But Lily wouldn't be affected either, and she'd probably be able to tell at a touch if any of us were. And the Edge people do know that. They know she's a touch sensitive."

"Which makes it unlikely they'll pull something, but not impossible."

"Oh, come on. I'm all for taking reasonable precautions, but—"

"Dammit, Cynna!" Suddenly angry, he spun. "Reasonable precautions? You're carrying my child. Have you forgotten that already?"

Her mouth opened—then closed again.

Temper sighed into exasperation. "You did. You really did forget."

"Look, as far as you're concerned, I've been pregnant for four and a half weeks. But for me, it's been . . ." She glanced at her wrist, then pushed a button on her watch. The dial lit up. "Nine hours and thirty-one minutes."

If she hadn't spent those past four and a half weeks denying reality . . . Cullen scrubbed his head with one hand and reached for the slippery reins on his temper. "I get it. You need time to adjust. While you're adjusting—"

You didn't ask if you could bring someone with you.

The voice was deep, disapproving, and oddly resonant, considering it happened inside his head. Inside Cynna's head, too, judging by her expression. "Hi, Mika," Cullen said. "The human with me is Cynna Weaver. I told you about her. We have a bargain we'd like to offer you."

"You can hear him?" Cynna asked. "You've dropped your shield?"

"Shields, plural, remember? One of them's specifically for mindspeech. I usually leave that one down." He still couldn't separate the other shields enough to use them individually. Shit, he wasn't even sure how many there were. But the mindspeech shield was the topmost, the easiest to peel away from the rest. Once he caught the knack, opening it was like opening the gate to the front yard while keeping the house locked. *Your timing is lousy, Mika.*

She is the womb-rich one?

Dragons could mindspeak one person, two, or everyone in their vicinity. This time the mental voice felt as if Mika stood at Cullen's shoulder, addressing him privately. The thoughts were, as always, clear and crisp as a knife blade.

Yes, he answered silently.

You may approach, Cynna Weaver. I have not yet met a gravid human person.

Cynna rolled her eyes. "Great. I'm a curiosity."

"Better than being a snack." *I've something to say to Cynna privately*, Cullen told Mika, and mentally closed the gate to his front yard. He grabbed Cynna's hand. "Two things I want to say before we join Mika. Don't look him in the eye—"

"I *know* that." She tugged at her hand.

He didn't let go. "And there's one more option I want you to consider for our child."

She stilled, watching him warily.

"You could marry me."

EIGHT

❦

A breeze tickled the naked trees, making limbs and twigs rub together like sandpaper fingers. The same breeze plucked at Cynna's hair and chilled her cheeks. Overhead, the sky was a watercolor smear, black with charcoal streaks where the city bounced its lights off ribbons of cloud. A few stars poked through the haze.

It wasn't enough. She couldn't see Cullen's expression, only the place where darkness paled into the smudged oblong of his face. "You proposed," she said blankly. "You just proposed to me."

"Yes."

"Marriage."

"It's a reasonable solution."

"Lupi don't marry. Ever."

"Oh, that's right. Thanks for reminding me. I'd forgotten."

Cullen's sarcasm slid right past in the total strangeness of the moment. She didn't know how she felt . . . yes, she did. She was happy. She didn't know why, but his proposal—pointless and mysterious as it was—made her happy.

Which made her as foolish as him, but who cared? Cynna smiled at their mutual folly and patted his arm. "I'm not going to marry you."

He frowned at her hand as if he'd never seen it before. "Why not? It's a tidy solution. We're friends, we enjoy each other sexually, and we've made a child. Marriage gives us equal rights to that child, and if . . . well, Lady forbid it should happen, but if you were injured, I'd have rights there, too."

She hooted with laughter. "You mean, if I end up brain-dead you can tell them to keep me on life support until the baby's born? Now, there's an appealing notion!" She shook her head. "Wow. My first proposal. Likely my last, too, but I never thought I'd have even one. Thank you."

He tilted his head up and sighed loudly. "Why do I get the feeling you're not taking the idea seriously?"

"Because you're deranged, not stupid. Are you wanting to cleave only to me?" She chuckled. "C'mon. Let's go see a dragon."

He turned away without another word and swung himself along the path.

She followed. It was lighter out from under the trees, and the concrete path was pale, making it easy to see where her feet belonged. As she walked, she wondered if she'd pissed him off by laughing.

Probably not. Cullen's temper was not subtle. When he got mad, you didn't have to guess about it.

She'd confused him, maybe. She hadn't reacted the way he'd expected. But what had he expected? Some women dreamed of wedding dresses and tossed bouquets from the moment they held their first Barbie. Cynna's first Barbie had learned kung fu and either beat up or protected the other Barbies.

She could have sworn Cullen knew her well enough to understand that she was not marriage material. This whole baby business must have unseated his reason . . . a comforting notion. Nice to think she wasn't the only crazy one.

Not that she was so insane she'd consider marrying a lupus. Cynna might not know much about marriage—or any long-term relationship, really, since hers tended to fizzle out pretty fast. But surely fidelity was nonnegotiable, and Rule was the only faithful lupus on the planet.

She wasn't cruel enough to marry a lupus, either. She didn't know what the other lupi would do to one who violated one of their most deeply held beliefs, but it wouldn't be pretty.

Maybe Nokolai would kick Cullen out if he went nuts and got married. God! Pain pinched at her just thinking about that. She didn't know what it meant to a lupus to be clanless—not in her gut, anyway, not the way another lupus would. But she knew it was the worst fate they could imagine.

Cullen had lived clanless for most of his life. He'd been Nokolai only a few months . . . three, she thought, maybe four. He'd been adopted into the clan shortly before they met.

What was he thinking? How could he risk losing that?

Maybe he wasn't. What did she know? And dammit, she couldn't ask. He'd tell her what he wanted to—probably not lying outright, but he enjoyed stirring the truth into a shape that suited him.

Besides, she didn't want him to think she was considering his proposal. She could ask Rule what sins got a lupus booted from his clan. She'd need to keep it hypothetical. If she . . .

Some stupid piece of nature tripped her while she wasn't watching. Cynna barely kept herself from taking a header. "Dammit!"

Cullen stopped, turned. "Oh, for crying out loud! Here." He made a gesture as if he were tossing something in the air—and a ball of light bounced into being, then hung there between them, glowing like an enormous firefly.

She stared. "Mage light. You know how to make mage light."

"Mika showed me. It was embarrassing, really. Turns out it's pathetically easy. Doesn't take more than a smidge of power."

"And you let me stumble along in the dark all this time."

"You had your hand in my pants at first. I liked that."

"You—"

Tell your mate to open his mindspeech shield so I can speak to him.

Cynna jumped—and stared. A ribbon of darkness peeled itself off from the shadows up ahead and padded toward them along the path. A very large ribbon. With eyes. The eyes were silvery gray; the pupils, slitted. They were about ten feet off the ground.

The whiff of fear didn't surprise her. How could anyone see a dragon without tasting fear? "Ah—Cullen? Mika wants to talk to you."

Cullen put his hands on his hips and frowned at the approaching dragon. "What?"

Your female wishes to attack you, but believes an attack would be unfair. Explain this.

"Quit poking your nose in our brains," he snapped.

My nose is not . . . ah. You employed metaphor. I do not need to poke my nose anywhere. Her thoughts are loud. Muddy, but loud.

Cynna had seen a dragon up close and personal before. She'd even ridden one on their mad flight from hell. That didn't detract from her fear, or her fascination. As Mika drew closer, the two feelings melded into awe.

The ball of mage light wasn't as bright as a flashlight would have been. She caught hints and shadows of the long body with its sidewise sway; the great wings were folded into a dark hump riding his back. His neck was long and muscular and as flexible as a snake. He held his head roughly level with his shoulders.

That head was triangular, the snout almost delicate. Mobile frills like those depicted by Chinese artists decorated his eye ridges, ear holes, and jaw like black lace. In the soft glow of the mage light, the scales on his face shifted through a dozen shades of red.

When Mika stopped, his lipstick-colored head was about five feet away—and he was looking straight at her. It took effort to avoid looking directly in the large, moist eyes with their double lids. *Fairness puzzles me. Humans think of it often, but they change the meaning of the word with nearly every thought. Sometimes "unfair" means wrong. Sometimes it mean unwelcome. Fair can mean receiving what is agreed upon, but fairness is at issue even when there are no agreements. Such as now. You had not agreed to avoid attacking your mate, had you?*

"Uh—no. But he's lacking a foot. It isn't fair to attack someone who's impaired."

One-footed or two, he is your superior, physically. He would win any fight between you.

"No, he wouldn't, because he wouldn't hit back. That makes it unfair to hit him in the first place."

The great eyes blinked slowly. *Do humans consider it unfair to attack one who refuses to fight back? That is insane. In such a case, only those who refused to fight would win fights, which is clearly not true.*

"I guess . . ." Moral questions were not her strong point. What would Father Michaels say? "I guess fairness is like justice, but more personal. People have different ideas about what's fair and what isn't, because it's personal."

Fairness is a subjective construction of justice?

"No," Cullen said suddenly. "Fairness is moral equity or balance. Unfairness is moral debt. That's why it seems subjective—morality's a slippery bugger. A child might think it's unfair that he has to do his homework when his friends are outside playing. He doesn't yet understand the morality of discipline. And, of course, some adults have no more moral understanding than a child. They'll cry 'unfair' when they don't get what they want."

Ah.

Silence fell, both mental and physical. The dragon neither moved nor blinked. Cynna could smell him faintly—a scent like cinnamon, hot sand, and musk. She fancied she could even feel the warmth of his breath. She thought of Dis and demons and a terrible, wondrous flight on dragonback. Her heart beat quickly.

At last Mika looked at Cullen. *During one conversation, we agreed that morality is a being's mental construction of right behavior.*

"We did."

Human morality is a morass of contradictions with teeth ever pointed inward, gnawing at itself. Debt, however, is a reasonable concept, one shared by most sentients. I shall consider fairness in that light. Your mate believed she would incur a debt if she knocked you to the ground, so she chose not to follow her wishes.

"That's pretty much it," Cullen agreed, slanting Cynna an amused glance.

Given the human preoccupation with and confusion over morality, fairness must be a complex construction, subjectively variable. It is susceptible to bargaining?

"To some extent."

What bargain do you wish to offer me?

"Three persons from Edge have arrived here, and—"

Edge? Where is—ah, I see. You refer to Dsighliai.

"Perhaps I do," Cullen said dryly. "I think Edge is the English translation."

Your mate is thinking she will go to Edge. How would she do this?

"They want Cynna to return with them, and apparently know how to open a gate to do that. Are you familiar with Edge?"

Do you bargain for knowledge?

"Maybe I will, later. Right now . . ." He glanced at Cynna. "The Edge people want to erect a shield before we discuss terms. One of them, a gnome, says he knows a shield spell that he can't perform himself, so I'm supposed to help. I'm gathering components tonight. You've shed some scales since you arrived."

Silence. It wasn't promising.

Cullen persevered. "Cynna is a strong Finder. She could locate any scales you've shed and we could gather them for you. In exchange for that service, you could give us a percentage—say half—of the scales she—"

In a flash, the great body lifted impossibly—fifteen feet, twenty, more—with the wings extended, the forelegs off the ground and that snake neck arched. Mika's mouth gaped in a hissing display of teeth. *My scales are mine!*

Cynna damned near peed herself.

Cullen looked up. "Yes, they are yours."

Mika didn't return to four legs, but he did stop hissing. *They can't be not-mine. What you propose has no meaning.*

"Humans—and lupi—barter what's ours in order to acquire something we want. I'm talking about an exchange."

What is mine is always mine.

The mental voice was utterly clear, utterly implacable. Mika wasn't interested in a philosophical discussion of the meaning of ownership. Cynna looked at Cullen. He frowned, gave a little shake of his head.

He didn't know how to get past dragon possessiveness, either. Was there a way to get the use of a scale without . . . "Copyright," she said suddenly.

"What?"

"Copyright law. That's the model that fits." She looked up and up at the dragon towering over them. "Humans don't feel the way you do about objects, Mika, but we do feel that way about some things. Things we create, especially. You, uh—do you know about books and plays?"

Of course. Lots of disdain in that thought.

"Maybe you've heard of Shakespeare."

One of your story makers.

"Yes, well, we still talk about Shakespeare's plays. Even though the man's been dead for a few centuries, we speak of those plays as his because he made them—just like you made your scales. Yet people have the use of his plays. They can perform them, talk about them, quote from them. Books are like that, too. And paintings. Creators own what they create, and that can't be changed, but creators can grant rights to others in exchange for something they want."

Slowly Mika descended. When he had his feet back on the ground, he said, *What do you mean by rights?*

"We want you to allow us to use a scale in a spell. The scale is still yours, but we'd get the right to use it. In return, I'd Find all your missing scales and return them to you."

You can Find them? All of them?

"I can, if they're within a hundred miles of me. I guess we should make that one of the conditions. I can't Find objects farther away than that."

The long body settled further. Mika reclined, his forelegs tucked up, the enormous tail wrapping itself around him like a cat curling up for a nap. *We will discuss this.*

Two hours and forty minutes later, Cynna's eyes were teary from the wind. Her face felt frozen, her fingers were numb with cold, and her thighs ached from gripping tightly to the heated body between her legs.

The rest of her was toasty warm as Mika settled to the ground once more. Leather blocked wind, and both the dragon she'd ridden and the man who rode behind her were warm.

God, but she loved dragonflight.

Cullen slid down first, which turned out to be a good idea. When she followed, her legs buckled the second her feet touched the ground. He caught her easily and grinned, his eyes lit with exhilaration to match hers. "Not used to riding?"

"Not this kind." Cynna grinned back, punchy with exhaustion but still soaring. "You do know how to show a girl a good time."

She'd Found seven scales. They'd brought back only five because two of them, it seemed, were no longer Mika's. They were very small, the size of her pinky nail. Cullen said the magic had drained out of them.

The other five were larger, including one as big as her hand with the fingers spread. That's the one Cullen wanted—it still held plenty of magic. Of those five, two had come off there in the park—those had been easy to recover. The other three must have fallen off while Mika was in flight. They found one on a quiet street, another on the roof of an office building. The last one . . . well, that guy really should have given it to them when they told him the dragon wanted his scale back. It wasn't their fault he didn't know better than to look into a dragon's eyes, and one brief spot of ensorcellment wouldn't hurt him any.

You are sure we found them all?

This was the third time Mika had asked that. "All of them within a hundred miles."

Better than a hundred, actually, since she'd checked again every time they set down to pick up one of the strays. Which was undoubtedly why she was so fucking tired now. She'd done a full cast each time, which meant doing a fresh Find over and over and over. But Cynna figured that when you bargained with dragons, you'd better be extra sure you kept your end of the deal. "Don't forget that I'll need my bag back."

The denim bag dangled incongruously from Mika's mouth. Once Cynna had put the first scale in it, he'd insisted on holding onto it himself.

The dragon turned, shifting his bulk as fluidly as a cat. *You will come with me and put my scales where I want them. Then you may have the bag.*

Cullen had said Mika had been redecorating. That was one way to describe it. Wholesale destruction was another, though Cynna supposed the new design was more functional for a dragon than the old one had been.

Carter Barron Amphitheatre used to provide tiered seating for about four thousand concertgoers. Only the topmost row or two of seats remained. The rest had been ripped up and piled like makeshift dikes on two sides of the concrete slope, the lower portion of which was now buried in dirt.

That's where they'd landed, on hard-packed dirt. Mika had built himself a level spot in front of his lair for landings, takeoffs, sunbathing, whatever. The level area dropped off abruptly into the deep darkness of what used to be a large stage, walled on three sides and with a lofty roof.

Mika simply flowed down the dirt bank onto the stage. Cullen jumped, landing lightly. Cynna might have managed a dignified descent if her leg muscles hadn't been so overworked from her dragon ride. As it was, she slid the last few feet and landed in a dusty thump. "Shit."

"You okay?" Cullen crouched beside her, the mage light hovering over his shoulder.

"Yeah." She stood and brushed off some of the dirt, looking around. Mostly she saw dragon. Mika didn't occupy every inch of the space. Just most of them.

The quiet *meow* made Cynna jump—and stare. A small gray tabby had appeared out of nowhere and was rubbing itself against one of the dragon's thick forelegs. "What the hell—?"

"Mika's cat," Cullen said. "Though I believe the cat sees things the other way around, and Mika is her dragon."

Mika's jaw opened, revealing teeth a great white shark would envy. Cynna's bag fell to the floor. Mika's tongue flicked out and stroked the cat. Who purred. For a moment the two beasts regarded each other, then the cat turned away, flirting her tail before she shot up the dirt incline to vanish in the darkness.

"That's . . ." Cynna's voice trailed off. "Dragons don't have pets. Do they? That cat . . . some of Mika's scales are bigger than her whole body."

"I wouldn't call her a pet. They have an understanding."

Mika, too, had turned. *I want my scales in this corner with my dust.*

The dust Mika spoke of wasn't the same sort covering Cynna's jeans. It was gold dust. The dragons had never explained why they wanted it or what they did with it, but each of them received seven ounces of pure gold dust a month as part of their payment for living where humans needed them to live.

Cynna exchanged another glance with Cullen, then grabbed her bag. The two of them made their way past yards and yards of sleek, scaled dragon flesh. Mika was facing the corner he'd indicated, his head lowered almost to the floor to look at four small foam containers like dollhouse ice chests. Three of the containers were lidded; the fourth was open.

Wait, he told them.

A low, throbbing note filled the space. Her mind clicked off and her whole body strained as if trying to open itself to the sound. Ears alone weren't enough to absorb the unearthly beauty of dragonsong.

Almost as soon as he'd begun, Mika stopped.

Cynna sighed in disappointment. Rule had told her about how the dragons used to gather in Dis to sing together. In this realm they lived more scattered, but Lily and Rule both believed they still gathered and sang.

It is open now. Put them here, next to my dust.

Cynna shook herself out of her near-trance and knelt beside the little foam chests. Sometimes dragons sang for dragon reasons, which might or might not be the reasons humans made music. Sometimes they sang to work magic. "You've spell-locked your gold?"

A whiff of disdain drifted through her mind. Mika thought it was a stupid question.

She put four of the scales in a tidy pile next to the open container of gold dust and made sure Mika knew which one she was . . . well, not exactly keeping, since it was still Mika's. Reserving for Cullen to use tomorrow.

Now that he had his missing scales safely locked away, Mika apparently felt chatty. He settled his body into a cozy loop and looked at her. *You are going to the realm you call Edge?*

"I think so," she said

Do not tell anyone there your secret name.

"Uh—humans don't have secret names."

Of course you do. Most of you do not live long enough to learn them. I think you will receive yours soon, but perhaps you will not know it.

Mika may have said something privately to Cullen then, because Cullen chuckled. Cynna heard the question he asked about the Edge delegation but didn't really pay attention. She was too busy yawning. The last of her adrenaline rush was gone, and she could barely keep her eyes open. She was happy to let Cullen do the talking.

When she woke up, the air was pearly with early light, her head was in Cullen's lap, and his lips were skimming hers.

By the time she'd blinked herself awake, he'd straightened. Involuntarily she ran her tongue over her lips, tasting him. She sat up quickly. "Why did you let me sleep so long?"

"You were tired. I wasn't, and Mika was in a talkative mood."

"I like sleeping in a bed." She ran her hands through the short spikes of her hair. "What did you two talk about?"

"Edge, mostly. He wants us to remember that demons are composite beings."

They were, of course, since they retained something of everything and everyone they ate. But what did that have to do with anything? "Why?"

Cullen shrugged.

She frowned, not liking the way she felt. Pouty. Messy. With morning mouth, no doubt. His breath had smelled fresh. Did lupi even heal bad breath? That would be so not fair. "Where's Mika?" Cynna asked, noticing belatedly that they were alone.

"Breakfast. He moves quietly when he wants to. You should know that I haven't been with anyone since we did the dirty in that hotel room."

"You what?" Sex. He meant he hadn't had sex. What kind of subject was that to bring up when she had morning breath? "Why not? I mean—why did you tell me that?"

He shrugged and rose, unwinding himself as fluidly as Mika had moved last night. "That sort of thing matters to many women. I thought it might to you."

"It doesn't." And then, because she couldn't stop herself: "It's been five weeks."

One corner of his mouth crooked up. "I suspect you have a seriously inflated notion of my randiness. When I was younger, maybe . . . hell, definitely. But I'm nearly sixty now, and not interested in constantly dipping my wick for no other reason than to get it wet."

Sixty. She kept forgetting that. He looked her age. "Yeah, I've noticed what a mushy romantic you've become in your dotage."

"That's me. Mushy as hell. Come on." He held out a hand. "You can buy me breakfast."

Cynna bought him breakfast. She rolled her eyes when their waitress nearly killed herself getting to the table— Cullen had that effect on women. On some men, too. She asked him what Mika had told him about Edge, and they discussed the spell he'd perform soon.

And all the while she kept hearing, "I haven't been with anyone since you." The words had woken something sharp and hungry and silent in her, something she wanted no part of. But it refused to go back to sleep.

NINE

~

SHORTLY before nine o'clock the next morning, Cullen was back at the big, ugly block of a building in an underground office with an old metal desk for company.

No one had threatened him with a strip search this time. He'd taken his clothes off all on his own.

Cullen's original training was Wiccan; he felt more comfortable going sky-clad when working a powerful spell. He could have worn a robe, but the bloody things were a pain to launder properly since they had to be cleaned of more than physical dirt. Naked was easier. If the sight of his bare ass upset anyone . . . well, a man had to take his fun where he found it, didn't he?

God knew he didn't expect much else to be fun today. Bloody ignorant government drones.

That so-called gnome expert had given away half a million in gemstones without getting any explanations for the shield spell. Zip, zilch, nada. They had the spell, sure—the gnome had drawn it last night. They didn't know what half the glyphs meant, much less how the overall design was supposed to work. The wrinkled runt had refused to part with one word of explanation, and the government had let him get away with it.

Cullen had damned near refused to cast the spell. Brooks had persuaded him to go ahead, mostly because he was right, dammit. They'd just have brought in someone else. Also, Brooks had a strong feeling Cullen needed to be the spellcaster.

So did Cullen.

On one point the councilor had been defeated, but he didn't seem to realize it. When told that Lily would not be going to Edge, he'd smiled and insisted she be present today anyway. He thought they might change their minds once they understood the situation.

Of course, he didn't know about the mate bond. He wasn't going to learn, either. That was none of his business.

Cullen might have been trained as Wiccan initially, but he had little patience with tradition for tradition's sake. He'd long since learned that full immersion wasn't necessary for full cleansing. Instead he washed his hands, his feet, and the major chakras—a mingling of Eastern and Western practices that would have appalled traditionalists in both hemispheres. But it worked.

He dipped his fingers in the bowl of salt water and touched the crown chakra at the top of his skull. A pulse of awareness prickled over his scalp; he both saw and felt the violet energy of that chakra flowing into balance with the other energetic centers of his body. He waited, letting that communion complete itself, then opened his eyes, grabbed his crutches, and swung over to the door, wearing a small diamond around his neck, a big one on his right index finger, and nothing more.

The hall wasn't empty. Two Secret Service types in dark suits eyed him. Give them points for professionalism—neither of them stared at the bits that were normally covered in public. One muttered something into his headset.

Cullen gave them his best professional nod and headed

for the door they were guarding. Earlier he'd spoken with the presidential adviser who was the reason for their presence. Marilyn Wright was fond of perfume, but otherwise seemed sharp and relatively unburdened by preconceptions.

A nice contrast to McClosky from Commerce. Unfortunately, it was McClosky who'd negotiated for the shield spell with help from that misbegotten gnome expert.

Parked beside the door was Ruben Brooks's wheelchair. Cullen left his crutches beside it, opened the door, and limped into what used to be a conference room. It no longer looked the part.

The gnome had fought to limit the number of people present. After serious dickering they'd agreed on the ten people in the circle, plus Cullen. Six humans and four other types of people sat on cushions on the cement floor like a kindergarten class playing hot potato. Every one of them turned to look at him. It amused him to see where they looked—or avoided looking.

Not that there was much to see at the moment, given his recent application of cold seawater. Later, with the magic surging through him like honey and storm, his fifth member would put on more of a show.

Lily kept her gaze determinedly on his face. The presidential assistant lifted her eyebrows. McClosky bounced a glance off him before returning to an in-depth study of his shoes, and Steve Timms was more interested in who had weapons than who wore clothes. Steve was very conscious of his increased responsibility today. He was bodyguarding both Brooks and Marilyn Wright.

Cynna gave Cullen a grin. She sat between Gan and Lily with that huge bag of hers on her Lily side. It held a supply of Hershey's Kisses to bribe the little not-quite-demon as needed. On Lily's other side, Brooks sat on a padded stadium seat instead of a cushion. He had a nod for Cullen. The gnome and the other guy were indifferent to nudity, and the tusked woman . . . interested. Definitely and sexually interested, which he found surprisingly disconcerting.

Gan said, "Hey! Nice cock."

"Thank you," Cullen said gravely. "I like it."

"How long does it get when—"

Lily hushed her, McClosky sputtered, and the presidential aide snickered. Cullen was pretty sure it was her, anyway.

He glanced at the clock on the wall. Seven minutes.

Clock time was an artificial construction, but numbers resonate magically, especially when used with intention. After some discussion, he and the councilor had settled on 9:05 to begin the casting. The two primes separated by a null suited the parameters of the spell.

"It's almost showtime, ladies and gentlemen," Cullen said, taking in the scent of the room. A couple of those present were frightened, but that wasn't unreasonable. They seemed to have it under control. "Any last questions?"

"Uh, do we need to clear our minds or something?" McClosky asked.

"Only if you're hoping to contact the dearly departed. This isn't a séance."

Marilyn Wright had a cool, dry voice that reminded him of Mika. "Are the rest of us likely to experience anything?"

He shrugged. "It's not my spell. Councilor?"

"If you is having a Gift, you is maybe having sight or feeling of shield. If no Gift, you seeing, feeling, nothing." He turned a wormy smile on Lily. "For the sensitive, as energies raised, she is likely feeling them on skin."

One of the many things the councilor had promised to explain once they were shielded was how, exactly, he knew about Lily. Cynna thought that Earth's gnomish elders must have learned about Lily's Gift from Gan and passed that information to the gnomes in Edge.

That was one possibility. Another was that the Edge

bunch was in league with a certain goddess—the one who wanted to destroy the lupi, find the Codex Arcanum, and copy it onto Lily's brain-wiped body and mind. Cullen didn't consider that likely. Lily would probably have picked up Her taint when she touched them if any of them were closely linked to Her. But it remained a possibility.

Dammit, Lily should not be here. Not that he expected anything to go wrong, and if it did, Lily's Gift should protect her, but . . . never mind. He had to deal with what was, not the way he thought things ought to be.

Cullen blinked slowly. Both types of seeing were always present, but physical vision was so vivid it normally drowned out the other. It took a moment's concentration to shift his attention to his other vision. He checked the altar, its contents, and the three circles surrounding it—his, still unset but marked by four black and four white candles; the shield spell itself, drawn in white chalk by the gnome; and the circle of people sitting on the floor inside the first two circles.

He also checked the silver pendant worn by the bald man and the stone set in the warrior woman's sword. He'd recognized them yesterday for charms—quite sophisticated, not terribly powerful, and only intermittently active.

As before, the power they did possess was directed at their wearers. He glanced at the clock again. And began.

The concrete floor was rough and cool beneath Cullen's feet. He limped heavily on the curled-up ball of his foot, but that was better than introducing crutches into the energy here.

They'd pulled up the carpet yesterday, and two witches from Sherry's coven had given the floor a seawater scrubbing . . . much to the gnome's amusement. Smug little bastard seemed to think cleansing was some quaint local superstition, but dammit, Cullen knew better. He could see the energy, couldn't he? An experienced caster of whatever practice didn't need to physically cleanse everything for most spells, but for the big ones, yeah. It mattered. And this was ley line magic. Achieving anything approaching real balance would be a bitch made bitchier by sloppy prep.

As he passed the first candle, he flicked a finger at it. It lit.

Someone gasped. He continued to move, his attention on the energies he drew with him as he walked sunwise around the circle. He would make three circuits.

The gnome had claimed Cullen didn't need a spell circle. Cullen had ignored him. Were all practitioners in Edge sloppy? Or were they so impossibly advanced they truly didn't need to set a circle to contain their magic?

He wasn't. The shield spell was supposed to keep things out. His circle would keep things in. Admittedly, he could set a circle a lot more simply, but this was one of the few things within his control, and by damn, he'd do it right. Besides, the FBI would be pissed if any magic leaked and crashed their computers.

He passed Cynna's leather-clad back in the third circle. She smelled faintly aroused, which made him smile. The fine webbing of energy covering her took the smile away.

Not that it wasn't a damned good spell. Sherry and three of her coven had spun an excellent protection spell on the leather coat. Those subtle filaments should tangle up any spells before they could touch the woman wearing it . . . any that weren't too powerful, that is. Enough power would burst those strands.

Feelings rumbled in him like distant thunder, assorted and strange. A web-spelled coat wasn't enough. He didn't want Cynna here.

But the gnome did. And the gnome kept getting what he wanted.

No one spoke while Cullen completed his three circuits over the complaints of his unfinished foot. Spell circles were set in two dimensions, but the protection they cast was spherical, so when he finished, he saw a ghostly dome over the lot of them, anchored by the candles.

Nice and uniform, he decided with a nod. He crossed the blank space left in the glyphs, heading for the altar. "I'll invoke the elements now," he told the others. He looked at the gnome. "Close the door."

The councilor sniffed, but he rose and moved to the unchalked portion of the circle readily enough. With quick strokes he drew a symbol Cullen knew: the *kryllus*, an Etruscan symbol for closure or completion.

Maybe the runt was on the up-and-up. Cullen wasn't taking bets on it.

The altar was a two-foot-square slab of granite borrowed from Sherry's coven. They'd used a trolley and four men to move it here. It held Cullen's athame, a glass chalice filled with water, a dragon's scale, a small oil lamp, and a double fistful of herbs sprinkled over a bed of damp earth in a stone saucer.

Two of the herbs had been beyond Cullen's resources, so the Feds had pulled strings. The yohimbe came from a lab in Canada; the aashringi had been flown in by Air Force jet from India. There were advantages to working for the government, Cullen acknowledged as he knelt in front of the altar. Not many, but a few.

The gnome had specified the components, but the manner of invoking the elements was up to him. He kept it simple, whispering the familiar words as he held his hand over each item in turn, moving clockwise, or sunwise: herbs, dragon's scale, lamp, chalice.

The others would see the small flame spring into being on the lamp's wick. They wouldn't see the colors that danced into life beneath his hand, or the single spot of uncolored intensity that was his diamond. Cullen picked up his athame. He drew a channel from color to color, connecting them—then touched the tip of the blade to his chest and pressed.

Blood trickled down, warm and liquid. And the colors streamed inside him.

Rocks fell down the slope of his spine. Wind blew through his skull. Water flooded his lungs. Fire burned his throat and mouth. His penis hardened and his lips pulled back from his teeth as power shuddered through him.

Dimly through the physical cacophony he heard Lily ask quietly, dubiously, "This is a blood spell?"

"It's okay," Cynna said. "The blood isn't for the spell. He's balancing the elements before doing the actual cast."

The councilor piped up, so shrill he sounded like Gan. "You is not saying you balance this way! Is—is primitive!"

You didn't tell me a few things, either, buddy. But Cullen was too caught up in sensation and sorting to speak.

Cynna again: "Physically balancing the elements is an ancient and effective tradition, and he's a dancer. He knows his body."

"But he is not telling me he does this! He is keeping secrets!"

"And you aren't? Right. Now shut up."

Cullen grinned.

"His foot," Brooks said quietly. "Look at his foot."

Hey, he *was* standing on his feet, wasn't he? Both feet. Flat on the ground. With his eyes closed. So he opened them.

The infusion of elemental energies had heightened and altered his other vision. Eyes open or closed, he saw color—wild, crashing color. His circle was a sheet of orange flame; the second circle was dull, inactive. And his feet . . . he looked down. The left one still ached a bit, but looked entirely normal, the parts properly situated.

Who knew swallowing the elements could accelerate healing? He'd figure out how later. Time to check out the others.

The gnome's power hugged him like a dun-colored blanket, as if hiding what lay beneath. Gan's magic was as in-your-face as she was—a shriek of orange punctuated by cerulean blue. A dozen shades of pink lapped over the tusked woman, glimmering into grape near the chakras. The clay-colored man's magic matched his skin—earthy, with ribbons of green and lavender.

Cullen checked the Edge party's charms and nodded. They glowed with faint, pastel lines, just as he'd expected.

Human magic was usually more translucent than that of those of the Blood, and more uniform in color. Power rose in a silvery fog from Ruben Brooks, sprinkled with sparks of black and violet. Rare colors, those. The silver was no surprise, of course, being the color usually associated with all types of clairvoyance, and Brooks was a strong precog. But the other colors . . .

Speculate later.

Cullen's eyebrows rose when he saw McClosky from Commerce. Magic hugged the man's ribs like wet moss, turgid and still—a Gift dammed up and denied.

Lily was the exception to the Technicolor display. Her magic looked much as it always did—like ice, colorless but reflecting hints of the colors around her. Beside her, Cynna sat with her long legs folded, the protection spell a fine net overlaying her own magic. Which danced. Like a lively sunrise, it sparkled in the pale palette of Air. Except . . .

Cullen stared. Over her stomach—her womb—a haze of lavender rested, cool and quiescent. He'd never seen magic coming from a developing fetus this early, but he'd never tried looking after in-blooding the elements. The energy was diffuse, the color pale, but it was separate. It didn't dance with her other colors.

Lavender, a soft purple. The color of those of the Blood.

"Cullen," Cynna said, "you breathing?"

No. He'd lost the balance. Flame licked at his fingers, roots twined up his calves, and his lungs sloshed with ocean, leaving him light-headed. Panic flickered at the edge of thought already dimming. He needed to *move*.

No. Air. Fire's first impulse was action, but it was breath he needed—to pull in air physically and locate the energy of Air inside him. It was there. He knew it was, however little he felt it. He dragged in a slow breath, belly-deep and ragged.

The next one came more smoothly as the sparkle of Air returned to his blood and Earth subsided back into bone and sinew. By the third breath Water had seeped back into his soft tissue, clearing his lungs. He continued to heed his breath, settling into the balance once more, and walked to the chalked circle and the glyph he'd been directed to use as entry.

Then Cullen reached for the ley line beneath his feet.

He couldn't see it. Too much earth lay between him and that wild current. He'd be working as blind as any other practitioner, reaching by guess and intention. But he felt it, oh, he did—keenly now, with the elements in him, a prickling beneath the skin and a drawing in his gut, power calling to power. His penis dipped like a dowsing rod.

He pointed his athame at the ground. *"Venio!"*

The word was a focus, a tool for his intention and will, which commanded the power to *come*. There were no real words of power—or rather, all words held power, but most practitioners preferred to use a language other than their everyday tongue. Still, it should be a language they knew. To match will with words, one must *feel* the words.

Cullen spoke to power in Latin, and power answered. Quickly.

It rolled up, up, through the earth faster than he'd expected. Faster than the thrice-damned gnome had warned him to expect, and stronger. The whole damned ley line answered his call.

No time to kill the little worm. No time even to hurry—if he lost the balance now, he'd die. So he spoke slowly, even softly, pronouncing each word with the fullest force of intention, quite as if his life depended on it:

"Res aqua repleo—
Res terra repano—

Res aero respiro—
Res ignus retorqueo.
Resero! Resero! Resero!"[1]

With the final repetition, Cullen touched the blade of his knife to the glyph the gnome had directed him to use. And all hell rolled up and smashed through him.

He didn't channel the entire ley line. No corporeal being could. But the power roared past him—firestorm, earthquake, tornado, flood—following the bend of his body, the aim of his blade. There was no way, no possibility of balancing this much raw energy.

The backwash was a bitch.

His muscles spasmed. He couldn't stop them, couldn't keep his blade touching the entry glyph. Power spilled—into him, the spell, the room.

Cullen collapsed to the floor, sinews shrieking, body convulsing. Vision stopped. There was only blackness, pain, and the roaring in his bones. He screamed—maybe not out loud—and Fire answered. *There, go there*—! He found the entry glyph again and stabbed it with his blade, and the portion of the wild energy that was Fire fled down the knife into the spell.

Then Earth: *Yes, go where you're told, yes. Repano*, he told it, and the rest of the earth magic shouldered past him to sink into the glyphs. He called Water and it answered, a turquoise flood rushing into the spell.

But Air—fractious, rebellious Air—was beyond him. It rushed around the room, lifting shrieks from the others, tossing hair and clothes, dancing itself into a vortex. He gulped it down and his muscles spasmed again, but weakly. His heart spasmed, too, a hard, hot knot in his chest as his

[1]*Res* is the usual salutation for the elements; it means everything from matter, relation, or condition, to the world or the universe. Thus, Cullen addresses the condition of Water or universal Water, not a specific puddle. The rest of the verse translates roughly as "Water, fill this; Earth, lay up here; Air, here exhale; Fire, twist and alter this—unblock, unclose, begin!"

body tried to give up. Which he would not allow. He got an elbow under him, grunted, pushed up—

"Goddammit!" Cynna screamed, on her feet now, her hair whipping around in the interior gale as she pointed at the entry glyph. "Go! Do as you're told!"

Air swirled around her once, twice, knocking her back a step. And did as it was told.

The silence shocked Cullen. He hurt. His right knee was the worst, almost enough to drown out the other aches. Apparently he'd wrenched it while flopping around like an electrocuted fish. His muscles felt like jelly. Slowly he turned his head to look at the spell.

"Cullen?" Cynna was halfway across the circle.

He waved her back. "Hold on a minute."

The brilliant colors of Earth, Air, Fire, and Water whipped around the gnome's spell circle, the lines of power weaving around each other so quickly he couldn't find the pattern . . . yet it seemed familiar.

"Are we in danger?" Brooks asked, as if the question held only mild interest for him.

"No, no," said the gnome, standing. "Danger over."

"You deceived us," Marilyn Wright snapped. "You said the spell was safe."

"Should have been safe, but the Cullen Seabourne called up whole entire ley line. I not knowing how he is doing this. But spell is excellent—swallowed all magic very good." He spread his skinny little arms wide. "Danger over."

As the power zipped around, twining in and out of itself, the colors were blending. Blurring. Turning back into the piercing, near-solid intensity of node energy, which wasn't possible. Magic did not return to its raw state, but this was. "Something's wrong."

"Not wrong," the gnome said happily. "Is working well. Whole entire ley line is much power, very thank you. *Kirelashidah!*"

And the power shook itself and melted out from the spell, ribbons shooting out to lock with other ribbons in a pattern he suddenly recognized. "Son of a bitch!" Cullen shoved to his feet, staggering as his banged-up knee tried to buckle on him. "Get out, get out! It's a gate! It's a fucking gate!"

The gnome shouted something unintelligible. Cullen slashed at the nearest power ribbon with his athame, sundering it. The loose end whipped around like a fire hose jetting water, and the center of the floor vanished.

So did the altar. And Cynna, who'd been standing next to it.

Cullen howled, gathering himself to leap across the widening chasm and kill the gnome. The clay-colored man tackled him.

The guy was strong and agile enough to crack his fist against Cullen's jaw as they fell. It cleared his head wonderfully. Cullen, too, was strong and agile—and lupus, and very fast, though with a bum knee and jellied muscles. Not good for jumping ten feet or more.

He belted the guy in the head with the heel of his hand.

Cullen's hand damned near exploded, but he'd knocked his opponent dizzy. A shot rang out, then another, hugely loud in the enclosed space. He shoved the man off him in time to see tusk-woman toss Steve Timms into the churning brightness that used to be a floor.

The gate was still growing, and he was kitten-weak from his battle with the loose ley line magic. He couldn't handle the diamond's energy, not in this state. With a flick of his hand he extinguished the candles. His spell circle evaporated.

The room spun for a second as Cullen reabsorbed the magic—Fire energy, and his. His vision cleared in time for him to see the two Secret Service agents who'd responded to the chaos by flinging open the door and drawing their weapons. "Get them out!" he shouted. "Don't shoot! Just get everyone out of here!"

Tusk-woman dropped Brooks into the bright chasm, and one of the idiots fired anyway.

The lights went out.

In the darkness someone screamed. "Back up!" he called to those who couldn't, like him, see the shining disaster spreading toward them. "Get your backs to the wall! The gate should stop at the glyphs!"

Large, strong hands seized his shoulders. The scent told him whose hands. He snarled and drove his fist where her stomach ought to be. Connected.

It hurt like hell, since that was the hand he'd bashed against her partner's thick skull. She bloody ignored the blow. He didn't even get an *oof* out of her, and she was wounded, too. He smelled the blood and knew Steve must have hit her at least once with that gun of his before she tossed him into the hole in reality.

Didn't seem to inconvenience her. She shoved him, and oh, Lady, but this woman could have arm-wrestled a demon.

Good thing he'd latched on to her arms. His legs went out from under him, but he held on with all the strength he had, and together they stumbled to the edge of the boiling chasm. Her own strength saved him—she jerked back before they could fall in, dragging him with her.

Cullen tried to trip her. She slapped him, and while his ears were ringing, she pried loose one of his hands. He used the other one to jab at her eye. She grunted and lost her grip, so he dropped to the floor and rolled, colliding with a pair of legs.

He knew that scent, too. "Get back, dammit!" he yelled at Lily. He staggered to his feet and made sure she did as she was told for once, dragging her past the roiling lines that marked the boundary of the gnome's spell. He pushed her against the wall. "Stay!"

Having done all he could, he turned, took four running steps and dived into the screaming whiteness of the gate.

TEN

Cynna fell through darkness. She fell and fell, for miles and years. Or maybe it was only seconds, and the darkness wasn't dark at all. Her senses refused to record what she was falling through.

Then it was air, bitter cold, rushing past.

And then she landed.

Her breath *whoof*ed out. She lay spread-eagled on something hard and cold. Nothing hurt, she realized in surprise. Overhead . . . that was way too many stars, whole beaming constellations of them in a sky like spilled ink. Except for right above her, where there was only black . . .

A black that someone was falling out of.

Gan landed with a *plop* near Cynna's feet and immediately jumped upright. "Better get out of the way. The others will be—no, wait. It's moving! It's not supposed to move!"

"What?" Cynna sat up slowly. Snow, she realized, looking around. She'd landed in snow. And that was about all she saw at first—snow glistening in a star-washed night. A great big rock very near . . . the altar. The altar had fallen through the floor, just like her. And behind it, she saw when she craned her head around, were a whole bunch of dark, scary trees, their branches dusted with white. A forest.

Another body fell. This one landed about twenty feet away.

"The gate, stupid." Gan propped her hands on her hips, glaring at the sky. "The gate's moving."

Right. A gate. She'd fallen through a gate. It hadn't felt like her previous experience of gates, but what did she know? Maybe there were lots of types of gates and each type offered a different experience.

Cynna steered for the body—which belonged to Mc-Closky, she saw as he groaned and sat up, looking as dazed as she'd felt. The snow wasn't deep, no more than a couple inches, but she was glad she'd worn her boots. "You okay?" she asked.

McClosky just shook his head. Another body fell, this one thirty feet off. The gate was moving away from the trees, she realized. Thank God. It would be bad to come down on top of them.

Timms hit and rolled like he'd practiced falling from the sky a dozen times, coming up on his feet with his weapon clutched in his hand and his eyes wild.

"Don't shoot!" she called, starting toward him.

He was making a slow turn. "Where the hell are we?"

"Not hell. Edge, I think."

"Of course it's Edge," Gan grumbled. "Though with the way that sorcerer messed with things, I don't know—"

"Sorcerer?" Timms yelped. "The gnome is a sorcerer?"

"Not the gnome." Cynna looked at Gan. "That's a secret, too."

"Did you bring the chocolate?"

Thirty feet away, Ruben fell from the sky.

Too high. That's all she could think, panic shooting her into a run as he landed. The gate had moved higher as well as farther away, and Ruben had landed hard. He was fragile, physically. She skidded to a stop and dropped to her knees beside him. "Ruben." He lay mostly on his side, eyes closed, one arm pinned beneath him. She put a hand to this throat, hunting for a pulse. "Ruben, dammit—"

He blinked. "I fell."

"Yeah, it was a gate. That goddammed gnome made a gate, not a shield." She found his pulse. Obviously he was alive, but his heartbeat seemed too fast and not all that strong. "Where are you hurt?"

"My wrist is broken. I suspect the left tibia is, also."

His voice sounded so much as always—calm, matter-of-fact—she almost burst into tears.

"It's moving higher," Gan said. "That's not going to work out well. Humans break too easily."

"What?" She looked up. A small, dark heap marred the snow at least a hundred yards away. "Is that someone? Who is it? Timms—"

"I'm on it." He took off running.

McClosky had made it to his feet. He looked like he might throw up. "We're in another realm."

"Yeah. You okay? I mean, are you hurt?"

He just shook his head, not moving. Shock, Cynna guessed, but she couldn't deal with him now. She turned her attention back to Ruben. "It's your left wrist? And your leg, possibly. I don't know what to do. Cullen would. He's claims to have gone to med school, so he'll be able to set it if . . . when he gets here."

"You might support my wrist while helping me roll onto my back."

She did, and he hissed in pain, his face turning the color of the snow. She started to shrug out of her coat. "You can't lie on that cold snow. That can't be good."

"The tibia," he said in a thin but steady voice, "is certainly broken."

"It's Ms. Wright," Timms called. "She's unconscious. Heartbeat's thready. I don't want to move her. Could be a neck injury."

Shit! "McClosky, come here." She had to say his name

again before he heard, but he did start moving. "I need to get my coat under Ruben. It will give him some protection from the cold and damp. His leg's broken. So's his wrist. I need you to help me move him."

Being given a task steadied him. "Yes. Yes, he shouldn't get cold. I'll take his shoulders."

No more bodies fell while they shifted Ruben onto the slight protection the leather offered. Fear kept trying to get her attention. *Not now*, Cynna told it. "I'm going to see what I can do for Ms. Wright," she told McClosky. "Stay with Ruben." She took off.

The snow wasn't deep, but it was slippery. She jogged carefully, wondering what in the world she could do. She wasn't a healer. She could, with difficulty, make fire, but she needed something to burn. And heat would just melt the snow, leaving them lying in mud.

God, but she hoped—oh, another one fell! And this one was naked. And male.

Cynna switched direction. "Gan!" she called. "Go curl up next to Ms. Wright!"

"Why?"

"You're supposed to help us, aren't you? She needs your body heat."

"Humans are so puny." But the little former demon did start trudging in that direction.

Cullen was nearly a football field away. Before she was halfway there, another body fell, even farther off. It didn't look like Lily, but with only moon and stars for light, she couldn't be sure. Then two more came through together—one large, one small. They fell on the other side of a slight rise, so she couldn't see them once they landed.

Cullen pushed up to his hands and knees, his head hanging. "Shit."

Relief pounded through her. "Where are you hurt?" she called.

"Everywhere." But he made it to his feet, though he swayed a bit. "You're all right?"

Winded, mostly. Snow was as bad as sand for running. She nodded.

"No bleeding?" He made that more demand than question.

Oh—right. A little jolt went through her as she realized what he meant. Falls weren't good for pregnant women, were they?

She came to a stop in front of him. "No bleeding. I'm fine. The gate was closer to the ground when I fell through. Ruben's back there. Broken leg and wrist. McClosky's with him—he wasn't hurt. Timms and Gan are with Ms. Wright. They're okay. She's unconscious. I don't know if Lily—"

"I got her away from the gate, I think." Cullen was grimly pleased about that. He looked up, scanning the sky. "Speaking of which, it's gone. Where's that damned gnome?"

"I think he fell on the other side of that rise. One them was really small, anyway. And someone fell just this side of it. I need to see if—"

"I'll check on them. Here, hold on to this for me." He handed her his ring, the one with the charged diamond.

"Why?"

"Because I'm bloody freezing. I want fur." He reached up to unfasten the chain at his neck.

"No!"

Cullen scowled. "What do you mean, 'no'?"

"You want to go rip out the gnome's throat, and it won't help. We're going to need him. He got us here, and he can damned well get us back. And I need you to have hands. I can't set Ruben's leg, and Ms. Wright is hurt and I don't know what to do for her, and . . ." She stopped, gulped, and shivered. "I know you're cold, but I . . . I need help. If you could wait a little longer, I could use some help."

The scowl lingered. He flicked a glance at the sky, where a half moon hung near the horizon, and muttered,

"She sings loudly here. All right. I can be cold awhile. But you—where's your coat?"

"Ruben's lying on it. I don't want him going into shock or something. Though maybe I should . . . I haven't done anything for Ms. Wright. I sent Timms to check on her, and Gan to keep her warm, but—"

Cullen put his arms around her. "Shut up, Cynna."

"We can't cuddle now."

"Warmer this way. Okay, Brooks is in charge, but he's injured, so it falls on you until he's well enough to take over. Does—"

"What does all that matter?" It was warmer this way. A lot warmer. "You're heating up."

"I can do it for a few minutes, take the chill off. Cynna—survival by committee doesn't work out well. Someone has to be boss. Rule's got the innate authority to pull that off with humans. I don't, so it's up to you. Does Steve have his gun?"

"He landed with it out and ready to fire. How's your foot?"

"Achy, but okay. Give me back my ring. I'll go see if . . . Guess I won't have to," he said, setting her aside. "Here they come."

Cynna saw two figures topping the rise. Both were too tall to be the gnome. Both seemed to be carrying something, but it was too dark for her to see what. "Is that Tash and . . . what is his name? Somebody of Wen."

"Not somebody of Wen," one of the figures said loud and clear. "Wen of Ekiba."

Cynna stared. "That's English. He spoke English."

"He's got a charm translating for him." Cullen raised his voice slightly. "Don't you, Wen of Ekiba? You've been pretending only the gnome understood us, but that was bullshit."

"Pretending?" sputtered a high-pitched voice. "Is pretending you, Cullen Seabourne! You pretending being lupus! Not telling us you being sorcerer! Only sorcerer calls up whole entire ley line, then cuts through part of spell. You messing ups everythings!"

Wen said something that wasn't in English, but Cynna got the gist. He was pissed, and not at them.

"My ring," Cullen said quietly.

Cynna handed it to him. She could make out the figures pretty clearly now. The big one was definitely Tash. Her size, her sword, and her tusks made her hard to mistake. Wen was carrying the gnome and something else . . . oh. She swallowed so she wouldn't start giggling. Her denim tote was slung over his shoulder, and it looked almost as funny there as it had in Mika's mouth.

"Cynna," Timms called, "Ms. Wright's not doing so well."

That wiped out any silliness. She raised her voice. "We've got injured. You kidnapped us. You'd better have some plan to take care of our wounded. We need shelter, too."

"Shelter is at City, where we would be if sorcerer fool not messing ups—"

"Who is injured?" The light, fluting voice cutting across the gnome's tirade came from Tash. She spoke much better English than the gnome. In fact, she sounded like a TV news anchor—no accent at all. "I am not a true healer, but I have some skill."

The gnome squawked something in his language.

"You will heal," the big woman said calmly. They were twenty feet away now, close enough for Cynna to see a dark stain on the woman's shoulder. Blood. "Humans don't heal well on their own. Who do you want me to help?"

Cynna chewed on her lip briefly. It could be a trick, but she didn't see why they'd bother. They'd gone to a good deal of trouble to get a bunch of humans here. Why turn around and kill them? "We've got two injured, but Marilyn Wright is in the worst shape. She's over there"— she pointed—"with Gan and Timms. What about you? You're bleeding."

"The wound is not significant. Wen clouded the man's reflexes. I will see what I can do for Marilyn Wright." She set off at an easy lope.

"Steve!" Cullen called. "She's going to help! Don't shoot her."

Good point. Cynna looked at him. "Maybe you can go see about Ruben. He thought it was his tibia—that's the calf bone, right? And his left wrist. I guess we'll need splints, but I'd like you to have a look."

He was watching Wen and the gnome. "I'll stay with you for now."

"Okay, I didn't make myself clear. That wasn't a suggestion. You wanted me to be in charge. If you won't do what I say, the others won't, either."

Cullen looked at her, his expression unreadable. He glanced at Wen, almost upon them now, his hands full of gnome and bag. "All right. If your ladyship pleases, though, you might come over and try putting your pain-block spell on him."

Cynna hadn't thought of that. She had a spell that blocked pain completely. Problem was, it also stopped healing, so it couldn't be used for most things. "Okay, but I don't know if he can learn it that fast. He's not a caster."

"It's worth a try. Getting a bone set hurts."

Cullen moved away just as Wen stopped in front of Cynna. She put her hands on her hips, glaring at the gnome. "For a change, you're going to try telling the truth. I want to know why you tricked us—about the spell, about speaking English, about pretty much everything."

"Not everythings." The gnome didn't look so hot. His legs dangled limply and his face was pasty. "Daniel Weaver is being in Edge, Cynna Weaver. He is fifteenth assistant to chancellor, very important position—highest status human in the City. The City where we is supposed to be. Also true we is needing you to Find something. Also needing the sensitive." His face spasmed in what might have been anger or pain. "She did not come through gate?"

"Nope."

He heaved a sigh. "We in big mess. I tell you more truths, but not now. Is not safe here. We supposed to be arriving in the City, but the Seabourne's messing change this. We not being certain where exactly we is, but too much away from river. Dangerous place. Wen has call his people. They arriving maybe three, four hours. I telling you all truths then."

Suddenly Wen stiffened. "Dondredii," he hissed. He said it again, louder, calling out to Tash in a string of non-English words. Then he looked at Cynna.

"Run!" Wen told her as he broke into a run himself, the little councilor grunting with pain at the jolting—but not complaining. "Get your people together! The dondredii come!"

ELEVEN

CULLEN looked up at the first shout. He got a good whiff about the same time. Not that he recognized the scent, but it said "carnivore" loudly.

Brooks was lucid but clammy. Cynna had done right to wrap him in her coat—shock was a real danger, given the man's physical fragility. Cullen couldn't tell about the tibia, but one glance confirmed that Brooks's wrist was broken—an obvious radial fracture needing immediate reduction and maybe surgery, judging by the visible misalignment. Only surgery wasn't among their options.

Neither was even crude bonesetting, not yet. "Sorry," Cullen told his patient, and slid his arms beneath the leather and the man, rising with Brooks in his arms like an oversize infant.

McClosky grabbed Cullen's arm. "What are you doing?"

Cullen jerked free. "Run, fool!"

Cullen followed his own advice. His knee hadn't finished mending, and his foot was still weak. He was slow. He lurched more than ran, but the group clustered around the presidential assistant wasn't far. His burden was still conscious when Cullen knelt and unloaded him as gently as possible beside the Wright woman.

Cynna and the rest were still sprinting toward them. McClosky puffed up just as Steve snapped, "What's our target? And where?"

"That way," Cullen said, nodding at the forest. "And I don't know. You—Tash—what are these—"

"Shit, shit, shit!" Gan piped, shifting from foot to foot, eyes wide and bright with fear. "Shit, shit, shit!"

Tash spoke calmly, her sword ready, facing the forest. "Dondredii aren't true sentients, but they have a rough group intelligence. Wen thinks this pack numbers twenty or twenty-five. We have a chance. You are injured?"

"Knee's banged up. It'll heal, but hasn't yet. You?"

"Not significantly." She looked at Steve. "Do you have more bullets for that gun you shot me with?"

"Eight rounds left in this clip, and seven more clips."

Seven. Good God. Cullen spared a moment to bless Steve for being such a paranoid gun freak.

"Clips?" Tash repeated.

"Lots more bullets," Cullen explained. "Do dondredii burn?"

"*Shit!*" Gan cried loudly.

They poured out of the forest maybe a hundred and twenty yards away. They ran with a swinging gait halfway between ape and hyena, using their upper limbs as a second set of legs, and they smelled like spoiled meat. They made no cries, no sound at all, as they ran.

Instinct struck, quick and brutal. *Change. I have to Change, to meet the enemy armed with teeth and speed—*

Cynna skidded into place beside Cullen, beating Wen and the gnome by a few paces. "Holy shit. Give me my bag, man." But she didn't wait for it to be handed over, grabbing the bag as Wen arrived and dumped the gnome on the ground beside Brooks.

A hundred yards and coming fast. They looked like

zombie apes—pale, necrotic skin, grossly heavy upper bodies, and the flat faces of apes or men.

Wen stretched out a hand. Tash slapped a knife into it. "Across from me," the big woman told him, adding something in her own tongue before switching back to English. "Wen will try to disrupt their group mind, but working alone, he may not succeed. They'll surround us before attacking. Those with weapons or killing magic will form a circle around the rest."

"What do I do?" Panic made McClosky's voice high and shrill. "I don't have a weapon."

Ruben spoke from the ground, his voice thin but clear. "You will move to the center of the circle and attempt to keep Ms. Wright alive. Agents Timms and Weaver, take direction from Tash."

"Cynna Weaver," Tash said, "can you kill?"

"Yeah, I'm not as good as Timms, but I can shoot something that wants to eat me when it's close enough." Cynna smelled scared. She sounded and looked ready, though, had her weapon out and steady.

"You will take my right. Sorcerer, what—"

"I want a gun," Gan said, hopping in place. "I really, really want a gun."

Eighty yards. Long, matted hair on their heads. None elsewhere, not even around the genitals. Some were female. That didn't matter. He couldn't let it matter.

"Do they burn?" Cullen asked again.

"Yes. You throw fire? Good. Stand between Wen and Cynna Weaver. Closer. Stand closer to each other. I need room for my sword. Yes."

Cullen's heart thudded against his ribs. He felt sick. He wanted to thrust Cynna into the middle of the circle. *No,* he told himself fiercely. *No. She has a gun. She can use it. The more of them we kill, the safer she'll be.* But it was hard, damned hard, to let her take her place with the protectors instead of the protected.

How the hell did Rule deal with this?

Sixty yards.

Tash said, "When in group mind, they ignore pain. Unless Wen can break them from the group mind, we must kill them to stop them."

Cullen could see their gaping mouths and the sharp, carnivore's teeth lining them. "My range is about twenty yards. Steve?"

"Fifty yards for the maximum stopping power." Normally Steve was a mercurial type—hot-tempered, driven, demon-ridden. He was calm now, as relaxed as Cullen had ever seen him. Nothing like the prospect of shooting monsters to settle a man down. "I'm waiting for forty yards, though, given the poor light."

"I don't want to get killed," Gan wailed. "I don't have much soul yet. I might be just dead if I die."

Wen shoved the little not-yet-gnome into the center of their circle. "Quiet." He turned to Cynna. "Shoot their heads, if you can. It will help me interfere with the group mind."

"I'm not good enough for head shots," Cynna said.

"I am," Steve said happily. He brought up his right arm, supported it with his left, and started firing.

The gun's blast shocked Cullen's ears, though the rest of him was prepared. Steve fired methodically. One after another, the creatures stopped, looking surprised as bullets tore out the backs of theirs skulls along with the blood and brains. Cullen stood with his right arm extended, most of his mind focused on the link between himself and the diamond in his ring. He'd draw on it, but wouldn't use mage fire, not for this—too hard to control, too many targets. He'd drain the stone too fast.

Part of him was amazed. He'd known Steve was supposed to be a good shot, but the little bastard didn't miss. Not once.

The ones Steve didn't kill were spreading out. Were there only twenty of them? Looked more like thirty. And they were getting close—

"Now, sorcerer," Tash said.

There, Cullen told Fire, pointing at the closest one. *Burn that.* Power leaped through him in a glad rush. The beast burst into flames.

So did the next one. He heard Cynna fire her gun, heard Steve slap a new magazine in his gun, and he kept pointing. *Burn. Burn.*

The second one he'd blasted wasn't dead yet. It was crawling toward them. Flames danced along the creature's blackened body. It had no face left, no hands, but crawled on its elbows and knees, and it was getting close. Cullen swallowed and pointed again—

Cynna's gun barked. The creature flopped onto its stomach and lay still, reeking of burnt flesh.

Brooks spoke firmly, his voice clear enough in spite of interruptions by the roar of Steve's gun. "Mr. Seabourne, concentr—*(gun blast)*—farther away. The others will—*(gun blast)*—closer."

Right. He needed to let Wen or Cynna kill any who got too close, or they'd have a flaming body stagger or crawl in among them. He wasn't used to fighting as a team. He wasn't used to trusting . . . *Never mind. That one. Fire, go there.*

Fifteen yards away, another beast burst into flame. Cullen pointed again. Another went up. And another. But Fire answered sluggishly the next time. Cullen's eyes stung, and he blinked sweat from them. Why was he sweating? Must have too much heat built up. Better burn another one, get rid of the heat. His diamond wasn't depleted. He could do this. *Had* to do this, couldn't let them get close to Cynna . . . but where was a target?

There. He saw one. It was running away. As his arm swung automatically to point it out to Fire, he swayed, losing his focus. Damn! Have to . . . what was that? Something large leaped out of the forest to take down his prey. It looked like . . . he blinked, trying to focus.

"Hey." Cynna's arm came around him. "You can stop now. They're mostly dead, except for a few that want to get away at least as bad as we want them to leave."

"You and the shooter left me little enough to deal with," came Tash's voice from behind him. She might have been disappointed. "Wen broke the group mind when they grew few enough."

Cullen blinked again and focused on Cynna's face. He didn't see any blood. "You're okay, then. Good." He nodded, frowned, and added, "Better let go now." And passed out.

TWELVE

KAI leaned against the runneled bark of an oak taller than her apartment building back home, breathing through her mouth. The mage light behind her head, the one she controlled, was bobbing in agitation. Her stomach hurt, her mouth tasted like something had died inside it several days ago, and her throat burned. And the smell . . .

Nathan had a water bottle in one hand, their small spade in the other. His colors were calm, the usual pool of indigo and purple with silvery thoughts swimming through them. The smell didn't bother him. The flaming bodies hadn't, either. Her vomiting had, but only because it was a sign of her distress.

He handed her the bottle and knelt in the leafy loam to use the spade, digging a hole next to her vomit.

Kai rinsed and spat the first two swigs, then sipped cautiously. Humiliation tasted almost as sour as what she'd just ejected, but was it harder to get rid of. She took a deep breath. "I'm sorry. I should at least be cleaning up after myself."

Nathan looked over his shoulder. "Why are you apologizing?"

"I'm betting you didn't puke your guts out the first time you killed."

"No, but humans are often squeamish. It's odd, considering your innate violence." He finished covering the former contents of her stomach with dirt and stood. "You didn't kill, Kai."

"They were killed because of me. Because I played with their minds, sending them here—where they damned near killed a whole bunch of people. If they hadn't had that Fire mage with them—"

"But they did, though I'm not sure he's a mage. Have you grown omnipotent while I wasn't watching?"

"All right, all right. I couldn't have known those people would be so close to the forest. But if I hadn't been messing with the dondredii they wouldn't have burned." Trying to learn how to use her Gift. That's what she'd been doing.

"If they hadn't been here being killed, they'd have been somewhere else killing. That's what they do. They are predators. Not very efficient predators," Nathan added, moving to the stack of saddles and saddlebags at the edge of the small clearing. He slid the spade back in one of the saddlebags. "Individually, they're weak and nonsentient. In group mind they approach real sentience, but—"

"Their group mind is insane. Yeah, I noticed. I didn't do their sanity much good."

"You have much to learn. That's why you were practicing on them rather than on true sentients. Kai, will you be all right by yourself for thirty or forty minutes?"

She nodded, though part of her wanted him to define "all right." In some ways she hadn't been all right for quite a while. "Why?"

"The people the dondredii attacked didn't wander too close to the forest. They gated in."

"Oh. Oh, shit. Though I guess I'm glad we found them."

"I need to make sure this is the group my queen spoke of."

"Of course. Go slink around. Ah . . . I guess you can be sure they won't see or hear you?"

Nathan's smiles always looked freshly minted, as if he'd just discovered the expression. This one blended amusement with pleasure: she didn't need to worry; he was glad he mattered to her. "I can be sure of that."

"Should we . . . a couple of them are injured. I know we're not supposed to contact them, but it feels wrong to do nothing."

"They have called the Ekiba, who have healers. You will be all right here?"

Kai glanced across the small clearing where their horses were tethered. From here she couldn't see Dell. The big cat's dappled fur blended well with shadows and darkness, and it was very dark indeed beneath the trees. Nor could she hear her, but she knew what the chameleon was doing. Feeding. Quite happily, too. Squeamishness was as foreign to Dell's nature as bloodsucking was to Kai's, and yet their bond remained strong. "Dell will know if anything gets close, and we haven't seen anything here she couldn't handle."

"I didn't ask if you would be defended. I asked if you would be all right."

She met his pale gray eyes, and just like that, she *was* okay. Loving him was easy. Sometimes it made the other stuff easier, too. She smiled. "I will."

He came to her and kissed her lightly. "So will I, then."

Nathan faded into the forest as easily as Dell, and even more silently. Kai walked over to the horses, moving far less gracefully. Thighs, hips, butt—everything hurt. She was in good shape and knew how to ride, but she hadn't done it in years.

They had three horses—a stolid chestnut they used for a packhorse; the bay mare that Kai rode; and Nathan's mount, a rawboned gelding with a bad disposition.

"Hsst," she whispered to the roan gelding, who'd snorted at her approach and backed off, his colors flaring into an edgy, annoyed orange. "Hsst, there, you're okay." She stopped and slid into fugue—slid quick and easy, which brought a prickle of fear. She let that prickle alone. Poking at it just made it stronger.

Fugue was a strange, glassy state where words didn't belong. She'd brought intention with her, though, and after a moment dreamed her way into her affection for horses. All horses, even big, bad-tempered geldings who tried to bite her. She held out a hand, sent a puff of a pink thought-bubble at him, and popped out of fugue. "See? Not saddling you now. Just coming over to tend your feet, and you need that, hmm?"

The pink wound its way into the gelding's thoughts. His ears came forward, and he snuffled at her hand. Kai chuckled. "Love means food to you, does it, big boy? Sorry—no treats." She scratched along his ear, though, which he liked, then took out her pocketknife. It had a nail file that served well enough for a hoof pick.

She picked up his near front hoof and dug out the embedded grass and dirt. The familiar chore soothed her. Nathan had to do pretty much everything for them here, and the dependence bothered her more than maybe it ought to. But at least she could do this. Grandfather had made sure she knew how to care for horses.

Most of the time these days she felt incompetent, and it was not a feeling she was used to. But so much of her life now consisted of things she wasn't used to. All-powerful queens. Traveling to another realm. Falling in love . . . well, no. She'd done that long before she knew what Nathan was. But being loved back, that was new.

She finished tending the gelding's hooves and stood back, her head cocked, looking for her pink thought-bubble in his colors. It had broken up, as she'd meant it to, its bits blending with the slow, simple shapes of animal thought.

Kai focused on the horse's colors until she slid into fugue again. Once there, she had trouble remembering what she'd meant to do . . . oh, yes. Reclaim her bits. She

liked the way they looked in his dusty colors, though . . .
No, she told herself firmly, the word itself almost enough
to tilt her out of fugue.

Slowly, gently, she *wanted* the bits that were hers. Like
wishes in a dream, the soft pink threads unwrapped
themselves from the gelding's colors and drifted toward
her. They sank into her own colors and dissipated.

She blinked. Swayed. In spite of her sudden exhaustion, accomplishment thrilled through her. She'd done
it. Twice now she'd been able to reclaim the thought-
bubbles she sent while in fugue. If she could take back
what she sent, she could be sure of not doing lasting harm
while she learned how to use her Gift.

Since her life depended on that, Kai could put up with
a little exhaustion.

THIRTEEN

CULLEN lay on something hard. The air smelled strange . . . humans, yes, several humans were nearby. One lay beside him, a quiet lump of warmth along his left side. It wasn't Cynna, though the air held her scent, too. And blood. Not fresh blood, and not much of it. The other scents . . . he should know some of them. Horses? Yes, but stranger scents, too . . .

He was very hungry.

Something creaked rhythmically. Someone spoke, but the words meant nothing. Somehow that jolted his memory back in place. Edge. He was in Edge. They'd been attacked . . . he'd burned so many. So many. He'd smell them burn in his dreams, he thought.

But bad dreams were an acceptable price to pay. Cynna was okay. His son was okay.

So was he, for that matter. Cullen opened his eyes.

The sky was still dark and star-blazoned. Automatically he checked the time, but what his moon-sense told him didn't add up. He felt disoriented, adrift.

He was moving. Whatever he lay on, it creaked and bounced over rough ground. He propped himself up on

one elbow. He was in a large wooden cart or wagon—
narrow with high sides and a gate of sorts at the back.
Ruben lay crowded up beside him, apparently asleep. The
blood smell came from him. His bandaged, splinted wrist
lay outside the rough blanket that covered him, Cullen,
and the woman on his other side—Marilyn Wright, still
unconscious. She smelled ill.

He *looked* at them.

A green haze overlay Brooks's magic. The woman,
too, wore a gauzy overlay. Healing magic. Cullen held
out his arm and checked his own energy.

Thin, but all his. And wearing a sleeve. He inspected
the rest of himself and saw that he was wearing a long
dress of rough, undyed wool, rather like a monk's cas-
sock or an Arab's thobe, but more narrowly fashioned. It
was slit on the sides to permit a full stride. No shoes. No
underwear, either, but the lack of shoes was more of a
problem.

He sat up slowly.

A number of clay-colored people mounted on horses
surrounded the wagon, which was pulled by . . . no, not
horses, though the large draft animals would have looked
at home pulling the Budweiser wagon. If not for the
horns, that is, and the curly hair. The scent reminded him
of horse. Also buffalo.

Fifteen feet ahead was another wagon drawn by a pair
of the not-quite-horses. Tash rode there with one of the
clay-people. Steve sat in the back of that wagon. Cullen
didn't see McClosky.

Cynna was in his wagon. She sat on the bench at the
front next to Wen, who was driving the wagon. He
wanted to touch her. He wanted her to be back here with
him. Why wasn't she?

Get a grip, Seabourne.

They were traveling on a road, he saw as he looked
around. Packed earth, not paved, and rutted. It wound
down from a range of low hills behind them into the grassy
plain they were crossing. Ahead, the land seemed to drop

off. No snow here, and the temperature was warmer—a blessing, given his lack of footwear. The riders were fanned out around the wagons. He counted sixteen, five of them women. They all looked fairly young, but that didn't mean much. So did he.

The women were as hairless as the men, which was a tad disconcerting, but not unattractive. They dressed exactly like the men, too, who all wore the same sort of loincloth Wen favored. Cullen took a moment to appreciate that.

They controlled their mounts with hackamores—bridles with a padded nose strap and no bit. Their saddles were thick leather pads with wooden stirrups, and their horses were more like ponies, sturdy and shaggy. No horns. They smelled like horses, too.

His stomach growled. His wolf had no objection to horse. "I need to eat."

"You're awake!" Cynna twisted around to beam at him.

"How long was I out?"

"Altogether? Eleven hours, if my watch is working. It might not be, given all the stray magic around here." She bent and dug around under her seat.

"More like thirteen, I think."

Her voice was muffled. "If you know, why did you ask?"

"Because it's still dark."

"Uh . . . yeah." Cynna straightened and tossed him something. Automatically he caught it. His mouth watered at the scent. Jerky, made from venison, not beef. He ripped off a bite while she went on, "We're in what they call Night Season. They don't have day and night the way we do."

He chewed, took another bite, and gestured for her to keep talking.

"It stays dark for three months. Lunar months, I mean—their moon acts like ours, so it's the basis for their timekeeping. After the Night Season comes the Dawning, which lasts a few sleeps. That's how they divide the time—into sleeps—since they don't have days. And after the Dawning it stays light for three months."

Cullen swallowed the last of the jerky, his hunger unappeased. "No doubt they call that the Day Season."

Her grin flickered. "Good guess. That's sorta why we're here." She tossed him another bundle. "Eat. I'll fill you in."

This bundle was wrapped in a greasy cloth. His nose told him it was bread, and so it was—dark, heavy, with bits of fruit and nuts baked in. None too fresh, but he was in no mood to be picky. He ripped off a hunk. "Start with the casualties. Marilyn Wright's in bad shape."

"Yeah." Her mouth thinned. "Head injury. They can't do much for her until we get to the City. Kryl—that's the Ekiba healer—stopped the bleeding and took down some of the swelling in the brain, but she doesn't dare try to wake her."

"Ekiba?" Cullen asked with his mouth full.

"Wen's people. They're sort of like gypsies, though they have some permanent camps, too. Fortunately we landed not too far from one of those camps. It took them a couple hours to reach us."

He swallowed. "How did Wen call them?"

"Ekiba can all mindspeak with each other. I'm not clear on just what their range is—either Wen doesn't want me to know or he doesn't know how to convert their units into ours—but it seems to be several miles. Anyway, they're like a telegraph system, passing messages along."

"Their healer set Brooks's wrist, I take it. What about his leg?" Cullen finished off the bread regretfully. He was still hungry.

"His leg didn't need setting—it was just a hairline fracture—but his wrist was a mess. She gave him this potion to knock him out because she had to cut it open to get the bones lined up right."

"Hey!" Steve called from the next wagon. "You're awake!"

"So I'm told. Brooks is drugged?" he asked Cynna, frowning. The man hadn't stirred once.

"No, that wore off a long time ago. Kryl put him in sleep—you know, like Nettie does. A healing trance."

In sleep. Nettie. Memory stirred dimly. "I woke up earlier, didn't I? I thought . . ." He'd thought it was Nettie tending him, chiding him for having emptied himself so badly. But Nettie, the clan's physician-shaman, was on Earth. It must have been the Ekiba healer who called him out of uncsonsciousness.

"When we made camp, yeah. Most of us weren't in any shape to go far, but Wen's people didn't want to linger so close to the forest, so we traveled a couple hours, then stopped to take care of the wounded and get some sleep." Cynna scowled down at him. "You scared the crap out of me, you know that? I've never seen anyone kill himself by abusing his Gift, but hey. Always a first time, right?"

"I'm alive, aren't I?" he snapped.

"You were in a damned coma!"

That startled him into silence . . . for a couple seconds. "Couldn't have been." Coma was not a restful state. He felt fine . . . aside from an ongoing wolfish interest in the horses. "Is there any more jerky?"

"Gah!" Cynna looked disgusted, but did bend and dig under the seat again.

Steve had unfastened the wooden gate at the end of his wagon. He propped it against the wagon's side so he could sit at the rear with his legs dangling. Behind him Cullen saw a couple of wooden crates and a couple of sleeping bodies. One was orange. The other was snoring.

Amusement tugged at Cullen's lips. There was a sight—McClosky bedded down with Gan.

"Sure looked like a coma," Steve said. "You were nonresponsive. I pricked your foot with my pocketknife, and it didn't twitch."

Maybe he was wrong.

Suddenly restless, Cullen stood, hitched up the skirt of

his thobe—he refused to think of it as a dress—and vaulted over the side of the wagon. His knee took the impact just fine, so it had finished healing while he slept. The pebbly road wasn't kind to his bare feet as he trotted up beside Cynna, but he'd had all the sitting he could take. "You believed I was in a coma."

She hurled another chunk of jerky at him. "Why are you grinning like that? What kind of an idiot grins when he finds out he was in a coma?"

"You were worried about me."

She rolled her eyes.

Steve, lacking all social sense as he did, continued cheerfully, "Everyone thought you were done for, especially when the healer woman refused do her woo-woo stuff. Cynna was frothing at the mouth, but the woman thought she'd get trapped in the coma with you. Say, is it true you people can empty out so much of your magic you up and die?"

"Theoretically," Cullen answered absently, biting off a mouthful of salty meat. How *had* he emptied himself so badly? He'd been using the diamond, not his own resources. Of course, it took some energy to draw from the diamond, but not much. But he had just finished wrestling with a ley line . . .

"Well, that's what they believe here. The Ekiba all thought you'd die soon. Tash thought you had a chance, being lupus, but the rest of 'em didn't believe it. Didn't believe you were lupus, I mean." He snorted. "They wouldn't listen to us. We're ignorant savages, werewolves aren't real, and we should quit lying. Gan set 'em straight."

Cullen finished chewing and swallowed. "Gan did?"

"They think she can't lie, so when Cynna got her to tell them about lupi, they believed her. What's this deal about you having been in hell?"

He waved that off. "Later. I may have looked like I was in a coma, but the healer couldn't tell for sure because of my shields, so—"

"Cullen," Cynna said quietly, "your shields were down."

That, he decided, was pretty damned scary. His shields would go down only if there was nothing left for them to draw on. Cullen had been taught that if a practitioner drained himself completely, he either burned out his Gift or died. "There goes that theory," he murmured.

"What?"

"Never mind. So Gan persuaded the healer I was lupus. I suppose the idea is that, being of the Blood, I'd gradually rebuild my magic."

"They argued about that, too," Steve said. "Can't agree on much, this bunch. You put an end to the argument by waking up."

"No, the healer woke me." His memory of that waking was as gauzy as a dream, but he remembered that much. He'd thought it was Nettie calling him back.

"You woke up on your own the first time," Steve said. "We heard you mutter something—"

"You told us to go away," Wen put in abruptly.

Cynna grinned. "That's when I figured you'd be okay. Only you went right back to sleep, and Kryl said. your shields were up again, so she had to wake you the old-fashioned way—by shaking you. She made you drink something nasty-looking and did some sort of energy sharing, then you went back to sleep. You didn't wake up again until now."

That still didn't seem right, but his memory was so fuzzy he decided not to argue about it. "Is there any more jerky? Water, too, or something else to drink."

"You've had two pieces and a loaf of bread."

"Healing takes fuel."

"If you can wait a short time, we'll be at the river," Wen said. "You have a wolf's needs?"

"Somewhat." If he didn't eat when he should, he got cranky. Real cranky. The need wasn't as strong now that he had a clan again, but it didn't pay to let a wolf get too hungry. "How soon, and what happens at the river?"

"We get shipped off to the City," Cynna said. "That's

what they call it, just the City. That's where out-realm traders come."

"Hostages and kidnap victims, too, I guess."

"Um, well, Bilbo explained—"

"Bilbo?"

"The gnome. I got tired of always saying 'the gnome' or 'the councilor,' so I've been calling him Bilbo. It pisses him off."

"To the gnomes," Wen said gravely, "names are of great importance. Birth-names are secret. Use-names are chosen carefully and divulged only within the family. Nicknames, as you call them, are bestowed on children by adults. By nicknaming the councilor, Cynna accords him the status of child."

Cullen had the feeling Wen didn't mind one bit if they insulted the gnome. "So Bilbo explained things. That's lovely. When we get to this city, will Bilbo and his buddies open a gate and send us home?"

"They can't. Or won't . . . Don't look at me that way! I'm not swallowing everything they feed me whole, not after the way they tricked us. But Wen and Tash and all of them say it's almost impossible to open a new gate in Night Season."

Cullen was very polite. "They FedEx-ed themselves to Earth, I take it."

"Is being two types of gate, sorcerer." The gnome had decided to join the conversation. He stood behind Steve at the back of the other wagon, glaring at Cullen. "Is new gates and old gates. Magic for old gates shaped over long time, years or centuries of using. Magic of old gates holds our shaping even during Night Season. Old gates requiring much more power during Night Season, but can being used."

"We used an established gate to cross to another realm first," Wen explained. "Twelve masters went with us to open a temporary gate between that realm and Earth. To return—"

"To return, you needed me." Anger and humiliation made a foul mix in Cullen's mouth as the pieces fell in place. He knew why he'd been so drained, damn them. "Or some other poor SOB who'd burn himself up giving you your gate. That's what you expected, wasn't it? *You* were the spell's final component," he said to the gnome. "The one I didn't know about. The gate was tied to you, but you couldn't power it. That was my job. What you didn't tell me was that your damned bloody spell needed my personal magic. Not just the raw magic. It ate my magic, too."

The gnome sniffed. "Such power. Such ignorance. No, sorcerer. Gate tied to me, yes. I expecting you to power spell, yes. Gate eats some of your magic, but mostly is using ley line. You not being harmed until you burning everythings in sight."

" 'Everythings' being the thirty or so creatures who wanted to eat us," Cynna put in sharply. "Including you, Bilbo."

"Enough." That was Tash, who spoke from her seat on the forward wagon without turning around. "The councilor, like most gnomes, is prideful and difficult. But he did not expect the gate to take your life, Cullen Seabourne. He expected it to consume his."

Cullen's silence lasted a few beats this time. He remembered how damned glad the gnome had been that Cullen brought up the whole ley line. He remembered, too, the pattern he'd seen in those last, wild moments as the gate opened. He'd recognized it, having built something much like it with three Rhejes—like it, but not exactly the same. But both gates had been tied to an individual who controlled them

His gate hadn't killed anyone, but it had been powered by a node. If there hadn't been enough energy . . . he didn't know, dammit. "Why open a gate the hard way, away from a node?"

The gnome sniffed again. "Such as you is not for questioning Harazeed. We is building gates where we wishes."

"What he means," Cynna said, "is that he won't tell you. I've asked. I think it's because he was so bent on bringing Lily along. See, this thing they lost, it—"

Bilbo hissed. Positively, that was a hiss. "Wait for wards."

"Wards," Cullen repeated. "Not shields?"

Wen's voice was cool. "Wards are all we have, too, sorcerer. True shields, if they are even possible, would require an adept."

Cullen was getting tired of being called sorcerer. "My name is Cullen. Call me that. Or Mr. Seabourne, or sir, or 'hey, you.' But not sorcerer."

"Don't sidetrack." Cynna leaned forward, speaking to the gnome. "We can't be warded every time we talk about the problem. We'll have to discuss it, ask questions, talk to people."

Bilbo erupted with a volley of words—some English, most not. Tash sighed, climbed down from her seat into the wagon bed and knelt beside him. When he paused for breath she spoke to him softly in a language Cullen didn't know.

"She is explaining to him that our secret is not so secret," Wen said quietly. "It is not widely known, *til Presti,* but any of those powerful enough to eavesdrop on us must already know what has been lost. We were gone longer than we wished to be . . . I tried earlier to tell him this, but—" He shrugged. "We have a saying: stubborn as a gnome."

Wen looked at Cullen, his eyes dark with some intense emotion Cullen couldn't read. Wen looked human, but he wasn't. His scent was alien, more alien than the gnome's or the woman with the tusks. "Edge is a high magic realm. Do you know what that means, Mr. Cullen Seabourne?"

"Not really," Cullen admitted. "Aside from the obvious—lots of magic, so much of the technology we have on Earth wouldn't work well here."

"Edge is very high magic, too high for most of it to sustain life consistently. Almost everyone lives along a strip of land five hundred *taloni* long and between fifty and a hundred *taloni* wide, where the level of magic is stable. This is the area around the Ka, the Sauwnosat, the Presti il Tó . . . we have many names for her, but she is life for us."

"The river," Cynna explained. "He's talking about the river we're headed for."

"Yes. The magical races have more protection from the randomness than humans, but only the Fey can venture beyond the area stabilized by the Ka."

"Not just the Fey," Cynna said.

Wen gave her a level glance. "No. A human with a strong Gift of the type you call 'sensitive' would be protected."

Cullen's heart did a funny skip thing. "So that's why you wanted Lily. She can go where you can't. But Cynna's human. So are Brooks and Steve and Marilyn Wright, and we landed well away from the river."

"Not far enough to be immediately harmful. They've taken no damage. Adam McClosky, Steve Timms, and Marilyn Wright will be treated well once we reach the City."

Very softly he said, "But not Cynna?"

It was Cynna who answered him. "I have to Find the medallion they lost, Cullen. Not much choice about that."

"What the *gnomes* lost," Wen said, and that sure sounded like bitterness in his voice. "For hundreds of years they have held it, claiming only they could be trusted . . . they call it the Chancellor's Medallion. It brings order, sorcerer. Among other things, it brings order to the seasons."

As Wen's meaning sank in, Cullen's hands clenched into fists. "It's Night Season now," he said slowly.

"Yes. Here, as in other realms, it gets cold at night. If night does not end, it will get very, very cold in Edge."

FOURTEEN

CYNNA walked along the rail, rocked by water. The Ka made the Mississippi look like a creek. She still hadn't seen the far shore, though she'd been on the boat for two days now . . . no, two sleeps. No days here. No daytime at all.

Not that it was completely dark. Aside from the vast smears of stars overhead and the glow of the moon, mage lights scattered along the barge's hull announced its dimensions to other vessels. More mage lights floated freely over the deck like oversize fireflies. One bobbed along beside Cynna as she made her way past boxes and crates and barrels to the front of the boat.

That one was hers. Cullen had shown her how to cast one. He'd been right—it was absurdly easy. She didn't understand how they'd come to lose such a simple and useful spell.

Near the lighted hull the river was brown and shiny, like suede rubbed slick by use. Away from the ship, brown rolled gently into black, its darkness interrupted by the running lights of other boats. The Ka grew crowded this close to the City.

The cant of the deck felt almost normal to her now. It dipped toward the prow because their means of propulsion stayed underwater most of the time, dragging it along against the current. Built for cargo, not passengers, the barge Bilbo had commandeered was a long, shallow-draft vessel with a shack at the rear, where Marilyn Wright lay, still and silent. Tash had spent most of the past two "days" keeping her alive. Once they reached the City, she'd be seen by one of the best healers in Edge.

Soon now. Ahead were the lights of the City—a million fireflies spreading along the left bank of the river, Most of the mage lights were white, but others were red, pink, green, purple. Like Christmas lights, she thought.

Cynna wondered what the Ka looked like in daylight.

Chances were, she'd never know. Edge was about halfway into the Night Season now. If things went well, she'd be heading home as soon as the Dawning arrived and the gnomes could open a gate to Earth. If things didn't go well, no one would see the Ka in daylight again.

She didn't see much point in thinking about that, so she didn't. Mostly.

Just ahead of the barge, a huge, pale shape rolled to the surface and exhaled, sending a spume of air and water from its blowhole. Cullen said the blowhole made the sea ox more like a whale than a manatee, which it resembled, because it breathed when it decided to.

He was such a knowledge magpie. She had the idea he'd been collecting facts all his life—all sorts of facts, not just those relating to magic. But he'd been around twenty-four years longer than her, hadn't he? Maybe by the time she was fifty-nine, she'd know a lot more than she did now.

God, she hoped so.

Of course, she'd also look fifty-nine. He didn't. He probably still wouldn't twenty-four years from now, either.

The sea ox wore a vestlike halter with a big metal ring on top that attached it by a chain to the barge. Clinging to a strap on that halter was the sea ox's rider, his scales gleaming wetly in the light from the ship, the moon, and the stars.

The triton looked over his shoulder, saw Cynna watching, and grinned. He called out something in his language that sounded like bat screeches. She grinned back. "You know I don't understand a word you say."

He laughed, waved, and sank below the water again as his enormous mount dived, its flat tail flipping up in what looked like its own parting wave.

"Flirting with your aquatic admirer again?"

She turned.

Cullen looked like an extra in a biblical movie in that long woolen dress. His feet were bare. He hadn't shaved, of course. None of the men could shave. The Ekiba didn't use razors.

On him, beard stubble, skirt, and bare feet looked good. On him, everything looked good. So did nothing, as she remembered very well.

Not just from having enjoyed that nakedness up close and personal, either. She'd seen him dance. He called himself a stripper, and it was true he danced naked—or all but, since the law insisted on a G-string. But what he did wasn't as crude as stripping. Carnal, definitely. But not crude. More as if the music had come alive so it could celebrate itself . . . "He is kind of cute."

"He's four feet tall and an excellent representative for Barracudas 'R' Us. Lots and lots of tiny, sharp teeth."

"Guess I won't French him, then."

"Good decision." He draped an arm over her shoulders. "Warm enough?"

He'd been doing that a lot the last two days—no, the last two sleeps. Whatever. He kept touching her. Not sexually, which was just as well, since there was no privacy on the barge. The sanitary facilities consisted of a damned chamber pot used in the meager shelter of the shack at the rear, then dumped overboard.

But lupi were touchy-feely types, weren't they? Physical contact came naturally to them. It was probably her own fault that all those casual touches kept her hormones churned up.

Unless, of course, he was doing it on purpose. "Are you doing that on purpose?"

"What?" His expression was all innocence. His fingers were skimming along the side of her neck . . . lightly, oh, so lightly.

"You are." And she really ought to make him quit.

"As a friend, I consider it my obligation to distract you from time to time so you don't wear yourself out with all your brooding." One finger dipped into the hollow of her throat. "I'm good at distraction."

"I don't brood. I've had a lot to think about, that's all."

"Mmm." He stood with her in silence a moment, forgetting about his distraction duties. "You think you'll know him?"

Cynna didn't have to ask who he meant. "How could I?"

The Ekiba they'd traveled with had passed on news of their arrival to Ekiba in the City. Word had come back that Daniel Weaver was eager for her arrival. That he was excited about meeting his grown daughter. "I was three years old when he left. I don't remember him at all, but . . . I've got a picture of him. I guess I'm expecting him to look like that, but it's been thirty years. He's probably fat and bald now."

"And wrinkled."

"Yeah." Cynna sighed and tucked away the longing. "How's Ruben?" Cullen had been talking to him the last time she saw him—about ten minutes ago. No privacy, none at all, on this barge.

"He wants some crutches so he can get around on his own."

"Well, that's nuts! He doesn't walk much when his leg isn't broken."

"But he can?" Cullen asked.

"Yeah, but not much. It exhausts him. I'm pretty sure it hurts, too, but he doesn't tell anyone when he's in pain. None of us, anyway. Deborah probably knows."

"Deborah?"

"His wife." Cynna had met Deborah Brooks a few times. She was short, chubby, and cute as a cocker spaniel. She looked like a cheerleader and possessed enough backbone for any two normal people.

She'd need it. Cynna tried not to think about how worried she must be.

"He says he's feeling different. Stronger. Maybe the Ekiba healer did something to help him with his condition . . . whatever that is." Cullen looked a question at her.

"I don't know. *He* doesn't know. He's seen so many doctors, been diagnosed with everything from muscular dystrophy to Lou Gehrig's disease, but none of the diagnoses help. Current medical opinion is that he's got some sort of autoimmune disorder, but it isn't lupus."

"A misnamed disease if ever there was one," Cullen murmured.

"From your perspective, I guess it is." Cynna sighed. "Sometimes he seems to get better, but it never lasts." And lately he'd been in his chair almost all the time. If the healers here could do something for him . . .

"He also said he's got a feeling about why he's here."

"Yeah?" As far as she was concerned, Ruben's feelings were gold. Precognition wasn't an unusual Gift, but accurate precogs were rare, and most of the good ones were involuntary visionaries, not intuitives.

Ruben didn't see the future. He just knew stuff. He tested at 70 percent, which all by itself blew the curve, but Cynna, like most of Ruben's people, thought the tests were bullshit. Precognition wasn't a Gift that could be summoned, yet in order to be "scientifically valid," the tests required the precog to perform on demand.

Idiots. "I'm betting it isn't because of the crush Bilbo has on him."

"Good guess. Though the gnome shows more respect for Brooks than for the rest of us."

"Ruben makes it hard to treat him any other way. So what did he say?"

"That he's supposed to be here."

"Oh, now, that's helpful."

"Also, he's sure you're needed here, which unfortunately puts him in agreement with Bilbo. But so am I. Needed, that is."

She grinned. "As something other than a black eye for Bilbo, you mean?"

"A worthy purpose, yet I'm hoping for a more active role."

Cullen's presence in Edge had not been part of the gnome's plans. He'd planned to shove Cynna and Lily through his gate, of course, and had decided to take Ruben, McClosky, and Ms. Wright along, too—as honored guests. Cullen insisted that "guest" and "hostage" were interchangeable terms to gnomes, but Bilbo was treating them okay so far. He claimed his council—the Harazeed gnomes who governed the City—really did want to open trade with Earth.

Assuming they survived.

A head popped out of the water near the barge. It was round, orange, and chewing something.

"You catching lots of fishies?" Cynna called.

Gan didn't bother to swallow before answering, treating them to a good view of partly masticated raw fish. "They're not as good as Lily's little fishies, but they're fun to catch. I like swimming."

No kidding.

One of the crew had taught Gan to swim their first day on the barge. She'd caught on fast, and after that wanted to spend every waking moment in the water. The crew weren't always available to swim with her, so Cullen had. A lot. No one went into this river alone, not even tritons, former demons, or restless werewolves.

Cynna hadn't gone in at all. She'd seen the crocs, and there were supposed to be bigger, nastier beasties in the river, so she hadn't argued when Wen told her humans shouldn't go in the river.

Especially pregnant humans. Her secret wasn't much of a secret anymore. Too many of these people could spot a pregnant woman instantly—by scent or magic or whatever. She didn't think Ruben knew yet. At least, he hadn't said anything. But all the Edge people seemed to know.

There hadn't been much to do on the barge except talk, but that worked out okay. They had a lot to learn about this place. No one would discuss the medallion, but that left a long list of other topics they were ignorant about. Ruben had asked each of them to concentrate on a specific subject. Cynna's task had been learning about the various races here. Wen and Tash didn't mind talking about that sort of thing, so she'd had an easy assignment.

She'd also learned the mage light spell and taught Cullen how to key his diamond so no one else could use it . . . then been keenly flattered when he keyed it to her, too. She'd gotten to know Steve better, too. They'd played many, many hands of poker with the deck of cards she'd dug out of her old denim bag.

"Better climb back on board," Cullen said to Gan. "We're nearly there, so your swim buddy will be—"

But Gan had ducked back underwater.

Cullen shook his head. "Guess she'll come out when the triton does. He'll have to come topside before we dock."

"We're nearly there."

Cullen sighed. "Bathtubs."

"Indoor plumbing, period. And clean clothes."

"Shoes. Pants. I grow eager for a pair of pants. And a toothbrush."

"Oh, man. I hope so." The Ekiba had given them these little sponges. First you wet one, then you chewed on it so it released this oozy stuff which was not at all like toothpaste. Then you scrubbed your teeth with it. She sighed, thinking of toothbrushes, and added, "Vegetables. Tash says they have plenty of fresh produce in the City."

Cullen looked at her quizzically. "You're longing for stir-fry, not pizza?"

"No, it's just that . . . it gets what I eat, doesn't it? The baby, I mean. I breathe for it. I eat for it. It's kind of like a parasite, only—"

Cullen made a muffled sound. His arm dropped away. "A parasite."

She felt herself flush and was glad he wouldn't be able to tell. "Maybe I didn't put that well. I mean, some parasites are helpful, right? Like bacteria. We've got lots of bacteria in our bodies that we need to survive, and they need us. There's a word for that, but I can't remember it right now."

"Symbiosis." Cullen barely got the word out. He seemed to be strangling. "You're talking about symbiosis."

"That's it. I guess the baby and me are kind of like that now—in symbiosis. It can't survive without me, and I . . . well, I'm not sure what I get from it, but I figure there's supposed to be an emotional payoff. I'm not there yet, but—"

The laughter he'd been choking on won. He laughed so hard he gasped for breath.

She stared at him coldly. "I'm ridiculous, am I?"

"Yes, but that's okay. I'm an ass." Grinning, he slid an arm around her waist.

She shoved it away. "Go play with yourself."

"Entertaining as that can be, I'd rather not. Cynna." He touched her cheek. "I'm glad you're coming to terms with the baby's presence. Sharing your body with another being, however tiny, must feel strange."

If she told him it reminded her of when she'd been a rider herself—of demons—he probably wouldn't laugh. Cullen wasn't easy to shock, but that ought to do it. "Yeah, it's pretty weird. Did I tell you what Gan said about how Bilbo and Company arrived right where Lily and I were?"

"How they knew where to open their gate, you mean?"

She nodded, pleased with herself for changing the subject so neatly. "She said it was a congruence problem. Well, she put it another way, but that's what she meant. Edge is geographically congruent to lots of realms, but not always time-congruent, and the realm they entered from wasn't time-congruent with Earth at all."

"I know. We went over that. It shouldn't be a problem on our return."

Or so the gnome said. They *had* learned a few things while on the barge.

The Edge people had spent a couple days in the neighboring realm they crossed to first, then another couple days on Earth. When they returned here, four weeks had passed—one week for every day they'd experienced. This had seriously freaked Cynna, who did not want to get home only to find it was 2050 or something. But Bilbo insisted the discrepancy happened on their trip to the less congruent realm, and that time slippage wouldn't be a problem between Edge and Earth.

"I know," Cynna said, "but Bilbo wouldn't talk about why he showed up where he did on Earth. According to Gan . . . well, I don't know why Bilbo won't admit it, but she thinks he used her as a beacon. Apparently what she does naturally makes her sort of an anchor, a way to get a time-fix between realms. Bilbo didn't target me and Lily. He targeted Gan."

Cullen got that distant look in his eyes that meant he was running her explanation over his own mental hurdles, checking it against what he knew of gates. Which, admittedly, was more than she did. After a moment he nodded. "That holds together. It would make even more sense if I knew how Gan can cross the way she does."

Cynna grinned. "It's because she's special."

His smile was softer than hers. "You'll be a good mother."

Cynna blinked and tried a laugh on for size. "Where did that come from?"

"You deal well with Gan, who's the child from hell if ever there was one. You care about her, look out for her, but don't try to squeeze her into your image of what she should be."

"Yeah, well, you know . . . she's a demon. Or was. I'm not sure there's a strong correlation here."

"You don't see the baby as an extension of yourself, the way so many parents do. Just the opposite. Yet you've accepted sharing your body with it."

"That doesn't mean I'll have a clue what to do once it's outside my body."

"No one does," he said, and moved so he could wrap his arms around her from behind. He pulled her up against him. "Or so I'm told."

She stiffened. "I'm not—"

"Relax. For a few minutes, turn off that busy and wary mind of yours. I'm not seducing you or trying to force you into a decision or a discussion you aren't ready for. Just . . . relax with me a bit."

"You're not so good at that, either."

He chuckled so low she felt it as much as heard it. "I'm a lively sort, it's true. Sometimes selfish."

"Sometimes?"

"It took me a bit to realize that I hurt you when I laughed. I'm sorry for that."

His mind was lively, all right, jumping from one thing to another without warning. "I guess it did sound funny."

"You compared our baby to beneficial bacteria."

She muffled her own laugh into a snort. "I get your point."

For a while neither of them spoke. Cynna found herself content with silence, with the slow rocking of the boat, and even with the darkness, marked as it was by so many stars. Up ahead she could see a line of piers stretching out into the water—dark themselves, but outlined by more mage lights. There were a lot of boats around and ahead of them, too, most of them small, but a few big barges like this one. And a couple sailing ships.

She wished she could see those better. They were pretty cool.

How did they decide which boats went where so they wouldn't bump into each other? Did they have a river version of air traffic control? Not that the river was as busy as an airport, but still . . .

Cullen was very warm along her back. His arms wrapped her loosely; one hand rested on her hip, the other on her belly. She liked the feel of him, and it wasn't all hormones. She admitted that. She wouldn't get too attached to this sort of thing, but it was okay to enjoy a friend's company, wasn't it? She wasn't mistaking this for anything more.

He'd damned near died.

Memory hit, cruel and breath-stealing. During the attack, she'd held together fine. She was good at crises. She'd done what she needed to do, deferring the emotions for later.

It was later. She'd dreamt of the dondredii last sleep, only in her dream they'd won through and eaten everyone. She'd probably dream again. And again.

Cynna had had close calls before. She knew how it felt afterward, the way her heart could start pounding when memory ghosted by. She knew the need to grab at life, prove she'd survived and life still raged inside her in all its heat and confusion. If there had been even a smidgeon of privacy on this damned barge, she'd have done her best to celebrate their survival with Cullen.

Only this time was different. It had hit her when those monsters swarmed out of the forest: she wasn't alone in this body now. A tiny rider needed the air she breathed, the food she ate, her very heartbeat to survive. If she died, so did the little rider.

Cullen's hand slid up to cup her breast.

"Hey!" She moved it. "I thought you weren't seducing me right now."

"I'm weak, and your breasts are temptation enough to trouble a eunuch."

"Pretty talk." He smelled familiar. She hadn't realized she knew his scent. It was disconcerting. Maybe that's why she blurted out the question that had kept her awake for a long time after she woke from the nightmare. "Does it look like a baby yet? Are there arms or fingers?"

"You're eight weeks along, so the fetus is about the size of a pinto bean."

"God. That's . . . I knew it was little, but that's *tiny*."

"But the heart has divided into two chambers, and there are buds that will become arms and legs. The arm buds have little elbows."

Cynna absorbed that for a moment. "Sometimes it's annoying, the way you seem to know everything. Sometimes it's handy. If I were at home, I could look it up on the Internet. Here . . ."

"Here you ask me?" His mouth crooked up. "The tip of the nose is present, and folds for the eyelids, but it doesn't yet have what we'd recognize as a face. The head is very large. The brain's developing and other organs are starting to, and in another week or so it should start moving."

She stared at him. "Moving! I thought it didn't do that until lots later."

"Women don't feel the movement until the baby is bigger and more active. That's called the quickening, and it's usually between three and four months."

"You really did go to medical school."

"I really did."

That, she decided, was extremely reassuring, under the circumstances. "We'll be home a long time before it's born."

"Before *he* is born. Yes, I trust so. Long before."

"You said you couldn't—"

"Achoo!" someone called out. Or something like that. Cynna had picked up a few words in what they called the Common Tongue, but mostly it still sounded like gargling to her.

All four sea oxen rolled to the surface at once, each

with its scaly rider. One of the smaller boats—long and narrow, with people rowing it—was coming straight at them. The two crew members who'd stayed on board the barge were suddenly very busy with ropes and things.

They'd reached the City.

FIFTEEN

❧

GETTING off the barge took a while. First an old man in a green robe arrived to take charge of Marilyn Wright. He was a healer, but not the VIP healer who'd eventually care for her. He was just supposed to keep her going until the chancellor's own healer could see her.

At least, Cynna thought the healer was a man. His hair was long and stringy, his face narrow and pointy with tiny scales where she'd expect to see whiskers. He didn't speak, not at all, and the robe hid his body. But he moved like a man.

The little gnome with him did all the talking. She didn't speak English, but she'd brought some of the translation disks with her, which were supposed to be standard for all newcomers to the City.

What was supposed to be true didn't always match with reality, especially with Bilbo in charge. Cullen accepted the disks for all of them. His shields would protect him from any tampering.

"Weird," he said after a moment of holding one in his hand. "A little voice is whispering in my ear, giving the English translation of every word spoken nearby. But it's the same voice for everyone. The lack of directional or volume cues makes it hard to sort out who's saying what."

"You detect nothing else at work?" Ruben asked.

Cullen shook his head. "Nothing's tickling my shields."

The gnomish woman said something to him. Cullen smiled one of his more charming smiles and thanked her for the advice.

Things got confusing after that.

Cynna's job had taken her all over the U.S. She'd been to Canada once and Mexico twice. Shit, she'd even been to the demon realm. She was an experienced traveler, or thought she was. But nothing could have prepared her for the sheer foreignness of the City.

Cullen said it reminded him of Cairo. Cynna felt more as if she'd walked onto a huge movie set that inexplicably mixed *Star Wars* with *Camelot* and a heavy dash of some old Sherlock Holmes movie. Take the horse-drawn carriage she sat in right now, with Ruben and Cullen. It seemed like something Holmes might have used.

The street itself was filled with *Star Wars* extras. She recognized some of the species—the three Ekiba on their ponies, for example. Also the phalanx of brownies giggling their way through the pedestrians and the gnome climbing out of his litter. Others were new to her. Some looked human, but that didn't tell her much. So did Cullen, but he was lupus.

The sky might be dark, but the street wasn't. There were so many mage lights bouncing along or clinging to the buildings that the entire street was brighter than a mall parking lot. This was a broad avenue, paved with stone and crowded with horses, carts, litters, and people. Mostly people. Horses and vehicles kept to the right, though their carriage, like Bilbo's ahead of them, rode smartly down the middle of the street. Maybe the middle was for government use?

Most of the streets they passed weren't broad, paved,

or nearly daylight-bright. Some were more like twisty sidewalks, too narrow for any but foot traffic.

The architecture was Art Deco meets the Arabian Nights. These people liked curves and domes and color; they liked their geometry both crisp and sinuous. There were arches and arabesques and tiles. Lots of tiles, large and small, arranged in intricate patterns, simple stripes, or a single emblem. Some buildings were covered entirely with mosaics. Cynna stared at the black-and-white harlequin design on a three-story structure that was flanked by buildings dressed up in purple, pink, green, and orange.

Their escort stood out for its sheer lack of color. A troupe of guards on horseback, wearing stiff gray jackets and black leather pants, had met them at the pier. If Cynna had thought that Daniel Weaver, so eager to meet his daughter, would be there, too, she'd been wrong. He was at the Chancellery.

So was Marilyn Wright, or she would be soon. Ruben had sent Steve Timms ahead with her in the ambulance—a gaily painted wagon that looked more like a gypsy caravan to Cynna than an emergency vehicle, though its four horses had moved off at a good clip.

Unlike the pair pulling this carriage. They never got above a sedate trot. Neither did the horses pulling the carriage ahead of them, of course, which meant she was free to blame their slow pace on Bilbo. He rode in that carriage with McClosky and Gan.

Once they finally reached the Chancellery, they'd meet the other councilors but not the chancellor. He was ill, they were told. Cynna wondered if the Council had tossed him in the dungeon for losing the medallion. They probably could. Ruben thought the chancellor's position was mainly titular—a ten-dollar word that meant he handled ceremonial stuff, but lacked real authority. Kind of like the Queen of England.

All the varied architecture, body shapes, and other sights might have been easier to process if Cynna hadn't been dealing with the damned translator charm. The street was noisy. Hawkers cried their wares, riders yelled at pedestrians who didn't move out of the way, pedestrians yelled back. Everyone was talking to someone, and the charm gave all of it to her at once.

Bilbo had assured them in his version of English that their brains would learn how to sort the translations they received in such a jumbled stream. But at the moment it was overwhelming, and this damned carriage was too slow. Much too slow.

Cullen leaned closer and murmured in the ear the translator charm wasn't using, "You know, your father probably won't drop dead before we get there."

Her head swung so she could scowl at him. "That isn't funny."

". . . Agent Weaver?"

That was Ruben, seated across from her with his splinted leg stretched out, his foot resting on a cushion. Unlike her and Cullen, he faced forward.

Cynna flushed. "Sorry. I wasn't listening—or was trying to listen to too many things at once."

"I asked if you were having trouble with the translator charm," Ruben said dryly. "I take it the answer is yes. Perhaps you could leave it outside your clothing for a moment."

The translation charm was a heavily scribed silver disk about the size of a half dollar, strung on a leather cord. It needed physical contact to work, so as soon as Cynna pulled it out from beneath her shirt, the whispering voice stopped.

Ruben was still talking. "Tash was just explaining that our charms will need periodic recharging. The spell is good for nine or ten sleeps."

Tash rode next to the carriage on a horse much larger than the ponies the Ekiba used. "Usually," she said, "the charm is supplied for a fee, and each renewal also has a fee. The councilor has said yours are free, however."

"Good of him," Cynna muttered.

If Tash heard, she ignored it. "Most people use the

charm as a tool to help them learn the Common Tongue and then dispense with them."

Cynna looked at her. "Did you learn English that way? You speak it really well." Unbelievably well for someone who'd been exposed to it on Earth for only two days.

"We, ah . . . there is another spell to impart a language. This was done to Wen and myself—the councilor had already learned your tongue from Daniel Weaver. But the spell is . . . there are difficulties. Most humans do not tolerate it well."

"I'm not human," Cullen pointed out pleasantly. "I might tolerate such a spell."

"I know little about lupi. Perhaps. You would have to open your shields."

"Ah. Well, we have many things to talk about, don't we? Obviously the Ekiba tolerate the spell's effects. And you . . ." He let his voice drift away, inviting her to explain.

"I am a half-half. Mixed breeds, you would call us. Some half-halfs are accepted into their mother's people. Most are not. I do not have a people."

"You clearly have status. Our escort saluted you. They gave you some title, but the charm burped. I heard reckon or recka or something like that."

"*Rekka* is my rank, which does not translate well. I am in charge of the City's guards."

Cullen had heard more than she had at the pier, hadn't he? She'd been too busy looking for someone who resembled that old photo, however old, fat, or bald he might be now. Or married. He might have remarried. Oh, God. He probably had, once he realized he couldn't go home. He could have had more children. She could have half siblings.

Please, God, don't let them be waiting for me at the Chancellery, too.

"Why didn't the councilor ever address you that way?" Cullen asked Tash.

"He does, when we speak among ourselves in Common Tongue."

But not when he introduced her to them. Was that because he habitually hogged the spotlight? Or had he had another reason to want them to think Tash was unimportant?

Ruben, as usual, spoke politely. "Perhaps you can explain something, Rekka Tash. Do I have the address correct?" He paused for her to nod. A nod meant *yes* to everyone here, just like back home, Cynna had learned. No doubt anthropologists would find that fascinating. "Why did the councilor insist from the start that he needed a shield spell that didn't exist? Why was he determined to trick us into coming rather attempting first to obtain our willing cooperation?"

"You would need to ask the councilor that question."

"I have, but his answers fail to satisfy me. To be blunt, they fail to make sense. Obviously he'd planned from the start to trick us into creating a gate. I don't understand his reasoning."

"The councilor does not confide in me." Tash's words were stiff, but her voice wasn't. She gave Ruben a long look, then added, "We, too, have seers, Mr. Brooks. And now perhaps you would like to look ahead. Awkward for those facing backward, but your first sight of the Chancellery is worth a strained neck."

Cynna twisted around. And gawked.

The wide street ended by making a circle around a huge building. It had to be a building, though it looked more like an enormous, sleeping beast sunk partly into the ground, or perhaps ready to rise from it . . . a beast its tenders had decorated lavishly.

All their love of curves and tile and color was here. Mirrored tiles, colored tiles, and colored stones or gems were inset in the patterns that swirled and clawed and climbed everywhere. There were no right angles, no clear delineation between wall and ground—the tilework spilled from wall onto earth, reaching delicate fingers across a stone courtyard.

The place easily covered three city blocks. Probably more. Parts of it reached higher than others, maybe three or four stories. It took Cynna a minute to notice how few windows interrupted the designs covering the structure. There were no plants. No flowers or grass or bushes in the courtyard, flanking any of the entrance, or sitting in pots on the three staircases she could see.

The Chancellery was a stunning, even overwhelming, work of art. Ruben and Cullen made complimentary noises. Cynna couldn't bring herself to. The place gave her the creeps.

There were several entrances. They rode past the biggest one, where a line of people snaked out through two huge, open doors. They continued to the side of the structure, where a long, narrow porch ten feet above the ground gave access to another entrance. Bilbo's carriage had stopped at the foot of those steps. McClosky was getting out. A small group of people were descending the steps—two gnomes and a man. A human man.

Cynna's heart began to pound.

The horses stopped. Someone took her hand. "You okay?" Cullen asked softly.

"I think I'm going to be sick."

"You won't," he told her firmly. "But if you absolutely have to prove me wrong—and I know you like doing that—aim for Bilbo's shoes."

"Good plan."

The man following the two gnomes wore the same kind of long dress Cullen had been given, only his was made of much nicer fabric—something with a sheen. It was a golden brown. Over that he wore a long, sleeveless robe or vest in a plush material the color of dirty snow. No hat. His hair was sandy brown; his complexion, fair; his features, pleasant but unremarkable.

He wasn't fat, wrinkled, or bald. A bit stocky, but otherwise he looked like his picture. Just like his picture.

Cynna didn't see what the others did. She did notice, barely, Cullen's hand at her elbow, supporting her when she climbed out of the carriage, as if she might have forgotten how to do that. She heard voices, but they were a mere buzzing, like insects.

The man moved up to stand in front of her. "Cynna?" His voice wobbled. He looked like he was trying to smile and couldn't quite bring it off. "You're my little Cynna?"

She nodded slowly. Her head might fall off if she weren't careful. "You're Daniel?"

"No!" His voice went loud and gruff, and he grabbed her. "No, not Daniel—I'm Daddy! Or Da, or Father, or Dad . . ." His arms closed tight around her. "Don't call me Daniel," he said, and there was a hint of tears mixed with the touch of brogue in his voice. "To everyone else I can be Daniel. Not to you. Not to you."

He was her height exactly. Five-ten. He smelled strange—smoky, with some spicy cologne mixed in. He was holding on too tight. She didn't think she could breathe. She pushed away. "Too fast," she said, almost panting, as if he'd sucked up all the air when he grabbed her. "You're going too fast for me. Until a couple days ago I thought you'd run out on us. Now . . ."

"Of course. Of course." He ran a hand over his head, smoothing back the sandy hair . . . hair she realized *was* different from her old photo, because it started farther back on his forehead. "I'm tripping over my own feet, aren't I, now? But you look so much like her . . . ha." He smiled, and mischief twinkled in eyes the color of whisky—eyes she recognized, having seen them in the mirror all her life.

He put his hands on her shoulders, beaming at her. "Now you're thinking, who is this man? He can't be my dad, who would know his sweet Mary is a small, round woman with dark hair and eyes. But you've her nose, you know, if not her build." He touched the tip of that nose with one finger. "And her generous mouth, as I can see in spite of all that fancywork you've put on your pretty face.

And something of her stubborn chin, too, I think. Though I flatter myself it's my eyes you've got, aren't they, now?"

Cynna felt herself nodding. Yes, those were her eyes in his face. Though he saw his eyes in her face, and wasn't that funny? Because they each had their own eyes, after all.

He heaved a great, meaningful, gusty sigh. "We've much to say to each other, but not, I suppose, all at once, or while standing out here in the cold. And my lord councilors wish to meet you."

One of the gnomes—not Bilbo—said something unintelligible, reminding Cynna of her charm. She closed her hand around it, and the whisper told her the gnome wanted Daniel to let their guests come inside and rest before some big meeting, and he could escort his daughter to her chambers.

Daniel glanced down at the gnome, nodded, and said something in the other language that the charm translated as polite agreement, then switched back to English. "Come, come inside. We will talk while we can, before you must . . . ha! It's hard, but you're here for more than the easing of my heart."

She was here because she'd been kidnapped. Reminded of several things, she took a step back and glanced around. Cullen stood beside her, his face as expressionless as she'd ever seen it. Usually he hid with smiles or words. Ruben was beside him, in a wooden wheelchair she hadn't noticed until that moment. One of the gray-dressed guards stood behind it. He was as large as Tash and the same color, but lacked the tusks.

"We would all appreciate a chance to rest and refresh ourselves before the meeting with your council," Ruben said. "But we will go to our rooms together. You have given us rooms near each other, as I asked?"

"But of course," said Bilbo. "We wishing for you all comforts. We—"

A laugh drifted out from the open door . . . followed by a woman. "Honored Councilor," she said in clear English in a voice like bells and fog, "their notion of comfort probably doesn't involve being dragged through a gate and thrown down into the snow to provide dinner for the dondredii."

"That," Bilbo said with some dignity, "was not being as we intending to happen."

"But they are here," she said indulgently as she floated down the steps. "Perhaps they will forgive, since your need is so great."

She was slightly less than Cynna's height and much more slender, her bones as delicate as a child's. Her skin was dusky, her eyes dark, her hair pure white. It was short in front and curled wildly around her face, but in back it bubbled below her hips like a frothy waterfall. She wore a long white dress, sleeveless, loose, and gathered at the waist by an embroidered sash the color of the sky at twilight. Her feet were bare, and she wore no underclothes. . . . which Cynna knew for certain because the dress was transparent.

Her face was exotic and beautiful and shaped like a cat's—wide at the eyes and cheeks, narrowing to a delicate, pointed chin. Her ears were long and pointed.

"I have long wished to meet a lupus," the elf-woman said, and she walked straight up to Cullen, stopping much too close. She put her hands on his chest and tilted her head to one side as she smiled into his eyes. "Hello."

SIXTEEN

CYNNA'S chambers consisted of two rooms. The bedroom was tiny, more like a nest than a room, being mostly bed. A huge, thick mattress overflowing with a whole rainbow's worth of pillows and blankets covered almost all the floor.

The sitting room was bigger, but no less colorful. Ocher walls extruded themselves to form a bench that made a U out of one end of the room. The wall-bench was wide enough for a human tush, but less than a foot above the floor—a good height for a gnome, she supposed. It, too, was crowded with cushions in many colors. There were two straight wooden chairs built for a human-size person—one orange, one purple. No cushions. Both looked uncomfortable.

The whole place was uncomfortable, and it wasn't just the colors.

At the other end of the room was a round table a lot like the one in her hotel room back home, only with shorter legs and painted bright blue. Four fat floor cushions surrounded it. Between the table and one end of the bench was a cupboard painted green and yellow and black.

A short, dark-haired woman stood in front of the cupboard. Her name was Adrienne. She wore a knee-length yellow dress with gray trousers and a long gray vest; her hair was long and braided. She was about fifty years old and she was human—she'd told Cynna that when she'd announced she was Cynna's maid. She'd shown Cynna how to control the mage lights drifting around the ceiling with a couple words in the Common Tongue, repeated what Cynna had been told about the location of the common rooms, explained that the baths were underground—where she seemed to think she was going to wash Cynna personally.

Not going to happen. But a shampoo would be nice.

At the moment Adrienne was holding up a dress she'd taken from the cupboard. It was long, shiny, and dizzyingly bright—green and pink and gold playing tag all over a lipstick red background.

It made Cynna's head hurt. "You've got to be kidding."

"Dalnee horra fall nutty sieve matta play, noresh," the woman said. Or something like that. The charm whispered to Cynna, "This would be appropriate for meeting with the Council, madam."

"Can't you get me some pants? Something . . . plainer. Like what I'm wearing, only clean."

Adrienne looked pained and launched into a long explanation about colors and caste and stuff. Cynna tried to pay attention, but her mind wasn't cooperating.

He hadn't known. That's what she kept thinking, over and over. *He hadn't known.*

Daniel Weaver had escorted them to their rooms, chatting amiably all the while about the problems with applying what he knew of science and engineering ("Not much," he'd said cheerfully, "but I was ever a history buff, and the older things work better here.") to innovations useful in Edge. Cynna hadn't really listened. She'd been thinking about that elf-woman and the way she'd put her hands on Cullen. Cynna had wanted to toss that frail, lovely body somewhere. Just pick her up and throw her.

That wasn't the reaction of a friend. Jealousy was stupid and pointless. It hurt. And it wouldn't go away.

Fortunately, the elf-woman had. After planting a kiss on Cullen's mouth, she'd murmured something too low for Cynna to hear and drifted off as absently as she'd arrived without speaking to any of the rest of them.

None of whom seemed to have noticed Cynna's reaction. *Please, God, don't let Cullen have noticed.* That's what she was thinking when her father followed her into her room. He'd asked about her mother, all excited and happy. Had Mary waited long before remarrying? Did Cynna get along with her stepfather, whoever that might be? Had Mary ever gone back to school the way she wanted to?

He'd been so eager, the questions tumbling out as if pent up all these years. "I'm sorry," he'd said, catching himself with a laugh. "I want to hear about you, too, my beautiful daughter . . . but Mary? She's well?"

So Cynna had told him. She had to, didn't she? His Mary had been dead for nearly twenty years . . . even longer in some ways, because Cynna didn't recognize her mom at all in the Mary he spoke of. She didn't tell him that. What good would it do? He didn't need to know the woman whose memory he'd cherished all these years had died as she'd lived. Drunk.

Had she just blurted it out, though? She'd wanted to be gentle. She'd tried, but he'd been so happy, and he'd left with his eyes wet and shocked . . .

"You will wear this, then, madam?" the charm whispered at Cynna.

She jerked her attention back to the matter at hand. Clothes. Really ugly clothes. "No, I won't." Someone scratched at the door. She turned away in relief. "Come in."

Cullen breezed in. "Ruben wants to . . . ah, what's that?"

He was looking at the red monstrosity in Adrienne's

hand. "The dress they think I should wear. Not going to happen. Ah—Cullen, this is Adrienne. Adrienne, Cullen Seabourne."

He was revved, not relaxed, not wearing the look of a man who's just had a quickie with . . . *Shut up*, she told herself fiercely. That kind of thinking would make her crazy. Well, crazier.

Besides, elf-woman had drifted away after greeting Cullen and ignoring the rest of them.

"Hmm." Cullen studied the dress, moving around as if he needed to see it from every angle. "I see," he said, nodding mysteriously, and told Cynna, "Go see Ruben. He wants to talk to you. I'll take care of this."

Lily could have helped with a wardrobe problem, but Cullen? Still, just thinking about Lily, picturing her reaction if she'd been told to wear that dress, made Cynna feel better for some reason. "I want pants."

"Trust me." Then he startled her. He brushed a kiss across her cheek. "Go."

The doors were the most ordinary thing about this place, being the right height and nicely rectangular. They didn't lock, though—didn't even latch. Either gnomes had no concept of privacy or they didn't want their guests indulging in it.

The hall was emphatically not normal. The floor tilted. So did the ceiling, which varied from a comfortable ten feet here to maybe six feet at its other end, where three stairs took it around a corner. Which was *not* a right angle. She took a deep breath, but that didn't help. The air felt oozy, as if the walls were breathing out oily vapors. Cynna gritted her teeth against the sensation.

They had this section of the Chancellery to themselves, eight little suites like Cynna's with a common room at one end of the hall and the bathroom—sans actual bathtubs—at the other. Presumably Steve and Ms. Wright would be moving into two of the suites eventually.

Ruben's door was a few feet down the hall from hers.

She knocked softly—a hard knock would open the door—and spoke her name. He told her to come in.

Ruben's room was laid out like hers, but the walls were purple and the floor was a mosaic of orange and yellow. His table was pale blue and held a bowl of fruit and nuts. His air felt oozy, too.

He was sitting on the wall-bench, propped up by pillows and with his splinted leg stretched out. The wooden wheelchair was an arm's length away. The scruffy look didn't suit Ruben the way it did Cullen, but beneath his whiskers his color looked good. If he was in pain, it didn't show. "You should see this dress they wanted me to wear. Ugliest thing I've ever seen."

"You refused it?"

That wasn't criticism. Ruben had had one of his feelings as they were disembarking from the barge. He wanted them to refuse to wear what they were offered at first. "It wasn't hard. That is one ugly dress." She moved restlessly around the room. "I wish we had windows, don't you?"

"My office in Mr. Hoover's namesake lacks windows. So does yours, as I recall. I'd ask you to sit," he added dryly, "but you might explode if you tried to be still, and then we'd have bits of burst Cynna all over. It wouldn't improve the color scheme . . . if we can call the random assault of color a scheme."

She managed a grin. "I wouldn't. Gan might."

"Are you all right, Cynna? The meeting wasn't too difficult?"

He'd surprised her, though maybe she should have expected this. Most of the time she was Agent Weaver. Now and then she was Cynna, and then it was okay to tell him things, if she wanted to. Personal things.

She did. "He didn't know about my mother."

"That she was dead, you mean?"

She nodded, though that was only part of what her father hadn't known. Why did it matter so much? Did she think he wouldn't have gotten himself lost if he'd *known* he was leaving her with a woman who'd die young?

"You told him. That was hard."

"It was like I'd hit him somewhere inside . . . he didn't stay after that. He said he'd be fine, he'd be all right, only he needed a little time to adjust to the news, but he meant he needed to be alone so he could cry. I took something away from him. Something important."

"Not you. You are not responsible for his pain."

Cynna knew that, but guilt was a familiar pit, one she'd long ago dug deep. One she'd learned to climb back out of. "I guess my mother took it from him. Or God. Or the disease that killed her."

"Did you tell him how she died?"

"He didn't ask. I guess he will, though." She took two quick steps, though there was nowhere to go. "I guess I'll have to tell him."

"Lies can be useful in our profession," Ruben said calmly, "but I think you don't want to use your father. Did you tell him about the baby?"

Cynna's mouth opened. Nothing came out. She felt her cheeks heating and decided she would sit down, after all. One of the hard chairs was right behind her, so she used it. "You heard."

"Tash mentioned it. She assumed I already knew."

No privacy, no privacy at all on that damned barge. "I only just found out myself, and I haven't told anyone. Except Cullen, that is, and he already knew. Everyone here seems to just know somehow. I thought . . . I should have told you."

"I'm sure you would have. Events have forced us along at a rapid pace. I take it Mr. Seabourne is the father?"

Cynna nodded, miserable. She felt like such an idiot. She wanted to tell him she'd been on the pill, that it hadn't happened because she was careless. She couldn't make herself speak.

Ruben waited another beat, giving her a chance to continue, than said crisply, "Tell me about the ugly dress."

He didn't call her Agent Weaver, but she heard the switch clearly—and with great relief, though she'd probably obsess over his reaction later. "They've got all these ideas about how color signifies caste and profession. Adrienne was explaining . . . ah, she's my maid. A human." She glanced around, then looked a question at him. He answered with a slight shake of his head, so she went on, "This room doesn't work so well for you, does it? Everything's too low. Makes it hard to transfer."

"My man is seeing about obtaining different furnishings as well as more appropriate clothing. I was offered a pale blue gown with an orange and green robe."

She grinned. He'd said "my man" like he'd had a personal manservant all his life. "I'd like to see that."

"You won't."

The door swung open. "It's boring here. Where's Cullen Seabourne? I want to go swimming."

Gan's fashion sense fit right in. She wore an electric blue robe over a snug little sheath striped in yellow and green and purple. No shoes, but she had added socks to the ensemble. "We can't swim now," Cynna said. "We have to meet with the Council soon."

"*You* have to meet the stupid Council. I don't."

"I do." Cullen sauntered through the doorway. He was looking very mild and peaceable, except for his eyes. Blue could burn. "I suspect you'd be bored, though, so you're right. No reason for you to go to the meeting. You trust us to make the right decisions, don't you? Or maybe it's the Council you trust."

Gan glared at him. "I'm not stupid."

"Then don't say stupid things. Your life may not depend on recovering the medallion, but your testing does."

Emotions did a quick-march all over Gan's ugly, expressive little face. She wanted to argue so badly. She settled for kicking one of the pillows. "I'll go to the stupid meeting, but I don't have to be *here*." She stomped out the door, leaving it open.

Cynna grinned. "Guess she told you."

"I'm abashed. You'll get your pants."

"Good. What has you so pissed off?"

"Me?" His eyebrows lifted. "Why do you say that?"

"Pissed may not be the right word. Temper's a quick thing for you—it comes, it goes. This is different. Something got to you."

"Your maid," he said in that light, pleasant voice, "offered me sex."

McClosky had come up behind him. "That upsets you?" He was dry, amused. "I would have thought—"

Cullen spun to face him. "That I enjoy coerced sex? Because that's what it would have been. She didn't want me. She's afraid of me. Afraid, period, I believe, but specifically afraid of me. Did your servant offer you sex?"

A hint of color flushed McClosky's cheeks. A veil of anger darkened his eyes. "He may have hinted, but I didn't get angry with him for it. This is a different culture. We can't judge."

"Cullen isn't angry at the servant," Ruben said.

Cullen turned. "What about you, Cynna? Brooks? Any offers?"

Cynna frowned. She'd been pretty upset when Adrienne gave her little "I am your servant" speech. Had Adrienne's offer to provide service in the baths meant . . . uh, yeah. It had. "I didn't pick up on it. She wasn't obvious."

"Interesting," Ruben said. "Did your own servant make a similar offer, Mr. Seabourne?"

"He did. He wasn't afraid of me, so I didn't think anything of it."

Of course not. Cullen got offers like that all the time.

"My servant did, also," Ruben said, "albeit somewhat ambiguously, so I asked him to clarify. He confirmed that sexual services were among his duties. I didn't detect any upset or embarrassment on his part, but I lack Mr. Seabourne's sense of smell."

Cullen stood very still for a moment. "I overreact, you think."

"Anger on behalf of the helpless or the abused is always appropriate."

Cullen held Ruben's gaze a moment longer, then nodded. "But not always helpful. Yes. This gives us one more point to bring up when we meet with the Council, however. You will allow me to deal with it."

And that, Cynna thought, was not a question.

Cullen frowned. "What about Gan? She wouldn't have any qualms about getting sex whenever and wherever possible, but she didn't seem to be in a postcoital glow."

"Cynna, you're on good terms with her," Ruben said. "Ask her when you have a chance. Right now, I'm curious about the way this was handled. We were each assigned a servant of our own sex who then offered to engage in sex with us. Apparently same-sex relationships are regarded differently here than in our culture, but why would they be specifically encouraged in our situation?"

"Babies," Cynna said suddenly, then flushed. "Well, it makes sense. They think it's okay to expect servants to give sexual pleasure, but not okay to risk making babies with them."

Ruben nodded. "Very good. That fits with other observations I've made . . . I believe it's time for private discussion. Mr. Seabourne, did you find that Agent Weaver's rooms are as we expected?"

"Just like yours and mine. The hall, too, for that matter."

Cynna frowned. "Does what you saw have something to do with the way this place feels? Kind of creepy, I mean."

Cullen shot her a glance, his eyebrows lifting. "You feel it?"

"The air is oily."

Ruben looked at McClosky. "Mr. McClosky, if you would get the door, please. Mr. Seabourne, are you able to secure our privacy?"

McClosky closed the door. Cullen closed his eyes and began chanting softly.

They'd discussed this, too, while on the barge. The shield spell might have been a ruse, but the gnomes were obviously aware of many forms of eavesdropping. They'd decided the chances were good their rooms would be magically bugged . . . an assumption that had proved accurate.

In less than a minute Cullen tossed up both hands. With a quiet *poof* the lights went out.

SEVENTEEN

"**NOT** again," McClosky moaned.

"One moment." That was Cullen, and a second later four mage lights bounced into place in the center of the room, making it about half as bright as before.

The room felt better. The air was just air—cool and dry and tinged with unfamiliar smells, but no longer oily. Cynna lifted a hand to run a diagnostic, curious about what kind of spell he'd used.

"Don't," Cullen said sharply, taking a seat on one of the floor cushions. "We're in a magical dead zone. It's temporary, and I left a loophole so I could pop out the mage lights, but if anyone else tries to use magic before the effect fades, the results could be . . . unpredictable."

"But what did you do? You didn't have time to set wards."

"No. They wouldn't work. The walls of this place are crawling with shaped magic—that's why you were un-comfortable, by the way. Gnomish magic is not a good mix with Air."

"That makes sense. It doesn't answer my question."

"The gnomes have had centuries to fine-tune the spells

in these walls. They've got an abundance of power. I couldn't outpower or outfinesse them, so I shorted things out."

Cynna snorted. "Magic is not electricity."

Cullen grinned. "Which means I had to be clever, doesn't it? Congruencies, Cynna. At the moment all the spells for about thirty feet around us are confused about where to draw power because of a little chaos I introduced in the system. It won't last, but for now no one can eavesdrop."

But how could . . . her breath caught. He was playing with raw magic again. That was the only way he could have done it. He'd sent a surge of power through the walls, disrupting the spells they contained. He'd shaped it some, she guessed, with that chant, but it was still dangerous.

He must have read her expression. "It worked, didn't it?"

She wanted to point out that the spells he'd disrupted might have other purposes—like, say, holding up the walls. But nothing seemed to be crumbling, and if it was temporary . . .

Ruben interrupted her worrying. "We can't be overheard now?"

Cullen gave a graceful shrug. "Not by the spells they had in place. I won't guarantee anything more."

"Very well. First, I want everyone to be clear on our roles while we're guests here." He gave Cullen a small smile. "However we define guests. We represent the government of the United States. We expect to be treated as such. They will likely concede to our demands with many smiles. They will patronize us . . . with the possible exception of Mr. Seabourne. They tend to discount humans. He is both lupus and sorcerer, and consciously or otherwise, they will expect him to be in charge."

"We're supposed to act important?" Cynna was dubious about her ability to pull that off.

"Don't act," Cullen said. "Their lives and the lives of everyone here depend on you. They know it. You just

keep that in mind and leave the acting to the rest of us."
His smile was chilly and not pleasant. "I'll play to their
expectations. Brooks, I suspect, will confound them."

She wasn't sure what he meant, but Ruben often
confounded people. She nodded. "Is that why we were
supposed to turn down the clothes? Because we're important?"

"Not exactly. The gnomes are trying to own us."

Ruben's eyebrows lifted. "You caught that, did you?
Yes, though I'd say 'claim' rather than 'own.' They want to
isolate us, then present us to the rest of Edge as if we'd already allied with them. Part of their plan involves dressing
us in clothes that speak with their cultural voice."

"Yes," McClosky said slowly. "That makes sense,
given what I've learned about the economic situation
here."

"Please summarize for the others."

McClosky's suit was dirty and wrinkled; his tie,
missing; his shoes, scuffed. Add that to his three-day
beard, and he looked more like a drunk coming off a
bender than the pressed and proper diplomat she'd first
met. He still sounded like an asshole sometimes, but not
as often.

At the moment he was earnest, leaning forward with
his forearms on his knees. "There are many factions in
Edge, as I'm sure you've all realized, but the gnomes are
top dogs. They control the City and the gates. Gates mean
trade, and trade is the realm's lifeblood. Their entire econ-
omy is based on it. They even import a percentage of
their food, which may be out of necessity. Given the limited amount of arable land, short growing seasons, and
relatively small number of crops that have adapted to
conditions here, I suspect they'd have a hard time feeding
their population without the gates."

"So the gnomes are power players," Cynna said. "I get
that. I don't see what that has to do with dressing us up
like their oversize cousins."

"We're game pieces. The Turning changed the political

situation here. I'm not sure how—no one would speak of specifics to me. But the balance of power is shifting, or they think it will."

Cullen was playing with one of the mage lights, sending it up and down with little pats of his hand. "Maybe the gnomes are afraid the Turning somehow made it possible for one of the other groups to open a gate. They'd hate to lose their monopoly. Though all this speculation and gamesmanship is moot, isn't it? If we don't locate their missing jewelry, no one is opening any gates . . . or so we're told."

Ruben looked intrigued. "You have reason to think they're deceiving us about the medallion's function?"

"Aside from the gnomish reverence for a good lie well told, you mean?" Cullen shrugged. "Not really. Under the circumstances, we have to proceed as if they're telling the truth about it. But I'm reserving room for a doubt or two."

"A sensible precaution. I do feel strongly we must locate it . . . though that's an incorrect usage of first person plural. *We* will not find the medallion. Agent Weaver will." Cullen and McClosky looked at her, but Ruben didn't give them a chance to ask how she expected to save the world. Instead, he asked her, "What have you learned about the various races here?"

"There's a lot of them," Cynna said promptly. "And like you said, humans rank pretty low on everyone's list. We're seen as useful but weak because we aren't of the Blood. Also, I've got the impression not many humans here have Gifts. I don't know why that would be true. Maybe it isn't. But they don't have a good Finder, do they?"

Cullen gave her a thin-lipped look. "Quit with the modesty. Your Gift isn't rare, but you are. I don't know of another Finder on Earth with your strength and training, and there aren't that many humans here. I'm not surprised they don't have a Finder of your caliber. I do wonder why they don't have any spells that can locate it."

"Have you asked about that?" Ruben said.

He snorted. "Bilbo turns purple when I mention the medallion at all. Tash says she doesn't know much about gnomish spells. Wen says the Ekiba have only the most basic search spells—their abilities lie elsewhere."

"What about the Ahk?" Cynna asked.

"The what?" McClosky said.

"Ahk. Large, tusked, bipedal, don't like anyone who isn't an Ahk. Warrior types with a closed culture and one of the power players here. They live in some mountains to the south. Tash's father was an Ahk."

Cullen shook his head. "Guess I didn't ask the right questions. No one mentioned the Ahk."

"What about brownies?" McCloskey said. "I saw some on the street. They're supposed to be good at finding lost things."

He'd surprised her. Most people didn't know squat about brownies beyond *oh, aren't they cute.* "They are, but their range is real limited, and they have very little power outside their own territory. Not much power, period, which is why they aren't considered major players even though there's a lot of them. They're territorial but not aggressive or acquisitive, and they can only use their innate magic."

"Meaning?"

Cullen answered for her. "Brownies don't cast spells, and spellcasting is Edge's technology. Power, wealth, prestige—they're all tied to magic here. Innate magic is respected, but if you don't or can't shape it, you don't get to play with the big boys."

Ruben spoke. "And the big boys are the gnomes, the Ekiba, and the Ahk?"

"Those are the ones everyone agrees on, yeah. And the elves, of course." Cynna darted a glance at Cullen. "There aren't many of them, and they mostly stay on their estates, but they've got power. Sometimes they use it, sometimes they don't."

"So we have a pastiche of power," Ruben said, "once

we leave the City. No common laws, no central authority, yet the various races trade, travel, and mingle freely. Are they culturally or inherently averse to violence, or is something else keeping them from war?"

"The elves," Cullen said. "Though we need to get in the habit of calling them 'sidhe.' They hate being called elves."

McClosky frowned. "She? They're all female?"

Cullen looked disgusted, but spelled the word for him. "Pronounced 'shee.' I'm not sure which group of sidhe we're dealing with here, but not the high lords—they'd be running things openly, not covertly."

"You believe they use their influence to prevent war?" Ruben asked.

"Wars they don't want, anyway. They disapprove of war on aesthetic grounds. The various factions here have probably learned the hard way to avoid open warfare."

"They have that much power?" McClosky said dubiously. "Cynna said there aren't many of them."

"It doesn't take many. Think of them as the guys with the stealth bomber and the A-bomb. No one wants to piss them off."

No one said anything for a moment, then Ruben spoke slowly. "Surely, if the sidhe are as powerful and proficient as you believe, the gnomes tried to enlist their aid to find the medallion. The sidhe live here, too. They must need this medallion restored, if it operates as we've been told."

Cynna had a highly uncomfortable thought.

"Maybe," Cullen said. "Sidhe are hard to predict, but some of them can cross without a gate, so . . ." He stopped, cocking his head. "We're about to be interrupted. Any last instructions?"

"Do any of them have hearing like yours?" Ruben asked.

"Tash," he said promptly, "which suggests that the Ahk do. None of the others I've met. Gnomes definitely don't."

In the pause that followed, Cynna heard the thud of many feet coming their way quickly. Cullen heard something more, because he grinned at Ruben. "That works."

"Good. Everyone, if you need to pass information privately, subvocalize to Mr. Seabourne. When—"

The door slammed open and half a dozen angry gnomes spilled into the room.

None of them were Bilbo. There was a great deal of babble, hard to sort because of the way the translator charm ran everyone's words together. The basis of their ire was, of course, Cullen's tampering, which had done something to other spells, not just the ones in this room. Some kind of chain reaction, Cynna thought. And something about toilets?

Yes. He'd made the plumbing all over the Chancellery stop working. Oh, my.

Cullen was polite in a way that turned courtesy into insult. He apologized for the inconvenience. He offered to help them fix their spells—the inference being that they needed help. Ruben was bland and immovable. Surely their hosts didn't expect them to leave eavesdropping spells operating in their private rooms.

In the midst of the commotion, Cynna edged closer to Cullen.

Subvocalizing felt awkward. You had to talk sort of deep in your mouth and throat without moving your lips, which mangled some of the consonants, but she did her best: *"Maybe the gnomes didn't ask the sidhe to search because they think one of the sidhe took it."*

He looked at her, and behind the arrogant mask he was wearing for their hosts, she saw grim agreement.

GAN didn't expect to enjoy the Council meeting, but she enjoyed *going* to it. She liked walking past the guards and sitting at the big table on a pretty embroidered cushion with all the other important people.

One cushion was left empty. Gan felt the bite of disappointment. She'd hoped . . .

"So what have you been up to?" Cynna Weaver said to her.

Cynna Weaver, like the lupus and the other humans, was wearing her same old boring clothes. Gan wondered why they hadn't changed into the pretty things they'd been given. "I've been at the market. They use money here, too. I want to get some money."

"I hope that means you didn't steal anything."

"Didn't you get a copy of the rules? In the City they cut off people's hands for stealing." Gan was pleased with herself. She hadn't quite been able to lie, but she had deceived the human woman.

"Thanks for the tip. I haven't seen any rules. I see you've got both hands, so you didn't get caught. What did you take?"

Gan looked at her, indignant. "Why do you think I took something?"

"Because I'm smart. How come you told us your minder's name earlier, if names are such big secrets?"

"Stupid. I didn't tell you Jenek's real name. I only know his call-name."

"Aren't those reserved for family?"

"Jenek is Hragash, not Harazeed. The Hragash aren't stuffy about call-names the way the Harazeed are." She sniffed. "They've hung around with sidhe too much. When I—"

"We is starting now." Thirteenth Councilor—the one Cynna Weaver had nicknamed Bilbo—glared at Gan and the human beside her. He didn't like either of them, but he had to put up with them. Gan stuck her tongue out at him.

The meeting started out like she'd expected—talk, talk, talk. The humans wanted the gnomes to get rid of the spy-spells in their rooms. They wanted clothing that suited them—they didn't like the clothes they'd been given. Humans had no taste at all. They also wanted a copy of the City rules that Gan had mentioned, and a map and more stuff like that. The councilors pretended everything was a big deal, but of course it wasn't, so they agreed.

Except about the baths. Humans were weird about clothes and being naked and all, but they couldn't expect the councilors to make everyone else leave the baths just so no one would see a naked human. That was just silly.

Finally Ruben Brooks said, "Very well. Let's proceed to the problem with your medallion. We have several questions."

The gnomes all looked at each other. Then they looked at the little door at one end of the room. It opened.

At first Gan was disappointed all over again. The gnome who came through that door was tiny and wrinkled. She had little round breasts and a little round belly and wore a really dull gown, a purplish gray with only a bit of gold on the sleeves. She had a lot of gems woven into the braids in her hair, but her face was so plain she looked almost human.

Nice teeth, though. They looked real sharp.

Then Gan saw her eyes and *üthered* her density and her hearts fell out of rhythm. "Eldest," she whispered. And that was all she said. All the questions she longed to ask, the ones she knew and the ones she didn't have words for, pushed up into her mouth and packed her throat so tightly she could barely breathe.

The Harazeed Eldest gave her a glance out of gray eyes swimming with secrets. "You are called Gan."

Gan nodded, terror and thrill mingling in a jellied mass.

"You will be quiet, Gan, until I am finished speaking."

Gan nodded again. She would. She would do whatever this one wanted.

The Harazeed Eldest spoke to the humans. "I am called First Councilor. I will tell you of the medallion."

She moved slowly, as if her bones hurt, but she settled onto her cushion easily enough. "At the end of the Great

War, the realms were in chaos. Much had been destroyed. Much knowledge was lost. Your realm," she said to the humans, "was entirely sundered, of course, save for its tie to Dis. The others were all but cut off one from another, also. The Great Gates were gone, and few remembered how to erect even the small gates.

"The Harazeed remembered. And so the medallion was given us, and we came to a realm that wild magic had made impossible to settle before. Our numbers were few. At first we lived here alone, save for the beasts. Even the sidhe did not linger in Edge in those days. Gradually the medallion settled patterns onto the realm. Even in the areas of high magic, day and night had meaning and season. Near the river, order strengthened its hold. We prospered, and others came to Edge.

"Then, as now, Edge was seen as a refuge for the outcast, the criminal, or the lost. In the early years there was much fighting, but Harazeed, like most gnomes, prefer trade and wealth to war. Eventually we settled into alliances that stabilized the distribution of power much as the medallion had stabilized the magic. But envy and covetousness can outshout reason. You will hear from the envious that the medallion does not have to be held by the Harazeed to work. Some who say this are merely ignorant. Others know this for a dangerous partial truth. Theoretically, the medallion imposes order no matter who holds it . . . but the type of order depends on the holder, and medallion and holder must form a true bond first. Very few are capable of forming such a bond with the medallion. In four thousand years, only Harazeed have been capable of this."

The Eldest paused, folding her hands together on the table in front of her. "There have been many attempts to steal the medallion. A few times one or another thief succeeded—but never for long. The medallion does not wish to be parted from its holder. This theft is different. When the power winds blew, the bond between the medallion and its holder was broken. One of the half-halfs who works at the Chancellery saw that this had happened, and seized what she believed was a gift from the gods. She took it."

"You know who took the medallion?" Ruben Brooks asked.

"Oh, yes." The Eldest looked at one of the other councilors. He got up and went to the main door, the one sized for humans and other biggers. He opened it and said something to those on the other side.

First Councilor spoke again. "Since the medallion was stolen, there has been a flood in Rhanjan and earth tremors in the Northern Mountains. A tributary of the Ka has changed its course."

Ruben Brooks asked, "You believe these things were caused by the loss of the medallion?"

"I do not believe. I know." She looked toward the door. "Here is the medallion's first thief."

The half-half the guards escorted through the door was one of those with bits from lots of species. She was taller than a gnome, smaller than a human, colored like the Ekiba, but furry on her neck and shoulders and arms. She was thin and naked, with the large eyes of a Makeen and the heavy jaw of an Ahk.

She was drooling.

Her body was empty, or as good as, according to Gan's *üther* sense. It was as if someone had eaten her without eating her flesh. Gan almost forgot and asked what had been done to her.

The humans hadn't been told to be quiet. "What did you do to her?" Cynna Weaver demanded.

"We did not destroy her. She did that herself when she laid hands on the medallion."

After a moment Cynna Weaver said, "I guess the chancellor isn't really ill."

"He died within hours of the theft. His mind was unable to recall how his body functioned. The medallion is *reshvak*."

Oh, that was bad. That was really bad.

Ruben Brooks shifted slightly. He reminded Gan a little of cautious old Mevroax, part of whom she'd eaten back when she was a really young demon. Ruben Brooks always put his words together carefully. Only she thought Ruben Brooks had more sense than old Mevroax, who after all had been stupid enough to get himself eaten by a really young demon.

"My charm was unable to translate that word," Ruben Brooks said in English. *"Reshvak."*

Cullen Seabourne answered before the Eldest could speak, which was rude and not smart. "She means it's alive, more or less. And a parasite. Madam." He did have the wit to speak with respect when he addressed the Eldest directly. "This medallion is one of the Great Artifacts, isn't it?"

The Eldest leveled a look at the young lupus. "You think you know what that means, sorcerer?"

"Not precisely, no. But they are said to be hungry."

Her mouth quirked up as if he'd said something funny. "Hungry. Yes. The medallion hungers for order. It is supremely able to create order because of that hunger, but it cannot order itself. For that, it requires the mind of its holder. Unless the fit is very good, however, it cannot form a permanent bond. Without that bond, it eats the minds of any who hold it."

"Madam," Ruben Brooks said slowly, "you are telling us that the medallion possesses a degree of sentience, but is an essentially disordered sentience."

"Precisely. From the moment its bond with the chancellor was broken, the medallion has been insane."

EIGHTEEN

❦

IT was late by the time they left the meeting. Inside the Chancellery all the lights had gone soft, as if they were on a dimmer switch. Outside, bells tolled. One of their escorts—three gnomes, none of them councilors—explained that the bells marked the "hours," which weren't terrestrial hours, of course. Each bell-period was one-tenth of the sleep-wake cycle that made up a day in Edge.

The sound, muffled by the walls near the meeting room, grew fainter as they proceeded through labyrinthine halls. It had vanished entirely by the time they reached the wing that held the guest quarters. Their escorts left them with polite wishes for a good meal and a good sleep.

Gan hadn't come with them. First Councilor had wanted to speak with her, and the little not-yet-gnome had gone off with her, all atremble, like a devout Catholic granted a personal audience with the pope. Cullen was ahead of Cynna and McClosky, pushing Ruben's chair. He had a preoccupied look on his face, as if he barely knew the rest of them were there.

Cynna was pretty preoccupied herself. "Did we hear the truth this time?"

"Mostly, I suspect," Ruben said. "Gnomes may prefer misdirection and prevarication, but I'm inclined to believe that First Councilor wouldn't lie about anything significant when so much depends on your finding their medallion."

"So Bilbo will be our traveling companion if we have to take to the road." Of all the gnomes, why did he have to be the one deemed most likely to form a good bond with the medallion? Of course, he might be thinking the same thing, considering the consequences if the medallion decided he wasn't such a great fit, after all.

"Take to the road?" McClosky said. "You think they're right about it not being in the City anymore?"

Cynna shrugged. "I'll find out tomorrow, I guess."

They'd reached a wide place where three halls and a staircase converged. Cullen came to a stop. "I hope someone has been paying attention," he said, "or I'll have to Change and sniff out our trail."

"It's this one," Cynna said, and started for the right-hand hall.

"I guess you don't get lost," McClosky said to her.

"Well, I can if I don't pay attention—knowing the direction doesn't tell me which road or hall or whatever will take me there. Or if I don't have a pattern for where I want to go."

He shook his head. "I don't understand how your Gift works." Then, as if the words had been pent up for hours, he burst out, "Can you do it? No one's asked that. Everyone assumes you can find this medallion. Can you?"

"Probably. I'm pretty good." It occurred to her that McClosky was the only one of them who had no idea how she worked. Since his life depended on her ability, she ought to explain. "Tomorrow I'll do the sorts. I'll need a pattern for the medallion, see—the better the pattern, the more likely I am to Find it. I'm hopeful there. A magical artifact as powerful as this sucker ought to leave strong traces."

"What does this sorting involve? Does it take long?"

"Sorting is a spell, not part of my Gift, but I learned from the best—an actual patterner." Cynna hadn't known that Jiri was a patterner back when she'd been Jiri's apprentice, but that was beside the point. "I expect it will take most of the morning. I'll have to sort the medallion's pattern from things it's been in contact with—"

"Like that poor female, whatever she is."

Or was. Cynna grimaced. "Yeah. And the chancellor's body. I'll be looking for a strong, magical pattern they have in common, see? Plus they've got an engraving of the medallion."

"And then you just go to it?"

"More or less, if we're lucky. If it's warded—which they think it is, since they can't locate it with their own spells—or if it's outside my range, I'll have to Find its trail instead of Finding it. That'll take longer."

"You can Find the trail even if you can't Find the medallion itself?"

"Probably. See, everywhere an object has been carries some trace of its presence. Inanimate objects leave so little behind, I can't Find 'em that way. A living being or something with a lot of magic leaves better traces. Something that's both alive and magical leaves the most. I can Find those if not too much time has passed."

"It's been missing for two months."

True. And that wasn't exactly optimal, but . . . "It's powerful enough to impose order on a whole realm," Cynna said firmly. "It will leave powerful traces. Speaking of which . . ." She glanced over her shoulder. "What's a Great Artifact?"

"A magical construct created shortly before or during the Great War," Cullen answered promptly. "By which I do not mean either of the piddly conflicts of the last century. The Great War was fought in multiple realms over better than a century by adepts and gods. Also lupi," he added. "We were created then to fight on behalf of our Lady."

McClosky's voice was thick with disbelief. "Created?"

Cullen made a graceful gesture. "All peoples have their creation myths. You will allow us ours."

The meal was served as soon as they arrived in the common room. The food was good. The first course was a porridge-like mush that looked awful but tasted like berries and nuts, followed by some kind of roasted meat that had not come from a cow. There were roasted vegetables, too—carrots, squash, something pale that looked like a potato, but wasn't.

The porridge went down fine. Cynna asked Adrienne to bring her some water, not wanting to drink the strong, dark ale they served with the meal. Pregnant women were supposed to avoid alcohol, right? She made herself eat plenty of vegetables—they were pretty good—and some of the meat while she talked with the others and listened to their ideas. There wasn't any dessert, but their servants brought them fruit at the end of the meal. Cynna grabbed an apple for later, yawned ostentatiously, and at last, thank God, she left.

Problem was, there was nowhere to go. Except her rooms.

Her damned, tiny rooms with the oily air. She didn't want to be alone. She didn't want to be with people, either. And they sure as hell didn't need to be with her. Wouldn't exactly reassure anyone to know just what a thin thread their lives all hung by, would it?

She paced. Anywhere else—back home in D.C., or in any of the other cities she'd stayed in while working—she'd go out when she felt like this. She'd walk or run or go to a club and dance for hours. Or maybe she'd go to a gym and work out until she wanted to puke.

These days, she did the workout more often; the club, less. It was too easy, too tempting, to pick someone up at a club. Easy to get in a fight, too. And that's what she really wanted to do—fight or fuck. The nameless feeling scrambling her insides like a cat clawing its way out of a bag would settle if she did one of those things.

No gym here. No nightclubs. Not even a goddamn TV,

a book, a DVD player. No, nothing at all to do in the garish little room.

Cullen was just down the hall.

No, she told herself. She'd made herself a promise, right? She was upgrading her taste in men, which meant no more desperate one-nighters. Not even on the bad nights, when she couldn't stand living in her own skin. Because she had nowhere else to live, did she? She had to find other ways of dealing with a really bad mood.

Cullen wasn't a onc-nighter. He was a friend.

That thought made Cynna want to put a fist through the wall. He was a friend, and she couldn't go to him because . . . because he was part of the explosion building inside her.

Besides, what if that elf-lady had beat her to it? The mood Cynna was in, if she saw the two of them snuggled up, she'd try to kill them both. She'd fail, of course, and probably wouldn't be lucky enough to die herself, and tomorrow she'd wake up with post-insanity humiliation.

This will pass, she assured herself. She just had to ride it out.

But how? There was no gym, no club where she could dance, and it would be stupid to go walking the streets of the City when she had no clue what the dangers were. Especially when so much was riding on her and her Gift. She could not risk herself that way.

She shouldn't risk her tiny rider, either. Cynna stopped, her hand resting on her stomach.

Crunches. She could do crunches and scissors and lunges and work up a sweat right here.

Here? She wanted *out*. Out of this room, away from the oily air and the damned walls and—

Someone knocked softly at her door. She spun. Dragged in a breath, dragged both hands through her hair, and prepared to do her best impression of normal and sane. "Yes?"

The door swung open. Cullen stood in the doorway, wearing what looked like tight gray sweatpants. No shirt.

He held out some cloth. "Put this on. We're going to go spar awhile."

CYNNA was staring at him as if he'd grown a second head. Cullen supposed that Rule would have worked out not just what to do, but why he was doing it. Not him. He was right to be here. He knew that instinctively, but the why escaped him

"Expecting a different sort of invitation?" he said sweetly. "Not tonight, luv. Aggressive sex can be fun, but you'd brood later. Here." He tossed her the knit pants and shirt his servant had scrounged up.

She caught them. For a moment he thought she'd start their sparring session right now. She thought so, too.

She settled for slamming the door in his face. He smiled and leaned against the wall and waited. So far instinct was working out okay.

Cullen's servant had arranged for them to use a room near the guard barracks. It was small and bright and empty. No windows—gnomes didn't like them—but the floor was covered with something with some give. Cullen didn't know what, but it should cushion any falls.

He meant to make sure Cynna didn't take any. But soft was still preferable.

"I'm not sure this is a good idea," Cynna said. Her voice was tight.

Cramming it all down, she was. Not that he knew what "this" was, but he had some guesses. "No throws in tae kwon do, right?"

"No. *Tae* means kick; *kwon* means hand or fist. It's all about kicking and punching. If you don't know how to do it, though—"

"Good. Don't try any flying kicks. Everything else should be okay."

"*I* know what to do to protect the little rider," she snapped. "I'm not sure about you. Have you ever practiced tae kwon do?"

Little rider, was it? "Some. We'll stretch first, then forms. Then we spar."

"Forms." She cocked an eyebrow at him. "So you do know something about it."

He hesitated. "Etorri is too small a clan to maintain a separate group of trained as fighters the way Nokolai does. We all trained. Our practice included tae kwon do forms."

She was skeptical. "Long time ago. You were pretty young when you lost your clan, weren't you?"

"Twenty-six." She always spoke bluntly of his *seco*— no sympathy, no mincing around his delicate feelings on the subject. He preferred that. His voice still turned harsh. "And I sure as hell needed to be able to fight. Some lupi see a lone wolf as a target. I needed the discipline, too, until I found I preferred the discipline of dance. You aren't the only one with anger management issues, you know."

"This . . . this whatever's wrong with me isn't anger. I don't know what it is, but—"

Cullen snorted. "Keep telling yourself that. Stretch," he told her, and dropped to the floor to begin his own stretches.

Truth was, he'd fought often enough in the years since he'd trained with Etorri, but he hadn't practiced the forms in so long, he didn't clearly remember them. They'd come back. He had excellent kinetic memory. Besides, he didn't have to be good at her particular branch of the martial arts tonight. Halfway capable would do as long as he knew how to spar and was fast. He did and he was. Fast enough to let her work out whatever was brewing inside her without hurting either of them.

"I should see if they've got ice. Ice would help. Surely they have—"

"Shut up, Cynna." Cullen snagged her arm and tugged her back down.

They were sitting on the floor, breathing hard. He

leaned against the wall. "It was a fine kick. A damned fine kick."

"I didn't think I'd connect. You said you could keep that from happening."

He turned to look at her and grinned, albeit lopsidedly. His jaw ached like fury. It wasn't broken, thank God. It would have been, if he hadn't pulled back in time. Well, almost in time. "No? And here I thought you were doing your damnedest to clobber me. No, don't try to look regretful. It's my fault you clobbered me. I underestimated you."

Her grin broke free. "Or overestimated yourself."

"Surely not."

"Maybe you were distracted by my breasts. You've got a thing for my breasts."

"Mmm." He smiled. "That I do, but I think it was your legs that got me this time, Wonder Woman."

Neither of them spoke for a few moments. Cullen's breathing smoothed, but hers was still uneven when she broke the silence. "You think the feelings getting to me are like yours, but they—it—whatever it is, it isn't anger."

"It's not regular anger a clanless lupus feels, either." It was loneliness, an unspeakable isolation that sometimes erupted as a red howling against the world. And himself. Always, always, it had been against himself as well, the vast, aching flaw of who and what he was.

That's what she felt. He knew that in the deep places inside him. She might not want to call it anger, but however she named the feeling, it rose from the same ache and fury of isolation, the same certainty of damage, that he'd felt while clanless.

Cynna's head was leaning against the wall next to his. She rolled it to look at him. "Is it okay for you here? The clan bond, the what-do-you-call-it . . . I should have asked earlier. I didn't think of it. I should have."

"The mantle. Yes. I feel it here. Not as strongly . . . we need the company of others of the clan to feel the connection clearly. But I'm all right." He could feel it still, and that was what counted. That was what the mantle did. It told him his place, told him where and how he belonged.

Fear or rage could still take him. They couldn't swallow him. "You should have been born clan."

"What?" She shook her head, mouth quirking. "Female clan don't experience the mantle, do they?"

"That's not what I meant. You like to fight. You like sex. If you'd been born clan, you'd see those as normal instead of something to worry about."

"Your female clan members fight?"

"Not all, but some do. One of the members of Canada's women's Olympic tae kwon do team is Etorri."

"Yeah?" That pleased her.

"Come on." Cullen pushed to his feet and held out a hand. "I'm sticky and sweaty, and so are you. Off to the baths."

Cynna let him pull her to her feet but released his hand immediately. "I'm not into public bathing."

"Tough. You may not feel them yet, but you picked up a few bruises yourself when I blocked some of your attempts to destroy me. You worked your muscles hard. You need a good, hot soak, and I want one. I'm told that at this hour the baths should be almost empty. A few trysting couples, perhaps, no more eager to be seen than you are. And I've reserved a private spot for us."

"Oh, you have, have you?" Her eyes narrowed. "No sex."

He could change her mind. He was sure about that, but . . . his mouth twisted wryly.

"What's funny?"

"I know when to fight with you, but my instincts are mute on when to seduce you."

She thought that over, then gave a firm nod. "Good."

NINETEEN

CYNNA hadn't expected the baths to be so beautiful.

They were underground, part of a cave system that included both hot springs and an underground tributary to the Ka. This struck Cynna as geologically suspect, but what did she know? Maybe hot springs happened all the time next to underground rivers near aboveground rivers Or maybe it was part of the general weirdness of Edge.

Cullen didn't know, either. She found that greatly reassuring. Here was an entire area of knowledge he was blank on. "You never studied up on geology?"

He shrugged. "Never had the need. I can identify some of the useful stones, of course."

Magically useful, he meant. She knew most of the magically useful stones, too. Cynna smiled, pleased with his ignorance, and closed her eyes, enjoying the warmth. She hadn't been this comfortable since she'd arrived in Edge.

They'd gone to their rooms first to get clean clothes—pants for them both, praise God. Cullen's servant—a small, dark-skinned man incongruously named Sean—had led them to the baths, which were a sprawling affair, encompassing several small chambers like this grotto as well as three large public areas. A few people of various species were in the public area they passed on the way to their own spot.

Sean had led them to this grotto, where Adrienne was waiting, reserving the spot for them. She had handed Cynna a small basket of toiletries, explained what was what, then left with Cullen's man, Sean.

"Should we tip them or something?" Cynna had asked once they were alone. "Not that we have any of their money, but the Council would probably give us some if we insisted."

"Ask your father," Cullen suggested. "We don't know if offering money is expected or insulting."

Cullen had stripped as matter-of-factly as if revealing that gorgeous body meant nothing. That was an act. He knew very well how beautiful he was, but Cynna chose to pretend along with him. She'd stripped, too. She wasn't as casual about nudity as a lupus, but she wasn't overly modest, either, and Cullen was the only one here. He'd seen her body before.

Both of them had washed with soft, mint-scented soap before losing interest in movement.

Their little grotto was as eerie as it was beautiful. It was only about ten feet wide and long, open on the water side but otherwise sheltered from other bathers by rock walls. The ceiling was high and vastly irregular. There was a wide ledge above the water and a shallow one below, where they sat in water warm as a bathtub. It lapped her shoulders, giving the illusion of cover.

The ledge she sat on was smooth and slick with moss. Hundreds of mage lights the size of fireflies skimmed rock formations above and below the water, many clinging to outcroppings of quartz as if attracted by its crystalline complexity. The colors were delicate and varied—multiple greens from moss; quartz in pink, purple, clear; stone in gray, sepia, cream.

"And to think," Cynna murmured, "they've resisted the temptation to paint any of this red. Or purple." She stirred her toes around, sending up a silty swirl. "The air isn't oily down here. What does it look like with your other vision?"

"Shiny. These stones have been absorbing magic for centuries. Not much worked magic, though. Aside from the mage lights, everything's pretty much the way it arrived from the maker." He looked at her. "You've a pretty glow."

"I've never been complimented on my aura before. No, don't explain. I know you see something other than a regular aura." Anyone could see those, with the right training. Usually not very well, but even a null could learn. And everyone had auras, even nulls. Cynna supposed it was like light—magic and life-auras came from different parts of the spectrum. "Did you see magic from the time you were little?"

"Mmm. My mum was thrilled. It almost made up for the complications of raising a child with an affinity for Fire."

"Started them, did you?"

"Fortunately, I learned to put them out pretty quickly. And Mum was Wiccan . . . think I mentioned that. Until I was six she kept a damper spell up around our flat. Annoyed the salamanders."

"How long has she been gone?"

"Just over ten years now. She lived to a ripe old age, for a human. Had me when she was older . . . Mum never admitted she'd cast fertility spells to conceive, but of course she had."

"My mother died young. She was only a year older than I am now when it happened." Cynna's mouth twisted with sadness, humor, a certain resigned fondness. She could feel that fondness now. She could even remember some of the lovely things about her mother.

"How did it happen?"

"She didn't drive drunk, but she walked drunk once too often. Wandered out in front of a taxi."

"You were very young."

"Thirteen." It had been a lousy age to lose a mother. Going to live with her aunt had probably saved her, but Cynna had been so busy hating her mother that it took years to recover from the anger and the guilt. So much left unspoken, unclear . . . "It took me a long time to see that she never stopped loving me. She just stopped being able to parent me."

"Who did parent you?"

"After Mom died? Aunt Meggie. Well, technically, she was my great-aunt. See, Mom was illegitimate. Her own mother died in childbirth when she was real young, barely sixteen, and her grandparents didn't want the little bastard who'd shamed them and killed their younger daughter. Assholes. But they had another daughter, and she—Mom's Aunt Meggie—wanted that baby. She was twelve years older than her little sister and worked for the phone company. She didn't make much, but Meggie pretty much did whatever she set out to do. Once she made up her mind to raise her sister's kid, that's what she did. Her parents freaked and wouldn't speak to her, but Aunt Meggie always said that was no loss."

"Humans." Cullen looked disgusted. "I'll never understand how anyone can hold a baby responsible for its birth. Your Aunt Meggie's dead, too?"

"Yeah, but not till she was eighty-three. One morning she didn't wake up, which was how she always said she'd die, God willing." Cynna snorted. "She always added the 'God willing' bit, but I figured God had better follow instructions just like the rest of us."

"She was a religious woman, then."

"Raised Catholic, but spent most of her life mad at the Church. She wasn't exactly thrilled about my decision to join it. She went around muttering under her breath and came damned close to breaking her own rule."

"Which was . . . ?"

Cynna smiled. "'Advice is like shit. Don't pass it around and don't take someone else's.' But . . . well, she knew why I needed the Church." The Catholic Church offered the best demon protection available. At the time, that had been an important criterion.

"Where was she before your mother died?"

Cynna's smile slipped. "She didn't believe in interfering, and . . . well, I always suspected she thought she hadn't done such a great job with Mom, and she didn't want to fail again. But when Mom died, she was there for me."

"I take it she didn't die all that long ago."

"Three years. Well, three and a half." She sighed. "I tried to get her to move in with me, you know? She was getting up there in years and her health seemed good, but . . . well, she wouldn't do it. Didn't even want to discuss it. She never would let me help her with money or anything, and she liked living alone."

"Was it after she died that you moved into a hotel? Or after she refused to live with you?"

Cynna opened her mouth. Closed it. Her throat felt tight. "That's not how it was. My apartment went condo and I didn't want to buy, so . . ." Lame. That sounded so lame. Especially with the way her eyes were stinging— which he would notice, damn him.

Had she moved into a hotel room because, with Aunt Meggie gone, she'd given up on having a home?

Duh.

Cullen stood, raising the smooth sculpture of his upper body above the water, and started toward her.

"What are you doing?" she asked, suspicious.

"I can't offer to comfort you," he said in the reasonable voice he used when he was being outrageous. "You'd push me away. So you'll have to comfort me for making me feel sad about your loss."

Cynna rolled her eyes. "Aunt Meggie died over three years ago."

He sat beside her and slid an arm around her waist. "That's not the loss I'm sad about. Quit squirming."

She shoved at his arm, not caring if she was being predictable. "I am so not in the mood."

He just pulled her closer and dropped a kiss on the top of her head. "Pretend I'm your gay hairdresser."

She twisted to stare in astonishment. "My what?"

"I'm going to wash your hair." With his free hand Cullen snagged the basket of toiletries. "Every woman I've ever known zens out when she gets her hair washed."

"Done it a lot, have you?"

"No." He shifted so that he was behind her. "But I used to wash my mum's hair after the cancer had her. She didn't much like being touched by strangers, and by then"—his voice turned wry—"she'd argued with or out-lived most of her friends. She was an ornery old bird. Loved me to hell and back, but she could have taught stubborn to a jackass. Tilt your head."

The shampoo was in a little jar, not a tube. It had a tangy, mineral scent and didn't lather at all. His fingers made soothing circles on her scalp as he rubbed it in, and the last tension drained right out of her. "Mmm. Your mum sounds a bit like my aunt Meggie."

"They'd have understood each other, I think." And that was all either of them said until he spoke again. "You'd better duck and rinse yourself."

The moss was slippery. Cynna took a breath, scooted her hips, and slid out flat on the shelf, her head bumping one of his legs. She ran her hands through her short hair, rubbing her scalp to get rid of the shampoo, then rubbed her head against his leg like an affectionate cat marking her territory. She stretched and came up smiling, eyes closed, water streaming in her face and down her back . . . and with his arms around her from behind, his hands on her breasts.

"I thought you weren't going to seduce me."

"I said I didn't know when to do it," Cullen corrected her, his fingers teasing her nipples. "But that's if I'm thinking about what you need. I'm pretty clear on what I need."

She stirred the water lightly with one hand. "It's late, and tomorrow will be busy. I need some sleep."

"Do you?" He said that idly, as if sleep were an odd thing to require, but he'd humor her. "Go ahead, then. I'll wake you when I'm done."

"As if." But she didn't move. She felt so tired and soothed and aroused all at once . . . it was just too much trouble to say no. She didn't want to go back to her rooms, where the air was oily. She wanted to lean her head back against his shoulder and let her body drift, half floating, while his fingers made her nipples happy, setting up a tugging deep in her belly . . .

He bent his head and drew his teeth along the tender cord of her neck, shooting a bolt of lust straight through her. "Drowsing off?"

"Any minute now." What was it about teeth? She loved teeth. He bit gently, then harder—not enough to hurt, but close. Her hips stirred restlessly. "Hope I don't snore."

Cullen chuckled and let his mouth soothe the spot he'd assaulted with his teeth, then drifted his lips along her shoulder, kissing, licking.

One of his hands drifted, too. There was no way Cynna could keep her hips still with what those clever fingers were up to now. "I thought this was all about you."

"Trust me, I'm doing exactly what I want to do."

Something else stirred within her. Something that made her need to turn, to see him. One of her legs dangled off the ledge as she twisted around. Her breasts, buoyed by water, brushed his chest. She met his eyes.

They were burning blue. Not playful. Not lighthearted. Her breath caught.

"Now," he said, soft and fierce. "*Now* I can get into you."

One little squirm of fear wiggled its way through her, but there was no time for more—no time even to wonder what she feared, because his hands curved around her bottom and brought her over him, her legs wide to admit him. His cock pressed at her entrance and sensation drowned her, purely drowned her.

For all the hard blue of his eyes and the tension along

his jaw, he went slowly. Cullen claimed he was not a patient man, and she supposed he wasn't, but he was thorough. He also claimed he was selfish, and that was partly true. Once he got inside her, he was selfishly determined to take his time.

She could have blamed the water. Cynna had never fucked underwater before. It was delicious, creating both buoyancy and resistance, altering the tempo.

But mostly it was Cullen who set the pace. Once he got her settled astride him, she should have been in charge. She wasn't. He controlled the ride with his hands, his thrusts, and the delicious things he did with his mouth. Her breasts bobbed along barely above the water, putting them within handy reach of his mouth. He took advantage of that.

Cynna took advantage of her position, too—looking at that beautiful face without having to worry about being caught at it. Letting her hands enjoy his wet, messy hair and strong shoulders. He smelled good. So good. Tasted good, too. She chased a drop of water down his throat with her tongue. Breathing him in while he thrust inside her, slow and firm and implacable.

He stopped her chase, cupping her face in one hand and making her look at him as his other hand reached down between them and touched her clit. And even before the climax hit, she burst—something inside her breaking and breaking, quiet and terrible and complete.

After, with her body collapsed against him, limp and destroyed, her face hid itself on his shoulder. Her eyes were wide and dry with despair.

How could she have let this happen? She'd meant to give him only her body and the pleasure bodies could offer. And he'd taken so much more. Too much.

TWENTY

THE market was an explosion of scent, color, and noise. Hawkers cried their wares in at least three languages that Cullen could pick out. His charm translated all of them, of course, the words tumbling over each other in an unholy din.

Not unlike the din in his head. He'd screwed up last night. Big time.

Cullen had known that the moment Cynna unwrapped herself from him in the baths. It had been abundantly clear as they walked back to their rooms. She'd scarcely spoken . . . which was better than what she did when they reached her door, bursting into bright, cheery speech. He'd stopped that with an angry kiss . . . proving that once he'd begun screwing up, he couldn't stop.

She'd responded, yes, but with confusion as much as desire. And wariness. Not that he blamed her. He'd known she wasn't ready, and he'd pushed anyway.

He hadn't been invited past her door. No surprise there.

This morning they'd all met in the common room for breakfast. Well, almost all—there'd been one missing and

one addition. No one had seen Gan since she went off
with First Councilor. The addition was Steve Timms. Last
night, while Cullen was getting his brains fucked out,
Brooks had gone to see Steve and Marilyn Wright. She
was still unconscious, but the healer had begun treatment
and was cautiously hopeful. Ruben trusted the woman, so
Steve was back with the pack for now.

They'd discussed what would happen if Cynna's Find
was successful—who would go on the trail of the medallion and who wouldn't. Cullen had some firm ideas about
that. Fortunately, Brooks had already decided he and
McClosky would be more hindrance than help. Timms
would go with Cullen, Cynna, and whoever the gnomes
sent; Brooks would stay behind to keep an eye on the
Wright woman's condition. McClosky would stay in the
City, too, of course, where he could talk trade to his heart's
content.

Cynna had accepted all that with a nod, adding only
that she might not know right away if she'd be able to
Find the thing. If her initial Find didn't work, she'd just
keep trying, refining the parameters, moving to other lo-
cations, until it did.

Cullen had assumed that, but the others probably didn't
know enough about how she used her Gift to realize how
many trials it could take. He'd asked if it would help her to
draw on his diamond. She'd said no. He'd asked if she
needed him for anything. She'd said no. He'd said in
that case, he'd head out, check out the market, see what he
could learn. She'd looked relieved.

Dammit.

Cullen stopped at a stall displaying stacks of paper.
Handmade, he judged, and not of high quality. Paper
mills probably required more tech than was possible in
Edge, and imported paper might be pricey, or not widely
available.

The gnomes had come up with acceptable clothing
this morning. Cullen wore leather pants such as the guard
here favored with a loose jacket in a finely woven indigo

wool. It had pockets, thank God. He'd missed pockets. From one he pulled out the cheap pen he'd borrowed from Cynna—she had six or seven in the bottom of that huge bag of hers—and began with the questions.

He'd been doing this all morning. The pen gave him a reason to talk to people. Supposedly he wanted to learn who might be able to duplicate it and who might be interested in selling such pens. In fact he was picking up gossip, putting together a picture of the society, and enjoying giving the gnome tailing him a hard time. The little fellow skulked about so obviously.

Edge was largely preindustrial, but magic made it more comfortable than, say, medieval Europe. They had decent health care, since healers were common. There was even a public health service to deal with broad issues such as clean water and epidemics. The sanitation system in the City was excellent, far better than in any comparable preindustrial society on Earth. Even the slums had clean water, waste disposal, and public toilets.

Printing presses existed, but most books and pamphlets were set the way Gutenberg did it. Metal was expensive. Edge had plenty of ore and magic helped with the smelting, but tempering and working the metal were done by hand. For the very best weapons you went to the Ahk, who were highly skilled artisans and spellcasters in all matters of weaponry and battle. Cloth was pricey; the best stuff was imported. You could tell someone's status by the quality of their clothing and their footwear. The poor wore sandals.

So did Cullen, at the moment. Of course, he qualified as poor, since he owned literally nothing here.

Plastic, of course, was nonexistent. Everyone he'd shown the pen to was fascinated by the substance. Some were dubious; some, excited. Cullen figured McClosky would have a great time with his trade treaties. Edge was going to have one hell of an effect on U.S. and global markets . . . assuming everyone here didn't die.

Great timing he had. Cynna was doing her sorting

today. The fate of all of them—of pretty much everyone in this world, save the sidhe—rested on her ability to get a good pattern so she could Find the medallion. Or so they'd been told. And he decided he had to get into her last night.

Oh, but he'd been honest, hadn't he? He'd told her he was doing exactly what he wanted, that he was serving his own needs, not hers. Aced that.

He was used to being selfish. "Thanks," he told the skinny, dark-skinned man at the paper stall. "I'll be in touch if I'm able to get the pens made." He ambled along.

Years. He'd spent years acquiring the wrong sort of instincts for what he needed now. He knew how to keep things light, how to keep a woman from expecting too much. He didn't know how to make a woman trust him. He'd never wanted that before.

And Cynna was not exactly prone to trust. He understood that. He wasn't, either. She'd modeled herself after the one dependable adult in her life, hadn't she? She'd even adopted her aunt's religion, though from what he could tell, she was blissfully unaware of that reason for her choice.

First her father deserted her. Never mind that Daniel Weaver hadn't intended to leave; the truth Cynna had grown up around was abandonment. Her mother had left her, too, slowly and infinitely more painfully. In a real sense, Cynna had lost her mother long before the woman staggered into the path of a taxi. Naturally Cynna wanted to be like her aunt . . . who'd died the way she'd lived. Alone.

Cullen scowled. Aunt Meggie had a lot to answer for. Even a lupus could survive alone. He'd proved that, but survival was thin gruel compared to actually living.

The market sprawled over several streets. Upscale and imported goods—imported meaning out-realm—were sold in permanent shops, but pretty much everything else was available from small stalls and wandering vendors. The section closest to the river was devoted to produce, with the fish market close by; another section offered both cloth and clothing.

There was no slave market. That was one of the things he had wanted to learn. The practice of slavery was outlawed by treaty throughout Edge, and the gnomes put real teeth in their law. Trafficking in lives earned the death penalty.

Point to the gnomes.

Cullen lingered awhile in an area devoted to charms, potions, and common spell ingredients. Some of them were clearly bogus, but others were intriguing. He'd persuaded one of the gnomes to supply him with some walking-around money, but it wasn't enough to buy the two charms that truly interested him, so he left without making any purchases.

From there, he turned onto a narrow, unpaved street. Still plenty of mage lights, but the people wore the kind of coarsely woven wool he'd been given by the Ekiba. Some looked downright ragged.

Most on this street were human. Especially the ragged ones.

Cullen stopped at a tiny stall and bought lunch—spiced, shredded meat of some sort mixed with cabbage and wrapped in flat bread. He bought two, chatted a bit, asked where to buy a drink to go with them, and wandered in that direction, putting together what he'd learned so far.

First, gossip was widespread about a gate to Earth being opened, and people were excited about the possibilities. Second, that's about all they knew. There were rumors that the people seen arriving on the barge had included Earth-realm humans, but most discounted that. Why would a trade delegation gate in anywhere but the City?

No one mentioned the chancellor's medallion. No one recognized Cullen. They assumed he was human, but from one of the other realms. It turned out that the majority of humans living in Edge weren't Theilo—the fall-through-the-cracks people—but were descended from them. And most Theilo hadn't come from the Earth realm. A few humans had migrated here by choice, but they were the exception. Which made sense, given the prejudice against them. That was more a matter of bias and stereotyping than violent oppression, but enough to keep them on the lowest rung of the economic ladder.

Back home, lupi had been actively hunted by humans for generations. That was now illegal—but only when lupi were two-legged. So it was odd that he found himself resenting the humans' plight here. Maybe he was constitutionally drawn to underdogs.

While sorting his thoughts—and watching his watcher; the little fellow was amusing in his attempts to duck out of sight—he'd wandered away from the mostly human area. He'd forgotten to get a drink and was in need of one, so when he saw what was unmistakably a tavern, he headed for it. He'd have some ale, he decided, listen a bit, and get back to the Chancellery to see how the sorting had gone.

A tall male something with an extra set of arms blocked the door and rumbled at him. His charm said, "Depart, human scum."

Cullen stopped, looking up at the ugly face looming over him. " 'Depart, human scum'?" he repeated incredulously. "You have got to be kidding."

"Humans are not allowed in the Gypsum."

He could have pointed out that he wasn't human. Instead he smiled sweetly. "But I'm thirsty. Of course you'll step aside."

The whatever-he-was growled.

It was the growl that did it. Cullen's wolf did not like being growled at, and he was in a mood to indulge the wolf. His smile widened. Wouldn't the oversize idiot look funny when the weak little human Changed? "I'm a peaceable fellow, so I'll give you to a count of three to get out of my way. One . . ."

A tinkling laugh interrupted him. He glanced over his shoulder, scowling . . . then caught a whiff of who approached, and his body went on alert in a completely different way.

She wore green today—a pale, silvery green, her gossamer gown styled like a sari, only without a blouse beneath. The exposed breast was small and round and lovely, the areola a pale, virginal pink.

And her scent . . .

"Quit playing with the poor half-half," the sidhe woman said, her voice rich with amusement and derision and suggestions. "He doesn't know what you are, of course." She tilted her head to one side. "I am not sure I do, either. Not in the sort of . . . detail . . . with which I would like us to be acquainted."

THE sorting had gone well. Tedious, but well. The first Find, not so great.

"No luck?" Ruben said softly.

They were in a kitchen garden, the only spot within the Chancellery where she could get her bare feet on the ground. That wasn't essential for a Find, but it helped when she was pushing her limits.

"No." She shrugged. "It's either too far away or it's warded. Time for Plan B."

"Your energies is not depleted?" Bilbo asked anxiously. He and two other gnomes waited just beyond Ruben on the cobbled path.

"No." She felt great, in fact, though she'd just done a full Find. She wondered if Edge's magic was keeping her replenished better than Earth's magic did. Or maybe it was the great sex last night. That, as any Wiccan would tell you, worked a treat to top off your magical tank.

"This will take longer," she warned them, and lowered herself to the ground. "I need to do some prep first."

Cynna had chosen a patch of creeping thyme for her grounding, in part because she'd do the plants no harm by standing, sitting, or stomping on them. The scent was pleasant, too. She closed her eyes and let herself drift on the mixed scents of the garden, the slightly damp, spongy feel of the plants and the earth beneath them, until she felt centered and ready.

Also horny. Squirmingly horny. Last night had reminded her body of what it had been missing, and it wanted more. But she could use that. Arousal was energy, and a lot more fun than pain. Theoretically she could use that, too, but she'd never been moved to try.

Her skin felt tight and lively. She ached pleasantly between her legs, bringing her attention to her root chakra.

Why wasn't Cullen here?

Shut up, she told her mind. Hadn't she told Cullen to go do his thing? She didn't need him to hold her hand when she did a Find. She'd wanted him out of her way, in fact, wanted time without him cluttering up her thoughts . . . and here he was anyway. And here she was, all annoyed because he hadn't shown up in spite of what she'd told him.

How very girly of her. Cynna sighed.

Once more she gave her attention to the thyme, the air, the sensations of this moment. After a few moments she had the calm, centered feeling back and brought her attention to her newest *kielezo,* the enspelled tattoo for the medallion. Carefully she trickled power into a *kilingo,* a spell that would connect the *kielezos.*

The usual way to Find a trail when she couldn't get a fix on the object itself was a slow, painstaking business. She had to keep Finding and Finding, moving around until she picked up whatever traces the object had left. In the last couple years, though, Cynna had been experimenting with another way, one that included time as a factor. In effect, she'd be hunting a space that "remembered" the medallion having passed through it about a month ago.

One of her *kielezos* stood for *time has passed.* That was her dial. Back home she'd set that dial by the number of nights that had fallen since the person—it was usually a person she had to Find—had gone missing. Here that wouldn't work, so she'd asked the gnomes to give her something that had been made in a single "day"—as precisely one day as possible. They'd given her a bit of knitting. She'd sorted it, abstracting the portion of the pattern that meant lifetime. Now she had to connect four *kielezos*: one for the *path*, one for *day*, the medallion's *kielezo*, and the one for *time has passed*.

She "drew" a firm line between the medallion's *kielezo* and *path*, then connected the two with *time has passed*, then tied the latter to *day* with a thread of power. She'd adjust the *day kielezo* through intention alone, setting the number of days she wished it to represent. When the connections felt right, she stood.

Cynna flexed her bare feet, absorbing the feel of dirt and plants and earth. She raised one heel and dropped it firmly. Then the other. Knees flexed, feet never fully leaving the earth, she stamped out an ancient rhythm, and as the rhythm built, she drew on her Gift, a process as simple and natural as taking a deep breath . . . *hold it, hold it* . . . power built and built behind her intention, gathered by her feet on the earth, focused by the arms she raised slowly . . . slowly . . . the patterns from the linked *kielezos* lifted with her arms, humming invisibly in the air around her.

Five and five and five and five and five and five, she told the *day kielezo.* She snapped her arms overhead. Exhaled. And Found.

There. Oh, yes. There, and all along there, heading that way. She had it.

Cynna grinned, a little dizzy, a lot tired. Triumphant. "I've got a trail. It's weak, but I've got it. The river. The medallion left on the river, headed south."

Ruben smiled. "Good job." There was, maybe, a whisper of relief in his voice.

The gnomes' relief was a lot nosier, but quickly subsided into orders and bustle. The trail definitely headed away from the City. They'd be traveling again. Bilbo assured them all would be ready for their departure in a bell-time, which was a little over two hours.

"I hope Gan shows up in time." She was a bit worried about the former demon.

Ruben looked at her. "Did Mr. Seabourne say when he would return? Or should we send someone for him?"

"Oh. No, you don't have to. He's back." She didn't have to do a full Find to know that. She didn't even need his pattern. With objects or people she knew well, she just had to wonder where they were. If they were close, her Gift told her. "I'll tell him we'll be leaving ASAP."

Cynna did take one wrong turn on her way back to their rooms, but otherwise navigated the maze quickly. It still took her long enough to wonder why she'd immediately offered to fetch Cullen. Just because her body wanted more of him didn't mean the rest of her was ready.

Maybe she was making too much of last night. What had changed, really? Sure, they'd had great sex, but it wasn't the first time they'd set off fireworks . . . as the little rider not yet pooching out her stomach testified. She cared about him, yeah, but she was supposed to care about a friend. Last night she'd felt vulnerable, but that didn't mean . . . she hadn't fallen for him, for God's sake.

Infatuation. That's what it was. It would fade in time.

Cynna was tired and wired when she reached his door. She knocked, forgetting to keep it soft. Her knuckles shoved the door partway open. "It's me," she called out, pushing it open the rest of the way. "Guess what?"

Her feet stopped just over the threshold. The weirdest feeling swept over her, like she'd mainlined a fire-and-ice slushy. And she said, "Oh, you're busy. Well, this will just take a minute." She strode forward, fire and ice fizzing in her veins.

Cullen was naked from the waist up. So was the elf-woman clinging to him. He had turned to look at her when the door opened, his eyes heavy and dazed. One of his hands covered one of the woman's dinky little breasts . . . perfect, dinky little breasts. The elf-woman had turned her head, too, but immediately dismissed Cynna, going back to what she'd been doing. Licking Cullen's neck.

Big mistake.

Four strides and she swung into a crescent kick, her back leg swinging out and up, the inside ankle aimed for elf-bitch's face.

Cullen blinked—and went into fast-forward. He *blurred*, dammit, moving impossibly fast to shield the elf-bitch with his body while his arms swung up, executing a perfect forearm block.

The ball of Cynna's foot smashed into his left forearm. He didn't follow through with the sweep that might have overbalanced her, so she used her momentum to pivot and come at the bitch again.

She wasn't there. A second ago she'd been standing smugly behind Cullen, her lovely lip curling in disgust. Now she just . . . wasn't.

TWENTY-ONE

THE chancellor's barge was way different from the one they'd been on before. They were headed downriver now, and the river had narrowed some, so the current was strong and fast. The barge was hitched to a pair of sea oxen, but they were as much for steering as for propulsion.

It was a luxurious vessel compared to the other one. The wood was dark and polished to a fare-thee-well, with intricate carving everywhere some gnome had found a spot to stick a knife. There were cabins, too, thank God, though even the ones supposedly sized for non-gnomes were tiny. Cynna had one to herself. Most of the others had to double up, and some slept out on the deck.

They were a large party. Tash led a small squad of the guard—always referred to in the singular for some reason—for their protection. Wen was along to keep the Ekiba comm channel open, and Bilbo had brought three more gnomes along. Cynna didn't know who or what they were. She'd been given titles to address them by, but what did "Third Assistant of the Red Jasper Collar" mean? Privately, she thought of them as Huey, Dewey, and Louie.

Her father was here, too.

That had come as a shock. Daniel Weaver said he wanted to be with her, get to know her. He hoped he would be useful; he was fluent in Common Tongue and had some understanding of three more of the languages here. He knew the customs and the politics. He worked for the chancellor, yes, but at the moment that office was vacant— though that was a deep, dark secret from the rest of their world.

At the moment, he was in the stateroom he shared with Wen. It was late, so they were probably sleeping. Timms was on the other side of the superstructure housing the staterooms. He was teaching Gan to play poker. Every so often she heard Gan yell in triumph or anger. The former demon was not a good loser.

Tash and three of the guard were bedded down on the deck—no cushy bunks for the guard, it seemed. The other four were looking alert and menacing in their medieval-meets-goth garb. Bilbo and Louie had retired, leaving Huey and Dewey still talking at the big table at the aft—or was it the stern? Anyway, the back of the boat. Everyone had eaten at a big table there earlier, then spread out maps to discuss their route.

Not that Cynna knew their route beyond "thataway." The medallion had gone at least fifty miles farther downriver than they were now, but she'd have to check again and again, resetting her "dial," to follow it. Still, the session with the maps had been useful; she knew more about Edge geography now.

She really ought to go catch some sleep herself. Instead she stood at the rail near the bow, staring out at the heavy darkness. Clouds had wiped out the sky, leaving them only their running lights, the personal mage lights of those who, like her, didn't see well in darkness, and the occasional sparkle from other river craft.

"I still had my pants on," Cullen said from behind her.

Her hands clenched into fists. She jammed them into the pockets of her duster. Hadn't she known she should go to bed? She really should start listening to herself.

"I know you don't want to talk to me," he said, moving up beside her, "but you can damned well listen."

He could talk. Didn't mean she'd listen. She kept her gaze fixed on the invisible shoreline.

"I didn't have sex with her."

Cynna practiced breathing. She was pretty good at breathing, and it paid to concentrate on your pluses.

Out of the corner of her eye she saw him run a hand through his hair. "I told you why she was in my room."

Yeah. Elf-woman could do the language spell. For Cullen, spellcasting topped pretty much everything else. "I believe you," she said without looking at him. "You wanted her spell, so you agreed to give her what she wanted."

"You didn't hear anything I said earlier, did you? She didn't agree to trade the spell for sex." His lips quirked. "I'm good, but I'm not *that* good."

It took Cynna a moment to suppress the urge to bloody that amused smile, but she'd been humiliated enough by her impulses for one day. "You're beautiful and you're new to her. Her first lupus. I imagine she doesn't get a 'first' very often."

He shook his head. "Let me be more specific. I did not agree to have sex with her."

"Then you were leading her on something awful."

"She agreed to give me the Common Tongue. To receive it, I had to lower my shields. When I did, she glammed me."

"She what?" Cynna's lips twisted on the question, but it was too late. Dammit, she was listening to him. "That's not a word."

"You've heard of faerie glamour."

She looked directly at him, disgusted. "Why do you think I was aiming for her, not you?"

His mouth opened. Nothing came out.

She found room among the emotional bruises for a thread of satisfaction. It wasn't often she'd rendered Cullen speechless. "What did you think, that I'd blame her and not you for consensual hanky-panky? The door opened. You didn't react. You saw me and still didn't react. You're an idiot, but not that much of an idiot. Just what were you supposed to give her if it didn't involve your cock?"

"Information," he said dryly. "Theera is a spy, so that's what she trades in."

"That's the elf-woman's name? Theera?"

"Her use-name." He shook his head, rueful. "I didn't think she could glam me. She's only half-elven, and I thought . . . Well, I was wrong, wasn't I? Anyway, she acts as agent for her half sister—business agent at times, but the double-O type as well."

He'd learned quite a bit about the lovely Theera, hadn't he? "You'd better tell Ruben about her, then."

"I did. You were busy avoiding me."

The sorry lump of feeling in Cynna's gut reminded her of when she was twenty. She'd had an abscessed tooth and no money. Rather than borrow from her aunt, who didn't have much, either, she'd tried to ride it out.

You could do that with some things. Not with an abscessed tooth, it turned out. She didn't know how it would work with the muddled ache inside her, but since there weren't any emotional dentists, she guessed she'd find out. "What kind of information did you give her?"

"She wanted to know what we'd agreed to do, what the gnomes had offered, how we planned to locate the medallion. I gave her two out of three."

"Meaning?"

"I didn't see any harm in her knowing what we'd agreed to, since that's basically nothing, aside from hunting the medallion. Or what the gnomes are offering—also nothing. We find their medallion and we get to survive and maybe go home. She made me an offer on behalf of her sister."

And what might that have been—a threesome? The words almost slipped out, but Cynna caught them in time. Her priorities sucked. She had to get her damned unruly mind to pay attention to the life-or-death stuff. "What kind of offer?"

"She claims the medallion doesn't have to be held by the gnomes to keep Edge stable. The gnomes warned us we might hear that, of course, but their warning doesn't make it automatically false. Theera's argument boils down to the inherent superiority of the sidhe at everything, especially all things magical, which makes them the proper custodians for the medallion."

"She doesn't object to the way it eats brains?"

"Sidhe do haughty better than a cat. I asked. She gave me to understand it was none of my business." Cullen paused. "If I tell her where the medallion is before it bonds with a holder, I get all sorts of goodies. Spells. Knowledge."

"She has your number."

"Actually, I've got hers. Or her call-me." He held out a hand. A small topaz rested in his palm. "This summons her."

In spite of everything, curiosity pricked at her. "How does it work?"

"I haven't figured that out yet." His fingers closed, and he slid the topaz into the pocket of the loose jacket he wore. "Haven't figured out how she vanished, either."

Cynna's heart kicked up into her throat. She swallowed. After failing to pummel the elf-woman, she hadn't stuck around for explanations. Once the faerie bitch vanished, so had Cynna—more prosaically, however, by running out into the hall. Gan had inadvertently helped by showing up just then, full of chatter. Then Steve had arrived, then their servants, then Ruben, and they'd been busy ever since, getting ready to travel the river again.

Cynna steadied her voice. "She must have faked disappearing. That's probably one type of glamour—disappearing."

"Glamour is illusion. She can probably make herself invisible, and maybe she could even fool my sense of smell, but she vanished to my sorcerous vision, too. I don't think that's possible unless she literally, physically wasn't there anymore."

"Translocation?" That was a mythical ability, one only adepts were supposed to be able to use. "We are so out of our league. If sidhe can do stuff like that, why can't they find the medallion themselves?"

"I don't know."

She caught herself heaving a great, huge, pity-party sigh. But if ever she was entitled to throw one, this would be the time. "I'm going to turn in," she said abruptly and turned to go, her personal mage light obediently tagging along.

He caught her arm. "Cynna—"

"Look, I'm not up to a heart-to-heart tonight. I know better, okay? You're lupus, and I understand what that means. I shouldn't have expected . . . well, anything. I *know* that. It doesn't help."

His voice was tight, frustrated. "She *glammed* me."

"Yeah. But you wouldn't see anything wrong with having sex with her. Only you've got it in your head you need legal standing over the little rider, so you're trying to convince me—"

"I won't be with anyone else. You've my word on it."

"You're not listening to me! I don't want you to squeeze yourself into some other shape. That won't work. It'll make you unhappy and you'll resent it and then we won't be friends any—"

He blurred and she went flying. Flying backward, courtesy of him tossing her through the air. Before she landed, he'd spun back around and sent reality whirling.

Cynna had seen lupi Change. She'd never seen Cullen do it, but she recognized the process. Still, what with landing hard on her ass and watching impossibility take slices out of Cullen's shape and whirl it into something new, it took her a second to see why he'd Changed.

Something—two somethings—were climbing over the rail, silent as ghosts and blacker than the night around them.

"Incoming!" she yelled and shot her mage light higher, slapping it with enough power to make it split into five spots of light.

Slugs. That's what they looked like, though they were man-shaped with the usual arrangement of limbs. They were tall and moist in a way that had nothing to do with the river, and their faces were strictly ugh—lumpy and misshapen, noseless, with no chins below the puckered sphincters that had to be mouths, though they looked more as if someone had gotten confused during assembly and put assholes in their heads instead of their butts.

Cynna took all that in while scrambling to her feet. She had a split second to glimpse some kind of harnesses on their chests before a huge red wolf launched himself at them.

Cullen was unbelievably fast in man-form. He was even faster as a wolf. The slugs were fast, too—just not fast enough. One of them had time to draw a sword from the harness she'd glimpsed. The other didn't. The wolf ripped out its throat.

A wordless shout went up behind her. She turned— and saw a pair of slimy black hands gripping the rail, drawing another slug up—but not yet over the rail.

Her body knew what to do. She turned sideways, drew her right knee up to her chest, and snapped that leg out. Her foot slammed into the thing's head and she felt the impact all the way up.

Slug-man felt the impact even more. With an ear-splitting shriek it fell backward into the river. The splash was drowned out by another yell. Cynna pivoted and saw another slug-man heading for her at an oddly gaited lope, a mean-looking blade in his hand, pursued by one of the guard. The guard—one of the two humans—shouted at her.

Her charm whispered blandly, "Don't touch them. They exude poison."

Now he tells her!

Boots. She was wearing boots, so the poison hadn't

gotten on her skin, but Cullen—"Hey!" she shouted at the guard. "Behind you!" Two more slug-men were racing at the guard's back. He whirled, leaving Tall, Dark, and Slimy free to swing his oversize knife at her.

Cynna skipped back. Couldn't spare a second to see what was happening with Cullen and the other slug—this guy was fast. He lunged, making a weird chittering noise with his misplaced anus, his blade weaving.

Shouts. A shot—Steve must have joined the fray. Her own gun was in her stateroom, but it didn't matter. She'd used up her ammo on the dondredii.

The slug-man lunged, and she hopped back. *Don't look at the blade. Look at the eyes.* That's what she'd been taught, but this guy's eyes were solid black. She couldn't tell where he was looking, couldn't read him at all.

The sword swished through the air where her gut had been. She leaned left just enough—but it had been a feint. The blade came back, and she almost overbalanced, dodging again—and tripped. On his dead buddy's foot.

Cynna went down. Three feet of sharp steel flashed through the space where she'd been. And a wolf went sailing over her and over the sword, twisting in midair to close his jaws around the slug-man's throat, sending out a geyser of blood as the two of them hit the deck.

She landed on her side, one arm pinned, the other searching for a piece of deck not covered by dead slug, slime, or blood to place her hand. Something grabbed that arm, flipped her onto her back. A dark body loomed over her, reaching for her face with one glistening hand. Blood ran from a gaping wound on the thing's arm.

An arrow suddenly appeared in its throat—feathered shaft poking out in front, pointy part sticking out in back. Hot blood speckled Cynna's face. The hand that had been reaching for her fluttered up as if to adjust the fit of the arrow. Cynna scooted back, clearing the way for that body to fall.

It landed across her left calf. She jerked her leg out, panting.

Cullen-wolf stood over the one he'd just dispatched. His fur was heavily spattered with blood. It dripped from his muzzle. His lips were pulled back, baring his teeth, and a deep growl rumbled up from his chest.

There was no one left to kill.

Not all of the lumps Cynna saw on the deck belonged to slug-men. Two guards were down. As she watched, Steve Timms leaped over one of those motionless forms, racing toward her. Tash stood about thirty feet away, a bow in her hand. She was barking out orders that the remaining guard scrambled to obey—*Get leather to protect your hand, fool,* whispered Cynna's charm. *Get those bodies overboard—fetch ash and salt—see what the hell happened to the tritons.*

Cynna wasn't listening. The huge wolf shook his head once, looked right at her, and his tongue lolled out in a doggy grin. Then he collapsed.

TWENTY-TWO

FLOATING . . . thoughts breaking up, shutting down, sliding off into gray . . .

I've got you.

Huh?

". . . don't touch him!"

"Where's the ash, dammit?"

Something splashed.

"Cullen? Oh, God . . . No! You can't have him!" That was Cynna's voice. He knew it, clung to it, through the haze dimming his mind. "Let go, or I'll—"

"Don't touch him." He knew that voice, too . . . Tash. "He's got the poison on him."

"My coat's leather. It will protect me."

Was Cynna touching him? Why couldn't he feel it?

Another splash. Funny. He could hear things going on but couldn't see anything, couldn't feel . . .

A sigh. "You can't help him, girl. He's gone."

"No! He can't be." Cynna again, stubbornness personified.

She was right, though. He wasn't gone. He couldn't move, couldn't see or smell. He had no sense of his body whatsoever. None. He didn't understand what he was, but he wasn't gone.

Tash's voice, very gentle: "His heart isn't beating."

Well, hell. That couldn't be good.

Footsteps, then: "I've got the salt and ash, but you're wasting it, using it on him."

Cullen didn't recognize the speaker, but the man had used the Common Tongue. He noted that with a quiet corner of his mind. The spell was still working even though, technically, he was dead.

Didn't feel dead. Where were the tunnel and the white light?

"Give it to me. Ash neutralizes the poison, right? I need to get it cleaned off—"

"It is too late, Cynna Weaver."

Tash was probably right. He wasn't astral traveling. He'd done that twice, and this was nothing like it. His astral form still saw and touched . . . well, it wasn't the same kind of touching he did with his body, but there was a similar sense. Not this . . . nothingness.

"He'll heal it," Cynna was saying stubbornly. "He can heal it. I just have to get the poison cleaned off."

"Healing doesn't work on poison," Tash said in that gentle voice. "Only with wounds. That's why the obab are so feared. Nothing stops their poison. It's a . . . I don't have your word, but it paralyzes everything. The lungs stop working, the heart stops beating."

"Lupi heal from poison. He can heal this. Dammit, Cullen!" Fury whipped her voice. "You *will* heal, you hear me?"

Doing my best.

Tash again. "It doesn't usually act this quickly. He must have swallowed some."

"I'm so sorry, sweetheart." Who was—oh, Daniel Weaver. "You have to accept that he's gone."

"No, but anyone who tries tipping him into the river will be. Steve, keep them back."

"Got you covered." That was Steve's voice. "No one touches the wolf."

"All right," Tash said, weary. "We'll leave him for last."

"Hail, Mary, full of grace," Cynna whispered. "Our Lord is with you . . ."

Cynna was praying for him? Couldn't hurt. Probably wouldn't help, but it couldn't hurt.

Another splash. Cullen knew what the sound meant now—dead obab being dumped over the rail into the river. Maybe some of their own dead, too. Couldn't be environmentally sound, but he was more concerned with Tash's intention of doing the same with his body. He wasn't finished with it. He just had to figure out how to get connected to it again.

". . . for us sinners now and at the hour of our—our— oh, dammit, Lady! Bring him back! You can't have him! If you're real, if you want me as your priestess or whatever, bring him back!"

At once he was *all* sensation. Pain. A giant had him in his grip and was trying to make lemonade from his chest. His ribs shuddered with the effort to draw in a breath. Alive *hurt*.

"He's breathing! Look, he's breathing!"

Scents flooded Cullen. His other vision came back, too, but dimly. He was about empty. He forced his eyes open . . . oh, yeah. He was still wolf, which meant his vision was black-and-white. And that was Cynna, her face shiny-wet, scrubbing at his fur.

Damn fool woman! She was going to get the poison on her. He drew another breath, found the moon's song, and forced the Change.

And oh, shit, but that *really* hurt. Took way too long, too. Changing always hurt. Changing away from Earth and right after a cardiac arrest . . . well, he'd survived. "Stop," he whispered.

"Stop?" She blinked damp eyes. "Stop what?"

Crying, he nearly said. That would piss her off, knowing he'd seen her crying over him. His lips twitched at the thought.

"Why did you do that?" She was kneeling beside him, her coat gathered carefully around her to keep her from touching any of the slime the assassins had left behind. Good. She wasn't completely stupid. Fear and joy and anger vied for control of her face . . . such an expressive face. Those tattoos she hid behind had never concealed her from him. "Why did you Change? You can't afford to waste your power that way. You need it to heal."

"Got rid of the poison," Cullen pointed out in the whisper that was all he could manage. Whatever was on him—clothing, blood, poison—couldn't follow him through the Change.

"Oh. Right." Her breath shuddered out. "God, but you scared me."

Scared himself, too. His eyes were trying to close. Sleep sounded like a fantastic idea, but first . . . "Steve's here?"

"Yes. He held them off with his gun so they didn't . . . we thought you were dead. Your heart had stopped."

Tell me about it. "Need to tell him something."

Hurt flashed across her face, but she motioned. A moment later Steve's face hovered over him. "Yeah, buddy?"

"They were after Cynna," he whispered. His eyes were trying to close. "Targeted hit."

"Don't worry," Steve said grimly. "I'm on it."

Okay. Good. He'd just rest his eyes for a bit . . .

TWENTY-THREE

A hand stroked the hair back from Kai's face. A warm hand, warm as the body propping her up . . . Nathan. She lay on the ground, her back against his front, her legs curled to one side. She heard one of the horses stamp, a tail swish.

The last time she'd checked in with her body, she'd been standing up.

"Are you all right?" he asked, voice low and worried.

Kai nodded. "That was . . . intense."

She didn't move or speak for a few moments. Nathan didn't, either. He must have had questions, plenty of them, but he was more patient than she was. Once assured she was back and okay, he relaxed, content to wait until she felt ready to talk.

"That's the longest I ever stayed in fugue," she said finally. "Not counting when I was little and got trapped there. This wasn't the same. I knew I could get out."

"What happened?" he asked softly. "Your warning worked. I could see that much."

She and Nathan had been ready to turn in. She was getting used to sleeping rough, though she had wistful thoughts of mattresses most nights. Their sleeping bags were excellent quality, but the ground did not remind her much of a bed.

Something had alerted him, some sound or stray scent—he hadn't been sure what. He'd gone to the river's edge to stare out at the barge.

They'd gotten slightly ahead of it before stopping, knowing the barge would pull well ahead while they slept. Couldn't be helped, and they hoped to make up the time tomorrow. The river bent around some low, rocky hills up ahead; they'd be able to go straight and meet it around the bend. So the barge had still been upriver of them, but not by much.

He'd seen or sensed the assassins. So had Kai—but her seeing wasn't like his. Or anyone else's. She'd seen the shapes and colors of their thoughts. She was, she reflected, becoming too familiar with the way the intent to kill shaped thoughts.

She'd told Nathan she was going to warn the people on the barge, and she'd fugued.

And now she didn't want to tell him what she'd done. He hadn't freaked over her other abilities, but this . . . "I guess I'm freaked by myself. I did something I could have sworn wasn't possible."

He waited. Nathan wasn't one to use words unnecessarily.

"Those—what did you call them? Obab? They went for the woman. You were right about the sorcerer. He's a lupus. I guess you saw that?" She hadn't exactly seen it happen. Unlike Nathan, she didn't have super-duper night vision, and the glow from a single mage light at a distance wasn't enough for her to make out much. But she'd seen his thoughts change.

"They killed him," she said flatly. "Or as good as. I've seen animals die. I saw the dondredii die a few days ago. I know what it looks like—the way the thought bodies start to fade, to break up . . . I hated it! I couldn't just let him die, could I?"

Nathan was startled. "You had a choice?"

"He's lupus, so I thought . . . it seemed that if I could hold his thoughts together, keep him *there* a little longer, his magic would finish healing him." Now she twisted to look at him. "I didn't do it by myself."

"You asked me for power. I gave it to you."

That's what she'd thought—though she hadn't asked out loud. Her own well had emptied too quickly, before the lupus's body had finished purging itself of the poison.

She'd been deeply in fugue. She'd touched Nathan's thoughts with one of hers—just a touch, nothing that would stay trapped in his thoughts and confuse or influence him. She'd asked, yes. And power had flooded into her.

Kai chewed on her lip. "You didn't know what I was doing. Shit, I didn't know what I was doing. I could have hurt you, taken too much—"

"I will always give you power if you ask. You wouldn't ask for evil reasons. For unwise ones, perhaps, but not evil."

"It was a lot of power."

Nathan smiled, the glint in his eyes pure amusement. Sometimes his sense of humor escaped her. "I have a lot of power, Kai. Better that you asked me than Dell. Her magic is strong, but shaped for her own use. And she doesn't replenish it as readily as I do mine."

It hadn't even occurred to her that she could draw from Dell. "I have so much to learn!"

"You are learning." He paused. "I'm glad the sorcerer lives. I think they may need him."

"You still think . . ."

"Oh, yes." He was certain as only one of his kind could be. "They are the ones my queen spoke of. They will find the medallion. Then, if necessary, we will take it from them."

TWENTY-FOUR

THE staterooms straddled the middle of the barge, with four on one side of the hall, three and a bathroom on the other side. Cynna followed the two guards who were carrying Cullen to her stateroom. She was chilly. Her coat and boots, contaminated by poison, were still on the deck. Her father had offered to scrub them with the salt and ash that neutralized the poison. He'd been upset, asking her over and over if she was okay, and seemed glad to have something to do to help.

One of the guard would show him how after their ceremony. They weren't as callous as it had seemed when they tipped their dead into the river. Not sentimental about bodies, obviously, but they mourned their dead.

Gan was right behind her. "I don't know why Tash is so mad. I checked out the tritons, didn't I? Even though it's very dangerous in the river, I did it."

After Tash threw her in. "You were brave. Did you catch any fishies while you were there?"

"Only one. And the tritons were dead, like I figured, so what was the point?"

The slug-men—obab, they were called—had taken out

the tritons first. No one was sure how they'd pulled that off. Tritons meshed minds with their mounts, but were also able to sense life directly, making them hard to sneak up on. Somehow the obab had managed it, leaving the barge tethered to riderless sea oxen.

Cynna supposed they were lucky the obab hadn't killed the sea oxen, too. Huey—turned out he was the barge's captain—had sent one of the two remaining tritons to ride the sea ox in turn, keeping them calm while the barge was at anchor.

"The point," Cynna said, "was that the tritons' bodies had to be released from their harnesses. You're immune to the poison since you're not fully converted, so—"

"That's what they say." Gan glowered. "But they can lie."

"You think the gnomes lied about your immunity? You're not dead, so—hey, careful!" she snapped at the two guard, neither human, who were maneuvering Cullen's stretcher through the narrow doorway. They'd nearly spilled him.

"Okay, they were right about the poison, but they could lie if they wanted to. Bilbo doesn't like me. He wouldn't care if I got killed."

Cynna didn't know what had Gan's tail in a twist. At the moment she'd didn't much care. She followed the guard with their sleeping burden into the tiny stateroom. Instead of a bed it had a padded, wraparound sofa-bench like the ones back at the Chancellery. Two sides were long enough for a human; the two guard deposited Cullen on one of them. She had to sit on the other side to give them room to clear out with the stretcher.

Sitting was okay. Her knees kept trying to knock together anyway.

Gan had followed her inside and was watching, her mismatched little face all broody. Cynna sighed. "Look, it's late. I nearly got killed and Cullen did die for a while. Can we talk about whatever is bothering you in the morning?"

"No morning here."

She grabbed for patience. "When we wake up."

"I guess." But she didn't leave. She looked at Cullen, then at Cynna. "You're all upset about Cullen Seabourne. I don't know why. He didn't stay dead."

"It's a human thing."

"Do humans always get weird about the people they fuck?"

Cynna swallowed a hysterical giggle. "Sometimes yes, sometimes no. We worry about our friends when they're hurt."

"I don't have any friends. Well, except for Lily Yu. She cares if I get killed or not, but she isn't here."

That punched Cynna right in the gut. *Don't anthropomorphize,* she warned herself. Maybe Gan wasn't quite a demon anymore, but she had been very recently. She probably wasn't capable of feeling lonely. She probably confused "ally" with "friend"—she wanted people on her side to increase her odds of surviving. Not because she felt adrift, cut off, alone in a strange place.

Logic did no good. She couldn't help it. Cynna got down on one knee and looked square into the absurdly large, pretty eyes set in that ugly orange face. At the moment those eyes were narrowed in a suspicious frown. " 'Friend' is a big word for me. It holds a lot of meaning. A lot of trust. You and I are maybe on the way to being friends. I don't know that we're there yet, but I would not like it if you were killed."

"Sure, because I can cross and you might need me."

Cynna shook her head. "Even if you couldn't cross, I would be sad if you died."

"Maybe you're lying."

"I'm not, but that's where the trust thing comes in. That's why people don't become friends all in one gulp. It takes a while to know if we can trust each other."

The scowl tightened a notch. "Would you be as sad about me as you would be if Cullen Seabourne had stayed dead?"

"No. But sad."

Gan stared at her a moment longer, then heaved a great sigh and ambled out the door, muttering, "This is confusing. This is really confusing."

Cynna followed to close the door behind her. Gan did not close doors.

"You got a license to practice demon therapy?" Cullen said.

"You're awake." She turned, a smile breaking out. "How do you feel?"

"Like a used lemon. Did you retrieve my diamonds?"

She nodded, suddenly swamped by an odd feeling that kept her silent. She couldn't think of anything to say . . . or maybe there was too much that she didn't want to say. Or even think. She felt . . . shy?

Cynna hadn't felt shy since the fourth grade, and she didn't want to handle it now the way she had then. Maria never had forgiven her for the bloody nose.

"C'mere." Cullen patted the crescent of space on the bench beside him as if her butt could fit there.

Her feet decided it was a good idea and carried her to him. Since she couldn't fit beside him, she sank to the floor. He raised his arm to make room, and she settled down with relief, her head on his chest, his arm looped loosely over her shoulders. He toyed with her hair.

This was enough. Right now, this was enough. He'd lived, and he was with her, touching her, wanting to hold her. She had plenty to think about, but for now she just wanted this. Her eyes drifted closed.

Maybe it was enough for him, too, because for long moments he didn't speak. Cynna would have thought he'd gone back to sleep if not for those warm fingers sifting her hair. Finally he murmured, "I heard pretty much everything. I was more or less dead, so I don't know why I could hear, but I could. You wouldn't let them dump me overboard."

Her throat closed up. After a moment she managed to say, "See? Denial isn't always a bad thing."

Cullen tugged at one strand of hair. "God knows I don't want to encourage you, but your denial worked out well for me this time."

"You're going to be okay, right? You can heal whatever the poison did to you?"

"Already healed that, or I wouldn't have woken up. Got some heart damage now, but—"

She squeaked.

He tugged her hair again. "That's what happens when oxygen flows back into heart cells when they've done without for too long . . . five minutes, according to recent studies. It looks as if the cellular surveillance system can't tell the difference between cancer cells and cells being reperfused with oxygen, so the mitochondria trigger apoptosis—"

"TMI, Cullen."

"I'll heal the damage in a couple days. What I don't understand is why my heart started beating again after it quit."

"I was doing chest compressions."

"You were praying."

"Well, yeah. But I was doing chest compressions, too. Got to give God something to work with."

"It was the Lady you called on at the end."

She remembered. *Bring him back.* "Your Lady doesn't do the miracle gig—or so you keep telling me."

"No, I keep telling you she isn't in the god business. She does sometimes respond to requests from a Rhej. Not often, but sometimes."

"I'm not a Rhej. I'm not even apprenticed to a Rhej."

"Take it up with the Lady. She seems to think you're hers." His voice was drowsy, fading.

"It was the chest compressions that did it." And maybe the Lady. Maybe Cynna wasn't hers, but Cullen was.

"Sure."

She needed to let him sleep. Needed some sleep herself, and God knew she was tired enough. But she didn't want to move.

Didn't want to think, either, but all the talk had kicked her brain into gear again, and it was presenting her with some facts. When she'd thought he was dying . . . dying, hell. He'd been clinically dead. There hadn't been room inside her for more than one big denial, and she'd spent it all on disbelieving in his death.

Cynna couldn't tell herself reassuring lies anymore. He mattered. He mattered all the way down, reaching places inside her no one had ever touched. Not even Rule. She was going to have to find a way to get over her notions about fidelity, because she wasn't getting over him.

Outside, a low chanting began. *"You who know Mershwin,"* Cynna's charm whispered. *"You who know our fallen comrade, gather him close . . ."*

"What's that?" Cullen said.

She pulled the translator charm out, letting it lie outside her sweater. The whispery voice ceased. Somehow it felt intrusive or rude or something to eavesdrop. "Funerals. In addition to the tritons, two of the guard were killed." She sighed. "We'd better get some sleep."

"Cynna." He curled his fingers around her arm. "When you tried to kick Theera's ass—or whatever you were aiming at . . ." His grin made a brief, weary appearance. "I didn't block you because of the glamour, or because I didn't want you to punch her out. I didn't want her punching back. Sidhe can punch pretty hard."

His words settled into her gradually the way a dog circles a spot before curling up to sleep. Her smile rose from that settled-in place. "Okay. Good." She hesitated a second, then did what she wanted to do, and kissed him lightly before repeating, "Get some sleep."

"I'd sleep better with you beside me."

So would she, Cynna realized. And was almost too tired to find that scary. "You see a full-size bed here?"

"Move the cushions to the floor."

She thought about that, or tried to. But her brain had turned to mush, and if he wanted to feel her close while he slept, why not? She hated the skinny little benches, anyway.

A few minutes later the cushions were lined up on the floor and Cynna was settling onto them. Cullen was already stretched out. With a flick of her hand and a murmured word she shut off the lights. The darkness was full and cozy, like a blanket in winter.

His breathing was even and soft, but he wasn't asleep. When she lay down, he lifted his arm and snuggled her close. *Fantasy number three,* she thought, her eyes closing. She used to fantasize about sleeping with someone all the time . . . not about the sex, but the sleeping-with. She'd picked up guys a few times back in her young and stupid days because she didn't want to sleep alone.

Fantasy played better than reality. Reality was having a stranger's elbow poke you when he rolled over. Reality was cover hogs, feeling crowded, and morning breath. A man she scarcely knew who wanted her to *talk* first thing in the morning, for God's sake. Reality was that she could feel even more alone when she wasn't technically alone.

Reality tonight was Cullen. Who'd died protecting her. No heartbeat, not breathing . . . that equaled dead, however temporary the condition turned out to be.

Protecting the baby-to-be, she reminded herself . . . but the reminder felt hollow. Did she really believe he would have stood back and let the slug-men kill her if she weren't pregnant?

He smelled familiar and welcome. He felt warm and living and *necessary,* which made her eyes burn.

All right, Lady, she told the one she knew existed, however much her existence complicated Cynna's life. *You brought him back. Now what?*

Though she listened as long as she was able, all she heard was the quiet sound of his breath, the gentle lap of water against the hull, and the soft chanting in a language she didn't know. It was soothing, somehow, that chanting.

She fell asleep, still listening.

TWENTY-FIVE

MAGE lights clustered thickly over the table, making breakfast as cheery as possible with no sun. It was a long, low table; the gnomes sat on low benches, but everyone else was on cushions. And everyone except Gan—who was apparently still asleep—was present for the meal.

No one was smiling much.

The barge was still anchored. Water lapped gently against its sides as it swayed in the river's current like a man in a hammock on a lazy summer day. Nothing else was summery. The air was cold and misty. It smelled of the river, smoke from the braziers the gnomes had brought out, and the yeasty scent of fresh-baked bread.

Turned out that Third Assistant of the Red Jasper Collar meant baker of the magical sort. "Collar" referred to a ring of red jasper stones used in lieu of an oven. Cynna had just finished eating two thick, warm slices of magically baked bread slathered with some kind of jam or marmalade.

She sipped at her tea, which she hadn't finished. She would, though. It was specifically for pregnant women—supposed to keep her from getting morning sickness, which so far she'd avoided without any tea. But nausea was one of her least favorite things, so she'd rather not take any chances. If she wasn't crazy about the tea's vaguely floral taste, well, it wasn't bad.

Lily would have hated it here. No coffee.

She missed Lily. She missed cars, too, and cell phones and NPR and Pop Tarts. And sunshine. She'd only been here a few days—no, not days. Sleeps. And she missed the sun something fierce.

How many sleeps? Suddenly anxious, as if losing track of that number meant losing something more nebulous and vastly more important, Cynna counted. "Has it been only six days?" she murmured.

"Sounds right." Cullen sat on the cushion next to hers. He was able walk this morning . . . slowly. "If you're talking about our sojourn here."

"I am." Cynna glanced at him. He'd broken his fast with smoked fish—three large smoked fish. Lupi were big on protein and needed even more when they were healing. "Does it smell good to you here?"

His sideways glance held surprise. He smiled. "It does. I prefer ocean, but the Ka has a rich bouquet. Much more pleasant than concrete and exhaust fumes."

Her eyebrows shot up. "You like Edge."

"In many ways, yes. I'm not crazy about the growing tendency of various groups to try to kill us, but the air is clean, the land and water smell healthy, and there's an abundance of magic."

Daniel Weaver spoke from across the table. "It took me a while to get used to the seasons here, and of course I spent the first year trying frantically to get back, or at least send a message . . . but your friend is right. There's much to love about Edge."

Daniel Weaver. Her father. Cynna wasn't used to that word having such an immediate and concrete meaning . . . "Will you stay here?" she asked. "If everything goes well and they get a gate opened to Earth, will you go back, or will you stay here?"

"I'd thought . . ." He looked down, fiddling with the knife he'd used to spread his jam. "But my Mary is gone where gates can't take me. I've built a life here, and not such a bad life. I'm guessing Chicago is very different from the city I left, eh?"

She nodded. "Computers, cell phones, TiVo . . . a lot has changed all over. In Chicago—well, Soldier Field looks like the Jetsons landed and smushed a steel top hat on the old building. And Millennium Park—you should see that. It's pretty cool. Everyone likes the Bean. But not everything has changed. There's still a mayor named Daley, and Cubs fans are still hoping."

Daniel let out a quick laugh. "Hoping? You mean in nearly thirty years they haven't managed to—"

"Hey!" Gan cried indignantly, hands on what might have been her hips, though given her lack of a waistline it was hard to say. "Aren't there any fishies left? Did everyone eat all of the fishies?"

"Sit down," Steve Timms said firmly. "You can have what's left of my fish, but next time come when you're called instead of throwing a pillow at me."

Cynna grinned. Steve had come a long way from wanting to shoot everything that wasn't human.

"Peoples." Bilbo tapped on his glass like a dinner speaker getting the attention of club members. "We is finished eating and is needing to talk."

Cynna exchanged a look with Cullen. Bilbo was right. It was time. But the discussion might not go the way the gnome thought it would. She and Cullen had had their own little talk before leaving the cabin. "We'll talk," Cynna said. "I'll start."

Bilbo shot her a frown. "I first. We have sending for tritons to compel barge onward. Soon tritons to be arriving, but—"

"But first I have to decide if I will go onward with the barge."

"Decide?" Bilbo slapped his hand on the table. "What is this deciding to make? We is all knowings that must proceed, or all die. My world it is in danger, yes, but you is in this world. All must go onward! Is only way!"

"I don't go on until I have some questions answered," Cynna said calmly. "We'll start with the question of betrayal. There's a leak somewhere, and I'm thinking it has to be someone on this ship."

Instead of anger or denial, she got confusion. The gnomes exchanged puzzled glances. Tash frowned. "You think we are leaking? Not a leak in the barge, but in the passengers?"

The charm and the learn-language spell must not cover every possible usage. "Leaking information. The slugs with assholes on their faces found us within a day of our leaving the City. They came straight for me. They—or whoever sent them—knew too much."

"Is troubling, yes," Bilbo said. "But is many spells could track somethings as big and well known as chancellor's barge."

"Yeah? Well, that makes the decision to travel on this barge pretty odd, doesn't it?" She looked around the table. "Unless you wanted me out here, grabbing the attention of every faction who wants to keep you from finding your missing medallion."

"Is not making sense for us to—"

"It would explain a lot," Cynna said, raising her voice to speak over him. "I keep wondering why you had to import a Finder. Why even the sidhe can't seem to locate it. You don't really expect me to Find it, do you? You just want me out here trying, drawing all the hostile attention."

Bilbo's frown was so fierce she wanted to warn him about his face freezing that way. "Why you is saying sidhe can't find it?"

"Any people who can perform a translocation spell flawlessly on an instant's notice could find a missing object."

"Who? Who is doing . . . Theera! She is translocating? When!"

The word came out as a demand, not a question. Cynna looked at Cullen. They'd been undecided earlier about whether to reveal Theera's approach to him. He gave the tiniest movement of his head—not a shake, but a negative. "I'm not answering questions now," she said. "You are. Tell me why you're upset about Theera translocating."

Bilbo didn't like it, but after a moment he shrugged. "We is thinking Theera is not knowing when we planning to leave City. If she translocated back to Rohen, is meaning she knows we about to leave and no reason for her staying in City."

"What's Rohen?"

"Theera's liege is being her half sister, she who is called Theil Ná Rohen. Rohen is being Theil's estate, her land, you understanding? All sidhe who is ruling is having tie to land. Theera is no mage—she is not casting translocation spell. Theil is mage, but not of degree to cast such spell, either. But Theil's lord—who is *true* lord of Faerie, as he is having land in Second Realm—is very skilled mage. He makes charm device, gifts it to Theil for using to return to Rohen. Theil is letting Theera using charm. Only goes one place—Theil's home in Rohen."

Untangling Bilbo's syntax was giving Cynna a headache. "So Theera's sister has this device and loaned it to her. It's the device, not her own ability, that lets her translocate?" When Bilbo nodded she continued, "But it still takes tremendous power. Translocation is like opening a gate within a realm."

"Theil is having much power. She is tied to her land in sidhe way, so has much power to drawing on. Theera not having such power, but her half sister is letting her use device, so is using Theil's power, not own."

Maybe the sidhe here weren't as powerful as she'd feared. Still . . . "But they—the sidhe—are kick-ass spellcasters. Why can't they find it? Or do you think they already have?"

Glances were exchanged—this time among Bilbo,

Tash, and Wen. Tash spoke. "The sidhe do not often act together. There are four major sidhe estates in Edge—Rohen, Gabotá, Leerahan, and Fa Nioth. They are sometimes friendly, always rivals. We think it possible that one of the estate lords has the medallion. If so—if it has reached that lord's land—neither the gnomes nor the other sidhe would be able to find it magically."

"And yet I'm supposed to."

Gan snickered. "That's your Gift, right?"

"Why is that funny?"

"It is!" Gan insisted, as if she'd argued with her. "Don't they all think humans are no-sums? Plain old worthless, huh? Now they have to admit they were wrong." She grinned at Bilbo—always an interesting sight, since she'd kept the pointy teeth of her demonhood. "Wrong, wrong, wrong. You were wrong."

There must be some powerful taboo against killing not-quite demons, Cynna reflected. Or Gan would be dead right now, judging by the look on Bilbo's face.

"Why not admit it, Councilor?' Daniel Weaver said suddenly. "After years of suppressing us, treating us like the bastard stepchildren you think we should be, you've had to admit a human can do what you can't. What the sidhe can't do." He looked at Cynna. Real anger—old anger—stirred in his eyes and tightened his mouth. "It's the nature of a Gift, sweetheart. It takes an adept to duplicate through a spell what a lupus does naturally—change his form. It takes an adept to duplicate what any of the Blood do naturally through their innate magic."

For a second Cynna was so preoccupied with the casual way he'd called her "sweetheart" that she didn't catch up with his words. "But humans aren't of the Blood."

Gan snorted. "You are so stupid. All of you. At first I thought maybe you knew what you were talking about, but you don't. There's no difference."

Cullen had quit slouching. "Human magic doesn't look the same," he said slowly.

"So? I guess demon magic looks different from lupus magic, too, doesn't it?"

Cullen nodded. His face was closed down, revealing nothing.

"What does 'of the Blood' mean?" Gan said. "Means you have inborn magic. That's what a Gift is. Inborn magic."

Cynna was trying to think of why that was wrong. It had to be wrong, didn't it? Everyone knew humans were not of the Blood. Everyone. Witches, shamans, lupi all agreed on that. Could everyone be wrong about something so basic?

Being of the Blood meant being born with magic, innate magical abilities that you just *did*, no need for a spell.

Being Gifted meant the same thing.

Cullen leaned forward, quiet and intense. "Most humans can't do magic. Are you claiming that Gifted humans have nonhuman blood?"

"Don't know and don't care." Gan stood up. "I want to go swim."

"Wait until someone can go in with you," Cynna said automatically.

"He could." Gan pointed at Cullen.

"No, he can't. He hasn't finished healing the damage from yesterday."

Gan sighed. "Boats are boring if I can't swim."

"Bored is okay. Bored means no one's trying to kill us today." Of course, the "day" had just begun. Cynna looked at Bilbo. "What will you do if the medallion is on sidhe land? Attack them?"

"No!" Bilbo looked genuinely horrified. "Is no attacking. Is political matter. Sidhe politics very complex, but Harazeed is knowing how to bargain. We is making known who has medallion, and if no true holder yet, others is making sidhe land-liege return to us."

"Others?"

"Other sidhe. Is complex. You is wanting lessons in

sidhe politics? Is having year or two for basic lessons in such?"

Sarcasm, used to distract her. "And if there is a true holder?"

"Is no holder yet. We is of Edge. Is knowing if medallion has formed bond with holder."

Bilbo hadn't exactly answered her question. Cynna looked at Cullen. They'd argued over which of them should play leader. He insisted it had to be her—she had the pull because of her Gift. Right now she wished she had a mindspeech Gift. She settled for arching an eyebrow at him.

Cullen shrugged. "Some truth, probably mixed with misdirection and leaving plenty out. Your decision."

Cynna didn't want to make the decisions. She wanted Ruben here. She wanted sunshine, hot chocolate, and a full-size bed—make that a queen-size bed. And for Cullen to be fully healed so they could put it to good use.

She wanted all sorts of thing she didn't have. She settled for taking a deep breath and letting it out slowly. "Okay. For now, I agree to keep up the hunt as soon as the tritons get here. But I want to talk about *how* we continue. Is it better to get more of the guard here? Should we leave the barge?"

Cullen looked at her, his blue eyes steady. "You're forgeting one question."

Her jaw tightened. She hadn't forgotten. Denial, much as she loved it, went only so far. She gestured at him to get it said. Asked. Whatever.

"Mr. Weaver," Cullen said, "why are you here?"

Her father's eyebrows shot up. "Why, to be with my daughter."

Cullen shook his head. "That might be your reason. But you aren't in charge, are you? Why have the councilors allowed you to come with us? Why do you even know that the medallion is missing? Every other human we've met has been a servant, a laborer, at best a small merchant. None have any authority."

Daniel's face reddened, but it was Bilbo who answered. "Daniel Weaver is bringing inventions to us, innovations from industry of his realm. We is profiting from them, so he is making deal, becomes adviser to chancellor. Cannot hide death of chancellor from his advisers. They notice," he finished with heavy sarcasm, "if they speaking with dead man."

"Bullshit," Cullen said.

Abruptly Daniel shoved to his feet. "They aren't idiots, Councilor." He looked at Cullen. "I know about the medallion because I found the chancellor's body, not because they trust me overly much. I'm on this barge because I am Cynna's father—which matters to me in one way and matters to them for quite a different reason. I suspect you've guessed why fatherhood bought me a ticket for this trip."

"You're supposed to persuade her to cooperate," Cullen said coolly. "If that doesn't work, you'll make a dandy hostage."

"No," Bilbo said sharply. "Daniel Weaver, you is telling him—"

"With all due respect, Councilor—shut up." Daniel looked at Cynna then. His eyes were hard and strange—not the warm whiskey color she was used to, but a brittle amber. "Don't let them use me against you. Don't let me do it, either." And he stalked off.

TWENTY-SIX

Two Sleeps Later...

CULLEN'S eyes shifted over those assembled to drive him out. Thirteen. Only thirteen proud Etorri had taken the trouble of coming together to rid themselves of the dangerous contamination in their clan.

Such a small clan, and so proud, so honored by the other clans. Such great du. They couldn't have their honor damaged, could they? If he wouldn't break himself to suit their notion of honor, they'd do it for him.

Thirteen present... but not his father. Surely he'll come. He's late, but he'll be here. Even if he doesn't understand, can't speak for me before the clan the way a father ought to, he didn't mean what he said. He won't leave me to face this alone...

Thirteen men... and one woman. Old, bent, her eyes filmed with cataracts, the Etorri Rhej spoke. "Cullen Seabourne, step forward."

It was happening. It was happening now, and his father wasn't coming. He'd meant it. He'd said Cullen would be dead to him if he refused the Rho's order, and he'd meant it.

Cullen held himself rigid and stared at the old woman, who seemed to think he'd cooperate politely. His throat burned. His eyes burned. "I'm right here and you're only half-blind. Surely you can see me?"

"Step forward," the Rhej repeated.

He shrugged. "No."

The man on his left was built much like him, with elegant hands and a neatly trimmed beard. His voice was much deeper than his appearance suggested, baritone heading for bass. "Don't make this harder on everyone than it has to be, son."

Son? Heat prickled over him like lightning waiting to strike. And he could have struck. He could burn them all—which was why they were so eager to be rid of him, wasn't it? "You're my Rho," he said to the man who was also his uncle. "For another few minutes, anyway, you're my Rho. You are not my father. I'm told . . ." He had to stop and swallow, which messed up his delivery. "I have it on good authority that I don't have a father."

"This doesn't have to happen. You can still renounce sorcery, remain—"

"I could renounce the Change, too, no doubt." He'd told them that, over and over. They didn't hear, couldn't understand, that the one was as much part of him as the other. No more essential than breathing, either one of them.

"No." The old woman's voice was sharp. "He cannot. Blame me, Cullen Seabourne, if you must blame. I have Seen that you are not to remain. Your Rho has hoped to change my seeing by persuading you to renounce what cannot be put aside. He meant well, but he offers false hope. You were born Etorri, but your fate does not lie with Etorri."

She'd been right. The old bat had been right. His fate lay with Nokolai, not Etorri.

With that thought came the knowledge that he was dreaming—same tired old dream, one his subconscious ought to have grown weary of playing with years ago. But

that knowledge was enough to shift the dream, not end
it . . .

*He was on the ground now, held down by strong hands
on his feet, his knees, his arms. Mist swirled over him and
them—they'd lost their faces to that mist, but the Rho's
voice was clear and certain: "I call* seco *on Cullen
Seabourne, born Etorri."*

"Let me go, fool!" cried a woman, unseen in the mist.

*Ah, yes—things were happening a bit out of order, but
that would be his mother, who'd shown up to berate the
Rho, the Rhej, the whole clan, bless her. Not that they had
let her attend the* seco *itself, but she'd tried. Cullen
braced himself for the next part—*

"Or I'll shoot every sorry-ass one of you."

*That was not in the script. Cullen turned his head as
the mists cleared, and saw Cynna standing a few feet
away with her legs wide, her .357 gripped in one hand
and braced by the other in proper FBI shoot-'em-up fashion. She was extremely pissed. "Maybe I'll shoot you all
anyway," she growled. "Bunch of damn idiots—let him
up this second."*

*He smelled Cynna, smelled the spicy musk of her. She
was aroused. And so was he.*

Cullen woke with his heart pounding, his skin damp
with fear-sweat, and the smallest of smiles on his lips.
The air was filled with the scent of Cynna curled up behind him, spoon-fashion . . . and her hand was on his
cock.

His breath hissed out as she stroked slowly up, the tip
of her finger stroking over the glans. Lust swirled through
him, hotter and so much cleaner than the mist in his
dream. "Cynna . . ."

"Shh," she said. "Go on back to sleep. Don't mind me."

He had to smile. She meant to turn the tables on him,
did she? And God knew he wanted to, wanted to sink inside her, ride her hard. But . . . "I can't."

"Um . . . you sure? Because evidence has come to
light . . ." Another slow stroke, this one ending at his

scrotum, where she scratched lightly. "That suggests you can."

Cullen closed his eyes. Her touch was sweet, the temptation clear and lovely . . . but he couldn't look at her. He couldn't. He held very still.

After a moment her hand retreated. "You worried about your heart?"

"Yes," he said, glad for the excuse. "I think it's healed, but better safe than sorry."

Cynna made a low sound, maybe skeptical. But she didn't push him, and for that, too, he was grateful.

Cullen lay awake far too long after that, sifting the shades of darkness in the tiny cabin with eyes uninterested in closing and a body disgusted with him for turning her down. Finally sleep began dragging at him once more.

That's just what she would have done, he thought as he drifted closer to the other darkness, the one that birthed dreams. If Cynna had known him back then, she'd have shown up, ready to kick ass. She wouldn't have let him face it alone.

HORSES were not Cynna's idea of fun. Riding one for hours in a drizzle kept her frownie face glued on. Once the medallion's trail left the river, though, horses became inevitable. Or so everyone told her.

"My ass is never going to forgive me," she muttered, shifting position for the thousandth time.

Cullen grinned. "Maybe they'll have some liniment in the village. I'll be happy to rub it in for you."

They were all keeping their mage lights near the ground so the horses could see where they were going. Cullen's pair of lights hovered near his horse's knees, and the underlighting made him look like a beautiful devil.

God only knew what she looked like . . . and she hoped He'd keep that info to Himself.

Cullen seemed entirely at home atop a horse, which

annoyed her no end. When they bought their mounts at the port where they left the barge, he'd expected to have trouble finding a horse that would accept him, since they mostly didn't like the scent of lupi. But horses here were used to odd-smelling riders, and his gelding had turned out to be a cheap date. A couple carrots and Cullen was its new best friend.

Cynna slid him an appraising look. After the way he turned her down last night, she ought to be pissed or hurt or both. Somehow she wasn't.

He met her eyes, wearing his bland face. Bland on Cullen looked about as convincing as a peacock pretending to be a sparrow. "Sure your heart's up to all that rubbing?"

"Did you say something about liniment?" Steve steered his horse closer. "Man, I'd kill for something that took the ache out."

If anyone was having more trouble with the horseback bit than Cynna, it was Steve. Not because he'd never ridden. Unlike her, he'd grown up in the country and had tootled around on a horse sometimes as a kid. But that was years ago, and he'd come off the injured list recently. Major injuries, too. Cynna at least had strong legs and a fit body . . . though curving those legs around a horse's barrel for hours at a time was teaching her about muscles she'd never known existed.

"Better save your ammo," Cullen advised him. "The way things are going, you'll need it."

The two of them fell to talking about the area they were riding through. Cynna's aching butt to the contrary, they weren't that far from the river—maybe twenty miles—in low, rolling hills dotted with trees. There was a road, fortunately. Dirt, like most roads here, but traveled enough to be maintained.

Ahead, though, were mountains. Not terribly high mountains, but they loomed large to Cynna. They were in Ahk territory.

The trail headed right up into them.

Bilbo was all in a lather about that. At first he'd said

they would wait for more of the guard to arrive. Then
he'd decided it would be worse to enter their land with
a lot of soldiers. They'd wait until they got permission.
Only problem was that, according to Tash, the Ahk didn't
get the whole notion of visitors, so permission might be a
long time coming. If you were on their land, you were either Ahk or a trespasser. They weren't kind to trespassers.

He was nattering away at Wen again, holding one of
those weird, relayed conversations with one of the other
councilors back in the City via two or three Ekiba. The
two of them looked pretty funny—the little gnome on a
baby-size pony trotting along beside the big, bald, nearly
naked Ekiba on his full-size horse.

"I'll check," Steve told Cullen, and bravely poked at
his horse's sides with his heels. The animal went into a
fast trot.

Cynna's horse had trotted a couple times. She did not
approve of trotting. "Check what?" she asked Cullen.

"Tash's scout is back, and Steve is fidgety. He's going
to see if that village we're aiming for is close."

"Please, God," she said fervently. "I think the drizzle
is working its way up to becoming real rain."

"In Ireland they'd call this soft weather. When it isn't
raining hard, you see, it's soft."

"You been to Ireland?"

"A few times. Mum had a cousin who married an Irish
lass. What they say about the incredible green of the land
is true."

"How about what they say about leprechauns?"

"Ah, now, that's another story." And he proceeded to
tell one, probably 90 percent fiction but entertaining.

Cullen didn't speak, act, or look like a man troubled
by nightmares or some hidden trauma. But last night . . .

Maybe she was imagining things. Cullen was a prime
manipulator. Maybe turning down sex was part of some
grand scheme to get her so hot and bothered she'd agree
to marry him temporarily so he'd have rights to his child.
She might have imagined the flatness in his voice last

night. Even if she were right about that, she might have read all the wrong things into it—that he was shook, bad shook, and needed time to pull himself together.

But she'd hadn't imagined the feel of his skin—clammy and cool, as if he were sliding into shock. Could a nightmare do that? Manifest so strongly the body reacted as if it were badly injured?

Nor had she imagined the tremors, if that was the right word . . . nothing as obvious as trembling, but before she woke him, he'd been vibrating like a tuning fork. She was pretty sure those tremors were what had woken her. When they hadn't woken him, she'd decided to do that herself.

So, yeah, her guesses might be all wrong. Guesses often were. But this time she didn't think so. She knew how sometimes the only way you make things okay is by pretending with everything in you that they were. Last night he'd needed her to pretend with him. He'd needed that more than sex.

But a wish ached deep inside her that he could have told her. Could have let her step into the pain with him and know what it was about.

THE village parked perilously near the mountains was called Shuva. According to Tash, Shuva existed because of its market. The Ahk were not farmers, so they traded for produce at the market here and in similar small villages near their territory.

Shuva was small, the stone cottages tiny. Many of the roofs gleamed darkly in the damp—slate tiles, Cynna thought. Some were thatched, their hats dull and dark in the damp night. They rode past some larger buildings, too—a school, a store, and what seemed to be a church or temple. No voices came from inside the last one, but light flickered in the windows, and as they rode by she heard music—the wild lilt of fiddles chasing some song to its end.

She glanced at Cullen. His head was cocked and his

face had fallen into an absent smile, the sort that means you don't know you're smiling. Lupi loved violins.

The light was thin here, not like the City. More candles and firelight, fewer mage lights. How did people endure three months of darkness?

Up ahead a tall man strode along beside Bilbo's horse. He was human, or looked it, with a bushy beard and long, dark hair pulled back in a rough tail. His features were Anglo; his skin, weathered in the way of a man who's spent much of his time outdoors. He had a Cossack look going— dark, heavy tunic with an embroidered band around the neck; furry vest; loose trousers tucked into workman's boots.

He was the sheriff. Sort of. One of the gaggle of children who'd met them at the fringes of the village had said, "Michael's gone to get the sheriff to meet your honors." At least, that's what Cynna thought he'd said, via the charm, but his words had gotten mixed up with the other kids shushing him, then insisting that Derreck wasn't a *real* sheriff. They just called him that sometimes.

The kids had followed them at first, but mothers and fathers had called them inside. Not many were out at this hour. It was probably about eight bells, which meant most people had eaten supper and were tucked up warm at home. Everyone she'd seen so far looked human.

"I thought humans stayed in the City," Cynna said to Cullen, who rode beside her. "At least . . . do they smell human to you?"

"Oh, yeah. They look human to my other vision, too." He widened his eyes in fake shock. "You don't suppose Bilbo misled us, do you?"

She snorted. "You think? Only I don't see why. He must have known we'd find out otherwise, so why did he bother? Habit?"

The guard riding behind them—one of the two humans—spoke softly. Cynna's charm whispered his words in her ear: "Humans are discouraged from settling outside the City, but do it anyway. They don't like it when we get out on our own because we start thinking we should be in charge of ourselves."

"Harry," the guard riding beside him said, warning in her voice. She was not human. Half-half, maybe, and sort of catlike, with those pointy ears and the short orange fur.

"What?" He glared at his friend. Cynna knew they were friends because she'd seen him humping her one night out on deck. She'd been purring, too. "Every other species in Edge has some region they dominate, where they rule according to their own ways. Not humans."

"Half-halfs don't," his friend said in the manner of one who's made the point many times before.

"Yeah, but almost all of you have human blood. That's why you're looked down on."

Cullen glanced over his shoulder. "This seems to be a human village, but the region itself belongs to . . ." His voice drifted off, inviting them to fill in the blank.

"Hoko," the guard named Harry said. "He's sidhe. Allied with Rohen, sometimes. Sometimes not. Hoko collects rent from the farmers around here when the mood strikes, but otherwise leaves people pretty much alone, so a number of humans have migrated to his territory."

Cynna tried a question. "Why is this Derreck not a *real* sheriff?"

"That would suggest they were governing themselves, wouldn't it? The village is in fief to Hoko, who probably hasn't bothered to appoint a sheriff, so the villagers elected one. Which isn't allowed if you're human."

"Why?" Cynna asked. "Why so down on humans governing themselves?"

"Because we're so damned warlike." Harry snorted. "As if the Ahk aren't."

"Babies," the female guard said suddenly. "That's the real reason. Humans are too bloody fertile—fertile with almost all the other species, too. If you were allowed to govern yourselves, you'd not regulate your reproduction the way it is now. In a few generations, Edge would be overrun with humans."

"Fertility is regulated?" Cullen asked sharply.

"Among humans, it is." Harry was bitter. "In every region of Edge. *Ashwa* is one of the few things everyone agrees on."

"Ashwa?"

"The practice of—"

"Harry," the female guard said, "remember when to shut up."

He shot her a sullen look. "You brought it up."

She faced forward, expression frozen. "Hsst."

Tash was riding toward them. As soon as Harry saw her, he shut up.

Tash told them about the inn. The bad news was that there weren't nearly enough rooms available. The good news was that those rooms did have beds—really large beds with feather mattresses. Cynna was excited about that as she slid off her horse at the nearby stable—and wobbled on legs suddenly turned to goo.

Cullen chuckled and slid an arm around her waist, propping her up. "We really do need some liniment, or you won't be able to move tomorrow." He asked the groom about getting some—which she knew because her charm whispered the translation.

Cynna's eyebrows went up. Obviously Cullen now spoke Common Tongue. Somehow she'd assumed the transfer hadn't taken place . . . but either the elf-woman had given him the spell before she glammed him, or even under a faerie glamour Cullen's priorities were clear: spell first, then sex.

"What was that word Harry used? *Ashwa*," she said as they left the stable, Cullen carrying a bottle of horse liniment. "Do you know it?"

He shook his head. "It wasn't included in the package I got from Theera, and I didn't hear any references to *ashwa* when I wandered the market in the City. He wasn't supposed to mention it, was he?"

Steve came up behind them. "Mention what? Hey, is that liniment?"

"It is," Cullen said, "and we'll share. Have you heard the term *ashwa*?"

"Nope." He put his hand on his hips and stretched, curling his back. "Man, I ache."

"I know what it means." That was Gan, who'd had no trouble at all with her little pony. "I can't tell, though."

"Not even for an extra chocolate?" Cynna had been giving Gan one Hershey's Kiss after supper every day that she behaved. Surprisingly, the former demon behaved quite well—for a former demon. She was by turns surly, selfish, mischievous, and rude, yet she didn't create havoc for havoc's sake.

When you got down to it, Cynna thought, Gan just wasn't mean. Not the way some people were. Real meanness was an inverted empathy—knowing what would hurt others and doing it. Gan mostly lacked empathy, but it was an innocent lack, one that might be slowly filled in.

Gan's face screwed up as she considered the nature of temptation. Finally she shook her head. "Not even for two more chocolates. They might find out. Ask your Daniel Weaver. He's not supposed to tell, either, but he might because of being your family. Don't give him any of my chocolate," she added hastily.

They'd reached the long wooden porch in front of the inn. Cynna paused, checking. "Yep."

"Yep, what?" Cullen asked.

"The trail. It's muddled for some reason, but the medallion was here."

"Here in the village? Or the inn itself?"

"The inn." She closed her eyes, concentrating. "Three weeks ago, maybe less. We're catching up." She opened her eyes. "And we might be able to get a description of whoever has it. They probably don't get a huge number of travelers staying here. Bet they'll remember who was here three weeks ago."

As it turned out, they remembered very well.

TWENTY-SEVEN

TASH straightened, shaking her head. "I can do nothing for him. No healer could—there's not enough mind left to heal. The only mercy I can offer is death."

Cynna's breath caught. "You won't, though. You won't just . . ."

Tash looked at Bilbo, who shook his head. "Is not deciding yet."

Tash, Bilbo, Cynna, and Cullen were in a crowded storeroom at the back of the inn. It stank of piss. A man—a human man—slumped on a huddle of blankets on a narrow cot, playing with his fingers. He didn't seem aware of his visitors. Every so often he whimpered. Once he giggled.

He had been good-looking in a brawny, rough-hewn way, Cynna thought. Now he was a bearded imbecile in a diaper.

"We can't keep him here," the innkeeper said through Cynna's charm. He kept wiping his hand on his apron—wanting to wipe his hands of the whole business, no doubt. "We've been waiting for an Ekiba to ride through so we could send out word, find his people. It's not our fault, what happened to him." He shook his head. "Not that I understand what happened. I can't believe what you say about Bell, though I guess . . . well, he did leave, but he always was something of a drifter."

According to the innkeeper and his wife, this man had arrived three weeks ago and paid for one night. When he didn't leave the next day, they checked on him and found him like this. Earlier they'd seen him talking to a kid, maybe seventeen, named Bell Hammond, who did odd jobs for them sometimes. Hammond had been a drifter, not a villager, but he'd lived here over a year. Suddenly he'd quit and left the village—hours before the innkeeper discovered his guest sitting on urine-wet sheets and counting his fingers.

"People don't drift into Ahk territory," Tash said, "unless they're idiots. You say Hammond was seen heading for the mountains?"

The innkeeper nodded unhappily. "I thought Derreck was wrong about that. Seemed like he had to be. Bell isn't all that bright, but he knows better than to enter Ahk land. Listen, you'll take this fellow with you, right? We can't keep him here."

Cynna backed out of the room, leaving Bilbo arguing with the innkeeper about whose responsibility the poor man was. If you could call what remained a man.

Cullen came with her. "Let's get some air."

She nodded. The stew she'd had for supper wasn't sitting well in a stomach turned raw by pity.

They didn't go far. The temperature had dropped, and icy pellets mixed with snow sifted through the frigid air. The porch was covered, though, and there was no wind; the cold, clean air did clear up her nausea.

Cynna stood at the porch rail watching the way white mingled with darkness in the wintry air. Cullen came up behind her. He'd let his mage light puff out, so the only light came from her own little ball of light.

"It occurs to me," he said softly, "that our thief didn't lose his mind until he lost the medallion."

He was right. The man had made it here, hadn't he? He'd seemed normal to the innkeeper until the next day . . . "The First Councilor said the medallion ate the mind of anyone it couldn't bond with. She didn't say the damage didn't happen until someone else got hold of it, but that's what it looks like."

"Maybe she didn't want us to think about grabbing it for ourselves."

Cynna shivered. "No temptation here. What I'm wondering is why this Bell Hammond would take it. How did he know it existed? The innkeeper never saw it. That poor man wouldn't have pulled it out to show the boy. Even if he did, Hammond shouldn't have known what it was."

Cullen shook his head. "We're missing something."

"A lot, I suspect." And her head was too thick to make sense of it tonight. Cynna sighed. "I need some sleep."

He moved up behind her, putting his arms around her. "In that damned crowded bed."

Turned out the beds were plenty big . . . big enough to hold three people apiece. More, if they were gnome-size people. Or that was the plan, since there were so few rooms. She and Cullen would be sharing with Steve. "Could be worse. We could have drawn Gan for a bunk-mate."

"Good point. I'm betting she's a bed hog. Ah . . . I'm not coming up with you yet. Tash has lost two guard and, while this inn is wonderfully comfortable compared to bare ground, it's not very defensible. Wen, Steve, and I offered to help with watches. I'm on first watch."

Cynna turned in the warm circle of his arms. Her mage light hovered near her shoulder, its glow falling softly over the beautiful contours of his face. Funny, she didn't always notice that anymore—how pulse-raisingly gorgeous he was. Mostly he just looked like Cullen to her. "I could take a watch."

"Pregnant women are excluded from guard duty."

She thought that over and decided it sounded right in principle. Applying it to herself wasn't easy, but . . . "I

guess I won't complain about getting my full eight hours."
Cullen slept eight hours only if he was healing. Otherwise, if he got in six hours, he thought he'd overslept.

The subtle ease in his features told Cynna he was relieved. He'd expected an argument. She tried to look se-
vere. "You're telling me I'm going to be sleeping with
Steve Timms for a couple hours."

His grin flashed. "You're safe. He made a point of
telling me he's of the 'don't poach' school of thought."

"Poaching is for bunny rabbits. I am not a bunny rabbit."

"I know, but Steve's not the brightest bulb, socially.
There is some good news—he's taking the last watch. So
if you can make do with slightly less than eight hours,
there will be a period when we have the bed to ourselves."

Oh. In that case . . . she ran a hand up his side. "How's
your heart?"

He didn't answer for a moment, then said softly, "Better. It's definitely getting better."

CYNNA stirred when the bed dipped. "Go back to sleep,
luv," Cullen told her softly, and he pressed a kiss to her
forehead. "Steve's shift doesn't start for another four
hours."

She did. She slept soundly, too, and was dreaming of a
cat-faced woman who wanted to hump Cullen. Cynna was
explaining to her that Cullen's penis was not shaped properly for feline intercourse when the door crashed open.

Cullen rolled to his feet on one side of the bed. Steve
did the same on the other. An eight-foot tusked monster
holding about six feet of drawn sword bellowed and
surged through the doorway. Cynna, bogged down in the
middle of the soft mattress, hadn't finished untangling
herself from the quilts when Cullen flamed him.

His scream went on and on, mixing with other screams.
His blackened body fell, blocking the door, as Cynna finally got her feet on the far side of the bed, next to Steve.

"Duck!" Steve cried—as a second monster replaced the first in the doorway.

Cullen ducked. Steve fired. The first shot seemed to startle the monster—its eyes widened, and it hesitated. The second shot hit right between those eyes.

"The window!" Cullen called, heaving one of the bodies away from the doorway. Maybe he hoped to block it if he could get the door shut.

Cynna spun, shoved open the shutter. "Shit! Two more climbing onto the roof of the porch. More—at least ten more on horseback—in the street below. Ahk," she added, her mind catching up with events. "They're Ahk."

A rumbling voice sounded behind her. Even as she whirled back to face the door, the charm was translating: "You fight bravely, but you are outnumbered twenty to one. Surrender, and we will spare all those still alive."

There was no one in the doorway. The speaker must have decided to lurk out of the line of fire.

Speaking of which, Cullen sent a jet of flame it through the doorway. "And we should take your word for that? Don't see why. I've got plenty more of this."

Rumble, rumble. The charm: "We do not kill you for that this time. You are new to Edge and do not know the Ahk. As for your fire . . . *grieegwashabettama.*"

Or something like that. At the sound of the last words, the ones the charm didn't translate, the blackened corpse on the floor reached out and grabbed Cullen's ankle.

He yelped, seized the enormous sword dropped by one of the monsters, and swung it. Steve shot at someone outside the window.

Obviously this dude had a charm, too. Or else he'd learned English. He'd clearly understood Cullen. "What do you want?" Cynna called.

"You," the charm said, "if you are Cynna Weaver. We want you alive. We are willing to spare the others if you surrender now. I make this offer so you may choose life for them, if you wish."

Where were the others? The five remaining guards,

Tash, Gan, Bilbo, Wen—all dead? Her father? God, she'd just gotten him, please . . . please.

She heard fighting downstairs. But several of their party had been here, on this floor. Daniel Weaver had been here, where all was so very quiet . . . "Tell your men to stop advancing, and we'll talk."

Her charm translated the bass gibberish as "Why should I do that?"

"Because you don't want them to die unnecessarily. Just as I would rather my people didn't die without reason. If they keep coming before we have a deal, we'll keep killing them."

There was a pause, then he bellowed something that translated simply as "Hold!" and added in what passed for a normal voice, "You are in charge? The others will do as you say?"

"Well, the councilor thinks he is, but yes, I am." Cullen kept telling her that, anyway. She'd find out if he meant it.

"The gnome is dead."

Her breath caught. She looked at Cullen. What now? Without the gnome to take custody of the medallion, what was even possible? They could kill some of the Ahk, but not all. They were too few, and there was no cavalry riding to their rescue.

Cynna shivered, and blamed it on the cold. "Then I am in charge. Except that Tash worked for the gnome, and I don't know who she—"

"The one you call Tash is also dead. She fought with great honor for those to whom her bond was given."

Dead? Tash was dead? The shock of it sent clammy fingers over Cynna, opening up a numb, empty place like an unexpected wound. She hadn't thought of Tash as a friend, exactly, but . . .

"Others are still alive. One of the humans is unconscious but not badly hurt. I believe he is kin to you. This little ugly one is also alive. I am unsure what she is, but perhaps you want her to live. Speak, little one."

"Cynna Weaver?" Gan's voice, even higher and squeakier than usual, came from the hall. "I don't want to be dead. Maybe I don't have enough of a soul yet to still be if my body's dead, and besides, I like being alive. I really like it. You said you'd be sad if I got killed. Do what he says, okay? So I won't get killed."

Her breath whooshed out. Her eyes stung as she met Cullen's eyes. He shook his head once, but she didn't know what that meant. Don't let them kill Gan? Don't trust them? Don't bargain away all their lives?

"Do you surrender?" the charm whispered.

She hunted for her choices amid this ruin. The Ahk were warriors. Did they have a warrior's code of honor—their word was their bond and all that? Cynna had the impression they were brutal but honest. But so much depended on her choice . . .

Cullen held up something. A gem?

Not just any gem. The one the elf-woman gave him. The call-me. Cynna swallowed and concentrated on not hyperventilating. Calling that bitch might be a mistake, but if anyone could take on the Ahk, it was the sidhe.

She nodded at Cullen and spoke loudly. "I have your word that everyone alive now will be spared if they stop fighting? No retribution?"

The rumble, and the charm: "Ahk do not take vengeance on those who fight with honor. Your people have fought honorably. You have my word."

"And you're in charge. The others will do as you say."

"They will."

She gave up.

Cullen disappeared.

TWENTY-EIGHT

GAN had been scared before. Lots of times. She'd seen lots of bodies, and while she didn't much like eating dead things, they held no horror for her. But as they walked past these bodies, she felt awful. Even the body of Bilbo, killed where he slept in the big bed, made her feel bad.

First Councilor had told her that might happen. Well, not specifically how Thirteenth Councilor would get killed, but that there was a chance he would be. So Gan had known this was possible, and she didn't even like Bilbo—and yet the sight of his slit throat made her own throat tight and unhappy.

Shouldn't she be feeling good? She'd survived. She wasn't hurt. Cynna Weaver had decided not to feel sad about Gan getting killed, so she'd surrendered like the big Ahk wanted. So she ought to be okay.

Nothing was okay.

They started down the stairs, her and Cynna Weaver and Steve Timms, surrounded by a bunch of Ahk. One of the Ahk was carrying Daniel Weaver, who wasn't dead. He'd been hit on the head and was unconscious.

There, sprawled on the stairs, was the guard who'd

played poker with Gan and Steve Timms sometimes on the barge. He had laughed a lot, even when he lost. He wasn't dead yet, but with a wound that big in his belly, he probably would be. A demon could heal that kind of damage. She didn't think people with souls could.

He was making an awful, groaning noise. He probably hurt really bad. Maybe he was scared about dying, too. Cynna Weaver asked the big Ahk if her people could tend their wounded. He was mad, though. He thought she'd tricked him because Cullen Seabourne had translocated someplace. Cynna Weaver had said she didn't know he was going to do that. She said Cullen Seabourne hadn't known he would do it, either, because some sidhe had tricked him, but the Ahk leader didn't believe her.

Gan stopped on the stairs, the awful feeling getting bigger and bigger until she thought she'd choke on it. "I want to help him! I want to help him, and I don't know how!" Why had she never learned how to do stuff like that? She was so stupid!

The Ahk behind her shoved her, but she set her feet and didn't move. She was still demon enough to be much more dense than she looked. "This is wrong," she said. "It's wrong."

"Gan." That was Cynna Weaver, her voice tired and achy. "The sooner we leave, the sooner those still alive can help the wounded. The only thing we can do to help them is leave."

At the foot of the stairs, in the big common room, were more bodies. Some were dead, some weren't. Two of the Ahk were tying up the injured guard with some rope. Only two of the dead were people Gan knew—had known—but one of them was Tash. Seeing her all bloody and still made the bad feeling swell up again until Gan thought it was going to swallow her, like being eaten from the inside.

There was a lot of blood. The innkeeper stood against one wall, wringing his hands. "I couldn't do anything," he said to Cynna Weaver. "I can't fight them. They're my neighbors. I couldn't do anything."

Cynna Weaver looked at him the way a full demon, maybe a Claw or one of the other big-deal fighters, looks at an imp or a bug. Like she might step on him, only he wasn't worth the trouble. "You told your *neighbors* we were here, didn't you? You call that doing nothing?"

"You have picked the wrong one for your betrayer," the Ahk leader said. "Wen of Ekiba told us where to find you. He told us a great many things."

Her eyes widened. She and Steve Timms exchanged a look. They kept walking, though. Maybe they wanted to get out of the place where all the bodies were, and all the blood.

Gan felt so weird. Not long ago she had really liked blood. Human blood, anyway. Demons got very silly and happy when they drank human blood, and she remembered how good that felt. But it was different when it was the blood of people you knew, and they were dead. She didn't like looking at their blood all over the place.

Was this what happened when you grew a soul? You could hurt, hurt a lot, even when you weren't hurt?

It was so confusing.

In front of the inn more Ahk waited. They'd brought the horses from the stable, but not the little pony Gan had ridden before. The Ahk leader said the pony would slow them down, and Gan would have to ride in front of one of his warriors.

Wen of Ekiba waited there, too.

"Tash is dead," Cynna Weaver told him. "Bilbo is dead. My father is injured. Two of the guard are dead, another is dying, and every bloody one of them is injured. You happy about all that?"

He just turned away. He didn't answer her at all.

It took several minutes to get everyone and everything loaded on horses. The Ahk wouldn't leave their dead behind, so those bodies had to be strapped onto their horses. Their healer worked on the two Ahk who were injured badly enough to need it. A third was deemed too far gone; the Ahk leader chanted over her, then slit her throat.

While all that was going on, others brought down all of their captives' belongings, including Cynna Weaver's bag with the chocolate kisses. Gan thought she might feel better when she saw that, but she didn't.

Daniel Weaver was a problem, being unconscious, and Cynna Weaver tried to persuade the Ahk leader to leave the man here. He wouldn't do it, though. He thought she'd cheated him out of the sorcerer and wanted everyone else for hostages so Cynna Weaver would do what he told her to do. Find the medallion.

Everybody wanted the stupid medallion. Gan hated it. It made people kill her friends before she'd even known they were friends. It made someone she'd thought was nice betray the rest of them.

Cynna Weaver stood very still and silent while they passed her father to one of the mounted Ahk, who would hold on to him while they rode.

"Cynna Weaver?" Gan said in a small voice. "Do you feel really awful, too?"

"Yes, I do. Thoroughly damned awful."

"Would we feel better if we killed Wen of Ekiba?"

Cynna Weaver looked at Gan, her expression all sad and strange. Then she did something surprising. She got down on one knee like she had when Gan said she didn't have any friends here. Only this time she hugged Gan. Gan knew it was a hug because she'd seen humans do that. She knew hugging wasn't always because they wanted to do sex, and she was pretty sure Cynna Weaver didn't want sex now because that would be stupid, but she didn't know what to do, so she just stood there.

After a few seconds of hugging, Cynna Weaver said, "I don't know. I kind of want to, but the—the wise people I know would say that killing him was wrong, and doing wrong things won't make us feel better."

"I don't understand."

The Ahk leader barked out an order. They had to go now.

Cynna Weaver sighed and stood. "Sometimes I don't, either."

TWENTY-NINE

THE gut-wounded guard had woken, and was moaning. Kai tried not to listen. At least her own patient was quiet, though the way she stared at Kai with those big, dark eyes . . . Kai raised her hand to brush the hair from her face, noticed the blood on her fingers, and didn't.

"His name is Harry," the woman she was sewing up said. "He's Harry. He doesn't have much of a chance, does he? He's just human. Humans don't heal well, and they got him in the gut."

"I don't know," Kai said. "I don't know what's possible here."

"You're a Theilo?"

"Sort of." Theilo meant a slider, one of the many who'd accidentally slid into Edge from elsewhere over the centuries.

"You speak Common Tongue well."

"Thank you." Kai knew the language for the same reason she knew what Theilo meant: Nathan. He'd given her the tongue one night soon after they arrived.

She finished her sewing, tied off the thread, and reached for the peroxide. The woman flinched when the liquid bubbled over her wound, but held as still as she had throughout. Kai appreciated a patient like this. The wound in her shoulder was shallow, no stitches needed, but the one in her thigh had gone to the bone. Yet she'd sat motionless the whole time Kai stitched her.

She was a pretty thing, rather feline looking, with a jaw that hinted at a muzzle and pointed ears. Then there was the fur—soft, short, and subtly striped like an orange tabby cat. Kai had had to shave it around the wounds, but it should grow back.

Kai carefully put the needle and thread back in her sewing kit. Nathan planned well, but the carnage that had greeted them when they reached the inn at Shuva needed so much more than their little medical kit. Not that the villagers hadn't been trying to help the wounded, but their only medical person was an herbalist who doubled as a dentist since he owned a pair of pliers. A real scary pair of pliers.

They needed more than a physical therapist—or former physical therapist. What was Kai's profession now? Wanderer? "Does your species heal well? Are you susceptible to infection?"

The woman shrugged one shoulder. "I'll heal. That's a beautiful cat you have. Well-trained."

All eight feet of Dell were stretched out as near the hearth as she could get without interfering with the two patients also laid out there. Her dappled coat was winter-thick, so she didn't really need the fire's heat, but like most cats she enjoyed it. "She is lovely, isn't she? She's not exactly my cat, though. She's my familiar."

The woman's eyes widened. "You're a mage?"

"No. Do people here have to be mages before they can take a familiar?"

"Huh . . . yes. I always thought so, anyway. Where are you from? You're human, but he isn't." She nodded at Nathan, who was with the moaning guard. "He looks human, but his scent . . . I've never smelled anything like him."

Kai just smiled and stood. Her back twinged and she twisted, stretching it out.

"Not going to tell me, huh?"

"No." She looked at the others in the room. Most of the villagers had cleared out when they arrived, taking the dead with them to the ice house to await burial, but the one they called the sheriff remained. He was the tall, bearded man sitting at one of the two intact tables, nursing a mug of ale and keeping an eye on them. He'd answered their questions honestly, if tersely. The man sitting with him was the innkeeper, who hadn't answered honestly—until he realized Kai knew it when he lied. Since then, he'd been more afraid of her than of Nathan.

Foolish man. She looked across the room at Nathan.

He sat on the floor between Dell and the gut-wounded guard, whom they'd laid close to the fire's warmth. He'd done what he could for the man—and that was rather a lot. The wound was neatly closed now, and when he laid his hands on the man's head, the moaning stopped.

Kai's anxiety shot up—but the man's colors were still there. Subdued now, with the pain colors fading. She started toward them.

Nathan met her partway. "I don't think he'll make it," he said softly. "I've done what I can with the wound, but he's lost a great deal of blood, and infection is likely. I put him back in sleep. It won't last. His pain will rouse him again in a few hours, but he will rest deeply until then."

Kai nodded, brushed her hair back from her face— then remembered the blood on her hand. She grimaced. "If only we hadn't been delayed in that last village! To miss them by only hours—"

"Couldn't be helped. And it may be just as well. Dell and I are very good, but I am not sure we could have killed fifty Ahk warriors."

"The sorcerer would have burned some of them." And maybe she could have changed their minds. Or maybe she would just have made them crazy. Fifty insane Ahk warriors would likely be even worse than the regular sort.

Kai chewed on her lip. "Nathan, I can't do this the way the queen wants me to. People are dying."

He was silent a beat too long, his expression stilling. "What do you mean?"

"She doesn't want us to reveal ourselves or let anyone know she sent us, but—"

"If the gnomes knew Winter was meddling in this realm, the power balance here and in other realms would be disrupted. More deaths, Kai. Possibly many more."

"There aren't any gnomes with the party from Earth. Not anymore."

He considered that. After a moment he nodded. "It's your quest. If you believe the time is right . . . we have to catch up to them first, of course."

She sighed. "I suppose we'd better eat before we set out."

Nathan laughed softly. "Kai, Kai. We will eat, yes, and also sleep. Even if you were able to go on without rest, the horses can't."

This was one of those times when their senses of humor didn't mesh. She knew Nathan wasn't heartless, but at the moment, laughter was very far away for her. She turned her head, swallowing the hard words she knew she'd regret later.

"Kai." He put his hand beneath her chin, stroking her there as if she were Dell. "I have lived long enough to know that I do not help others by taking on their grief. We are doing what we must. These people will do as they must, also."

"I guess I—"

"Hsst!" That came from the innkeeper's wife, who was tending the other patient laid out near the hearth. "She's waking up," the woman said. "You said to let you know if she did."

They crossed to see. Nathan had spent most of his time working on the guard because this woman, while she'd looked dead, had been unconscious from a blow to the head. The deep, bloody wound in her chest from a sword thrust had miraculously missed anything vital, and Nathan had said that the woman's own healing ability was sufficient. Since Kai could see from her colors that she had a minor healing Gift in addition to whatever natural healing ability she possessed, she hadn't argued.

She was not as pretty as the feline woman. Though Kai had yet to see an Ahk, she'd been told what they looked like. This woman's skin and short tusks proclaimed her kinship to them, though she'd fought on the side of the party from Earth.

"Who are you?" the woman demanded weakly when Kai knelt beside her.

"I'm Kai, and this is Nathan. What is your name?"

"I'm . . ." Her eyes widened when she looked at Nathan. "You! You're a—"

"Eh!" he said hastily. "I'd rather you didn't say it. You're the first to recognize me, and I'm wondering how."

"Then it's true?" She looked shocked. "I didn't know you could—"

"As I said, I don't wish it spoken of." He spoke with authority this time, a subtle shift that was probably not simply a matter of voice. He looked at the innkeeper's wife, who was staring, her colors turned fearful. "You may go now."

The woman gathered herself to her feet and hurried away without a word.

Nathan looked down at the injured woman. "You may tell me how you knew me, now. And your name."

"I shouldn't have said anything about recognizing you." She was bitter. "My brains are addled from the blow."

"But you did speak of it," Nathan said gently. "Your name? You may give me a call-name, if you wish."

"I am called Tash."

"And you recognized me because—?"

At first it seemed she might not answer, but finally she gave a small sigh. "I've a bit of a healing Gift, nothing major, but it lets me sense bodies directly . . . I saw the Hunt once, you see."

"Ah." Nathan nodded. "I'm afraid I must make sure you don't speak of this." He bent and reached for her head with both hands.

THIRTY

THE Ahk were beyond hardy. They were machines, Cynna concluded, every muscle in her body protesting the need to stay in the saddle. Stupid, bloody, barbarian cyborgs.

It was Cynna's third solid "day" of riding up winding mountain trails, and the first when the snow hadn't stopped. Her poor horse wasn't happy, either. It had to be a bitch, climbing up this miserable excuse for a trail where the snow was several inches deep in places.

The mountain trail coincided with the one only she could sense. But she hadn't told her captors that. Chulak—the big son of a bitch who led them—had told her scornfully that he did not need her to tell him where an intruder had crossed Ahk land. He could follow that trail himself. She would be needed, he said, only after they left the mountains.

Before they'd reached those mountains, Wen had ridden off in the other direction. She still didn't know why he'd done it. Money or wealth of some sort, she gathered; Chulak had said something to him about his payment. But what payment could have made him betray so many? His own people would hunt him down if they found out. The Ekiba's wandering existence was possible because of their neutrality.

Maybe he hadn't seen it as betrayal. She'd learned that the Ekiba were the only exception to the "no outsiders" rule about Ahk land, and Wen had served as one of the Ekiba communicators in these mountains several years ago. He'd lived with them; maybe his loyalties had shifted.

Probably she'd never know. But she'd liked him, dammit. She'd liked him.

No one had died since they left the village, at least. Cynna reminded herself of that, hunting for something to lift her spirits from dead zero. And Cullen had gotten safely away, even if that hadn't been what he meant to do . . . and even if she wished fiercely that he were here with her. Stupid thing to wish, since the Ahk were determined to kill them all slowly, from exhaustion.

She flexed her fingers on the reins, trying to get some feeling back. They'd given her mittens, even a furry cloak with a hood, but the higher they climbed, the colder it got. Even Chicago wasn't this cold . . . though admittedly she'd never tried riding through that city on horseback for hours in the middle of snowstorm.

At least she was uninjured. Cynna gripped the horse's barrel as firmly as she could with her aching legs and twisted to look behind her.

Through the snow she saw the dark horse of the Ahk behind her, the one riding double so he could support Daniel Weaver. Daniel had woken from his concussion soon after they left the village, but the damned Ahk wouldn't stop. Daniel had thrown up twice that first day and been unable to eat before the sleep period last night.

The next morning, though, the Ahk who doubled as healer had done something for him. His face was still the color of freshly churned slush on a city street, but he no longer threw up.

He smiled at her now, trying to reassure her. Cynna

stretched her lips in the best smile she could manage, and faced front again.

Ahead of her was a horse's rump, partly covered by the fur cloak of the Ahk riding it. Not much of a view, no distraction at all when her mind wanted to cruise back over everything that had happened, dipping into horror like it was a loose tooth, picking at the places where she might have done things differently. As if that could change anything.

The horse's rump rounded a curve of rock and vanished.

That wasn't especially interesting, since she'd seen it happen dozens of times. This trail wound around like crazy. But a moment later her horse rounded that same curve, and she saw the cave ahead. It was deep, with a wide mouth and a fire. A big, blazing fire, and people were in it and getting off their bloody horses.

Her mount got excited, too. It picked up its weary head and moved a little quicker, eager for shelter and warmth. Moments later she was out of the snow and one of the Ahk caught her horse's halter. She swung her leg over . . . or tried to. Her muscles cramped and refused to obey. She bit her lip.

The warrior shook his head in disgust, reached up, and lifted her off. She promptly slid to the damp, rocky floor of the cave.

"Liniment," Cynna said, her eyes closed. And to her disgust, tears seeped out from under her eyelids as she thought about Cullen getting her that liniment, laughing at her for needing it, promising to rub it in for her . . .

"Humans are very puny," said her charm.

It was speaking for the Ahk leader. The Ahk were divided into clans, and Chulak—unlike most people in Edge, Ahk didn't keep their names secret—was the leader of his clan, only more like a combination of Rho and Rhej: the big boss and the high priest. She opened her eyes and glared at him. "You'd better take good care of this puny human or she'll die, and then what will you do?"

"You are not dying." He was indifferent.

"You'd better take care of the other humans, too. If my father dies—"

"You will refuse to find the medallion for me?" Chulak smiled, or gave his version of a smile. It looked pretty ghastly. His tusks were longer than Tash's had been. "I think not. You will wish the others to live. And yourself."

"Maybe. Or maybe I'll decide that the death of an entire realm would be a fitting memorial to him."

He hesitated just long enough to make her think he might buy it. "Get up. You are not injured, and you make yourself ridiculous and shame my niece's sacrifice."

"I liked your niece. I don't like you." As comebacks go, that one wasn't much, but it had the benefit of being true. Tash had been the niece of this overgrown bully of a religious zealot—unacknowledged because he wouldn't allow tainted blood into his clan, and Tash had been half human. Once she was safely dead and unable to reproduce, though, he claimed her. Bastard.

He'd already turned away to give other people orders. Steve approached. He walked stiffly, but unlike her, he'd stayed upright after dismounting. It made her feel like the weakling Chulak had named her. "I've got the liniment," he said, and held out a hand.

"Bless you." She took it and let him help her to her feet, not bothering to stifle her groan. Everything hurt. "Thanks. And that liniment would be where—?"

He reached inside his fur cloak and pulled out the green bottle. "Just give it back when you're through." He looked over his shoulder at Chulak, his narrow face tight with anger. "Unless you can figure a way to poison him with it."

"If it didn't kill him straight off, he'd probably decapitate someone to show his annoyance."

"Sooner or later," Steve said, staring at the big Ahk. "Sooner or later, we'll get a chance."

He meant it, which worried her. Trying to kill Chulak was a short route to having all your questions about the afterlife answered.

This cave was apparently a planned stop, or maybe one they used regularly. They had hay and oats stored here for the horses and dried food and water for the people. There were skins of the thin, sour wine the Ahk liked, too, but Cynna was avoiding alcohol, so she stuck with the water.

The horses were lined up around the front of the cave, where their bodies blocked the wind and their body heat contributed to the warmth of the fire, making it almost comfortable inside.

Cynna had discarded modesty almost as thoroughly as a lupus. She simply found a shadowy corner where she could partially strip and, shivering, rub in the liniment. It burned worse than Bengay at first, but subsided to a gentle heat that helped. After she pulled her clothes back on, she did some stretches while the Ahk tended the horses. They were big on caring for their horses before anything else.

Two of them had gone back into the storm with short shovels; before the last horse was lovingly rubbed down, the captives were escorted, one at a time, to the freshly dug latrine pit.

Cynna went first because of her supposed status as their leader. She didn't object. The guys could stop along the trail and empty their bladders if they had to without slowing everyone down—or treating the entire company to a view of their freezing backsides.

When she returned, she took her rations to the side of the cave designated for her party and sat. She was too tired to be hungry, but she chewed the jerky and journeycake methodically, washing down each bite with water, knowing she needed the fuel. So did the little rider.

That made her tired eyes water again, dammit. She thought of Cullen and how much the baby meant to him.

Gan came back from the latrine next and ate in grim, hasty silence. Sure enough, she hadn't quite stuffed the last bite in when Chulak called her. The Ahk had decided Gan would do for a servant—or slave—and had been giving her chores at every stop. Cynna had protested, but Chulak was, as usual, massively indifferent. The little one was strong and hardy, he said, unlike the humans; she could do her share of the work.

Her share included anything the Ahk didn't want to do—encouraged by a kick or blow if she balked.

Daniel came back next and settled beside Cynna. He looked ill, but smiled at her. She wanted to tell him to quit doing that. She knew he hurt. "Eat," she said instead, handing him one of the journeycakes.

He looked at it and sighed, but dutifully broke off a piece and put it in his mouth.

Moments later, Steve joined them. "And to think I used to like mountains," he said glumly, ripping a bite off his jerky with his teeth. "Rock climbing, anyway."

"You do the pitons and belaying and all that?" Cynna asked. He nodded, his mouth full. "Well, there's just one mountain left, and we're on it." She finished the last of her journeycake and eyed the jerky. It was her least favorite component of the meal. Oh, well. She popped it in and started chewing.

"You memorized the maps that well?"

Cynna shook her head, chewed some more, and finally swallowed. "I'm a Finder, remember? If I can Find mountains, I can Find not-mountains. I think we'll be off this one sometime tomorrow."

"I didn't know you could Find something as general as mountains, much less not-mountains."

"Most Finders can't." Finding the generic rather than the specific involved doing multiple Finds simultaneously— not easy, but she hadn't had much else to do other than avoid falling off her horse. She flashed him a grin, only a trifle forced. "I'm good."

"More to the point, maybe, is where will we be when we come down from the mountains?" Daniel said. "I know Edge geography generally, but not with the kind of specificity that can tell me where I am now. Other than in Ahk territory, obviously."

"That, I can't tell you. Not for sure. But I think we'll come out in Leerahan, maybe close to where it butts into Rohen."

No one said a word, but they all exchanged glances. Leerahan was one of the big sidhe estates. Rohen was another. Rohen was also where Cullen had gone, snatched up by what he'd thought was a communication charm. Or so they assumed. All they really knew was that he'd vanished.

It was possible, just possible, that he'd persuade the Rohen liege . . . what was her name? Theil. That he'd persuade Theil to come to their rescue. Even if he did, the sidhe would have to find them, and if they did, they'd probably insist that Cynna Find the medallion for them.

Better them, though, than Chulak. Better anyone than Chulak. Edge would be in deep shit if he managed to form a bond with the thing and started remaking the realm to suit him.

Cynna realized she was feeling less exhausted. Almost alert. "You think there's some drug in these journeycakes? Or maybe some kind of recuperative magic?"

"They sure taste nasty enough to be good for you." Steve had finished eating. He pulled out the deck of cards Cynna had long since ceded to him, and began shuffling.

Gan looked over from where she was scooping up horse shit and glared. Cynna hid her smile. "Better not start the poker game until Gan can join us. Should be soon. They're moving into their worship circle." Every night the Ahk sat in a circle and chanted. Cynna had listened in, of course, but the charm didn't translate most of the words. Still, it was obviously a religious ritual.

"Okay if I join you for a few hands tonight?" Daniel asked.

Cynna looked at her father. She was getting used to thinking of him that way—*my father*. He had some color in his face for once, maybe the result of the journeycakes. "Sure. But, um, if you're feeling up to it, I have some questions."

He studied his hands for a moment, then sighed. "I don't have many answers, but you're welcome to what I do know."

"What do you know about the Ahk religion? Chulak wants to remake Edge in his god's image or something. That's why he wants the medallion. I figure I ought to know more about this deity of his."

Daniel glanced over at the Ahk. He spoke softly. "They aren't interested in converts, but from what I can tell, Hrvash of the Ninety Names—that's what they're chanting now, his names—is a lot like the Ahk themselves. Hard, even brutal, but strictly honorable within the framework they understand. I, ah . . . I'd say Chulak is not a typical priest." He lowered his voice even more. "More of a fundamentalist. Extremely devout, wants his people to return to the old ways, which he considers the basis of all honor."

Great. "We have problems with that type back home, too. A lot of them live in the Mideast, but some—oh, never mind. I'm so tired my brain's derailing. The main thing I want to know is, what is *ashwa*?"

Daniel's eyebrows lifted. "Where did you hear that word?"

"I heard it, that's all. What does it mean?"

His gaze flicked quickly to Steve and back. He didn't answer. Just then Gan came hurrying up. "I'm ready to play poker. I want my chocolate, too. Maybe I could have two chocolates this time. I really need two chocolates."

Cynna pulled her bag over. "Tell you what. I'll give you two chocolates if you'll go play poker with Steve up near the horses. I want to talk with my father by myself for a little while." She looked at Steve. "Okay with you?"

Steve shrugged. "I guess."

Once the other two had left, Cynna looked at her father. She didn't say anything. Just raised her eyebrows and waited.

For a minute she didn't think he'd answer. That anger was in his eyes again, the anger she'd glimpsed once before. Finally he nodded once. "You might as well know. *Ashwa* is the agreement signed by the five major power groups in Edge that Gifted humans are to be sterilized."

"What?"

"Hush!"

She lowered her voice. "It seemed strange I never encountered any Gifted humans, but I thought it might be something about Edge itself. I never dreamed . . ."

"They're afraid of us." The bitter twist to his mouth might have been a smile. "Not without reason, I suppose. Look at what's happened on Earth, where humans have had free rein. The other races have mostly died or been driven out."

"Because the magic died! God, are they just ignoring that? We've been cut off from the other realms, but surely they know about ambient magic being real low until the power winds changed things."

Daniel shrugged. "I'm telling you what everyone here knows—or thinks they know. Humans tend to take over by virtue of numbers. We're the most fertile of the races, and if they didn't take steps to keep our population down, we'd outbreed them all. If Edge were part of Faerie rather than being autonomous—"

"Wait, wait. You mean Edge isn't part of Faerie? It's high magic, and sidhe live here."

"To be part of Faerie, a realm must belong to the two queens, Winter and Summer. The queens don't govern their realms directly, but they have some essential laws— they're called, jointly, queens' law—that are binding on all those in their realms. Edge was given to the gnomes. Queens' law doesn't apply here."

"And what does queens' law have to say about humans?"

"It's not what it says. It . . . parts of queens' law are actual laws the way we think of them. Written rules. There aren't many. There's one about death magic, for example. It's utterly forbidden. But other parts of queens' law are, well, more like natural laws that are imposed on the realms by the queens."

Cynna was beyond skeptical, but kept her voice polite. "They can impose natural laws on several realms?"

"Sounds godlike, doesn't it? I have to say, when I first came here, I thought that's what the queens were—not actual gods, but a religious mythos used to explain the way things worked. I was pretty damned superior then." He shook his head, rueful. "Didn't I have the answers these backward souls lacked? But the queens are real, sweetheart, and they're not gods, however they may seem to mortals like us."

She knew someone like that. Sort of. The lupi's Lady, the one who'd created them and who they insisted they didn't worship. They just did what she said on the very rare occasions she deigned to speak to them through their Rhejes.

For a moment Cynna remembered a voice, *the* voice, the one she'd heard in a church one night . . . "They don't, uh . . . I mean, these queens haven't created any races, have they?"

"No!" Daniel was startled. "No, as I said, they aren't deities. They're High Sidhe, which means they're both immortal and extremely powerful, but they can't create life. Except in the sense all beings do, I suppose."

Cynna dragged her mind back on topic. "And these queens have imposed a natural law on their realms that affects human fertility?"

"It affects all fertility, I'm told, but the ones most affected are humans. If the population of any race in any of their realms grows too large, they stop having babies for a time."

"Jesus."

He nodded. "Here, lacking queen's law, the other races came up with a different way of limiting our numbers. In high magic realms, those with magic are more fertile than those without it. By sterilizing all humans born with Gifts, they limit our overall fertility."

"Everyone knows this, right? It isn't some deep, dark secret, but they tried to keep it secret from us. From those of us from Earth, I mean."

"Were you likely to trust them, help them, if you knew about *ashwa*?"

"Hell, no." Not then, anyway. But she'd seen more of this world. Specifically, she'd seen the Ahk up close and personal. Cynna chewed on her lip. "You work for the gnomes. You wanted me to Find the medallion for them."

Daniel sighed. "The gnomes enjoy deceit. They prize a good lie, but they are basically fair. They say the medallion will cause havoc in other hands, changes no one can predict, changes that might devastate the people here. I think that's probably true. They're also the least likely to instigate a war over the bloody thing. They can fight, don't get me wrong. But the Harazeed gnomes remember the Great War too well. They'll go to great lengths to avoid open conflict."

She considered that and several other things in silence, rubbing idly at her stomach.

Cynna couldn't feel any change there yet. No pooch. She hadn't had morning sickness or noticed any other physical sign of the little rider's presence. And yet, the baby was becoming real to her. Still mostly a future reality, a matter of looking forward and thinking things would go a certain way and there would be a baby.

Her baby. Hers and Cullen's.

She looked up. "Dad?"

Daniel's breath caught. His smile wobbled. "Yes, sweetheart?"

"Cullen said you had a bit of a Gift. A charisma Gift."

His face went through so many emotions she couldn't sort them all. "Yes. Yes, I know about *ashwa* personally. That's what you're asking, isn't it? You're the only child I'll ever have."

"Did the gnomes do it?"

He gave a single nod.

Cynna dragged in a huge breath and let it out slowly.

He'd been sterilized by the gnomes, and he still thought they were the best bet to hold the medallion. "I need to think things over."

Tentatively he reached out and touched her hand. "You need some sleep, too."

She found a smile. "Of course."

But her mind, slippery thing that it was, didn't help her line up plans for escape or locate any previously over-looked options. As soon as she lay down, she was too tired to think at all . . . almost too tired. Because one thought did intrude just before sleep dragged her down.

Those with magic were more fertile in high magic realms.

Earth was becoming higher magic . . . not as high as Edge, certainly, but more than it had been for about three thousand years.

Cullen had gotten her pregnant right after the power winds blew.

Maybe the lupi wouldn't have such a big problem with fertility anymore.

Oh, my. She really hoped she saw Lily again, so she could tell her. Or warn her.

THIRTY-ONE

THEY were better than halfway down the mountain the next day when the mountain moved.

Cynna had been through an earthquake before. She'd even been outside when it hit—in a forest, of all things. A forest in California, part of a national park, where she'd been hunting a missing twelve-year-old. It was been a small quake, but still pretty spooky.

She hadn't been on horseback, though. Horses do not like earthquakes.

They were spread out when it happened, headed across a tilted cup of land with a fairly shallow grade. Trees surrounded the cupped meadow—mostly evergreens, but a few stubborn oaks, too, their winter-brown leaves still clinging to their limbs. It was probably pretty here in the Day Season. Beneath the thin snow cover was lots of dead grass.

Grass and snow, with dirt beneath rather than rock—it could have been a lot worse.

The moment the land started to dance, so did Cynna's horse. The screams didn't help. Those big, bad Ahk warriors were yelling like crazy. Cynna had a few moments to think she was doing okay, staying on her frantic horse in spite of everything. Then the animal reared.

She lost the stirrups, felt her butt leave the saddle, and grabbed—but there was no pommel on the saddle, and the fistful of mane she did seize slipped right through the stupid mitten. She ended up on her back with the breath knocked out of her.

By then the ground had stopped moving. She lay flat, caught in the wide-eyed terror of a spasming diaphragm. She could not inhale. Endless seconds later Steve's face hovered over her. "You okay? Cynna! Hey, you okay?"

Suddenly she sucked in a huge gulp of air. Blew it out. Did it again. Oh, air was sweet. "Yes, I'm . . . breath was knocked out. I don't think anything else . . . hey, no groping." Steve was running his hands up one of her legs and down the other. She managed to push up on one elbow and grin. "You'll give me ideas."

"You're all right?"

That was Daniel, who'd also dismounted. He knelt beside her as he spoke.

"Fine. That damned horse . . ." A weird keening got her attention. She sat up the rest of the way, staring. "I'm not so sure about them."

About half the Ahk were prostrated on the ground, their voices rising in an eerie ululation. Some of the horses liked that about as much as Cynna did—they were shying away.

Some horses were just plain gone, she realized. Including hers. "I guess they aren't used to earthquakes here."

Chulak hadn't dismounted. He bellowed something the charm didn't translate, then more words that it did: "This is not the displeasure of Hrvash! The mountain trembles because some fool has the medallion, a fool who does not know how to use it—or who uses it against us!"

The keening faltered. Stopped. A couple of the prostrate Ahk sprang to their feet and waved their fists in the air, yelling things about killing those who attacked them.

The others liked that theme, adding to it that "they" had offended Hvrash by attacking his holy mountain.

The mountain was holy? Someone should have told her. Maybe she wouldn't have cursed it so often. Cynna pushed to her feet, looked around for Gan. The little not-quite-gnome had been riding double with one of the Ahk, as usual. "You think the earthquake was caused by the medallion being in the wrong hands?"

Daniel grimaced. "I hate to agree with Chulak about anything, but it's possible. These mountains are supposed to be geologically stable."

Steve spoke slowly. "The Council thought the flood in that place—what was the name?—was caused by the disruption the medallion is experiencing."

"Experiencing? More like causing." Cynna frowned. She didn't see a small, orange body anywhere, either moving or still. "Where's Gan?"

"Some of the horses spooked, ran off ahead," Steve said. His own horse was placidly nudging the snow aside, hunting for grass to crop. "Her rider must have lost control of his mount."

"We'd better look for her. For my stupid horse, too." Cynna set off, limping slightly. Her hip hurt. She hadn't noticed that until she started moving. More liniment tonight.

Chulak assumed they were trying to escape. On foot. At a slow walk.

She glared up at him on his horse. They were surrounded by seven of the mounted Ahk. "Idiot. We're looking for Gan. For my horse, too, and I think you've got a few of those missing yourself. We'll be sure and let you know if we see them."

Ahk were so armored by their own superiority that they scarcely noticed insults—at least Chulak didn't. The big leader gave orders and his minions snapped to obey, trotting their horses toward the downhill exit from the little meadow. Rock and earth humped up at that end, with a single opening. Runaway horses would react like anyone in a panic, Cynna supposed, taking the easiest route—downhill, not up, and through an opening rather than clambering up the sides of the rocky hummock.

As soon as the horses and their riders moved out of her way, Cynna started walking again. So did Steve and, after a moment, her father, the two men leading their horses. Chulak stared at them with that massive indifference Cynna hated. He didn't bother to stop them.

"Guess someone gave him a clue," she muttered.

"You like to push it, don't you?" Steve said.

"Sometimes." When she was pissed all the way down. Like now. Why now, rather than at any one of a number of moments in the last days—or weeks—she couldn't say. She just knew she'd had enough.

Not that it changed anything.

She heard some of the Ahk calling out up ahead, but they were on the other side of the rocky hummock, which kept the charm from working, so she didn't know what they said. They sounded cheerful, not upset.

A few feet beyond the opening in the hummock the trail veered left, running between masses of trees. She hurried along it. Up ahead a bunch of horses blocked the path. She heard rocks falling. Laughter. A screech— Gan's voice. That had to be Gan. No one else was nearly that high-pitched.

Cynna lurched into an awkward run, her hip making her slow. Steve shot ahead of her.

More voices, and this time the charm worked: "Catch this one, then, little one!"

Gan screamed.

"Arkhar, you missed! Such a bad shot you are—she can't catch them unless they come much closer!"

"Try it with a bigger one, Sithell. Maybe she can catch a bigger rock."

Steve shoved his way past the horses. "God damn you!" he yelled. "Stop it!"

Cynna squeezed between big, smelly horse bodies, getting switched in the face by one animal's tail, and came out in a wide spot in the trail. Or what used to be the trail.

Five Ahk were gathered at a drop-off where there should have been more trail. After ten or twelve feet of hole-in-the-ground, the trail resumed. A lone Ahk stood on the other side with his horse, running his hands over one of the animal's back legs.

On this side, one of the Ahk stood at the edge holding a rock the size of his head in both hands.

Steve stood beside him, quivering with anger. He didn't seem to be aware that the Ahk was two feet taller and a hundred pounds heavier than him. "I said put it down, motherfucker!"

The Ahk didn't have a charm to translate Steve's words, but he had a pretty good idea what the human was saying. That was obvious from the way he sneered when he spoke.

Cynna's charm said, "Maybe you want to catch it this time? But we didn't ask you to play, human." And he dropped the rock over the edge.

Gan screeched again, an ear-splitting howl that mixed with the sound of the rock crashing down and down and down.

"Chulak!" Cynna screamed "Get your ass over here! They're killing one of your hostages!"

Steve wasn't waiting on Chulak to sort things out. His fist shot out in a punch to the gut that startled the big rock-dropping warrior more than hurt him. The others started laughing even as Steve rammed his shoulder into the Ahk's belly, twisting his body—and shoving.

The Ahk teetered on the edge. And started to fall.

One gray hand shot out and seized Steve's arm. Steve threw himself back, pulling them both away from the edge before he was dragged to the ground. The big Ahk swarmed over him, teeth and tusks bared in a snarl made for nightmares.

He went for Steve's throat with those tusks.

Cynna's boot landed on his temple. Hard.

She hadn't been positioned right, so the kick wrecked her balance. She fell against another big, gray body. Two huge hands seized her arms, holding her upright. The Ahk she'd kicked shook his head once, as if puzzled. Then collapsed.

The one holding her spoke thoughtfully. Her charm said, "Good kick."

"Steve Timms?" Gan's voice rose from the hole, thin with fear. "Cynna Weaver? Are you killed?"

"Not yet," Cynna called back. She jerked away from the Ahk holding her, moved to the edge, and peered down.

Some kind of sinkhole, she thought. But it was dark down there. She couldn't see a thing, not even a bright orange thing, so she sent her mage light down.

"Cynna," Steve said, his voice muffled, "when you get a chance, I could use some help getting this asshole off me."

"I'll do it," Daniel said. He sounded out of breath.

"You okay, Steve?" Cynna's mage light drifted down, and at last she saw Gan.

"Fine. Sure, I'm fine."

The hole was round. Was that normal for sinkholes? The sides were almost smooth, almost vertical. Impossible to climb. Cynna couldn't see the bottom. She did see the tree that, collapsing when the earth beneath it suddenly vanished, had wedged itself across the hole about twenty feet down. Gan clung to one of its branches.

Those miserable assholes had been chucking rocks at her. Big rocks. Even if they didn't hit her, they could have dislodged the tree.

Chulak's distinctive rumble made her turn. He still sat his horse, staring down at his men. Her charm whispered, "Sithell. Report."

The one who obliged with a terse account was short for an Ahk and built like a tank. The Ahk carrying Gan had, as they thought, lost control of his horse. The animal had been running flat out, with no chance of stopping when he saw the sinkhole. They'd jumped it—but the rider lost his grip on Gan. When the others arrived, they'd been so relieved that the horse took no hurt that they'd felt playful.

Chulak did not. "Which of you *leathin* thought I did not need so many hostages?" He paused. "Did one of you—any one of you—think at all?"

Sithell spoke respectfully. "It seemed the mountain had decided to swallow the orange one. We did not wish to argue with Hvrash's mate."

"But you thought she would not object if you chucked rocks down her throat?"

Looked like the Ahk knew a rhetorical question when they heard one. No one said a word. So Cynna did. "I need rope. Now."

Chulak's head turned slowly. "Come here."

That did not sound good. Balking wouldn't help, though, and she wanted that rope. She walked up to his horse.

His hand shot out. A sledgehammer hit the side of her head, knocking her down. Dimly, through the roar in her ears, she heard him rumble, heard the charm whisper: "I do not like the way you speak to me."

She didn't quite pass out, but she wasn't fully there, either, as they discussed Gan's rescue—and the punishment of those who'd risked losing one of Chulak's hostages. Three of them lost a finger. One—the one she'd knocked out—lost two fingers. They waited for him to come around so he could chop them off himself.

While they went about their bloody business, Cynna distracted Gan from her plight by describing the way Steve had championed her. Her father sat behind her, propping her up. That felt weird, but it was a nice weird.

Finally they gave Steve a rope, and he hauled Gan up.

The former demon was scratched, bruised, and bloody. Her blood was red, as red as anyone else's. Her eyes were huge. "You saved me," she whispered to Steve. "You fought the Ahk to make him stop. He's huge and could kill you, but you fought him."

She lurched forward suddenly and clasped him around the knees. Hugging him.

Steve made a strangled sound and staggered. "Little too tight." He sought Cynna's eyes wildly, his expression pleading.

She smiled with the half of her face that wasn't broken and made a patting motion.

He got it. He bent and patted one bare, scraped orange shoulder. "Had to do something," he told her gruffly. "Dirty bastards. And you're one of us, right?"

The round, bald head bobbed in a nod. As suddenly as she'd latched on, she let go. She limped over to Cynna and threw her short arms around Cynna's shoulders, squeezing—which hurt. Gan was a lot stronger than she looked.

Fortunately, she let go quickly. She stared at Cynna, her ugly little face fierce. "I understand now. I understand."

Cynna didn't, but whatever revelation had come to Gan, it was important. So she smiled with half her face and reached out and squeezed one dirty, stubby-fingered orange hand. "I'm glad."

THE Ahk wouldn't consider risking their horses by jumping the sinkhole, a sentiment Cynna heartily—if silently—agreed with. They had to find another route down. By the time they halted to make camp, they were in low, rolling hills, partly forested. And Cynna was dizzy with exhaustion.

The only reason she hadn't keeled over from pain was that she'd finally given in and used her no-pain spell a couple hours earlier. It was for emergencies only because it stopped pain completely, but also stopped the healing.

But the son of a bitch who'd hit her refused to stop, and falling off her horse wouldn't help her head much.

Of course, she probably could have told Chulak she couldn't stay on the horse any longer. He wouldn't have stopped, but he didn't want her falling off and damaging herself. He'd need her to find the medallion's trail again, so he'd probably have had one of his people ride behind and support her, the way they'd been doing with Daniel until today.

Turned out she was just stupid enough, just stubborn enough, to try to out-tough three hundred-pound bipedal rhinos who cut off their own fingers to show remorse for endangering their leader's possession. And then rode for hours and hours and hours without complaint.

Bastards. And she was an idiot, which was abundantly clear the moment she dismounted and cut the juice going to the no-pain spell . . . took three steps, and threw up.

Concussion. That's what Chulak's healer said, via her charm, when he checked her out. He had her lie down in her blankets and did a warm-hands thing, cradling her head, that made her sleepy. She had barely a second to think, *oh, he's putting me in sleep, just like* . . . before she conked out.

That's how she came to sleep through the battle.

The next thing Cynna knew was another pair of hands on her face. These were cooler, the fingers long, the palms smooth. These hands stirred her awake instead of sending her away, cool hands that warmed her from the inside out.

She blinked her eyes open and looked up at dark, long-lashed eyes . . . full lips, parted in a small smile. Black hair with silver wings was pulled back, revealing a face so exquisite it stole the breath she'd just taken. Honey-colored skin and pointed ears. . . . dazed, she lifted a hand but didn't quite dare touch him.

"Who are you?" she breathed. Her pulse pounded in her head. It hurt. The pain distracted her somewhat from the pulse pounding elsewhere, but not entirely. No, not entirely.

"Why, I am your prince, Sleeping Beauty," he said in a voice like fog and mist, a voice she could have listened to for hours. A voice with a hint of huskiness, as if he, too, felt the delicious stir of arousal. "Come to kiss you awake."

THIRTY-TWO

CULLEN shifted in the saddle. His horse stamped, protesting his restlessness. He told his mind to stop thinking. Like most minds, it disobeyed, throwing up possibilities, scenarios, nightmares.

Cynna wasn't dead, he told his mind. She wasn't. They had no reason to kill her and every reason to keep her alive.

His mind noted that people died in battle even when that wasn't intended. And this had recently been a battlefield, and a number of people had died here, judging by the stink of blood and death soaking the ground, even if the bodies were AWOL for some reason.

But not Cynna. The Ahk—may they all be damned to the lowest circle of hell—were warriors that even the sidhe respected. They would have protected their prize.

The Ahk had been among those who died here, though. And someone *had* tried to kill Cynna on the barge. Someone able to hire obab assassins to take care of a problem for them. Someone who didn't want her Finding the medallion.

In spite of his fear and urgency, Cullen didn't speak.

He didn't want to distract the two peering into the recent past. A pair of sidhe—male and female, but almost identical otherwise—stood in the center of the trampled, blood-soaked ground, holding hands. Their eyes were closed. The magic swirling around them was mostly purple tinged with gold. Now and then it dipped into a muddy brown.

It had taken *days* to get here—bloody, be-damned days, too many of them spent arguing, beguiling, manipulating while trying desperately not to be manipulated in turn. And probably failing. The sidhe prized subtlety, and manipulation was warfare at its most subtle. Given the centuries they'd practiced on each other, they'd developed it into an art form.

He'd been at a disadvantage in many ways in their delicate negotiations, but perhaps his chief liability was that they knew what he wanted. He could only guess at their goals. Being sidhe, those would be varied and shifting. In the end, the deal they appeared to make was simple enough. He would dance for them, and they would rescue Cynna.

The sidhe prized subtlety, but their passion was beauty in all its forms. Still, Cullen didn't fool himself. Being both lupus and beautiful made him interesting to them, but not interesting enough to risk their lives. He danced well, but their dancers were grace itself. No, his performance had been either a tangible excuse to do what they intended to do anyway, or a cover for what the Rohen liege truly wanted. Or both.

As for what Theil of Rohen really wanted . . . he glanced at the tall woman sitting so lightly on a horse the color of smoke, surrounded by members of her court. He wasn't sure—how could he be?—but he thought he'd guessed right. She wanted the medallion, yes, but even more important was making sure none of the other sidhe lieges in Edge obtained it. She claimed that the medallion was moving from one person to the next intentionally, that it was seeking its proper holder. She might be telling some form of the truth about that.

But Cullen thought there was something she wanted just as much. He had shields the sidhe couldn't break, couldn't affect at all. The first time Theil had tried tickling his shields, he'd seen shock in her eyes, however fleetingly.

He suspected she'd wanted badly to learn how he acquired such shields.

Not that she'd asked directly. The testing of his shields had been mild and gentle and constant, but she'd made only a single comment on them three bloody days after he'd been yanked to the court of Rohen. How amazing, she'd said with the small smile that was her usual expression, to find such shields on one from Earth. Did all lupi possess natural shields?

That question had, at last, tipped her hand. She knew the shields were an artifact, not a natural ability. Cullen wasn't sure how sidhe perceived magic. Not the way he did—he knew that much. Their awareness of it was visceral, or perhaps it comprised a sense for which he had no analogue.

God knew they were unlikely to explain, had he been foolish enough to ask. But Theil would have been able to tell the difference between an innate ability and craft, however sophisticated.

"Not at all," he'd answered Rohen's liege. "There is quite a story attached to my shields. Perhaps I will attempt to entertain you with it once we are on our way. There should be time for storytelling. Cynna is over a day's ride away."

"Perhaps a little less than a day," Theil had told him, smiling. "We travel fast when we wish to."

Cullen had known where Cynna was because of a map—theirs—and a hair. Cynna's. Bleached along most of its short length, dark at the root, it had clung to his shirt, riding with him through the miserable maelstrom of translocation.

Not his preferred means of travel at all. He'd damned

near thrown up first thing upon arriving at Rohen's court. Sheer stubbornness had kept the contents of his stomach inside long enough for the nausea to fade.

Cullen supposed he couldn't blame all the delay on the sidhe love of indirection. It had taken him two days to set up the location spell, using that hair as a focus. And they had cooperated, giving him whatever ingredients he needed. Theera had even made a useful suggestion or two . . . probably laughing behind her beautiful gray eyes all the while. His spell must have seemed very crude to them.

Actually, they'd offered to locate Cynna themselves, using their doubtless more sophisticated spells. He'd politely refused. If he gave up the hair and let them find her, why should they take him along?

He didn't think Theil was behind the murder attempt on the barge, but he didn't know, not with certainty. He'd held on to Cynna's hair, and of course they'd made no attempt to take it from him. That would have violated the laws of hospitality—which were indeed laws among the sidhe.

Oh, he'd been treated well. Theera might have lied about the function of the charm she gave him—and it turned out that translocation charms were very few in number, but not as singular as Bilbo believed—but once he used it, he became an honored guest. He could have left at any time.

They'd known he wouldn't, of course. Not while they could dangle the possibility of help for Cynna in front of him. Finally he'd become convinced that was all they meant to do—tease him with possible aid, keeping him away from her.

He'd requested a horse so he could leave. They'd promptly agreed, asking only that he take leave of their liege first. Courtesy being almost as important as beauty to the sidhe, he'd known that would be necessary. When he did, she'd expressed her sorrow at losing his company, mentioning that she had hoped to see him dance before they parted . . . that had led somehow to the comment about his shields, and an agreement. He would dance for her court; she would ride with twenty of her people to the aid of his lady.

Nothing was said or even implied about Cynna Finding the medallion for them. But she wouldn't be a guest on their land the way Cullen had been. No laws bound them once they left Rohen, and Theil's word bound her only to rescue Cynna. Cullen was grimly aware of that.

He'd worry about what to do next after they found Cynna. Which—please, Lady!—had better be soon. Or he was going to blow whatever reputation for courtesy he'd established. The urge to burn something, anything, was growing.

His horse stamped. He shifted his weight. Who would have thought he'd ever long for a mate bond? With such a bond, he'd know, dammit. Know where Cynna was. Know she was alive.

She had to be alive.

Cullen's crude little location spell had worked until Cynna left the mountains and entered Leerahan. Leerahan's liege had smeared something like a "don't see me" over his entire land—or that's what it felt like, as if he had spread a muffling blanket over the area, one that smothered Cullen's location spell.

But it wasn't hard to follow the tracks left by thirty horses. They'd done just that, trailing the Ahk, until they reached this spot. Where the Ahk had been attacked.

Finally the hand-holding twins opened their eyes. "We are sorry, liege Theil," said the female. "But—"

"—we can pick up only snatches of what happened," the male continued. "Leerahan *oduelo* lies thickly here. But we did see who attacked the Ahk."

"Leerahan, of course," his sister said. "Two sleeps ago. They cloaked their arrival and slit several throats before the Ahk were aware of their presence. Very odd for an Ahk war party to enter Leerahan, but perhaps—"

"—they thought they would go unnoticed. There are traces of a masking spell, not of sidhe crafting, as you no doubt are aware. Leerahan, of course, prevailed. The images are patchy after that—"

"—but we concentrated, as you asked, on the human woman. She left here alive—"

"—and willingly, riding with Leerahan's liege, he who is sometimes called Aduello."

"But we cannot mark their path in any way. That is too well hidden by the *oduelo*."

Theil looked at Cullen, a trace of sympathy in her cool blue eyes. "Cynna Weaver is under a glamour, of course. Aduello casts a most lovely glamour, beautifully crafted. A human would have no defense against it. Unless, of course, she has shields like yours?"

Cullen shook his head. "No. But she's alive. That's what counts."

There was said to be one other defense against glamour. One that had nothing to do with shields, and everything to do with an old, old story, told in many forms . . . "We will learn soon enough if he holds her in a glamour, won't we? Assuming you continue to ride with me," he added politely. "You may believe Cynna no longer requires rescue, since it is sidhe who hold her now, not Ahk."

"Of course we ride with you. I prefer not to endanger my given word with assumptions. You understand there will not be a battle? I do not wage war on a brother liege."

"Battle is a broad word, Liege Theil. Some battles employ physical combat. Not all."

Theera, sitting a magnificent white mare alongside her half sister, regarded him with sympathy verging on outright pity. Theera did not like him. "I hope you also understand that we cannot wrest your sweetheart from Aduello for you, if she chooses otherwise. Even if that choice is the result, in part, of a sexual glamour, we must respect it. Glamour cannot compel one to act against one's nature, after all."

"That's true," Cullen said sweetly. And left it at that, since the implication was that he'd broken free of Theera's glamour because desiring her was very much against his nature.

That wasn't precisely true. But neither was her spurious sympathy.

There might have been a hint of amusement in Theil's eyes as she turned her horse to the west. "We cannot follow them magically. Their horses left a trail, however, that . . ." She turned her head as one of her male sidhe called out softly.

Two riders came over the nearest low hill, pausing at its crest as if to make sure they were seen. One was male, with coppery skin and black hair that reminded Cullen of Benedict. He wore a suede jacket of the sort seen everywhere. The other was female and bundled up against the cold in what he could have sworn was L.L. Bean winter wear.

After that brief pause, they put their horses back into motion. The woman led a pack horse as well. No one else moved. As they reached the bottom of the hill, Theil spoke clearly, her voice raised just enough to be heard. "My sentry did not report your arrival."

"Your sentry is undamaged," the man said in Common Tongue. "I did not wish to be seen until now."

"You—" Theil broke off. Her eyes widened.

A second later, Theera gasped. About then Cullen caught the faintest wisp of a scent, one he'd never encountered before. One that made the hairs on his nape bristle.

The two riders steered their horses through the staring, motionless sidhe. The woman was human. Cullen was sure of that, though she possessed a Gift of a sort he'd never seen before. He had no idea what the man was, but he had power. Great gobs of it.

"Liege Theil," the man said courteously, "I would introduce to you Kai Tallman Michalski of Earth and offer you two of my names. I am known as Nathan Hunter."

The liege had her expression under control. "I greet you, Nathan Hunter and Kai Tallman Michalski. I would offer no discourtesy, but I am . . . extremely curious . . . about your form and your presence."

"I feel sure you have heard the tale about my form."

"Winter's hound," one of the sidhe whispered.

Theil stiffened. She gave the one who'd spoken a single glance. The man flung himself from his horse to kneel. "My apologies. I should not have . . . I did not think."

The man called Nathan nodded once. "Forgiven. My identity is not a secret among sidhe."

"It damned sure is to me," Cullen drawled.

Theil gave him a look that ought to have sliced him in two.

Nathan Hunter, however, had only a small, rueful smile. "Your kind never like the way I smell. I am not Challenging you, wolf. Stop bristling at me."

"You are delaying me, though. Never mind what you're called. *What* are you?"

The man exchanged a glance with the woman, and she spoke for the first time—in clear English with a slight Texas accent. "He's a hellhound. I know he doesn't look like one, but that's a long story, and we're running out of time. If we're going to save your Finder friend and keep Edge from falling into chaos, we need to get moving. Nathan?" She gave her companion an inquiring look.

"Yes, I think so. There is one other I would like you to meet," he said to the rest of them. "Her name is Dell."

On the hill behind them, a grassy hump shifted. And stood. And a huge cat with the husky build and oversize pads of a lynx padded down toward them. A cat he couldn't possibly have missed seeing earlier, yet he had. A cat that looked exactly like the one he'd thought he'd glimpsed at the end of the dondredii attack.

"I was sent here," Kai said, "because the realms have shifted. With that shift, the needs of the medallion changed. It's searching for a new holder. I'm supposed to help it find the right one."

"You?" Theil's left eyebrow arched slightly in subtlest scorn. "You are human."

"The realms have shifted," Kai Tallman Michalski repeated. "And I am sent by the Winter Queen. Perhaps she sees something in me you do not."

Did she realize she'd offered insult and challenge as subtle as any sidhe might conjure? Cullen's mount shifted. His saddle creaked. "I'm following Cynna's trail," Cullen said abruptly, turning his horse's head in the direction of those tracks. "Feel free to join me when you're through chatting."

All at once Theil laughed. The sound was silver and wind, and he had a sudden image of a hawk stooping on its prey. *"Ki rel abathium!"* she cried—which meant, he thought, something along the lines of *why the hell not?* "We ride, Rohen!"

Her horse spun and leaped into a gallup. Within a single heartbeat, so had the rest.

THIRTY-THREE

LEERAHAN Court was stone and it was forest grove. It was both garden and sculpture, structure and meadow and quiet little brook. The fluting edge of one wall rose above the trees on Cullen's left like a giant bird's wing. On his right, twenty feet away, was a staircase. Between wall and staircase was grass—thick, lush, and brilliantly green. Never mind that elsewhere grass was winter-dead. Cullen walked down the wide swath of greensward that was the Leerahan great hall with Rohen's liege, twenty of Rohen's sidhe, a hellhound who looked exactly like a man, and two women. One of those women was not quite a telepath.

There had been time to talk some on the way here. Not as much as might be expected, because Theil had spoken the truth when she said her people could move quickly when they wished. It was damned hard to hold much of a conversation at full gallop. But he'd learned what Kai Tallman's Gift was, and why she was here.

It was the hellhound who'd gained them entrance to the court. Without him, Aduello might have allowed Theil and her half sister to enter, but not with so many of her people. Certainly not with Cullen. But no one was willing to tell the hellhound no.

Not because Nathan Hunter was—or had been?—a hellhound. Because he was Winter's hound. Said in a certain tone, "winter" meant only one thing—the Winter Queen, one of the pair of immortals who ruled all Faerie. The queens didn't rule in Edge, but if Winter's hound wished to visit Leerahan alongside two human women, twenty sidhe from Rohen, their liege, and a bedraggled lupus sorcerer from Earth, no one was of a mind to turn him away.

At the end of the greensward was a stone dais thirty feet wide. Not carved stone, and not precisely a dais, for it was platform and furnishings in one. It looked as if bedrock had been bidden to rise and fold itself into shapes comfortable for sitting, standing, or sprawling, depending on the whims of those who waited there. Cushions were strewn casually among the dips and benches, cupped seats and steps.

Aduello lounged on a stony bench cushioned by thick white fur. He was a tall, languorous sidhe of predictably inhuman beauty—black hair striped with silver falling like rain to his waist. He wore a pair of low-slung black pants that were silk and snug with a loose, flowing shirt and a cropped vest, heavily embroidered. Three of his court stood nearby—two men and a woman, all wearing swords. As did most of the sidhe assembled along the sides of the greensward, watching.

Beside him sat Cynna. In a dress.

That gown—long, gossamer, the color of the Hershey's Kisses Gan liked so much—shook Cullen. It made him doubt. *She's playing the bastard*, he told himself. She'd let him dress her to please himself because she was pretending to be trapped, enraptured by the glamour he cast.

She was a knockout in it. A thin crimson scarf crossed between her breasts and wrapped her waist, showing off her Amazon's figure. A slit up one side gave a long glimpse of leg. He wanted to lick his way up that leg.

Aduello stroked Cynna's arm casually, as one might pet a cat. She didn't move. She didn't even look at Cullen. Her expression was blank, dull. "Theil," Aduello said with a polite nod, "it is good to see you, of course, but you come in strange company. Or perhaps I should say, in strangely numerous company. And you, sir"—another nod, this one for Hunter—"I am unsure what to call you."

Hunter stepped forward. "My most recent name is Hunter. That will do. Thank you for allowing us entry, Liege Aduello."

"I'm told"—another lingering caress of Cynna's arm—"that you are not here hunting breakers of the queens' law."

"I am not on a hunt, sir. But I am here at my queen's behest. My purpose is to escort one she has sent questing. I present to you Kai Tallman."

The tall, broad-shouldered woman stepped forward and bowed her head briefly. "Liege Aduello, I understand the woman beside you is not the only one you rescued from the Ahk."

"That is true."

"I would like you to have the others brought here."

"Would you?" He'd possessed himself of Cynna's hand and toyed with her fingers. This touch seemed to call her back to herself. She cocked her head, giving Aduello a heavy-lidded smile. "And yet I feel no need to do so."

Cynna spoke suddenly. "They're all right." She was still smiling like a fool, but at least she looked at them now instead of the man playing with her. "They're fine. Aduello gave them the rose quartz suite—that's what I call it, anyway. You should see it. It's gorgeous. But . . ." She looked at the sidhe beside her. "Aduello, they'd like to see Cullen. Can't they come see him? In fact . . ." She frowned slightly, as if puzzled. "They may want to return with Cullen and these people. They aren't as happy here as I am."

"Ah, well." He patted her hand, all indulgence. "Why

not, if you wish it? Ertho, you'll see to it?" He gave the edge of his smile to one of the men on the dais with him. The man left, using an artfully concealed crevice in the stone wall behind them.

"Liege Aduello," Kai Tallman said clearly, "I must ask you not to mindspeak to your people. Give them their instructions out loud, please."

He froze for a second. There was no trace of a smile on his face when he looked at her—looked much more closely than he had before. "I have never met a human who could use mindspeech, much less overhear it when another did so. I suspect you are imagining things."

"I do not use mindspeech. I know when it is used, however. I also know when lies are spoken."

Aduello's eyebrows went up. "That would not make you comfortable company at most gatherings," he said with polite disbelief. "But what am I thinking? I have offered you no refreshment." He looked around as if he might have misplaced a servant among the cushions.

"Aduello." Theil smiled at him. "You know why we are here, and it is not for refreshment."

His eyebrows rose. "To collect the humans I collected? And that other one . . . something like a gnome, yet not."

"We are here about the medallion."

There was blunt speaking. For a sidhe, shockingly blunt.

Aduello's lazy smile didn't falter. "Of course you are. You tried for my lovely Cynna yourself, didn't you? Tried to kill her, that is. And with obab." He shook his head. "Such a messy way to operate, my dear. You must have felt quite desperate. It's not like you to abandon subtlety so thoroughly."

"That," Kai said coolly, "was a lie."

Aduello's eyebrows lifted slightly. "You grow tedious."

"Which leads me to suspect you were the one who tried to kill her. Otherwise, how would you have known about the obab?"

"But Cynna tells me everything." He stroked her cheek. "Don't you, sweetheart?"

She had that puzzled look again. "The obab . . . that's the slug-men, right? The ones whose touch was poison?" She looked at them again—right at Cullen, in fact. And her left eyelid dipped in a slow wink.

Fierce and strong, victory shot through him.

"Of course Aduello didn't do that," Cynna continued. "I don't know why he accused you of it, ma'am, because he knows who did it. The humans." She sighed. "There's a cabal of them, humans unhappy with their place here in Edge. They tried to kill me because they hope to lay hands on the medallion themselves, poor fools."

She looped her hand around Aduello's arm and turned a smile on the bastard so saccharine it was all Cullen could do not to laugh out loud. Or warn her not to overplay it. "Aduello would never hurt me."

Aduello didn't see what Cullen saw, perhaps because he wasn't looking. He patted Cynna absently, his attention on those confronting him. "I will allow you to take my other guests away with you, if they wish to go. I will allow you to question Cynna concerning the medallion—that is what you wish, I assume? I will even wish you well in your search. But then I must insist that you leave."

Kai looked at Cynna. "Ms. Weaver, do you know where the medallion is?"

Cynna glanced first at Aduello. He nodded once. She met Kai's eyes then and said quietly, "After the Ahk captured us, I decided I couldn't let them find it. I misled them. We came out of the mountains well away from the medallion's trail."

Kai glanced back at them. "She's speaking the truth."

"But I do know where it is."

Did Cullen imagine it, or had Aduello's hand suddenly tightened on Cynna's arm?

"At least I think I do," she went on. "The trail leads back toward . . ." Her eyes lifted as Cullen heard movement to his left, near the grand staircase. She glanced that way, where her father, Gan, and Steve were emerging . . . and smiled. A real smile, a Cynna smile, cocky and reckless. "This rat bastard beside me."

She jerked her arm free, pushed to her feet, and jumped.

"He's calling them!" Kai cried.

The sidhe lining the walls burst into action, swords flashing from their sheaths as they charged.

Cynna landed on the grass at the foot of the dais and rolled. Fire shot out from Aduello's clenched fist, missing her by inches.

And the woman standing silently beside Cullen—the husky woman who hadn't spoken, whom no one had introduced to Aduello—turned into eight feet of pissed-off kitty cat.

The sidhe flowed around Cullen, moving into the defensive circle they'd planned—but Cynna wasn't within that circle.

Neither was Cullen, by then. He walked forward, concentrating on fire. Fire was *his*, dammit—and so was the woman that rat bastard was trying to burn. He flung out his hand and sent a rope of fire to meet the one menacing Cynna.

The two flames kissed. Clashed. Cullen felt sweat break out on his forehead. Rat bastard was strong. He opened the diamond on his finger. His flame went from orange to blue . . . and the tips flickered into black. Aduello looked at him, startled and furious. He spoke a word, made a gesture, and his fire vanished—replaced by a wall of water shooting up from beneath the ground.

Mage fire could burn anything. Even water. But mage fire was damned dangerous to play with, and Aduello wasn't his job. Cynna was, and right now she had a problem with a sidhe slicing at her with four feet of steel.

Cullen throttled way back on the power and sent the fire that way. The sidhe screamed and fell back. Cullen raced to Cynna. "You're okay? You're all right?"

"Watch out!" she screamed.

He spun and sent fire at the pair of sidhe advancing on them. Then called it back, fast, as a huge silver-gray cat leaped on the pair.

"My father," Cynna cried. "And Steve and—hey! He's really something!"

As soon as things broke, the hellhound had drawn his sword and raced to where Steve and Daniel stood beneath the overhang of the staircase. A single guard, realizing the value of hostages, held a sword at Daniel's throat . . . for a moment. Then he was on the grass, watering it with his blood.

Hot damn. Hunter was as fast as *he* was. And a helluva lot better with a sword.

Another pair of sidhe advanced on Cullen and Cynna. There was no way he and Cynna could get inside the protective circle the Rohen sidhe had formed. Too many pressed them with both blades and magic. Lots of magic. The air was thick with it. Theil, with the power of her land-tie to draw on, was carrying the brunt of that battle from her place beside Kai.

So Cullen circled Cynna with his arm—and circled them both with a ring of fire. It would discourage the ones with blades, and for the moment, no one was pressing them with magic. Probably because they knew where the real threat lay, because their liege knew. With the still, silent woman in the center of Rohen's circle.

Kai Tallman did nothing visibly, not even to Cullen's vision. Her power lay in an area he couldn't see. The power of mind.

Aduello's wall of water vanished. He pulled a chain from beneath the silk of his shirt, closing his fist around the silver medallion that dangled from it. He wore a look of intense concentration.

Nothing happened.

"Nathan!" Kai cried. "I can't hold him!"

"What's she holding?" Cynna gasped.

"His thoughts. She's not letting him tap into the medallion to—oh, good."

The hellhound flew at Leerahan's liege in a leap any lupus would have been proud of, sailing up from the grass and through the air, the arc of his leap carrying him past Aduello—and that shiny black sword of his swung in a quick, clean stroke.

Aduello's head fell to the stony dais a second before Hunter landed. His body toppled second later, a geyser of blood shooting from his neck.

Everything stopped.

Hunter walked to the edge of the dais and spoke loudly. "Leerahan's liege was insane, driven mad by what he tried to hold. My lady tried to control his madness, and could not. I killed him. If any here dispute my judgment, you may make your claim to my queen."

"That," Cullen said very softly, "was part of the deal. Hellhounds are the only ones allowed to go around executing sidhe lords. A land liege isn't precisely a lord, but close enough."

A dark-haired sidhe—the first visibly aged one Cullen had seen—stepped forward. "I am called Raellian. I accept your judgment. My brother tried to master the medallion through his land-tie." The sidhe's face worked briefly. "He changed. He began to believe . . . to do things that made little sense. I was pledged to him, but I argued . . . he would not listen. The medallion drove him mad."

A murmur of voices rose. The sound, overall, was accepting.

"Leerahan," Theil called out strongly, "I have no desire to make claim on your land, but your land wants claiming. Your liege is dead. One of you must make the tie. Your three days begin now. Rohen will stay to witness, if you wish."

That steered the murmurs in a whole new direction.

Raellian spoke, his voice firmer now. "What of the medallion? Even I can hear it calling. Its voice will only grow louder as its need grows. Who can take it back to the gnomes safely?"

Cullen sighed. This was the part he didn't like. "I think that would be me."

"What?" Cynna's head spun. She scowled at him. "No way are you touching that thing."

"Shields," he said simply. "No one else has shields like mine. I'm the only one who can—"

"That won't be necessary," Kai said. "Look."

A small orange Buddha sat on the dais, chubby legs dangling over the edge. Smiling. The silver chain around her neck was spattered with blood, as was the heavily inscribed disk hanging from it. "Hey," Gan said, swinging her legs. "This is pretty cool."

"Gan!" Cynna sounded like she was about to cry. "Oh, no, Gan. Oh, no." She walked up to the dais. "What have you done to yourself?" she whispered.

Kai walked up and put an arm around Cynna. "She's all right. She's the true holder. I can see the bond forming already, and it's . . . it's quite lovely, really."

"It's okay, Cynna Weaver," Gan said kindly. "I thought it wouldn't be, when First Councilor told me I had to do this if Bilbo got killed. I wasn't going to. First Councilor thought the medallion wouldn't eat me because of me still being partly demon, but maybe it would. She wasn't all the way sure, so I wasn't going to do it. But then Steve Timms saved my life, and you helped, and I understood. Getting a soul hurts because then you start getting friends, and things that hurt them hurt you, too. I couldn't let my friends get their brains eaten. Just like Steve Timms couldn't let the Ahk throw those rocks at me and kill me. Because maybe I'd be okay, but none of you would be."

She looked at Cullen then, and there was something . . . more . . . in her eyes. "Not you, either, Cullen Seabourne. Your shields are good, but the medallion has been very lonely and very confused. It would have kept calling and calling, and people would have killed you to get it. And I'm one of you, so I couldn't let that happen." She giggled. "I'm one of a lot right now, but that's okay. It feels good. Like having lots of friends. Hey." She cocked her head to one side. "Cynna Weaver? Do you have any of that chocolate left?"

THIRTY-FOUR

CYNNA collapsed onto a grassy mound. Cullen sat beside her. They'd escaped from the court proper to a space that was more outdoors than in, though the enchantment of the court lingered here. The air was warm and summery.

The sky overhead was still dark, of course. Cynna stretched out in the grass. "You think they'll be talking long?"

"For at least the next three days. I'm not sure how sidhe settle who will make the land-tie, but I'm pretty clear that it involves a lot of talking." Cullen eased down onto his side, propped up on an elbow to smile at her. "Don't worry. We'll leave long before then."

"I guess that means on horses."

"I'm afraid so. Cynna . . ."

Something in his voice worried her. "Yeah?"

"I know you were playing Aduello. Pretending that his glamour had stuck so he wouldn't kill you and maybe the others. I want you to know that it's okay. Whatever you had to do to keep him from guessing you were free of the glamour, it's okay. I don't mind."

She searched his face and found it . . . blank. Showing

nothing at all. Happiness dawned slowly inside her at what she saw. "Yes, you would."

"Lupi don't—"

"Maybe not, but you would. You wouldn't hold it against me, but you'd mind."

Cullen didn't move or speak for a long, long moment. Then his smile cracked the blankness. "I damned sure would. I've been fighting my own mind for days, and fighting it worse once I knew . . . trying not to think about what he . . . I knew the glamour wouldn't stick, but you were in his power. And, uh, sometimes the glamour does stick for a little while."

Cynna laughed. "Stuck to you at first, didn't it? Well, don't worry. He didn't really want me, just wanted me dazzled. And the glamour didn't last long." Within an hour of being woken by her self-proclaimed Prince Charming, she'd gone from being desperate to jump his beautiful elf bones to thinking Aduello was a gorgeous, manipulative bastard.

Instinct had kept her quiet, warning her not to let him know she'd come unglammed. Instinct . . . and a lifetime's accumulation of cynicism. Or maybe that was a distinction without a difference.

"One thing I don't understand," Cullen said. "Why did Aduello keep you around? Just so you could send everyone off on a wild-goose chase for where the medallion was supposed to be?"

"Since he wasn't lusting after my body, you mean? That was the idea. I was supposed to tell you that the medallion's trail led back to the City. What I think, piecing together some of the stuff he said, was that he'd arranged for a group of would-be rebel humans to take the blame for a while by dying in a terrible fire or explosion or something. He wanted more time to solidify his control of the thing. He'd just have gotten crazier, of course. The hellhound guy was right about that. It didn't eat his brain the way it did the others', but it sure unbalanced him."

"Hmm." Cullen settled down the rest of the way, sliding one arm beneath her so he could rearrange her to suit him. That turned out to be laying her head and shoulder across his chest, which rose and fell with the slow ease of his breathing.

For a while Cynna lay there in silence, amazed by survival and the beauty of lying here with him.

"You going to miss Edge?"

She snorted softly. "I like cars a lot better than horses, and hardly anyone tries to kill me back home. I can't wait for them to get a gate up. But . . ."

"Your father."

"Yeah. Though maybe . . . Aduello kept me with him a lot. I think that was part of the whole glamour business, keeping me nearby to keep the effect strong. But I was able to talk to Dad sometimes. He thinks he might get to visit. The gnomes are going to need someone to handle their trade stuff, right? Someone with a trace of tact and maybe a bit of a charisma Gift. Unlike poor Bilbo." She sighed. "I didn't like him, but he had courage. And Tash . . ." She blinked quickly to get rid of the dampness.

"Tash is alive. She's on her way back to the City."

"What?" Cynna lifted her head to stare at him. "How do you know? How do you even know what happened to Bilbo, for that matter?"

"Kai and Nathan have been trailing us ever since we arrived. They came upon the inn and found . . . the remains of the battle. Tash was injured, but alive." He grinned. "She says she has her father to thank for that. Praised his skill. It seems he was one of the warriors Chulak led, and he mercifully slid his sword through her chest right where an Ahk heart would be—but hers is located higher, like her human mother's. Then he conked her on the head, knocking her out. She was unconscious, with a hole in her chest where they expected her heart to be. They assumed she was dead."

"Son of a bitch," Cynna said, amazed.

"She won't remember Hunter and Kai," he warned her,

"so don't mention them. Hunter had to adjust her memories. No one except sidhe are allowed to know that the Winter Queen meddled here."

"I'm not sidhe. Last time I checked, you weren't, either."

"But I've got shields," he said smugly. "Even Nathan can't get through them. And we aren't staying here, so he's settling for us taking a vow of silence on the subject. But, ah, your father . . . I'm afraid he'll have to adjust Daniel's memories a bit. He's staying here, and his allegiance is to the gnomes."

Cynna didn't like that. She didn't like knowing anyone could do that. "So I'm not supposed to mention Kai or the hellhound guy to him?"

"You can mention them, but what he'll remember is that Rohen and Leerahan acted together to, ah, solve the problem of Leerahan's liege, who'd clearly been driven insane by the medallion. He'll remember Hunter vaguely as a wandering mercenary we brought with us, and Kai as his female companion."

"With a big cat. Who sometimes looks like a woman. I didn't imagine that part, did I?"

"Her cat is . . . well, they wouldn't tell me what she is," he admitted. "Whatever Dell's species, though, she's Kai's familiar."

"Kai's from Earth. How could she get a whatever-it-is for a familiar?"

"How did she get hooked up with a hellhound?" Cullen shrugged. "Apparently Hunter's spent a lot of time on Earth. He met Kai there. I don't know about Dell."

"She and Hunter are a team?"

"They're lovers, Cynna."

Something in his eyes made her heartbeat pick up. She licked her lips. "How did you know the glamour wouldn't stick?"

"It didn't stick to me." His eyes were intent. Telling her things. "I knew it wouldn't stick to you, either."

"But why?"

"I think you know," he said softly. His words, his voice, sounded certain. His eyes . . . wary, watchful. And open. Vulnerable.

"I've heard stories," she began. And had to stop and swallow. Her heart was going crazy. "Old stories about how the glamour can't stick if . . . if . . . oh, I can't." She punched him on the arm. "Why do I have to say it? You say it."

His eyes were very dark. His lips quirked up at one side, but his eyes stayed so dark. "I've been telling you all along. Since before we left Earth, I've been telling you in the only way I thought you could hear."

Cynna wondered if she'd start hyperventilating. "You saved my life. More than once. You didn't . . . didn't just save the baby, did you?"

His head moved once in a negative.

He'd done other things, not just the risky heroic stuff. He'd stayed away when she was still deep in denial about the baby, but called. Letting her know he wasn't going anywhere. He'd understood about her father and her need to come here and meet him. He'd come with her, stayed by her, promised her things. Understood her. Been there for her.

Like Cullen said, he'd been telling her. All along he'd been telling her with his acts, not his words. Maybe that was the only way she could hear it, like he claimed. It was also the only way he could say it.

Her voice sank into a whisper. "The stories say that a faerie glamour can't stick to someone who . . . who has found their true love. You love me."

Light slipped back into his eyes, easing itself around his face until it had formed a smile there—lazy, amused. Happy. "Yeah, I do. And you love me."

"But when . . . I mean, when did you know? Because I didn't. Not until—"

"The night we fucked each other's brains out in

the baths?" This grin held a hint of smug. "Yeah, I knew I pushed your buttons then. Scared you pretty good, didn't I?"

"When did you know?" Cynna persisted.

He scowled. "This is one of those stupid questions that no man can answer without getting in deep—all right, all right. Don't hit. I liked you from the start. I wanted you. You got under my skin pretty quick, too. But . . . this probably isn't what you want to hear, but I don't lie to you, and you asked. It wasn't until I knew you carried my baby that I . . . I don't know." He flipped a hand as if demonstrating some kind of either/or thing. "I couldn't keep you out anymore. Becoming a father, that blew me open, and afterward, you were just there. Inside me. Everywhere I looked, everywhere I went, you were in my head. And now I guess you'll be back to thinking it's all about the baby—"

"No." Cynna kissed him. Just once, and softly, to shut him up and tell him some of the things that were hard to say. "No. I understand. The baby made you see things inside you that you could have ignored otherwise. I think it's been doing that to me, too, only more slowly. I couldn't keep you out, either. And Cullen?"

"Yes?"

"I'm sticking. You won't get rid of me, so get used to it."

"Good." His breath sighed out and he gathered her close again, stroking her hair. "That's good. You're a hard woman to court, Cynna Weaver."

She grinned at his notion of courtship. And then just lay there, satisfied with the moment, with him . . . with herself. Happiness was a slippery thing, but sometimes, if you had the courage to reach for it . . .

She yawned.

Oh, how romantic. But she hadn't slept well since Cullen got zapped away from her, and she was so very tired . . .

"Hey, I just remembered something."

"What's that?" she asked, drowsy.

"The dragon. Mika. Remember what he told us? That demons are composite beings. I'm guessing that's why Gan suited the medallion so well. She's used to organizing her various parts."

"Composite is too big a word when I'm asleep, but yeah, I remember. Only how could he . . . well, he couldn't know about the medallion or any of this. Could he?"

"I don't know. But he told me one more thing—just me, male to male, while you were asleep."

Another yawn cracked her jaw. "What?"

"He's never seen a human mating ceremony, and he's curious. He wants an invitation to the wedding."

"**THAT'S** it?" Kai said, weary and disbelieving. "We just go? Right this minute?"

"She's calling me, Kai," Nathan stood close, his hands on her shoulders, one thumb stroking quietly along her collarbone. His face was quiet, but his eyes smiled. He'd draped one of their saddlebags over his shoulder. "Her summons is immediate, but not urgent. Still, we had better go now."

They stood beside their horses, poor tired beasts. Dell sat beside Kai, grooming herself complacently. She was very pleased with herself for her part in the battle, and her satisfaction blunted some of Kai's distress. "I . . . I thought we'd have a chance to see how things turned out. We should say goodbye, at least."

"We've followed the others so long we feel a connection to them. They just met us." Nathan shrugged. "They are grateful, but they don't know us well enough to miss us."

Kai swallowed. "I didn't do things the way your queen wanted."

"She'll be pleased. The medallion is with its holder, and the gnomes are unaware of Winter's interest in their affairs." He ducked his head to kiss her softly on the mouth. "You've learned much about your Gift, too."

"I used it to control someone." That's what a binder did. And the queen killed binders.

"For which an entire realm might be grateful, if they knew." His smile eased from his eyes to the rest of his face, giving it the shine of love, mingled with amusement. "Kai, do you still not know what you are?"

"No. And if you do and haven't said anything—"

"You feel no urge to tamper with minds that are healthy. When you see imbalance, disorder, madness—then you are compelled. You want to tidy wrongness when you see it. You're a mind-healer."

She blinked. A healer? Not a monstrous danger to others, but a healer? "I don't think I've healed any minds."

"Perhaps not. You've barely begun learning your Gift, but that's the direction it pulls you."

A healer. Kai took a deep breath, feeling his words settle inside. Feeling their rightness. "So where are we going?"

"To one of my queeen's private places, away from court. You'll like it. Can you pull Dell closer now?"

Dell took that moment to cease grooming herself and rasp her tongue along the back of Kai's hand. Kai smiled and reached with her mind—with her love—as easily as she stretched out her hand to touch the big cat's head. "Ready."

He handed her the other saddlebag. "Let's go."

THIRTY-FIVE

THEIR route back to the City was different from the one that had brought them to Leerahan, thank God. Cynna never wanted to see Ahk territory again, and maybe not mountains.

Horses, though, were inevitable. They rode to a small port on the river where the chancellor's barge awaited them. A combination of sidhe mindspeech and the Ekiba hotline had arranged that, as well as passing on the basic events to those waiting back in the City.

Gan was full of herself at times, but she still enjoyed swimming in the river and eating the fishies.

Cynna caught up on her sleep on the barge. She and Cullen did their best to catch up on . . . well, sex and lovemaking both, she supposed. The two of them were good at sex. Making love was new.

She liked it.

Ruben and McCloskey met them at the dock. Ms. Wright was conscious and out of danger, but still tired very quickly. The healer didn't want her leaving the Chancellery until it was time for her to leave Edge entirely.

Ruben was walking.

"Hey!" Cynna forgot herself and hugged him. "Look at you! This is wonderful. You look wonderful."

Ruben smiled. "You look wonderful, too, if somewhat overstimulated. Mr. Seabourne looks extremely ... rested, also."

She blushed, dammit. He wouldn't see it, though.

"I'm very interested in hearing your report."

"It will have to be ears-only, sir. There's a lot that can't be put in writing."

"That's true of most of your reports, or so you like to insist."

Cynna did not like writing reports. "Cullen, look how great Ruben's doing."

"So I see." Cullen's smile came easily these days. "You're moving well, too. Not limping. No splints."

"The arm and leg are still a bit tender. I'm afraid I'm showing off. The chancellor's healer sped the healing of my bones and in the process discovered the cause of my progressive weakness." Ruben gave Cynna a gentle smile. "I hadn't wanted to worry you, but back home, my prognosis was not good. Now, with care, I should be fine. I have a rare allergy to certain metals, you see. Particularly iron and steel."

Cullen nodded. "It's that trace of sidhe blood, no doubt. Most of them aren't troubled by cold iron—that's a myth—but a few are allergic to it."

"Wait a minute," Cynna said. "Trace of sidhe blood? Ruben?"

"I saw it in his magic," Cullen said, "after in-blooding the elements, when my vision was heightened. Traces of violet and black. The violet's uncommon, but it was the blend of it with an iridescent black, like flecks of mica, that clinched it. The only place I've ever seen that is in sidhe magic."

"A metal allergy," Cynna said slowly. "That's going to be hard. Steel is everywhere."

Ruben nodded. "Even being around large amounts of steel may be debilitating for me, which will prove a challenge. But primarily I must avoid touching it. The healer is unfamiliar with aluminum, so she can't say whether that's included on my 'do not touch' list, but I suspect it is."

"Aluminum? Your chair. Ruben, your chair has aluminum and steel!"

"Yes." He looked embarrassed. "I had a strong feeling I should be at that meeting with the gnome, if you remember, when we expected him to give Mr. Seabourne the shield spell. It turns out that was my first precognition utterly about myself. I wasn't needed for the mission, but I did need very much to come here. Being forcibly separated from my wheelchair has probably saved my life."

IT took the gnomes another two weeks to build the gate. It was a small one, only large enough for two to go through at a time. But it was permanent. They left at the start of the Dawning.

They were escorted to the new gate by three of the councilors, a troop of the guard, and Tash. She wasn't recovered from her wound yet, but she'd informed the healer she could mend just as well sitting in a carriage as lolling around in bed.

Gan accompanied them, tricked out for the occasion in a new dress. This one was silk in an eye-popping combination of reddish orange, cinnamon, and fuchsia. The chancellor's medallion hung from a shortened chain around her neck.

She waved a lot at the people they passed—some of whom were waving or pointing at her. "Sometimes it's fun, being important," she confided to Cynna. "Sometimes it's annoying. You'll remember about the chocolate? And to tell Lily Yu she can visit? And you and Steve Timms and Cullen Seabourne will come see me sometimes, too, right?"

"I'll remember," Cynna said, and kissed the top of her bald, orange head.

They went through the gate in pairs. Cynna and Cullen went last, at their request. The last thing Cynna saw of Edge was the sun rising over the river, making sky and water dance with color.

The first thing she noticed about being home was wet feet. The management of Fashion Center mall had finally gotten around to fixing their fountain.

TURNED out the gnomes were wrong about all the time slippage happening between the other realm and Earth. They'd left Earth at the very end of February, and their adventures in Edge had taken just under four weeks. When they returned, Cynna's breasts felt heavy and tender and she couldn't button her jeans anymore. And it was the middle of June.

"Missed the cherry blossoms," Cynna said, shaking her head.

"They were beautiful this year," Rule assured her.

The two of them sat at the big, round table in the kitchen at his house three days after the big return from Edge. Lily was working. Cynna had planned her visit to avoid Lily; she'd told Rule that and that she needed to discuss clan business with him. That had surprised him.

He was drinking coffee. She had a tall glass of orange juice. It was a cloudless day, and while they exchanged the kind of nothing-talk friends do, she kept looking out the window at all the sunshine. She didn't think she'd ever take sunny days for granted again.

"I don't wish to rush you, but I do have an appointment in about an hour," Rule said at last.

"I'm having trouble jumping into this," she admitted.

"Is it about the Lady?"

"No! Well, not really. Not yet, anyway."

"The *ashwa*?"

Cullen had told him about *ashwa* and what it might mean for lupi—the possible increase in their fertility as the level of magic on Earth rose. She looked him in the eye and got it said. "Not really. I need to ask you about lupi who get married. What would Nokolai do if one of their members got married?"

Rule's eyebrows flew up. His voice turned gentle. "Cynna, Cullen isn't going to marry you. I don't know if he's hinted or implied such a thing, but I hope—"

"Actually, he's already asked, and now he's just assuming. He's like that—if you don't beat him back with a club, he figures that means he'll get what he wants. But before I make it official, I need to know for sure Nokolai wouldn't kick him out or anything." She made a face. "He wouldn't lie to me outright, but this might be a subject he's willing to bend the truth on."

The shock on Rule's face was everything she'd feared. So why did it make her giggle?

"Cullen?" he said at last, incredulous.

"It's a kick, isn't it? And it isn't just about the baby." She still marveled over that.

"No, it wouldn't be." He waved that aside as obvious. His face was very serious. "Cynna, you understand that this not up to me."

She nodded. "Your father, mostly, right? And the Rhej. I, uh, I've talked to her."

She'd surprised him again, but this time he smiled. "You were able to persuade her to come to a phone?"

"Yeah. She said . . . well, she had a lot to say."

Rule's smile deepened. "You agreed to become her apprentice."

"Sort of. On a trial basis," Cynna added quickly. She still couldn't believe she was the right one for the job, and she figured the Rhej would see that soon enough. But . . . "Everyone keeps telling me it's not a religious vow or anything, but . . . well, according to the Rhej, the Lady does sometimes intervene in ways that look pretty miraculous. She's got that kind of power, only she's bound by lots of rules about what she's allowed to do, and she can't act unless she's asked, she might not do it anyway, and mostly the only ones she can hear asking are the Rhejes. Or . . ."

"Or someone she's chosen to become a Rhej."

"Yeah." Cynna sighed. When Cullen died, Cynna had called on the Lady. A second later, he'd drawn a breath. Maybe that was coincidence. Maybe it was a debt. "Anyway, the Rhej said that as far as she's concerned, Cullen is Nokolai and will stay that way."

"That makes a difference. Let me think a moment." Rule drummed his fingers on the table once, a habit of Lily's he'd picked up. "He won't lose Nokolai," he said at last. "My father is not easy to predict, but he's extremely unlikely to go against the Rhej on such matter. But it will be difficult. Some, both within and outside the clan, will shun Cullen. This is a vital moral issue for us, Cynna."

"I know." She said that with sympathy, because this put Rule in a difficult position. But she'd marry Cullen anyway, and not because she had to have the ring. Because he did. He needed her to be family, to be his.

Well, okay, she admitted privately as Rule walked her to the door. She needed that, too.

Cynna found something new to marvel over. For years, Rule Turner had been the standard against which all other men were measured. He'd played a part in saving her, whether he knew that or not. Until him, she'd had no idea how a good man treated a woman.

She'd been a bit in love with him long after he left. It had never really died, not for her.

"Have you told Lily?' Rule asked when they reached the door.

"Not yet. I thought you needed to hear first because it affects the clan, and I needed your answer." Oh, this was going to make trouble for him. "Rule." Impulsively she reached for his hand. "I am sorry about . . . well, the problems. I know this causes problems."

He nodded, but found a wry smile. "I'll cope. I'll even come to the wedding."

And that was a major concession. She beamed at him. "We'll probably hold it outdoors someplace. Not many inside spots big enough for a dragon."

Cynna all but danced down the sidewalk to her car.

Now when she looked at Rule, she might remember what he had been to her, but she didn't want him. Oh, she did in one sense—the my-body-likes-sex way any healthy woman feels around an attractive man. A little more alive, a little more female. But she didn't *want* him.

She wanted to hurry back to the brash and bold, arrogant and tender, often annoying man who loved her. And haul him off to bed, where she could propose to him properly.

Want to attend Cynna and Cullen's wedding?
Visit www.EileenWilks.com.
A link to a free short story about their wedding day
is available on the NIGHT SEASON page.

Turn the page for a preview
of the next lupi novel
and the return of Lily Yu and Rule Turner in

MORTAL SINS

by Eileen Wilks

Available Now from Berkley Sensation!

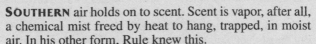

SOUTHERN air holds on to scent. Scent is vapor, after all, a chemical mist freed by heat to hang, trapped, in moist air. In his other form, Rule knew this.

In this form he knew only the richness. The world was more scent than sight as he raced through silver and shadow woods, through air heavy with moisture and fragrance. Layers and layers of green overlaid the complex stew of water from a nearby stream with its notes of kudzu, rock, and fish. Goldenrod jumbled with loosestrife, dogwood and buckeye, and the sugary scent of maple, punctuated here and there by the cooler tang of pine.

But it was the musk, blood, and fur scent of raccoon he chased.

The moon hung high overhead as he leaped a fallen log, muscles reaching in an exhilarating approximation of flight. His back feet skidded in mud when he landed. Ten feet away, his quarry shot up a tree.

He shook his head once, disappointed. Had he been truly hungry, raccoon would have served, but it was the chase he wanted. Damned raccoons preferred to climb instead of running. Good for their survival; bad for his pleasure tonight.

A deer, though . . . He decided to course, searching for that scent.

Coursing was as much excuse as action. He'd eaten well before Changing, so hunger was distant; the real delight was simply being in motion, four-footed, reading the world through his nose, ears, the pads of his feet.

The human part of him remained, a familiar slice of "I" that was not-wolf. He remembered all his two-legged thoughts and experiences; they simply ceased to matter as much. Not when the air slid through him like hot silk, laden with a thousand flavors. It was, perhaps, that part of him that felt a pang for the wonders of these Southern woods, remembering the hotter, drier land claimed by his clan in Southern California. His grandfather had made the decision to buy land there for Nokolai's Clanhome. In that place and time, the land had been cheap.

It had been a good decision. Nokolai had prospered. But most Nokolai wolves ran on rocks scattered over hard-baked ground, not on loam as rich as the summer air that streamed through him, nor through tree shadows surprised here and there by the tumble of a little stream.

Rule had run as wolf in other places, of course, but not in these woods. Not with Leidolf so near.

The spike of worry was real, but fleeting. Wolves understand fear. Worry is too mental, too predicated by the future, to hold their attention. The slice of him that remained man would have held on to that worry, gnawing it like an old bone that refused to crack. The wolf was more interested in the day-old spoor of an opossum.

Which was why he ran tonight: too many worries, too much gnawing at problems that refused to crack open and release their marrow. Lily said they hadn't come up with the right questions yet.

Rule paused, head lifted. Thought of her was sweet to man and wolf both. If only she could . . .

He twitched his ear as if a fly had bitten it. Foolishness.

Man and wolf agreed on that. Things were as they were, not as he might wish them to be.

An hour later he'd found no deer, but had enjoyed the distraction of many other scent trails—a pair of wild dogs, a rattler, all sorts of birds. But there was no one to share them with. He was wistful, wishing for a clanmate to romp with.

Wishing, though he tried not to, for Lily—who could never share this with him.

At the base of a low hill he found another scent. One that reminded him he had two clans now. The scent was old, but unmistakable. At some point in the last few months, a Leidolf wolf had marked the spot with urine.

Inside Rule stirred something more visceral than recognition as the portion of mantle he now carried rose, *knowing* the scent. Welcoming it.

For a moment, Rule was confused. Always before that scent had meant enemy. But the message of the power curled within him was clear: this wolf was *his*.

The man understood this change had expected it, so the wolf decided to acknowledge it and move on. He wound up the little hill, anticipating grass. His nose told him there was a grassy place nearby, a spot where some change in soil had discouraged trees. He liked grass. Perhaps it would be tall and home to mice.

Hunger had grown closer as he coursed the night. Mice were small and tricky, but they crunched nicely.

A thought sifted through him, arising from both ways of being: a few months ago he wouldn't have noticed a trace as old as that left by the Leidolf wolf. Was it one of the mantles coiled in his belly that made it possible to sort that scent? Or both mantles?

Perhaps the night and the woods were magic because he carried more magic within him now.

He would think on that, he decided, in his other form, which was better suited to it. For now . . . at the crest of the hill he checked with the moon, aware of time passing and a woman who slept in a small town nearby. He would enjoy the grass awhile, perhaps catch some mice. Then he'd return to the place he'd left his clothing and the shape that fit those clothes.

The grass was indeed tall and the pungent smell of mice greeted him as he approached the tiny meadow. Rabbits, too, but rabbits never ventured out at night.

For the first time that night, a breeze stirred, whispering in the grass and carrying a host of smells. He froze, more in curiosity than alarm. Nose lifted, he tested the air.

Was that . . . corruption? Yes, the stench of rot was unmistakable, though very faint. It meant little. Animals died in the woods often enough. Besides, the smell came from where he thought the highway lay. Animals were hit by cars even more often than they died in the woods.

Still, he wondered idly if the mantles would make a difference. They slept now, unneeded and uncalled, but he could try. Why not?

With a wisp of attention, he woke the twin powers in his gut. He asked—not with words, nothing so indirect—about the wisp of scent the breeze had brought. It sharpened in his nostrils immediately.

His body went taut. *Go.* The breeze might die, or this new acuity fade. *Go.*

He launched himself into a run.

Wolves are largely indifferent to death, as long as it doesn't threaten them or theirs. The body he chased was certainly dead, so the wolf felt no urgency.

The man did. Rule ran for over a mile—not full-out, not over unfamiliar terrain with no immediate danger or prey to force him to top speed. But he was fast in this form, faster than a born-wolf.

By the time he slowed, he knew he'd been right about the highway. He heard cars cruising along, perhaps a half mile ahead. But what he sought lay within the woods. The rankness of rotting meat made his lip curl away from his teeth as he approached.

Surely even humans would smell this.

Some other scent hid beneath the putrefaction, one he couldn't identify right away. But it brought his hackles up and started a growl in his throat.

Wolves are not natural scavengers; only a very hungry one would consider eating anything this rotten. And Rule was too much a man even now to feel anything but a sad sort of horror at what lay between a pair of oaks.

Not all beasts are so picky, however. And he hadn't been the first to find them.

COMING SOON FROM
USA TODAY BESTSELLING AUTHOR

EILEEN WILKS

BLOOD MAGIC

**Eileen Wilks's novels of the Lupi are a
"must-read for anyone who enjoys werewolves
with their romance"**
(Patricia Briggs, #1 *New York Times* bestselling author).

As they plan their wedding, Lily Yu and Rule
Turner, a prince of the Lupi, are facing a great deal
of tension from both of their families. Not everyone can accept their mixed marriage: She is Chinese; he is a werewolf. Even Lily's grandmother is
acting strangely distant, though Lily and Rule are
about to discover that her behavior has nothing to
do with their upcoming nuptials....

penguin.com

EILEEN WILKS

USA Today **Bestselling Author of**
Mortal Danger **and** *Blood Lines*

NIGHT SEASON

Pregnancy has turned FBI Agent Cynna Weaver's whole life upside down. Lupus sorcerer Cullen Seabourne is thrilled to be the father, but what does Cynna know about kids? Her mother was a drunk. Her father abandoned them. Or so she's always believed.

As Cynna is trying to wrap her head around this problem, a new one pops up, in the form of a delegation from another realm. They want to take Cynna and Cullen back with them—to meet her long-lost father and find a mysterious medallion. But when these two born cynics land in a world where magic is commonplace and night never ends, their only way home lies in tracking down the missing medallion—one also sought by powerful beings who will do anything to claim it…

M110T0907